I0719035

Prince Edward Island

Love Letters & Legends

Prince Edward Island Love Letters & Legends

The Complete Collection

A series of sweet contemporary romance

JESSICA EISSFELDT

Prince Edward Island Love Letters & Legends: The Complete Collection:
A series of sweet contemporary romance
Jessica Eissfeldt

Paperback Edition
ISBN: 978-1-989290-35-4

ALSO BY JESSICA EISSFELDT

Sweet Historical Romance:

Sweethearts & Jazz Nights
Dialing Dreams
Shattered Melodies
Fancy Footwork
Unspoken Lyrics
The Sweethearts & Jazz Nights Boxed Set: The Complete Collection

Love By Moonlight
Beneath A Venetian Moon
Beside A Moonlit Shore
The Love By Moonlight Boxed Set: The Complete Collection

Sweet Contemporary Romance:

Prince Edward Island Love Letters & Legends
This Time It's Forever
Now It's For Always
At Last It's True Love
Prince Edward Island Love Letters & Legends: The Complete Collection

Collections
Love & Lattes: A Sweet Romance Short Story Collection
Pieces of Me: A Poetry & Lyrics Collection

Chick Lit
Love, Your Fangirl

To Prince Edward Island—
thank you for the inspiration.

JESSICA EISSFELDT

This time it's forever

This time it's forever

A Novel

**Book 1 in the
Prince Edward Island Love Letters & Legends Trilogy**

JESSICA EISSFELDT

This Time It's Forever: A novel
Jessica Eissfeldt

Chapter One

RUBY ZALONSKI GLANCED out the wide windows at the rain-soaked Simmons College campus lawn. The black umbrellas most students carried intermingled with the occasional pink polka-dot or sunny yellow one, in the heart of downtown Boston's Fenway neighborhood.

Gray clouds scuttled across the August sky. The fat raindrops plopped against the windowpanes of LeFavour Hall, which housed the library at Simmons College.

Ruby sat in an overstuffed chair in the archives room of the library. She took a deep breath and inhaled the cozy and familiar scent of musty paper and waxed hardwood floors. A smile flitted across her face as her eyelids fluttered closed.

For a second, she imagined herself ten years in the future: a nice tenure-track archival position here at Simmons in the library and information science department, living in a historic brownstone, and married to a nice man. She sighed. Then maybe she'd finally feel like she belonged here? Had a real *home*?

She fiddled with the antique heart-shaped locket she wore around her neck.

Never mind that she'd lived in Boston all her life. So it *was* her real home. She let the sterling silver necklace slide through her fingers. But this place, this city, just didn't feel like that.

She didn't quite know why. But she'd always had this vague sense of restlessness. As if she belonged somewhere else. Should *be* somewhere else.

She tapped an unpolished fingernail against her chin as

she looked down at the antique love letter fragment. Its edges were torn and what looked like smudges of dirt and gunpowder obscured the neat, curving script.

Though the iron gall ink had faded to a reddish brown, the flourishes of the t's, dots of the i's and flowing lines of the f's remained strong. Defiant.

She broke into a grin.

Even...revolutionary.

Boston   2 Dec. 1775

My darling Edwina,

In the fortnight since I was taken from you, I can but think only of the August night we met, when such horrors of war were furthest from our minds, and I daresay, our hearts, as well.

Though I must confess, I did not think of you as attentive to my affections when I was greeted by dawn gleaming off the blade of your cutlass that November morn. How the compass of the heart points in new directions when time and distance have no little significance.

News in Charlotte Town travels at speed, especially among those who frequent Cross Keys Tavern, myself among them. I know you can imagine my state of appal when I, one week prior, learned of your Situation. That General Washington and his Rebellious Colonies should treat Callbeck and Wright with such deference and kindness, but leave you to your fate in the hands of those Loyal to the Crown, I do not conceive.

I fear that I may never again see your sweet face—

Ruby sighed. It was too bad Dr. O'Neil hadn't had the other half of the letter fragment like she'd hoped he would. But this couldn't be a dead end. It just couldn't. Her dissertation was riding on Revolutionary War love letters like this one.

Where was the other half of this letter? What did the

rest of it say? And, most of all, *who* was writing to Edwina?

Ruby's eyes traced the jagged, ripped edge. Her contact at the rare books store on Cambridge Avenue found this fragment in an old family bible they'd had on display.

Just then, the library clock tower gonged the hour. She scrambled to her feet. How had it gotten to be 5 p.m. already?

She had to hurry or she'd be late for that first date to-night.

After she gathered the rest of the notes she needed, Ruby made her way out of the library and back across the green expanse of lawn to the library sciences department.

She wove her way through the maze of graduate and doctoral students, dropped backpacks and makeshift desks before she finally reached her own desk, shoved into a tiny alcove under the eaves, to transcribe what she'd found.

She lifted the lid of her old, somewhat glitchy silver Macbook. Its edges bristled with bright pink, blue and yellow sticky notes to herself. The ding of an incoming email made her pause.

To. ruby.zalonski@simmons.edu
Sent: Monday, August 12

A note to all current staff and students. The position of special collections & archival librarian, payband 12, has been posted as of this email, with the retirement of long-time employee Marianne Schwartz, who has been with us for 30 years.

There will be a retirement party on Tuesday after-noon for her. So don't forget to stop by the staff lounge for some cake and coffee, and a chance to find out what Marianne will be doing with her retirement!

The position was finally opening up? A little thrill ran through Ruby. She opened up a new outgoing message and attached her resume and cover letter, then hit send. She grinned.

Now, she had to finish transcribing her notes.

She readjusted the No. 2 pencil that secured her messy brunette bun and pushed her cat-eye tortoiseshell glasses further up on her nose. Her fingers stilled on the keyboard as her mind strayed back to the letter fragment.

The bold, sweeping handwriting formed in her mind's eye. No one wrote like that these days.

The way the quill pen had formed each word with a hint of a flourish.

She found herself holding her breath as she recalled the writer's firm belief in Edwina's love. The tender words...

For a second she wished whoever it was had been addressing her. Because she'd never find a love that grand. That sweeping. That, well, legendary...

"Ruby? How's it going?"

She glanced over her shoulder. Dr. Jill Burton, the department head—and Ruby's academic advisor for her doctoral dissertation *In Love & War: A Discourse on Women's Love Letters During The American Revolution*—leaned into the half-open doorway. Dr. Burton crossed one lime-green ballet flat over the other.

"Pretty good, Dr. Burton. Did you know that the special collections position just opened up?" Ruby shuffled the pages of notes on her desk before looking back up at the older woman.

Dr. Burton nodded. "Saw that a minute ago—was about to tell you."

"I just applied." Ruby blurted. "I know I haven't completed my Ph.D. yet. But if I could be considered for that job, it would be a dream come true." She grinned.

The older woman smiled. "While I'm all in favor of your enthusiasm, you do know that a Ph.D. is one of the requirements? They do consider non-Ph.D.'s at a university of this size. But it's rare that someone without a Ph.D.—even someone like you who's almost completed her doctorate—would be chosen. Besides that, competition will be fierce. There hasn't been an opening like this in 30 years."

"I know." Ruby said, and pushed up her glasses.

Dr. Burton smiled again. "Well, if I hear anything about

when they want to start interviewing, I'll definitely keep you in the loop. So how's everything coming? Your dissertation is in committee review right now. Which means your defense date is coming up pretty fast. Early next month."

"If I could find more of Edwina's letters, it would definitely support my main theory about women's love letters in the American Revolution as a vital means of communication and self-expression." She paused. "I'm not prone to conspiracy theories, but whoever was writing to her, I think there was something going on...I know that it doesn't exactly have a direct connection to my original love letter research, but it might be an interesting side note or sub-theory to work in."

"Just make sure there's enough money left in your research grant to go ahead with it. They won't be giving out more funds any time soon." Dr. Burton cocked her head. She tapped a French-tipped fingernail against her chin, a sparkle in her eye. "But you're right—that sounds pretty interesting. It certainly wouldn't hurt to explore that angle. It might even add new evidence you could work into your defense. Make it stand apart."

Ruby laughed. "Thanks! So, what's the latest on those papers of Dr. O'Neil's?"

"It's too bad about his passing away so suddenly." Dr. Burton shook her head. "I just got back from a meeting about the late professor." The older woman crossed her arms, and a frown formed between her perfectly plucked brows. "I don't know how it happened in this economic climate—especially with so much money being re-directed to the sports program."

"But," Dr. Burton continued, "the university lawyers have all been consulted, and the paperwork's all drawn up, so it's been given the go-ahead. Which means our department will finally be able to receive his donated papers. Now we just need someone to go up and catalog them."

Wait a minute. A smile spread across Ruby's lips. Special collections..."You need someone to catalog Dr. O'Neil's

papers—why not me?" Ruby's heart thudded. "After all, I initiated contact with Dr. O'Neil in the first place—eight months ago—asking him about that love letter fragment to Edwina."

If she cataloged his papers, then it'd be apparent to all of them here on campus that she was the ideal candidate for that special collections position, Ph.D. or no Ph.D.

"He had so many historical documents," Ruby added. "If I went up there, maybe I could find other love letters written by and to, Edwina, that would help my overall research and add to my supporting documents."

And it would be the perfect opportunity to distinguish herself from the other candidates. She could prove she'd gone above and beyond. Acquired and cataloged this special cache of documents. It'd be easy enough to organize the professor's papers, surely.

"Well, Ruby, you have a good point. All right, the cataloging job's yours. But just remember, you need to be back here by next Thursday so you can prep for your doctoral defense."

"Right," Ruby said. "I'm sure the cataloging won't take long."

THE SALTY AIR riffled the sparkling blue water of Charlottetown Harbor and buffeted against the forest green of Nathan O'Neil's jacket. He stood on the grassy slope of the earthworks of Fort Amherst, at the Skmaqn-Port-la-Joye-Fort Amherst National Historic Site, which nestled against the red cliffs of Prince Edward Island.

He took a deep breath. Couldn't imagine living anywhere else than here on the island. It was home.

This view was one he'd always loved. Bathed in August afternoon light, the boats trailed wakes through the waves. The Charlottetown cityscape was just barely visible from across the bay.

In fact...this would make a great drawing. On impulse,

he pulled out the tiny spiral-bound notebook and pencil he always kept in his jeans pocket.

Hmm, the cliffs would look better if he moved more to the left. He applied pencil to paper and sketched the sparkling waterfront scene. He paused. Looked up again. Cocked his head. If this sketch was going to work, he'd need to add just a bit more detail to the waves...

He glanced at his watch. How had twenty minutes gone by? His coffee break was definitely up. Well, that server issue wasn't going to fix itself. He needed to get back and reboot everything.

He strode up the grassy slope. Then headed onto the gravel path that wound its way through a pine grove leading up to the site's interpretive center. The scent of wild roses drifted to him. He glanced at the row of bushes that bordered the pathway. The plaque near them stated they were descended from original plantings done in the 1700s.

"Hi, how are ya, Nathan?" the man behind the counter said, "Before you go over to the servers, can you check in the back room?"

"Rick, we've known each other since we were eight. You know I'm not exactly a handyman."

Both men chuckled.

"The men's room ran out of paper towel with that last tour bus load. There's another set to show up any minute. The janitor doesn't come on shift for two more hours, and I'm swamped answering calls and giving tours. Otherwise I'd run in there and do it myself."

"All right, I'll go do it. But only because you saved me from getting a swirly from Bobby McPhee back in grade five."

Nathan unlocked the storeroom and rummaged through the cardboard boxes until he found a box full of brown paper towelling. He re-locked the storeroom and headed toward the men's room.

His head brushed the brick ceiling as he stepped inside the washroom. Going into this place always unnerved him. He glanced around the cramped space. Its walls, ceiling and

floors seemed to slough off more crumbling brick every day.

God, how old was this place? He didn't know.

But he did know it was always damp. And that this section, converted in the 1960s before they'd been so vigilant about conservation, used to be part of the old jail, back when Fort Amherst was in use.

He rubbed his arms against the chill that had crept under his forest green fleece jacket. Then again, he was pretty much always cold.

He shifted the box of paper towelling to the rough, uneven floor, and leaned over it to get to the paper towel dispenser.

He jiggled the lock, but it wouldn't budge. Even with the key.

With a muttered curse, he nudged the paper towel box aside so he could stand as close as possible to the dispenser.

He slid the key into the tiny lock again and twisted. Still nothing. He shook the dispenser gently and hoped it would jar something loose.

Still nothing.

Maybe there was another way to open it? Nathan inspected it from all angles. He finally spotted a narrow gap along the bottom, one that would just fit his fingertips. Worth a shot. He slid his fingers into the slight space and pried upward.

Nothing.

He tugged a little harder. With a bang, the dispenser front flopped open, hit the brick wall and caused Nathan to jump backward. He lost his balance, and held onto the only thing that kept him upright: the towel dispenser.

But it pulled away from the wall with a grating and scraping noise. Nathan fell backwards. He landed on the rough brick floor.

He winced. Caught his breath. Hmmm, nothing...broken.

He got up. Dusted himself off and put the new paper towel roll into the holder then glanced down at the box on the floor.

He glanced back up at the wall. And swore.

There was a gaping hole in the wall.

He leaned forward to inspect it. He brushed aside the crumbling mortar and brick dust as his fingers explored the empty cavity. Well, he'd have to—

His fingers brushed something soft. Cloth, he realized. Tucked in behind the left edge of the cavity.

He tugged on it, and it ripped. He swore again.

He tugged on it more gingerly this time and finally pulled it free. It was a tiny, lightweight bundle, wrapped in some sort of yellowed fabric.

He coughed at the swirl of dust as he unfolded the cloth. It was...a book?

No, he realized, not a book: a notebook of sorts. A journal? He eased open the cover. No name there.

Hmmm.

He opened the first page.

But there was nothing written on it. He flipped to the middle. Nothing there either. The book's pages were completely blank. Every last one. Hmmm.

Just then, the door swung open and an Asian man stuck his head into the room.

On an impulse Nathan couldn't explain, he shoved the small book into the inside pocket of his jacket. "I'll let you just—uh, there you go." Nathan gestured to the paper towel and ducked out of the washroom.

After he brushed the mortar and dust off his jacket, Nathan headed back to the desk. "I think the maintenance guy will have to be called in a bit sooner than his usual shift. That paper towel dispenser needs looking at."

THE LIBRARY CLOCK tower gonged a final time and Ruby looked up from the computer screen. It was 6 p.m. She really had to get going. But before she shut down her laptop, she glanced once more at the final email Dr. O'Neil had sent her.

From: goneil@upei.ca
To: ruby.zalonski@simmons.edu
Subject: 1775 letter fragment
Sent: January 12

Dear Ruby,

Thank you for your email last week. I apologize for the delay in responding to you. There have been a few issues that have come up, but I'm sure they will blow over. I've weathered such storms before. The dean and some of my colleagues don't seem to like the theories I'm formulating about Edwina Belliveaux. (Another reason I'm planning to donate my papers to your department at Simmons instead of here at UPEI, once I finally decide to retire for good.)

Anyway, after studying the letter fragment scan you enclosed, I'm sorry to say that I don't have the other half. Though women's love letters during the American Revolution certainly makes for intriguing research.

Because we're both researching Edwina—though for very different reasons—I did some digging in my personal papers since we last corresponded.

And came across General Washington's signed order of Nov. 23, which mentions Edwina. I thought it might be of interest for your own work, so I've attached a copy to this message.

This order is the last remaining original copy. You know, it was only by chance I came across it, pressed between the pages of a psalm book I'd gotten at a rare book auction near Boston some years ago. I've been working on my theory ever since.

You mentioned you don't know the story behind Edwina's role in trying to prevent the theft of the Great Seal of Prince Edward Island, so allow me to fill you in. My version is a bit more complete than the Wikipedia entry.

Near dawn on November 17, 1775, a group of

American privateers, helmed by Captain John Selman and Captain Nicholas Broughton, both under the command of General George Washington, disobeyed a direct order from Washington (which I've also attached), and set sail for Charlottetown, Prince Edward Island. (But back then it was called St. John's Island.) They were supposed to lay in wait for British ships carrying arms and supplies to Quebec, along the St. Lawrence River, but for reasons lost to history, decided to head to P.E.I. instead.

Two American tall ships were in the harbour that morning. Governor Walter Patterson was away in England. So the acting governor, Phillips Callbeck, went down to the docks, hoping to talk some sense into the Americans. Poor man—he'd only been at the post four months. He couldn't stop the Americans. They began raiding and looting the town. Callbeck got kidnapped. Thomas Wright, the town surveyor, who just happened to be in the wrong place at the wrong time, got kidnapped too. Such was the fate of another young man, who got kidnapped as well. But his name, unfortunately, has been lost.

The Americans took all of Charlottetown's winter supplies. They also stole the Great Seal of Prince Edward Island, which was made of silver. But not before Miss Edwina Belliveaux tried to stop them.

I don't know about down there, but up here on Prince Edward Island, people see Edwina Belliveaux as a heroic historical figure. She is famously known for saying, "Unhand that seal, good sir. It is not, nor ever shall be, yours."

But they took it anyway.

The privateers sailed back to Massachusetts. Washington demoted the two captains and freed Callbeck and Wright. Nothing is said of what happened to the young man. But the Americans did keep all the winter supplies, as well as the Great Seal. The seal's never been found. Not only that, there's still a reward of

£1000 for its safe return.

I believe that the lost seal can be found and that the reward money may be partial proof of this. I'm also inclined to speculate that the seal may be part of something larger—perhaps a treasure of sorts? (My family seems to think I spend a little too much time speculating on this. And my colleagues, well, let's just say they think I'm completely wrong. But I say what's academics if you don't have a little disagreement?)

What's more, after reading the love letter fragment, in conjunction with Washington's Nov. 23 order, I think my theory about Edwina stealing the seal is correct. (For the treasure?) If so, it just may change the history books, and lead me one step closer to finding the lost seal...I'll be in touch soon.

Dr. Gordon O'Neil
Professor Emeritus of P.E.I. History
Department of History
University of Prince Edward Island

Ruby shut her laptop. She stuffed the last papers into her bag and headed outside. She dodged puddles as she hurried across the lush green lawn. Just as she headed off campus and caught a tram headed in the direction of Boston Common, her phone buzzed. She glanced at it and grinned at the name on the caller ID. "Hey, Maggie!"

"Hi, Ruby. How's it going?"

"Oh, good, good. Just running late for a first date."

"This the one with that banker tonight?"

"No, that was last month." Ruby sighed. "I ended that after the third date."

"He hit the third-date cliff, did he?" Maggie teased.

"Yeah...I don't know why I do that. Seems I'm always ending things after the third date. Who knows? I'm probably just afraid of commitment or something." She bit her lip. "I'm afraid that—I know this sounds kind of ridiculous—the guy will just disappear on me. So I guess I feel safer if I end things before he gets a chance to."

"Aww, well, good luck with this one."

"Thanks. How's that new jewelry design coming?"

"That antique locket of yours really got me inspired. Oh! I have to run. Got a meeting with one of my suppliers but just wanted to wish you luck tonight."

AFTER WORK, NATHAN jumped in the shower. Fifteen minutes later, he tucked a blue paisley-print towel firmly around his waist.

He wiped away the steam from the mirror in his bathroom. He flicked on the electric razor and started to run it across his dark stubble. Why did he keep breaking things off with perfectly good women? Especially after going so far as to get engaged. Twice.

He shook his head.

He finished shaving and flicked off the razor. Maybe this woman would turn out to be his true love... Where had *that* come from?

Because true love, well, it didn't exist. It was a myth. A legend. Just like that island poem called *The Fair Isle Lovers*. Something beautiful, but something unreal. A figment of the imagination. And most of all: impossible.

Women loved that poem. It was full of passion and romance.

He pursed his lips. And tragedy.

He shook his head. He could never figure out quite why every schoolkid on the island—including himself—had to memorize it in grade six. It had a pretty depressing ending, now that he thought about it...

Kind of like his relationships. Hadn't all his relationships, if you could even call them that, taught him that? Love was always a disappointment. Love was pain. And after the initial high, the initial hope, it all fizzled out.

Fell apart.

When he realized, yet again, that he couldn't drum up the depth of feeling for any of the women. No matter how

much he wanted to. No matter how long he stayed.

No matter what, the emptiness persisted. Grew, even. And once he'd broken up with the latest woman, he was inevitably alone. Left picking up the pieces of his disappointment. Yet again.

Just because he'd had two broken engagements didn't mean there was anything wrong with him. Did it?

He ran his fingers through his damp hair but didn't bother with gel. He slapped on some aftershave and then paused. The woodsy scent brought up the usual sense of longing and restlessness he couldn't quite place. Yet he'd bought this bottle because he'd loved the way the aftershave smelled.

A smile flicked across his face. The woodsy scent somehow reminded him of Fort Amherst. He'd always loved it there. Not the fort itself but the woods around it. Well, he shrugged, it was a beautiful spot.

Nathan walked into his bedroom and shrugged into a periwinkle-blue button-down dress shirt and pulled on a pair of dark-wash jeans.

He slipped into a pair of deck shoes. Then he grabbed his keys off the counter by the front door, didn't bother to lock it, and got into his late-model Lexus.

He headed downtown to Piatto's Pizzeria. But he circled the block three times without finding a parking spot—a sure sign of tourist season on the island. He grinned.

He finally found a parking place along Queen Street when a minivan with Iowa plates pulled out of a spot.

Nathan walked along the red brick sidewalk. He nodded hello to the people he passed. Mostly, in early August, tourists with cameras slung around their necks.

The sounds of clicking silverware and people laughing drifted to him.

He caught the scent of oven-baked pizza and sun-warmed petunias as he strode up to the bright red wooden door of the pizzeria.

He was just about to pull it open when he heard a voice behind him.

"Hi, how are ya, Nathan?"

Nathan turned in the doorway to see a thin bald man in a blue windbreaker, with even bluer eyes. "Robert. Good, good. And you?"

"I'm fine. But I hear a congratulations is in order."

Nathan moved aside and opened the old wooden door wider so a Japanese couple could go inside.

The older man continued, "That's no small feat, winning the Premier's Award for your design of the new Charlotte-town Girl Guides site. Great work."

Nathan smiled. "Thanks. It was a fun and challenging side project." His gut tightened.

It was great. He enjoyed what he did. And after all the time and money he'd put in to getting his double degree, he should.

And yet... He fiddled with the hem of his untucked button-down. Something was missing. What, exactly, he wasn't quite sure...

But he set those thoughts aside. "You've done pretty well for yourself, too, Robert. Getting elected to deputy mayor."

The other man grinned. "Thanks. I feel I can do a lot of good for this city."

"I'm sure you can," Nathan replied and clapped the older man on the shoulder.

"Well, I'm off to the post office. But congratulations again. And if you ever come by city hall, the coffee's on me." Robert winked and then continued down the street.

Nathan's gaze darted inside the airy restaurant with its copper-plate ceiling and large windows along the front.

He spotted a slender blonde woman who sat by herself at a table near the door. That must be... What was her name? Oh, right. Vanessa. He should've remembered that.

He walked over to her, cleared his throat, and extended his hand. "Hi, how are ya?"

She grinned up at him, then got up and gave him a hug that lingered a few seconds. "Really good."

Nathan took a step back. "That's great." He picked up a

menu as he sat down. "Decided on what I can get you for lunch?"

"Hmmm." She studied him over the edge of her menu. "I think I'll have their Salsiccia con Gorgonzola pizza. Would you like to share?"

"Uh, sure." Then he ordered a coffee. Black. Well, she was cute but he preferred brunettes.

"So," he said after he placed their order and leaned his arm against the table, "have you been here long?"

"Depends on what you mean by 'long.'" She laughed. Scooted closer. "I'm a born and raised Islander, if that's what you mean. But I've been here at Piatto's," she glanced at her watch, "about ten minutes so far. You?"

"Well, I'm a native Islander too. And I only just got here."

She laughed again. "I knew that." She touched his arm for a second. "So," she tucked a strand of already-neat hair behind her ear, "what high school did you go to, then?"

Their orders arrived before he could answer.

He fiddled with the coffee stir stick even though he never added cream or sugar. Then took a slice of pizza and bit into it.

After finishing the piece, Nathan again stirred his coffee that didn't need stirring. He glanced out the window in time to see a man in a tricorn hat consult a pocket watch as he crossed the street toward Cross Keys Condos. Must be one of the costumed Confederation Players doing a tour.

Nathan glanced down at his coffee cup. Looked out the window again. Blinked. The man was gone. He looked around. Had the Confederation Players changed their outfits from the 1860s to the 1770s? Nathan frowned. He probably just hadn't gotten enough sleep.

"Nathan?"

"Oh! Sorry. Um, it was Colonel Grey High."

Vanessa darted a glance his way over the rim of her water glass. "Colonel Grey, huh?" She took a sip then blinked up at him, her eyes wide, her lips slightly parted.

He shifted in his seat. "And you?"

"Oh, I went to Charlottetown Rural." She started digging through her purse. Took out her business card and handed it to him. "I'm free tonight." She paused. Looked up at him. Lowered her voice. "That is, if you are?"

Nathan felt a wave of disappointment wash through him. "Vanessa," he said. "You seem really nice. And you're cute. But...I can't go on any more dates with you. I'm just not that interested. I'm sorry."

"AND SO THEN," the 30-something man across the table from Ruby waved his fork, "I got the supervisor award. For the third year in a row. Plus, I got a fifty percent pay raise and a company car." He leaned forward. "A Mercedes. S Class." He grinned, and Ruby could see a slight gap between his front teeth. But the dimple in his cheek was rather appealing.

She fiddled with the stem of her wine glass. "Oh, that's, uh, great for you."

The man nodded. "Thanks!" He took a bite of his salmon.

Silence stretched between them. Ruby's mind strayed back to the love letter fragment. Such a romantic phrase: *the compass of the heart points in new directions*...No one talked like that any more. Least of all, to her...

Ruby placed her unused knife neatly on the edge of her plate. Then moved the wine glass from one side of the table to the other.

As if suddenly realizing she was still sitting there, the man said, "So, what is it that you do?"

"I'm currently a doctoral student for Simmons College. My focus is archival and preservation studies. I want to become a special collections librarian." Hmmm. But who wrote that romantic phrase? Whoever it was must have had a poet's soul...And did Edwina know it? Appreciate it? Return the sender's affections just as ardently? *Ardently*? What? She shook her head. She'd been reading so many antique documents that she'd started to think like that.

The man took another bite of his salmon. "Don't you like your job?"

"Oh! Yes. I love it—to me, discovering antique documents is like a treasure hunt." Hmmm. Would Dr. O'Neil's papers provide any new connections between Edwina and whoever she was receiving letters from?

"That's great. So what are you working on now?"

"Well," Ruby said, and made a wry face. "I was running late to this date, actually, because I was researching. So I actually have a few photocopies here." She paged through her notes. She came to her copy of Washington's signed orders Dr. O'Neil had sent her, and handed the first one to her date.

Headquarters   October 16, 1775

...Should you meet with any vessel, the property of the inhabitants of Canada, not employed in any respect in the service of the ministerial army, you are to treat such vessel with all kindness, and by no means suffer them to be injured or molested.

George Washington

He glanced up at her as he finished reading, a questioning look on his face.

"Oh, I'm not really concerned about George Washington. I'm hoping that I'll be able to find out more about a woman named Edwina Belliveaux, who actually isn't mentioned in that."

Her date frowned. "So why do you have this one?"

"Since I'm researching love letters, and not George Washington, I only have this order because it's one link in the paper trail that I'm hoping will lead me to more information about Edwina. She's the subject of a fragment that I'm wanting to use in my research on women's love letters in the American Revolution."

"Oh. Well, that's...great. And where is this Edwina mentioned?"

"In a different document. I have it right here, actually."
Ruby handed him the other printout from Dr. O'Neil's
emails.

Headquarters   November 25, 1775

*Now that Captains Selman and Broughton have been
dealt with and their ranks stripped from them, you are
to send Miss Belliveaux back to the Island of St. John
and Charlotte Town at once.*

*Though she has done a great disservice by being
under my employ as a so-called privateer, and in truth,
disobeyed the earlier direct order from me after having
set sail for Charlotte Town, now that the true loyalties
of Edwina Belliveaux have been discovered to lie not
with the Crown nor the Patriots, but with those of Acadian descent, you are not to harm her.*

*While she has not persuaded the French-Canadians
to be favorable to our Patriot cause, as I had hoped she
might, let the Loyalists in Canada seal her fate. Her
blood shall not be upon the hands of the Patriots.*

George Washington

"So what was the connection, exactly, between Washington's second order and the love letter fragment?" her
date asked.

Ruby leaned forward. "That question had been going
through my head ever since I started corresponding with a
professor in Canada eight months ago. It seems pretty clear
that the Edwina in the love letter was the same Edwina who
appeared in this order."

"Well, sounds like a fascinating mystery for you." He
handed back the photocopies. Straightened his tie. "So. Did
I tell you about the time I went scuba diving in Bora Bora?"

Ruby fought down a surge of disappointment. Why had
she expected him, even for a moment, to be as excited as
she was about this?

She flicked her eyes to her watch. What would she find
when she went through Dr. O'Neil's papers? Ruby had

already been in touch with Evie, Dr. O'Neil's daughter. She'd said Ruby would be welcome to stay in her dad's now-unused place at Cross Keys Condos downtown. So her accommodations were taken care of. Now she just had to pack.

As Ruby's date looked down at his plate and took the last bites of his meal, she cocked her head. From this angle, his jawline looked appealing. She squinted, and decided that it pretty much cancelled out the fact that his hairline had started to recede.

No. A man's hairline had nothing to do with his character. She had to look past that.

A few minutes later, the waiter arrived with the check. Would he want to split it like the last guy had?

Ruby's date smiled at her. "My treat." He took the bill and paid in cash. "Are you all set?"

Ruby nodded.

"Can I walk you to your car?"

"...Sure."

He held open the restaurant door for Ruby and they walked out into the cool summer evening.

"Well," he said, as they came to a stop in front of Ruby's black Toyota sedan, "I had a nice time. Let's do this again sometime."

Ruby's smile faltered but she reached for polite words. "Thanks for dinner and uh, that sounds...nice."

He opened the driver's door for her and then headed off to his own car. Ruby got in and drove back to her apartment.

This guy was nice enough. Had paid for their meal. Even if he did tend to talk a bit too much about himself. Maybe it didn't matter that he hadn't asked her any follow-up questions about herself. And he was decent looking...

She withheld a sigh. She couldn't expect more than that. What did it say about her love life that the only thing that got her pulse to race these days was a centuries-old love letter? And not even a whole one, at that?

She shook the thoughts off, unlocked her apartment and

let herself in. Time to pack for Charlottetown.

She walked into her bedroom, pulled out her battered flowered purple suitcase, and unzipped it.

First, though, she should probably change out of her work clothes and into something more comfortable.

She slipped off her blouse and slid out of her slim gray trousers. She folded them and put them away in her dresser drawer before she realized she still had her jewelry on.

She took out her rhinestone earrings and slipped off her imitation Cartier watch. Then she pulled on her favorite jeans and blue tank top, careful to lift up the locket to avoid its chain catching in the knit fabric.

As she settled the locket back into place, she slid her fingers around the cool sterling silver etched with tiny flowers.

Out of habit, she flicked it open. On the left, a miniature painting of a handsome dark-haired man with brown eyes looked back at her, his hair neatly tied in a queue. On the right, a miniature painting of a beautiful woman with green eyes and blonde hair in neat ringlets. Ruby smiled. Who were these people? She had to admit, she loved to speculate about it ever since she'd picked the locket up at that flea market in the North End.

She noticed the picture of the man had somehow gotten a bit off-center, so she moved a fingertip to adjust it. Hmmm. That didn't work.

She unfastened the locket. She held it in both hands and tried to get a better angle to adjust the picture. Well, maybe it'd be easier to take it out and slide it all the way back in again.

She gently tugged on the thick antique paper. It came out easily. But behind the miniature was a small square of folded paper. Ruby cocked her head. She put the locket down then unfolded the small square:

Cardinal directions of the heart
Impart the way toward True North
Good-hearted General's Orders did put forth;

Crowned Head of Justice, strong and brave
Cradled on the wind and waves

Huh. What was this? How had it gotten in there? She readjusted the miniature and put it back into place, now centered then snapped the locket shut.

*Cardinal directions of the heart...*Why did that sound so familiar?

She'd have to look at it more closely after she'd finished packing. Could it be some sort of poem? Or possibly a rhyme? Or...she grinned. A riddle?

She pushed up her glasses. Nah. Nothing that exciting ever happened to her. She turned back to her packing.

As Nathan strode back to his car after his failed date, he unwrapped a white chocolate Hershey bar—the last portion of his lunch—and took a bite. But the sweetness of his favorite chocolate brought up a bitter memory.

He and Dad had been in the study, had that argument... He sighed and his mouth tightened. The last one they'd had before he'd died in February. Was that really six months ago?

And now he couldn't take it back. Couldn't say, "I'm sorry," and then swipe the white chocolate Hershey bar from Dad's desk drawer to offer him half.

His lips rose in a crooked half-smile. But it faded. Now both of his parents were gone...

"Are you even listening to what I'm saying, Nathan? You can't just loaf around here like some teenager or homeless person."

Nathan had crossed his arms and hunched his shoulders, but kept his voice calm. Rational. "Dad. I got fired. It's not the end of the world. Just because jobs are hard to come by here on Prince Edward Island doesn't mean that I won't get another one. Statistically speaking—"

"Quite being so damn logical, Nathan." Dr. Gordon

O'Neil's voice grew louder. "Sometimes life is more than numbers and statistics. Sometimes you have to let that go and figure out what you want to do with your life. You can't just keep working these dead-end jobs. You need to actually use your graphic design degree—"

Nathan had taken a bite of the chocolate and clenched his fists. "I'm 33 years old, Dad. Please don't talk to me like I'm 17."

"I'm still your father."

"Sometimes I wonder."

"What's that supposed to mean?"

"It means that on this island, family is the most important thing. Roots. Connections."

"Yes, well, you'd better start exercising some of those connections or you'll be working at God knows where—McDonald's—the rest of your life!" A vein ticked in Dr. O'Neil's temple.

"Calm down, Dad. You know what the doctor said."

"I won't calm down. I need to make this point to you! Can't you see? I'm on your case because I care about you. Your future. You're not going to be the only O'Neil on Prince Edward Island who's failed."

Nathan had snapped off another piece of chocolate and chewed furiously. "Just because this family has roots in this place going back to 1768, doesn't mean I have to be like every last one of them!"

"Yes, well, you've already proven that quite nicely now, haven't you?"

"Dad." Nathan had raked a hand through his hair, fought down the surge of anger. "You know I love you. But should you really be the one to talk? Everyone thinks your theories about the Great Seal are, well, crazy... Even I think that and I know how much work you've put into them. And let's not even talk about your ridiculous ideas about the seal being part of some sort of treasure."

"Good idea. Let's not talk about that. Because finding the lost seal isn't the point of this discussion, son. Though I do have reason to believe I'm about to find it."

"You can't find it, Dad. That's impossible. It was melted down for bullets long ago. And there is no treasure, either. You should realize that and stop wasting your life on—"

"Wasting my life?" Dr. O'Neil raised his brows. "At least I'm using my education. At least I'm making something of myself."

"Thanks, Dad." Nathan had blinked rapidly. But then his blue eyes, the exact shade of his father's, flashed. "Just because I made a few mistakes, took a few risks in university, doesn't mean I'm only capable of being the black sheep you seem to think I am."

"So that means those broken engagements, that pot smoking, and those reckless driving tickets mean nothing?"

Nathan had hunched his shoulders. "I only broke off two engagements. And I don't smoke pot any more. People can change."

Dr. O'Neil had opened his mouth to reply but sagged against his desk instead, and let his head drop to his chest.

Nathan's heart felt squeezed in a vise. "Dad?" He touched a hand to his father's shoulder.

"I'm fine." Dr. O'Neil shook off his son's concern. "Just a little...out of breath."

Nathan suddenly hadn't been able to catch his own breath. "All right, Dad," he had said softly, "if it means that much to you, I'll start looking for something else right away."

Dr. O'Neil had straightened up. Nathan's shoulders had relaxed. "One of my buddies from uni works at a software company here in Charlottetown. Maybe they need a graphic design guy."

A seagull wheeled and called overhead. Nathan blinked away the memory and took a deep breath. He crumpled up the empty Hersey wrapper and tossed it into the trash can. He wished he could toss out the guilt and regret just as easily. Because now he'd never have the chance to make things right.

Chapter Two

NATHAN SHRUGGED OUT of his green jacket and slung it over the back of the antique Windsor chair in the cream-tiled hallway of the split-level he'd inherited from his grandma.

This evening, he could transpose bits and pieces of the initial sketch he'd done at Fort Amherst onto a larger piece of real drawing paper.

He went to the fridge and fished out the last bottle of Beach Chair Lager behind a carton of Chinese takeout and headed out the screened-in back porch.

He inhaled the scent of freshly mowed grass from his neighbor's yard. He took a seat on the old wicker porch swing, its faded blue gingham pillows ones his grandma had stitched from her mother's rag bag.

His lips lifted in a half-smile. Another Island trait—mending and making do.

He leaned back against the pillows. Took a sip of his beer. A light breeze played across his face and carried with it the scent of impending summer rain.

His mind returned to his date earlier in the day.

People around here liked to think he was a heartbreaker. And it was true.

He raked a hand through his hair. But that had never stopped women from throwing themselves at him.

A fact he wasn't proud of. In fact, he'd broken the heart of his most recent ex when he'd walked away after six months.

She'd asked him to be her boyfriend after the fourth date.

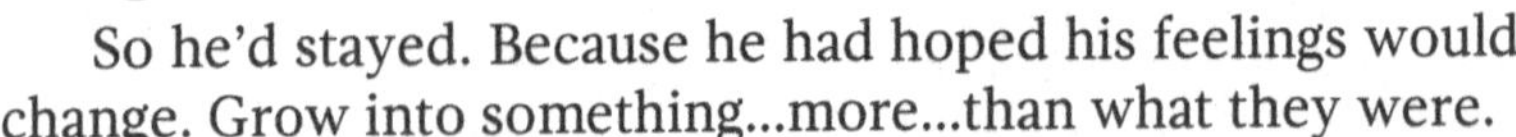

So he'd stayed. Because he had hoped his feelings would change. Grow into something...more...than what they were.

But it just became six months of emptiness. At least, for him. But for her, it'd become six months in which she'd grown to love him so much that she'd basically proposed marriage one night as they lay in the dark of his bedroom.

Somehow, you could say things in the pitch black that you couldn't quite find the courage for in the light of dawn.

He never should've let it go on that long. It really wasn't fair. To either of them. He sighed. He shouldn't be this dissatisfied in his love life. It didn't make any sense. Wasn't that the nature of love, anyway? To make compromises? To be a bit...disappointed?

Because the whole notion of true love was just a fiction. People were happy enough together. Could even have fulfilling, satisfying lives together if they simply liked each other. Right? Of course they could. It happened all the time.

He took another sip of beer.

Then why didn't that seem like enough, for him? As irrational as that sounded.

He pushed aside his negative thoughts and got to his feet. He drained the rest of the beer and tossed the empty bottle into the blue recycle bin by the back door.

In the kitchen, he had just flicked on the dishwasher when he heard a rumble of thunder. All at once, it was pouring rain.

The rain beat down on the roof. Outside, treetops bent in the force of the wind.

Cold and wet blew through the kitchen, and Nathan shut the window just in time.

He dashed around the rest of the house to make sure no windows were left open. He eased the small leather-bound book out of his back pocket and placed it in a half-empty drawer of his nightstand. He'd look at it later.

But that's when he remembered he'd left the window to his dad's office open earlier that day after he and his sister had gone over there to consult with the contractor for some renovations.

He dashed out the door and across the lawn to his car. It wasn't that far to the condo. The rain started to filter through his heather-green cotton V-neck T-shirt during the short sprint to the car. He sped over to the condo but didn't bother to roll up the car windows as he drove.

As he pulled into the lot, the rain came down in sheets. Well, the secondary entrance was closer. He jumped out of the car, reached the building's back door and pressed down on the brass thumb latch of the curved door handle. It didn't budge.

He could feel his shirt start to stick to his back as the rain pelted down.

He searched his jeans pockets for the key. It wasn't there.

Damn.

He jogged back over to his car, his shirt now pretty much soaked through.

He shook the water out of his eyes and grabbed the right key ring after he fished around a minute or two in the jumble of odds and ends in his console.

He ran back across the parking lot and then the sidewalk. It took him three tries but finally he fit the key into the lock.

He shook his head at himself. He was usually better at this. Well, maybe that was only when he was unhooking a woman's bra with one hand.

Not that he'd done that in awhile...

As the Air Canada jet angled a little to the left to circle the Charlottetown airport, Ruby peered out the small window. Late afternoon sunlight sparkled on the blue Northumberland Strait. Patches of gray rainclouds interlaced with the dark green of pine trees and the lighter green of rolling hills. Even from this height, she could see red sandstone cliffs topped with bright green grass. The surf curled and ebbed against the uneven shoreline of the island.

The plane touched down. Ruby's pulse thudded in her throat.

What if Dr. O'Neil's papers didn't contain any more of the information she needed? What if she was completely wasting her time and this didn't make any difference in qualifying her for the position? What if she'd have to re-do her whole 300-page dissertation?

She shook her head. Lifted her chin. It wouldn't come to that.

"Ladies and gentlemen," the flight attendant said, "it'll just be a second while the ground crew brings around the stairs. No skybridge at this airport. Please watch your step as you go down."

After a few minutes, the fasten seatbelt sign dinged off, and Ruby stood.

She made her way down the steps of the airplane. The afternoon sunshine glinted gold off the metal of the airplane and tinged the expanse of sky. As Ruby crossed the tarmac, a fine mist of rain started to fall.

With the rain came the scent of salt air and she inhaled. A smile spread slowly across her face.

Was it her imagination or did the ocean smell different here than in Massachusetts? She closed her eyes. She could almost imagine herself walking through a pine forest, carrying a woven basket filled with bread. The fine cotton of her green-striped summer dress swished around her, the sounds of the surf off to her left as seagulls called and wheeled overhead.

A wave of longing and homesickness surged through her. A seagull called again, and she startled. Her eyes opened.

What? How could she feel homesick for this place when she'd only just arrived? Besides, she'd grown up in the city.

She frowned and shook away the feeling. Where had that come from? But she shrugged. Just due to the time difference, that's all. She yawned. And the long trip.

A *Welcome to Prince Edward Island* sign caught her eye as she walked through the sliding glass door to the tiny arrivals area.

As Ruby headed to the baggage carousel, she looked around. On her left, displays showed photos of rolling green hills and fields of blooming pink lupine. Other images depicted smiling children who dug clams on the beach. The wet red sand squished between their toes. More pictures illustrated laughing couples seated on outdoor patios with red-brick paving stones and old-fashioned lampposts.

A sense of lightness filled Ruby's chest, and her heart beat faster.

She retrieved her overstuffed purple flowered suitcase from the baggage carousel. But as she set it down, it wobbled and pitched over.

She righted it and noticed that one of its wheels had snapped off. Well, the suitcase was old. And baggage handlers could be a little rough on luggage. She dragged the damaged suitcase along and headed out the arrivals door as the rain began to fall harder.

NATHAN TOOK THE stairs to the fourth floor and stepped inside number 415. He shut the door quickly behind him and heaved a sigh of relief.

Until he realized he had dripped water all over the faded Oriental rug in the foyer.

He took off his leather flip-flops and wiped his feet before he went into the bathroom and rooted around for a towel.

Nothing.

A knot settled into his stomach and his fingers clenched. As he closed the linen closet door, he caught the familiar scent of Downy as he did.

He swallowed.

Water settled around his bare feet and he headed into the kitchen to grab a dishtowel.

The tea towel drawer squeaked on its runners. It'd been doing that for as long as he could remember: the sound of

childhood. He gave the drawer a pat as he shut it.

After he towelled off his hair with a faded tea towel printed with lavender sprigs, he shoved the towel into his back pocket and shut the window over the sink.

The rain pounded on the roof.

The wind suddenly shifted and began to keen through the open living room windows. He darted over to shut both of them, then turned and started down the hall.

His footsteps slowed, though, as he approached the first door on the left.

With his lips pressed together, he pushed open the door and got a whiff of cherry tobacco and leather-bound books.

He stood there for a second and looked at the mess.

Overfull boxes piled on top of drawers piled on top of accordion file-folders, which bulged at the seams, full of every sort of scrap of paper, newspaper clipping and online article printout.

If a messy desk was a sign of genius, then his dad must have truly been an Einstein of his field.

RUBY DASHED TO the nearest cab. The driver rolled down his window. "I've got another fare heading downtown, but you can hop in if you're headed there too."

Ruby nodded, and the man got out to stow her luggage.

"How are ya?" he said, as Ruby got in. "Where you headed?"

"Cross Keys Condos, please."

The man pulled into traffic. "So where you from?" he said.

"Boston."

"Ah," the man grinned, and the bobble-headed yellow duck on the dash seemed to grin, too. "Got a few cousins down that way. Haven't been there myself, though. What's your name?"

"Ruby." Ruby glanced out the window as the car turned on to North River Road and dropped off the first fare. It was pouring rain now. "Zalonski," she added.

"Hmmm. Can't say I know that last name."

"No, it's not too common. It's my adoptive last name."

The man nodded, and so did the yellow duck on the dash. "My wife's adopted. Can't imagine not knowing who your father is, myself, though. How long you in town for?"

A wrought iron fence surrounded one brightly painted blue house with red geraniums that hung in baskets on the wide white porch.

"About a week," Ruby answered. "I'm hoping to make this a fairly quick trip—I have a dissertation to defend back in Boston soon. But I'm here on university business. Cataloging some papers." She turned her head and saw a weathered gray clapboard house, shaded by broad leafy oaks and maples.

The cab slowed and turned right onto Euston Street. They passed a three-story red brick home. It had white columns and what must be a 300-year-old oak tree in the yard, with roots that almost spilled out onto the street.

But the car kept going.

More houses. More big trees. Ruby grinned. She couldn't help but remember the big oak that her adoptive father had hung a rope swing from. She'd spent every second that she could, during her childhood summers, outside in that big swing.

The taxi turned onto Queen Street. "Here we are." The driver pulled into a parking spot in front of a four-story red brick building with a bronze plaque affixed to it. Ruby noticed the date—1773.

A bistro called Terre Rouge shared the first floor with a gourmet olive oil store.

Baskets of pink and purple petunias hung from old-fashioned cast iron lampposts.

The driver got out and pulled Ruby's suitcase out of the back. Ruby got out too. She pulled up the hood of her light summer jacket, and paid the driver. She made sure to tip him.

"Have a good one. The condo's around to the side

there," he said, as he pointed to Ruby's right, before he drove away.

Ruby sprinted around the corner. She pulled her battered suitcase behind her and opened the door of the condo entrance. She noticed the hand-painted, gold-lettered, wooden sign with two old-fashioned brass keys overlapping one another. She'd arrived at Cross Keys Condos.

In the lobby, a large carriage-lantern hung overhead, which threw the marble floor into a flattering, mellow light. Ruby punched the code that Evie had given her into the keypad by the door. She let herself into the foyer before she pressed the call button on the elevator.

NATHAN COULDN'T HELP glancing at the *Globe & Mail* article documenting his father's discovery of yet another elusive historical tidbit about some famous dead person.

Like Edwina Belliveaux. Nathan reached out and automatically straightened the framed yellowed newspaper clipping on the right-hand corner of the desk. It had been there for as long as he could remember. He picked it up:

One of the island's most recognizable forebearers, Edwina Belliveaux, gets yet another honorable mention today, as a plaque with her name on it has been installed—

God. He blinked rapidly and set the framed clipping down. Now that famous dead person was his own father. Nathan pressed his lips together and moved to the wall of windows opposite the roll-top desk.

Rain blew in and made circles of damp on the highly polished hardwood and the red-and-blue Aubusson rug. It filled his nose with the scent of damp wool and lemon floor wax.

He reached into his back pocket, pulled out the kitchen towel and began to mop up the mess.

It'd probably be easier if he shut the windows first, though. He got up from his crouch and moved to the window.

It stuck a bit, swollen slightly from the humidity and the rain.

He pushed harder. He'd just gotten the old six-by-six wavy glass to move down an inch when a loud banging sounded in the hallway.

Nathan crossed the study and stubbed his bare toe on the leg of an antique writing desk that sat by the room's entrance.

But he couldn't help smiling at it even though his toe throbbed. His mother had bought the Federal-style desk at an auction in Rustico. He ran a finger along its cherry-wood surface.

He'd always wondered about the series of notches on the underside of the writing surface. Who had owned it?

More banging.

He made his way to the front entrance and put his hand on the doorknob just as his skin broke out in goose bumps.

He shook it off and opened the door. No one was there. A sense of déja vù coursed through him.

He paused but then leaned out further into the hall.

A young woman stood in the hallway with her back to him as she tried to lift a heavy-looking suitcase. One of its wheels, he noticed, had sheered off completely. She struggled up the stairs.

He took a step out into the hall. But before he could offer help, she'd lugged the suitcase over the final stair step. She spun around. Her eyes widened behind her glasses as she realized someone else was in the hallway.

He met her gaze. The hairs on the back of his neck stood up as the sharp tang of sea salt and the sweetness of wild roses filled his senses.

His throat constricted. He cleared it. That was quite the perfume. Shampoo. Or—hand lotion?

A sting of tears prickled his eyes as he continued to hold her hazel gaze.

He tried to force himself to look away. But couldn't.

The blood pounded in his veins, and he felt as if he'd just jumped off a cliff. A sharp, sweet sort of joy clutched at his heart while regret and longing rose within him. His throat worked. Two words, deep and resonant, coursed through his heart and mind—*I'm sorry.*

What?

He held his breath. Frowned. What *were* all these emotions? Nothing. He blinked away the sting of tears.

He was probably just tired. He actually hadn't slept well the past few nights. Yet he found he couldn't speak.

He watched, wordless, as she took a step backward while her lips formed an O. But no words came out of her mouth, either.

He cleared his throat again. Finally managed, "Don't go." Huh? He swallowed. Chuckled and rubbed a hand across the back of his neck then said, "I mean, can I help you?"

She shook her head, and her glossy blonde curls shimmied and fell in shining waves down the smooth satiny skin of her bare back—He blinked. No. That didn't make any sense.

Her hair was in a ponytail. Yes. She had brown hair, not blonde. Right. And she was wearing a yellow T-shirt. She took a shaky breath. "Y-yes. I'm looking for Dr. Gordon O'Neil's condo."

His fingers gripped the doorframe. He couldn't stop staring at her. As if he'd never get his fill. As if, when he blinked, she might disappear. What? That was ridiculous. Of course she wouldn't disappear. "This is it."

The young woman shifted the bag to her other hand. "Well, his daughter Evie told me I could come by."

"My sister?" Nathan shifted his weight. Forced himself to concentrate. "I hadn't heard anything about that."

"Oh. And who are you?" The woman lifted her chin.

"I'm, uh," he riffled a hand through his damp hair. Frowned. "Dr. O'Neil's son. Nathan."

"Oh," the young woman repeated. Crossed her arms. "Well, can you please let me inside? My name's Ruby Zalonski. And I've come to catalog his papers."

RUBY WAS NOT going to stare at the way Nathan's rain-soaked heather-green cotton T-shirt clung to the contours of his chest. She had important work to do. Or how something in his gaze seemed to speak of moonlit beaches, wild roses and second chances.

She frowned. Huh?

He looked like he'd just stepped from a movie set: ripped jeans, tousled black hair, soaked T-shirt and all. Her heart leapt to her throat. How could anyone this gorgeous be for real?

Well, she was smarter than to get carried away by something like good looks. Looks didn't tell you anything. Evie's warning about her brother's reputation told her everything. She straightened her spine. Pushed up her glasses.

"What's this about?" Nathan's eyes narrowed, and as he tilted his head, a few strands of his damp, dark hair fell across his forehead.

Ruby lifted her chin though her heart raced. She couldn't help staring at those stray strands of thick dark hair.

She shoved her hands into the pockets of her white capris so that she wouldn't smooth away the stray strands for him. "For my doctoral dissertation. I'm from Simmons College and I'd arranged to catalog Dr. O'Neil's papers for—"

"Well, I have no idea what you're talking about." Nathan started to close the door.

"Wait," Ruby said, and put her hand on the doorframe near his. "Your sister told me I could stay here. Now that...now that there's an unused bedroom?"

Nathan's gaze flicked down at the suitcase at her feet. Something about the way his lashes rested on his cheekbones as he glanced down at her suitcase had a fierce sadness washing through her. Like she'd gotten here too late. That she'd missed her chance—

His gaze flicked back up to her. Held.

She caught her breath.

He blinked. "Uh, come in for now." He paused. "I'll just confirm with Evie in a bit."

"Thank you," she managed around the lump that suddenly lodged in her throat. She took a breath. Cleared her throat.

Saw him swallow. "You're welcome." A beat of silence. "Here, let me take that." He leaned forward to take her broken suitcase and she watched the cotton of his T-shirt stretch across his bicep as he picked up the luggage.

Ruby forced herself to take a deep breath. Then she followed him inside as he turned and shut the door to the condo behind them.

"Watch yourself," Nathan said, "it's a bit messy in here. Renovations."

She bent her head and slipped off her faux alligator-print wedges.

A quick look around revealed a short hallway with a gold-and-cream Oriental rug. It was only then she noticed his feet were bare, too. She felt her cheeks turn pink.

She curled her toes into the thick wool as she saw his broad shoulders tense underneath his shirt when he turned to glance over his shoulder.

In reply to the unspoken question in his gaze, she followed him down the short hallway. When she looked to the left, she saw what he meant.

Ladders and paint cans were strewn around, and a big plastic drop sheet covered the flooring. Long sheets of drywall leaned against the exposed-brick walls, and big plastic trashcans were heaped up with plaster and lathe.

"That must have been the living room?"

"Yep. We're having it redone. The roof started to leak awhile back, and up here on the top floor, it somehow went unnoticed."

He stopped suddenly at a door on the right. He pressed his palm to the smooth surface of the burnished wooden door and pushed it open. Ruby felt a shiver go up her spine as she watched his fingertips caress the wood. She peered inside.

It was a study—and a complete mess.

"Dad had his own filing system, if you could call it that. Only another academic could figure it out. If they had a lucky day."

Which, she was rapidly discovering, wasn't today for her.

NATHAN PUSHED AWAY from the doorframe and shoved aside the strange sensations and irrational emotions as he did so. Those feelings didn't make any sense. Therefore, he wasn't going to pay any attention to them. He had to deal with what was in front of him.

And right now, it was this woman.

"So you're here to catalog my dad's papers?"

She passed him on the threshold. He had to shove his hands in his jeans pockets to stop himself from reaching out to smooth back the stray strand that had come loose from her ponytail.

"Yes. But don't worry, they've only sent me here for a week. Academic budgets, and all that."

He mentally shook his head. Took a deep breath and let it out slowly. She wanted to catalog Dad's things. That meant she was going to be here in the middle of these renovations.

"Wait. Wait."

She paused. Turned her head to look at him.

"Where did you say you were from, again?"

"People ask that a lot around here." Ruby laughed lightly and tucked the stray strand of hair behind her ear. "Boston. Simmons College." She cleared her throat and shifted from foot to foot.

This woman was an outsider. From away. He winced inwardly. He'd always disliked that term, 'from away.' He wasn't of his grandfather's generation. He shouldn't feel any sort of suspicion or distrust for her just because she was from off-island.

He crossed his arms. Studied her unruly brunette waves, her tortoiseshell glasses, and the yellow cotton T-shirt that fit her so perfectly.

He swallowed. But how could he trust this tidal wave of emotions she'd plunged him into, just by...just by standing in front of him?

And if she was from away, then why did it feel so good to have her here? "So you're an academic too."

Ruby put her hand on her hip. "Not yet. But I soon will be. I'm working on my doctorate."

"That wouldn't happen to be a doctorate in P.E.I. history, would it?"

Ruby frowned and crossed her arms. "No. It's in archival studies, actually."

"But you were corresponding with my father."

"...Yes."

"Let me guess." He also crossed his arms. "You probably think the lost seal can be found too. And that Edwina Belliveaux had something more to do with it than what history says."

"You know," Ruby said as she un-shouldered her carry-on and set it down by her bare feet. Nathan saw the polish she'd used was a pale pink. "Some people happen to think your father's work was revolutionary."

She held his gaze. Continued. "He wasn't afraid to stand up for what he believed in, no matter what other people thought. No matter what other people said."

"Well, those other people had plenty to say." Nathan frowned and regarded her.

She didn't break eye contact. "They thought he was crazy. A crackpot. All his conspiracy theories about the Great Seal, the pounds sterling and that 'famous quote'"— Ruby made air quotes with her fingers—"from Edwina."

"Exactly. So I wouldn't waste my time if I were you. That's what got him his reputation in the first place." Nathan raised his eyebrows at the memory. "He seemed to think the lost seal meant something more than what everyone thought." He shook his head. "And that Edwina stole it instead of trying to save it."

She continued as if she hadn't heard him. "That's why we started corresponding in the first place." She crouched beside her carry-on. Took out a glossy black leather folder, which, Nathan saw, contained a brand new legal pad, a freshly sharpened No. 2 pencil, and an array of rainbow-hued sticky notes.

Nathan waved a hand in the general direction of the mess. "Well, I'll save you the trouble of sifting through all these—"

"—valuable resources?" She straightened up. And the glance she shot him held just enough fierceness that he lifted his palms.

Ruby flicked a page in the legal pad over to a clean sheet then picked up the pencil and licked the tip. God. His gut tightened. What the hell was happening to him?

He watched her jot the date, and—she glanced at her watch—the time, onto the page in neat, curving script.

Nathan shifted to lean back against the glass top of his father's massive oak desk. "Don't tell me you're here to *find* the Great Seal? Chase down some ridiculous notion about a treasure?"

Ruby raised her brows. "And if I was?"

Nathan shook his head and opened his mouth.

"For your information," Ruby said, and crossed her arms again, "I'm here to catalog his papers, not make judgements. My research is focused on love letters. I'm hoping to find out more about one particular love letter, actually. One that Edwina received from...someone." The color rose on her cheeks. "I want to figure out just who. And if there's something in your dad's papers that can help me, so much the better."

"You like that, don't you?" Nathan said. He rested his hands, palm down, against the smooth glass-topped surface of the desk. He studied Ruby, his head cocked. "The romance of it all..." He rubbed one hand up and down his opposite arm.

"There's nothing wrong with that." Ruby shot him a

look filled with annoyance.

"Love letter research?" Nathan tugged at his earlobe. "Isn't that a little..." He shrugged, rubbed the back of his neck. "I don't know—"

"No." Ruby frowned. "That's right. You *don't* know. This is my research, not yours." She tapped her foot. "I thought Canadians were supposed to be polite."

"Don't believe everything you hear."

Chapter Three

RUBY'S GRIP TIGHTENED on the plastic grocery bags. It had finally stopped raining. She carried her bags down Queen Street toward Cross Keys Condos later that evening as she dodged puddles.

She walked through tree-lined Victoria Row, with its paving bricks, brightly colored picnic benches, and white fairy lights strung between leafy tree limbs.

But it wasn't the sound of the live jazz band playing on the outdoor stage that caught her ear, but Nathan's name.

She turned her head, and spotted two older women seated at a bright yellow picnic table under a maple tree.

"That Nathan O'Neil, I heard he broke up with yet another one just the other day. And after only the first date. Are these Island girls not good enough for him?" The woman shook her head.

Ruby paused mid-stride.

"That man never changes," said the other woman. "He's 33 and still acts like a teenager. At least he quit smoking pot. But he's still breaking hearts at every turn. One day he'll wake up and realize he's thrown his life away. Old and lonely, I tell you."

Ruby's eyes widened, and she strained to catch their words. Was that true? The tiniest bit of disappointment made her stomach dip. But then she shook her head at herself. Evie had warned her about Nathan's reputation... Yet why had she had such strong emotions around him?

"But all the women run to him. Girls these days have no sense to let a man do the chasing." The other woman clucked her tongue.

The first woman nodded. "Hard to believe he's an O'Neil. Who would break off two engagements?—not like any of his ancestors, that's sure."

Two engagements? No. Ruby lifted her chin. She shouldn't just stand here and listen to idle gossip. It wasn't right. And it wasn't true.

"Shame about what happened up at UPEI with his dad. Too bad the poor man had to pass away so suddenly."

Although, *that* was definitely true...

"And did you hear? Apparently Nathan got a $300 ticket—talking on his phone and driving at the same time. He always was a bit of a reckless driver. I should know. My Marvin was his driver's ed teacher."

Ruby adjusted her grip on her grocery bags. She couldn't keep standing here, listening.

"Anyways, how was your doctor's appointment...?"

Their voices faded as Ruby walked on by. It was none of her business what kind of person Nathan was. After all, she was only here for a week. If he had a bit of a heartbreaker reputation, so what? It wasn't like he'd shown any interest in her.

And even if he had shown interest, she was smarter than to get involved. She'd only end things after the third date, what with her commitment issues, so the whole thing would be going nowhere from the start.

But Nathan's blue eyes flashed through her mind anyway.

NATHAN HEADED BACK to his own house after Ruby had gotten settled in at the condo, and ambled into the kitchen to make himself a sandwich.

Where had she come from, Ruby? Boston, she'd said. That was somewhere he'd never been. He hadn't been off-island except once, for a work conference in Toronto.

She'd probably been all over. Seen interesting people and places. And discovered all sorts of history...

His heart beat a little faster. He wanted to sit down and talk to her for hours. The conversations they could have. The places she could tell him about, and then that they could discover, together. Take it all in. Take her all in, gather her up in his arms...

He could just imagine her in a long skirt...She picked up the damp hem and laughed as she ran along the shore. The sunlight in her eyes. The expression on her face as she looked over her shoulder at him. The feel of her long legs, smooth and silky under his touch...His heart pounded. He blinked. Stared at the contents of his fridge.

Wait, what was he doing again? He tried to dislodge the errant images.

Right. Sandwich.

Nathan got the bread, meat and mayo from the fridge and set them on the counter. He gave a frustrated sigh. What was going on here? There had to be some logical explanation for it. Had to be.

Otherwise...

He slathered mayo on two pieces of Wonder Bread.

Otherwise—he shut his eyes, and all he could see was Ruby's hazel eyes. Looking back at him.

He shook his head. No doubt she was just like his father. Probably just as crazy as Dad, too. All that talk about love letters and research. He frowned. Who researched love letters?

He slapped a slice of turkey between the pieces of bread and carried the plate to his small dining room table.

He snorted. Next she'd want to run around and try to actually find the seal or something. He wasn't going to waste his time on any more thoughts about her. No matter how beautiful her hazel eyes had been.

Wide. Green flecked with golden brown. Deep and wise and rimmed with dark, long lashes that reflected an expression almost as startled as his own—What the hell was happening?

He ate the sandwich. Got up and put his dirty dishes into the dishwasher.

Shook his head. Shoved his hands through his hair. No. No.

Otherwise—the only logical explanation would be—"Completely illogical. Completely irrational. This has no grounding in any sort of...sense."

And now he was talking to himself.

He had to go pick up the last of Dad's papers from his office tomorrow and go through the rest of Dad's stuff there. Hmmm. Ruby would be there at the condo, probably—maybe she'd be there when he dropped them off? A grin snuck across Nathan's face.

Which he immediately straightened into a thin line.

The only logical explanation for this was...lust. Of course. That was it.

The grin snuck onto his face again.

He crossed his arms. Pursed his lips.

No. He cocked his head. It was as if he'd already known her forever, even though he'd never met her before in his life.

It was a knowing. *Beyond* knowing. It was a rightness. A...a...Completely illogical and crazy notion. He didn't feel anything for her. Besides maybe a bit of attraction. A bit of lust—

Buzz. Buzzzz.

Nathan jumped. Reached for his phone.

"Evie?"

"Nathan, hi. Listen, Ruby got there okay and everything, right?"

As Evie spoke, Nathan could hear the twins' whoops of glee in the background. *'Let's play post office! Grandpa said I got to keep his old paper. Here, now you can mail it.'*

"Girls," Evie's voice was muffled. "Mommy's on the phone. Shhh. Go in your room and play with the dollhouse."

Nathan smiled to himself as he leaned against the wall between the kitchen and living room. "Yeah, yeah, she got here just fine. I was going to call you in a bit and ask. Cuz I didn't know anything about it, so I was a bit...surprised."

"Sorry, Nathan. I meant to text you about it yesterday.

But with the twins' new dance lessons starting and this bicentennial celebration documentation at work to organize..."

Nathan rubbed the back of his neck. "It's okay."

He heard Evie sigh with relief. "You're okay with her staying there, right? I know we're working with the contractor to do those renovations." Evie raised her voice as the dog barked and peals of laughter followed.

Nathan's heart clenched. Evie didn't have time to handle any of this. The least he could do was agree to help her out. "Evie, don't worry about it. I'll take care of everything."

A pause.

"You're sure? I mean, I know we agreed to do it all together. I can drop by if you need to..."

"No, no," Nathan said, his voice gentle. "You have far too much going on. I'll handle everything."

"Well...if you're sure you think you can."

Nathan swallowed back a retort. Even his own sister sometimes thought he was still the reckless, irresponsible sibling. "I'll let you know if I need anything, ok?"

"Thanks, Nathan. Listen, don't forget Sunday dinner this week is at my and Dave's place."

"Right," Nathan said. "I'll be sure to look up a really good joke for the girls."

"They loved that one you told them last time about the ducks."

Nathan chuckled. "I'm glad. See you then."

LATE WEDNESDAY MORNING sunlight spilled through the faded lace curtains of the six-by-six window in Dr. O'Neil's study. Ruby was dressed in denim shorts and a lavender-colored cotton T-shirt, with her hair pulled into a ponytail. She stood in the doorway. The patch of light pooled onto the hardwood floor.

She glanced at her phone. Nothing from her advisor in the last 24 hours. She sighed. Bit her lip. When would she hear if she'd gotten selected for an interview?

Ruby's stomach rumbled and she checked her watch. She had to eat something. Even if that chewed up precious time when she should be going through the mountain of paperwork in Dr. O'Neil's office.

She fought down a flutter of panic. She'd stay up every night she was here, if she had to, in order to catalog all of this. She had to get back by next Thursday like she'd promised Dr. Burton.

Her phone buzzed. She picked it up. Maggie.

"Hey, Ruby! How's it going with the professor's papers?"

Ruby gave a laugh. "Uh, I'm feeling a bit overwhelmed, actually. P.E.I.'s beautiful, just like you said it would be. Remind me again why you left?"

"Sometimes I wonder. But that's a long story, actually. So, what do you think of Dr. O'Neil's son?"

Ruby pulled the phone away from her ear and looked at it with raised eyebrows. "How did you know I met him?"

"I figured you were bound to. That city's only 30,000 people."

Ruby fiddled with the hem of her T-shirt. "He seems..." She sighed. The memory of Nathan's blue eyes that first second she'd seen him flashed through her mind. "I've never seen anyone quite as good-looking as he is. No, that isn't true," she said as she realized it with a jolt. "I've never *experienced* anyone as handsome as Nathan is."

"Really?"

Ruby nodded. "You know me. Lukewarm attraction's normal. Chemistry's just for romance novels. And I'd been truly content to keep it firmly between the pages."

"But now?"

"Now it's...more than just physical attraction." She cocked her head and remembered how something in his eyes spoke of second chances... "It's strange. Like, in a way I felt as if I'd missed him. No, not missed him... More like, hadn't gotten there in time. That makes no sense, though. In time for what? Because I've only just met him."

"Wow. Sounds intense."

"No." Ruby shook her head. "This is *just* attraction." And that, well, that was easy to dismiss. Because she couldn't let herself be attracted to him. She was leaving in a week. And he did have a reputation, if the stories were true. Of course, there was always some kernel of truth in every fiction.

"Well, I need to run. Sourcing some semi-precious stones right now. But send me a text or two, okay?"

"Sure. Talk soon."

She smiled as she ended the call. Stretched and yawned. Her stomach rumbled again, but there was a leaden feeling in there too. What if she couldn't get all of this wrapped up this week? Would that affect her status as a candidate for the special collections position? She had to call Dr. Burton and tell her what was going on. But first, she needed to get some lunch.

She got up and grabbed her purse. The floor slanted slightly underfoot and the boards creaked. She grinned. She'd always loved old buildings. But this one hadn't always been condos.

Ruby looked around. She hadn't gotten an opportunity to check out much of the place last night.

According to the plaque on the sidewalk outside, it had originally been a place called Cross Keys Tavern, built in the 1770s. Now if only cataloging Dr. O'Neil's papers would be as easy as that.

She navigated around piles of papers as she made her way toward the study door. But as she passed the window in the dormer behind Dr. O'Neil's desk, a flash of something caught the corner of her eye.

She turned her head. Nothing.

She started to move away from the spot when the sparkle caught her eye again.

She stepped up to the wavy glass. A tiny crack had somehow caught the sunlight, which caused the glass to shed rainbows through the small space.

She peered closer.

No, she realized. It wasn't a crack.

It was multiple sets of...initials? Done in crude etched lines. Her fingers traced the letters. She rubbed the goose bumps that had suddenly sprouted on her arms and dropped her hand from the window.

Ruby walked out of the study and into the living room, with her purse slung over her shoulder. Just then, the doorknob rattled in the entryway and the door swung open.

Nathan stood on the threshold. "I'm on my lunch break and came to see if you wanted, uh, a sandwich?" Ruby felt a blush creep into her cheeks. That was nice of him.

He held up a Subway bag. Ruby took in his blue eyes fringed by dark lashes; his thick black hair—windblown; his tie—askew. She bit her lip and tried to ignore the way her toes curled. And how she felt like she'd just jumped into a Tilt-A-Whirl. "Thank you." She put a hand to her stomach.

"You okay?" Nathan put one hand on her elbow. With the other, he put the bag of food on a side table.

"Yes," she managed after a moment. She mentally shook her head. He couldn't be affecting her like this.

She felt the warmth of Nathan's fingers seep into her skin.

But she jumped when she realized his thumb had begun to stroke the thin skin on the inside of her elbow.

"Oh, uh, I'm sorry." He dropped his hand and shoved it into his pocket. Rubbed the back of his neck with his other hand. "You know, I don't normally do that, but you probably wouldn't believe me if I said it, seeing as how...I was doing it."

He trailed off. "Now I'm just making this more awkward." His gaze darted around the room, and his tone became more formal. Distant. "I brought in the last of the boxes. Where would you like me to put them?"

Ruby glanced over her shoulder and followed his line of sight. Five battered banker boxes were neatly stacked in the hallway, a Subway cup tray balanced on the very top box.

Nathan picked up the boxes.

"Nathan, there's—"

But the Subway cup tray had already wobbled and tumbled to the floor, sending a flood of Nestlé Iced Tea and Mountain Dew all over the box and the floor.

"Damn it."

"Here," Ruby said, as she crouched down beside him and picked up the now-soaked top box. "Maybe we can salvage some of it." She placed the wet file on the floor and began to take out all the papers. "You're right," she said, "your dad really was disorganized. Oh." She paused, a receipt she held, poised mid-air between the file and the floor. "I didn't mean—I'm sorry."

"'S'ok," Nathan said, as he continued to mop up the puddle.

Ruby continued to pull out random bits of paper.

Tattered, crumpled electric bills. Outdated reminder postcards from dentists. Clippings from out-of-print academic journals. Torn, oil-stained gas receipts from 1975. A crumbling, handwritten bill of exchange for a compass.

She'd emptied almost everything from the box and placed it in neat piles on the floor by size and shape.

She peered into the bottom of the box. A red spiral bound notebook, its cover warped by coffee stains, lay in the bottom. She pulled the cheap notebook out and it fell open to the last page filled with cramped yet meticulous handwriting:

> *"According to an article about Phillips Callbeck in 'The Story of Old Abegweit,' published in 1932, mention is made of a £1000 reward still being in effect for the return of the Great Seal of Prince Edward Island.*
>
> *I have long speculated as to why this is the case. Academics believe that the Americans melted it down for bullets, hacked it into pieces for coins, or both.*
>
> *I have begun developing a theory. What if the American privateer captains came to Charlottetown, raided the city and made off with the seal for another reason than the one presented by history? What if they were on the hunt for a treasure?*
>
> *I'm still gathering evidence and I can't say for cer-*

tain what that treasure may be."

"What's that?"

She handed him the notebook and their fingers brushed. Again, that sense of regret edged into her awareness. Huh? She shook it off.

Nathan scanned the writing. "Just another one of his unscientifically supported ideas."

Ruby readjusted her ponytail and stood. She put her hands on her hips. "Why is it that you think your dad was so crazy, exactly? It's not like this is hurting anyone or anything. He was trying to figure something out, here."

Nathan's blue eyes bored into hers. She wasn't going to be the one to look away first. Nathan crossed his arms. "You want the truth? He was wasting his time. It's just a legend. It's not real facts. Sure, there might've been some truth to it, buried deep, but...come on. Be realistic. Logical. Just because there's some letter that happens to name this woman Edwina, doesn't mean she was some sort of spy for George Washington and had something to do with the Great Seal being stolen. Not to mention that whole speculation about treasure he had. I mean, that sounds like something out of a novel, not real life."

Nathan began to pace. "And now you're here, asking these same questions that my dad did, and—" Nathan sighed and raked a hand through his hair. A flicker of what looked like worry, mixed with anger, flashed across his expression. "I just hate to see anyone waste their life on something that isn't anything more than...than...a colorful island legend."

"Well, I appreciate your..." Ruby narrowed her eyes and shoved her glasses up her nose as she watched Nathan's pace increase, "...concern, but what some people view as 'a colorful island legend,' others have spent years researching and categorizing. It's a part of history, legend or not. Someone had to write the letter. Someone had to be inspired, had to have that kernel of an idea. And someone had to have heard something that gave them the reason to write it all down."

"Yes, that's all fine and good, but it doesn't mean that every fictional piece of literature is based in fact!" Nathan clenched his hands into fists.

"I know the difference between fairy tales and facts, you know." Ruby tapped her foot.

Nathan had shoved his hands into the back pockets of his charcoal-colored dress pants and turned away to stare out the window.

Ruby couldn't help but admire the fit of those tailored pants—she frowned—even if the man wasn't talking sense.

Nathan turned away from the window to look at her again. "*Do* you?" He rubbed a hand across his stubble. Swallowed. "My dad put all his attention on his research and none on his family. He got so carried away that he forgot about everything else. And I had to pick up the slack."

Ruby watched the sadness, anger and finally resignation, flash across Nathan's face. All at once, she wanted to wrap her arms around him and never let go. To bury her fingers in his hair and nestle against him, to keep him safe and warm.

Her breath quickened. Where it didn't matter what anyone else thought of them or who they were, or where they came from. A surge of righteous indignation washed through her.

No one was going to stand in their way. Not if she could help it.

Ruby mentally shook herself and tapped a finger against her chin instead. Forced aside the strange thoughts. "What're all those letters doing on the window?"

Nathan uncrossed his arms and cocked his head. "What?"

"I'll show you."

Just then, Nathan's cell phone buzzed. He glanced at it and frowned. "It's Evie. She never calls this time of day. I have to take this."

He held his phone up to his ear. Listened. Nodded. "Okay, Evie. I'll come right away." He turned back to Ruby. "Listen uh, hold that thought, will you? I have to get to a meeting with my lawyer."

NATHAN ADJUSTED HIS too-tight tie. He hunched his shoulders. The last time he'd worn this suit, he'd been practically married.

And look how that had turned out.

But the small leather-bound notebook he'd found at the fort reassured him, somehow. Which is why he'd tucked it, on impulse, into the inside pocket of his suit jacket that he'd thrown on last-minute before he'd headed over here.

Nathan stretched out his long legs in the solicitor's office and glanced over at his sister in the chair next to his.

Evie didn't look too much happier about this. His heart clenched at the sight of his sister. Her short curly brown hair hung rather limply against her forehead. She fiddled with the paperclip that attached all the pages of the hearing documentation together.

"Can anything be done?" Nathan said to his father's long-time friend and attorney.

"My answer, Nathan, is the same as the last time you asked that question," the lawyer answered, her hair cut into a sleek steel-gray bob. "Now, we both know he was a little...eccentric in his ideas, especially in academia. But I don't want to live the rest of my life knowing that I didn't do my duty for him and his family."

She held up her hands. "As you know, his work was very important to him. As was his reputation. And so," the older woman shook her head, "this unfortunate business at the university has threatened everything your father has worked so hard for."

But instead of the paperwork the lawyer was talking about, Nathan found himself thinking about how his pencil had flown across the page so effortlessly. How he'd gotten to that point of euphoric joy as he'd focused completely on the sketch that had seemed to almost draw itself, there on the cliff-top.

He rubbed the back of his neck. The graphic design job definitely didn't do that for him.

Nathan chewed on his lip. Why was this happening now? He'd been perfectly content before this whole thing with his father's research had come to light...

He frowned. Remembered how his dad had appeared to be a caring father but really, he'd only wanted more time to work on yet another research project for his precious tenured position.

Nathan's hands clenched into fists. Dad had always cared more about history and long-dead people than his own family. Nathan swallowed. Than his own son. Maybe that was a little unfair to judge him so harshly. But Dad's actions hurt.

The lawyer pushed up her horn-rimmed glasses and continued. "UPEI's Board of Governors has come to me."

Nathan shifted in his seat. "Go on."

The lawyer nodded and pushed up her glasses again. "You see," she moved the papers in front of her on the table, "this letter," she held one up for Nathan and he could see the official UPEI letterhead, "accuses your father of falsifying and forging documents."

Nathan frowned. "What the hell is that supposed to mean?"

The lawyer cleared her throat. "I quote one of his colleagues: 'Dr. Gordon O'Neil has severely erred in judgment. Not just once, but multiple times in his career. He should never have received the honor of emeritus, nor should he even be a professor at this institute of higher learning.'" She shuffled her papers. Picked up another one. "This is from another colleague: 'Dr. O'Neil's research is not about legitimate history.' And another: 'O'Neil is wrecking the historical and cultural heritage of the island.'" She met Nathan's gaze. "These are all previous claims. But now, combined with this..." She indicated the official letter and shook her head.

Her glossy bob gleamed in the light from the window behind her. "The thing is," she said, then shrugged and spread her hands wide in a gesture of surrender. "Everyone knew what your father was like. But as time went on, his colleagues began to suspect he was helping himself out to bolster his credibility in the theories he was formulating about the theft of the Great Seal in 1775."

Nathan stared at her. "What?" His jaw clenched.

"These charges claim that your father forged the signed order of General George Washington—dated 23 November, 1775—about Edwina Belliveaux."

"What I don't understand," Nathan said, as he leaned forward in his seat. His eyes flashed, "is why. The O'Neils have always had a stellar reputation on the island here." A muscle in Nathan's jaw ticked. "My father may have been a crackpot," he said between clenched teeth. "But he has never done anything illegal." Nathan crossed his arms.

"I'm sorry, Nathan, but that's why I asked you and your sister into the office here. Because it looks like this is really quite serious. Before your father died, he'd published a paper on his latest findings. It raised the ire of those colleagues of his who I quoted earlier. They claimed he'd forged the order. Now," the lawyer rubbed her temples and took off her glasses, "this could lead to a serious investigation. Against not only the paper he'd published and his claims about the seal, but also against his whole life's work."

"So," Evie said, "what are we supposed to do about it?"

"Well," the lawyer said, "you have two options."

Nathan perched on the edge of his seat.

"One," the lawyer raised a hand and ticked off the points on her fingers, "you can ignore it and hope it goes away. Which it won't. Or," she adjusted a strand of her hair, "you can take the governors to court. Sue them for defamation of character, that sort of thing..."

"Or," Nathan said, as he stood and began to pace, "we can disprove these claims." He glanced over at his sister and then at the lawyer. "You both know I hate to fight. But," he ran a hand through his hair. "This isn't right."

He put his palms down on the table. The smooth mahogany surface gleamed. "Because," he said, as his eyes met the lawyer's, then his sister's, "we all know Dad was an upstanding citizen."

"Exactly," Evie said.

Nathan fiddled with the spare change in his pocket. Began to pace faster. "But if we don't do something, then no one will remember Dad that way. We can fix it." He paused. "We just need to gather the evidence. And show the governors that they don't know what they're talking about." Nathan rubbed the back of his neck and clenched his teeth. Injustice had always bothered him. Wrongs *had* to be righted. Dad was *family*.

Evie cocked her head. "He was working on that research project about the Great Seal."

The lawyer tapped a fingernail against her temple. "Dr. O'Neil told me that he was beginning to realize that the lost seal, if it could be found, may be the key to figuring out Edwina's real role in history. That she was somehow connected to it in ways people hadn't imagined.

"But—" she paused and shuffled some papers, "—we both know how stubborn Islanders are about changing their outlook." The lawyer continued. "The hearing's two weeks from today."

"Well, there's only one thing to do." Nathan put his hands on his hips. "I need to find the original order. It's the only way to clear things up." This had to be made right. His fingers brushed the small leather-bound volume. He couldn't—he wouldn't—let those in power take away what wasn't rightfully theirs. He gripped the book. Not from someone he loved. Not this time. Not again. He looked down and discovered he had clutched the small leather-bound book so hard his knuckles had turned white. *Not again*? He frowned. Where had that thought come from?

His mind strayed back to Ruby. Wait. He could ask her...for help? He could ask her what she thought they could do about it, anyway.

She'd found that letter fragment, after all. And she believed Dad. She had a copy of the order he'd sent her...

It'd be a place to start, anyway.

"It's the only way to clear Dad's name. So I'd better get started."

There was no way he was going to let his father's good name be dragged through the mud. He had to set things right. And if that meant working with Ruby, figuring out if there really was something behind all this, well, so be it.

RUBY LOOKED AROUND at the vast piles of paperwork on the floor next to the desk. Now that she'd made a bit of a dent, and organized the late professor's desk, she realized she needed some sort of filing system for these piles on the floor.

She tapped a forefinger against her chin. Snuck a look at her phone. Still nothing from her advisor. She sighed. Best to focus on her work and put that out of her mind for now.

Well, in reverse order by date was always a good place to start. She rifled through the pages of her legal pad until she found a clean sheet. Then she began to write dates in back-slanting, block letters and made sure to leave space between each entry.

The easy part was over.

Ruby reached for the nearest box, the one that looked the messiest. She pried the lid off and peered in. A moldy half-eaten gingerbread cookie lay inside.

She hadn't thought to bring rubber gloves.

Using a spare piece of paper, she reached in, picked up the cookie and threw it into the trash. Underneath the grease stains was a series of pages bound together with rubber bands. Photocopies, from the looks of it.

She flipped through them. They all seemed to be talking about the same thing. A reference to that thousand-pound reward. From an article in *The Island* magazine dated... Ruby pushed her glasses up her nose and squinted at the almost-indecipherable scribble in the margin...2 May, 1875.

She withheld a sigh. So far, nothing had come to light having to do with the love letter fragment or just who Edwina had received the letter from. Not that she should be surprised. Dr. O'Neil had said he didn't have the other half.

Maybe she'd come all the way up here for nothing.

Ruby glanced at the time on her phone. Nathan's meeting with the lawyer was taking awhile. Was it about Dr. O'Neil? Or something else entirely? She shrugged. It wasn't really any of her business.

And it didn't really matter, except that he said he'd help her sort through more of the boxes. Which was nice of him. Not that she needed any help. She'd devised her own particular filing system so that—

A short knock on the door to the condo interrupted her thoughts. A second later, she heard the door open and then shut.

She glanced over her shoulder. Nathan had come back.

He walked into the room, and Ruby's heart fluttered. He nodded in her direction as he rubbed a hand across his unshaven jaw. "How's it going?"

"Uh, pretty well," she said, "But now that you're back, can you tell me about those initials in the window?"

"...Uh, sure." He glanced at his phone. Put it back in his pocket. "Where?" She showed Nathan the spot she'd been standing in earlier.

He reached a fingertip up to trace the tiny series of letters. "Been there as long as I can remember." He cocked his head. "I think it started back when the tavern was built. Couples would etch their initials in the glass when they got engaged."

He leaned against the window ledge behind his father's desk. The window, Ruby noticed, looked like it was original to the 1700s. She smiled. "Well, that's certainly romantic."

"Yeah. It's a bit of a tourist draw, actually. Dad would never let anyone up here, but it's been mentioned on the walking tours around downtown."

Nathan rubbed a finger along a heart carved into the window ledge. "This has been here for ages too."

"Really?" Ruby peered over his shoulder. "That's so neat."

Nathan's lips curved up. "Yeah, I guess it is. Funny how you don't think much about things you've seen all your life.

Like this study." He paused. Looked around. "I remember Dad would make me stay up here for hours when I was in high school. On hot August days like this. When I'd rather be bridge-jumping along Covehead Road with my buddies."

Ruby's eyes widened.

"You jump off at a certain angle so you don't knock yourself out, and the bridges aren't that high from the water." Nathan grinned and raised his eyebrows. "Everyone did it. The cold Gulf of St. Lawrence feels great when it's hot out. Much more fun than sorting through dusty documents." He raised a palm. "No offense to present company."

Ruby laughed. "Back in high school—and even now—I'd *rather* sort through dusty documents or read at the library than do crazy things like that. Libraries have air conditioning." She shot him a grin. "Though I do like going to the beach. Especially at sunset. Walking barefoot through the surf..." She leaned back against the desk. "Although the New England coastline isn't anything like the shorelines up here. At least, from the photos I saw and the view out the airplane window. It's all sandy beaches and high dunes."

"Along the north shore, yep." Nathan nodded. "That's something I don't take for granted. The natural beauty around here."

Ruby sighed. "It's so gorgeous." She straightened up. "So. How was the meeting with the lawyer?"

Nathan sighed. He rested both palms on the wooden window ledge, which creaked with the weight. Ruby couldn't help but notice the line of muscle on his arms flex as he did so. She cleared her throat.

"Not so good. My dad's been accused of forging documents." His hands tightened into fists. He leaned back further, and eased his full weight onto the ledge. "So I'd like to help you find that November 23 order of Washington's. It's the only way I can clear Dad's name. Prove he wasn't forging it. He might've been a crackpot, but he wasn't a criminal." Nathan compressed his lips then glanced at Ruby.

"Oh." Ruby's mouth suddenly went dry and she rubbed

her palms on her jeans. Nathan? Here? In her space? How was she supposed to think, with him around all the time? She had a method. A strategy. He wasn't an academic.

She glanced at him and tucked a strand of hair behind her ear then wet her lips. No. No. Be a professional. She'd just think of him as her...assistant. Right. That would work. He was asking for her help. She could give it. "Okay," she said at last.

Nathan's shoulders relaxed. He met her gaze. "Thank you," he said.

"You're welcome." She pushed up her glasses.

"I appreciate your...giving me a chance. Some credit." His smile was lopsided. "Dad never did."

Ruby just nodded. "Well, he said he found it originally in a psalm book. So maybe if we look there first..."

"Okay. Whatever you think."

Ruby brought a hand up and absently played with the locket around her neck. Having Nathan around felt like the right thing to do. The right choice.

"That's pretty. Where did you get it?" Nathan nodded in her direction.

"What? Oh—" She glanced at the locket. "A flea market a couple years ago in Boston's North End. Got a great deal."

"Deals are always good."

"Yep. Turns out, when I had it appraised, it was made in the 1700s. The jeweller thought it looked like Paul Revere's work. I just like it for the sentimental value. Though the possible historical aspect is pretty neat too, I thought." She flicked open the locket. "See? The two pictures?"

Nathan took a step closer. "Those have great detail in them. That's amazing."

"Yeah. In fact, I found something underneath the man's portrait just the other day. Some sort of rhyme or puzzle or something."

"Really? I love puzzles and stuff like that. Can I see it?"

She rummaged around in her pocket. "Here."

Cardinal directions of the heart
Impart the way toward True North
Good-hearted General's Orders did put forth;
Crowned Head of Justice, strong and brave
Cradled on the wind and waves

Nathan bent his head to examine the slip of paper. Ruby couldn't help but notice the way the afternoon light glinted off his black hair.

"The whole thing sounds like some sort of..."—he laughed—"...riddle."

"That's what I said when I first saw it."

"Cradled on the wind and waves..." Nathan murmured to himself.

"Do you know what that means?"

"I'm not sure. But I do know that the Mi'kmaq people called Prince Edward Island *abegweit,* which means, basically, 'cradled on the waves.'"

Ruby's eyes widened.

"Look." Nathan pointed to the phrase. "*Good-hearted General's Orders.* It's capitalized..." Nathan began to pace. "Orders. General..." He held up his hands. "Of course. Washington was a general during the war, right?"

Ruby slowly nodded.

"Didn't you say he had those two orders? It's more than coincidence. One of which refers to the seal. And the other refers to...

"...P.E.I., maybe?" Ruby flipped to a clean page on her legal pad.

"Yes," Nathan said, "that's it. So crowned head would be referring to, well, someone in authority."

"Crowned...that means royal." Ruby commented, as she began to affix paperclips to the neat piles of papers she'd stacked on the professor's desk. "Royal. Like, a queen."

"Or king." Nathan ruffled his hair. "King George III. That *could* to be a reference to the seal."

Ruby slipped the unused paperclips into their paper

container. "So King George III...what about the justice part?"

"He commissioned the seal, and the seal is what makes legal documents official. So, justice refers to that. It only makes logical sense." Nathan grinned.

Ruby nodded. "...Right. Yes. That does." She cocked her head and held his gaze for a moment.

"But what about cardinal directions of the heart?" She bit her lip. "That phrase sounds so familiar...but why? Of the heart..." she murmured and tucked a strand of hair behind her ear. "Cardinal directions..." Her eyes widened. "Of course. It's that same phrase as in the letter fragment. Well, not exactly the same. But similar. That means this could have something to do with a compass."

"And true north," Nathan added, "that's a direction on a compass. The compass pointing toward north."

"Yes, but true north. Capitalized."

Nathan shifted. "Well, there *is* an island legend about a compass that's supposed to point toward your true love, instead of true north. So I think you're right—it's definitely referring to a compass."

"Wow."

"Yeah. And speaking of lovers, it's speculated that Molly McDuff, the first postmistress in Charlottetown, wrote a poem called *The Fair Isle Lovers*. It's thought she was writing about someone she knew. But that hasn't been proven. She lived and worked here in the tavern all her life. That's what these condos used to be. Up here was the storage area for the tavern. They probably kept barrels of rum and salt pork and things like that up here. Anyway, Molly was sort of the unofficial postmistress at the time, too. Over the years, people have discovered the occasional postcard or letter lying around this building."

"You know quite a bit."

Nathan shifted beside her. "Yeah, well, listening to Dad all the time, I guess I picked up a few things."

She leaned forward and her eyes lingered on his mouth. She tore her gaze away. No. She was being ridiculous. How

could she feel so attracted to him? She was leaving next week. Besides, they lived in different countries.

Not only that, she had a job to do. She had to be professional. She was just here to finish cataloging these papers.

She didn't have time to get involved with some local. Especially not this local. The conversation between those two older women ran through her mind again.

Not only that, she'd read enough romance novels to know that bad boys on the page and bad boys in real life were two different things.

Nathan raked a hand through his hair. "That poem's just a bunch of romantic nonsense. Made up before there was TV or the internet to entertain people." He shook his head. "When will people see sense?"

"Speaking of seeing sense—what about this?" She pointed at the page again. "This means..."

Nathan looked down at the page too. "Well, based on what we've figured out...this riddle is talking about the lost Great Seal of Prince Edward Island. This could help clear Dad's name."

Ruby frowned. "But we're already trying to find that order. And I have all these papers to catalog. We don't have time for this."

ALONE IN HIS house that evening, Nathan tugged at the hem of his white cotton T-shirt and then pulled it over his head. The movement made his hair ruffle as he tossed the shirt in the general direction of the laundry hamper.

Then he unzipped the fly of his dark-wash, slightly faded jeans. He shucked them off too, which left him in just his Calvin Kleins.

God, he couldn't stop thinking about her. Ruby. He shook his head.

No. He needed to get back to his sketchpad. That's what he really needed to do. It was the only thing that kept him centered these days.

But somehow, that seascape he'd so eagerly sketched had fizzled and lay in uninspired flatness in his mind.

The way the light had reflected Ruby's glossy waves, and the gold flecks in the hazel depths of her eyes—His fingers twitched.

He had to draw her.

Huh?

He'd never attempted a portrait before. But...that would get her out of his thoughts and onto the paper. Then maybe he could concentrate on his work again. Keep making progress with his new site design for Parks Canada's offices on P.E.I.

He couldn't imagine living anywhere else than this island. Just look at it. The sand dunes. The seagulls. The feel of the sun on his skin. Why would anyone want to go anywhere else? It had everything he needed. But perhaps not everything he wanted...

Nathan ruffled his hair even further. As he jammed a hand through it, he ambled into the master ensuite bathroom and squeezed toothpaste onto his brush.

Nathan's mind wandered to the way Ruby had looked at him behind her brown tortoiseshell glasses. He couldn't suppress the way his gut wrenched.

God. Those big hazel eyes... Full of intelligence. Spirit. He grinned. He liked that about her. And she was smart. Smarter than he'd ever be. Going for her doctorate. Wow. But that was okay. He liked smart women.

He leaned against the sink.

What the hell was going on? Nathan spit out the toothpaste and turned on the tap.

He shook his head. She wasn't an Islander. She was American, besides all that. What's more, she would be gone soon. Out of his life.

He didn't need to complicate things by adding the disappointment of yet another failed relationship to his list.

He swallowed.

Just like all the ones before.

But this hollow space in his heart had somehow grown

in the last few days and he wished he had someone to at least...talk to.

He let the tap run for a second then he leaned forward and splashed cold water on his face. The cool droplets brought back a sense of centeredness. Normalcy.

He took a breath and reached across the mirrored medicine cabinet to grab a towel. He began to dry his face when an image rose in his mind's eye.

He froze. Then yanked open the bathroom vanity drawer and fished out the small sketchpad and pencil he kept there for times like this when inspiration struck.

In one swift movement, he flipped the pad to a clean sheet and put pencil to paper.

He could see her in his mind's eye, as if through an out of focus camera lens. A woman's face. A beautiful face. A haunted face. He began to sketch in long, fluid strokes.

His breath quickened.

Bringing her to life.

A shiver ran through him.

He watched his pencil move across the paper. Watched, as if looking at someone else's hand, not his own, began to shade in details.

Her cheeks, streaked with dirt and tears. Though her eyes were hidden by the brim of a battered tricorn hat, he could almost *feel* her features: taunt with anger and hope. And her handkerchief torn and speckled with...was that blood?

Nathan swallowed down the sudden lump in his throat, as he now felt that same surge of longing and regret he'd experienced in the hallway.

His head began to pound as if he had a migraine. His heart throbbed and ached, like he had just lost his best friend and his only true love. As Nathan continued to sketch the picture in his head, he saw, in his mind's eye, the woman's lips move.

His pencil moved even faster across the page as he raced to capture the curve of her lips, the hint of a tender smile underneath all that sadness.

She brought a crumpled piece of paper up to her heart. Her hand clenched into a fist as she did.

He shook his head and clenched his jaw. But kept sketching.

At last, he stopped. A bead of sweat trickled down between his shoulder blades. The blood pounded in his veins.

He stared down at the page. He'd done it. She was absolutely beautiful. How was this possible? He'd never drawn anything like this in his life. He'd never even drawn people before. Only landscapes.

And even those looked nothing like this. Nothing this...good. This lifelike. It wasn't logical.

Because this...this wasn't a picture of Ruby, as he'd intended to draw. This was a picture of a woman from the 1700s. He swallowed. Dug his nails into his palms. What if logic couldn't explain what had just happened?

Chapter Four

THURSDAY MORNING, RUBY'S cell phone buzzed. She glanced at the caller ID. Dr. Burton.

"Ruby, how's it going?"

"I was going to call you in a little while because I have some, uh, news." Ruby bit her lip. "Dr. Gordon O'Neil's papers are a bit more...messy than I thought. This could take awhile. But," she hurried on, "I'll be back to prep for my defense."

As Ruby opened her mouth to explain more, her advisor said, "Actually that's not why I called. Have you checked your email?"

"I, uh, haven't had a chance to yet."

"Well, congratulations! You got selected for the job interview."

Ruby sank onto the wingback chair. Her heart hammered. "But this cataloging may end up taking two weeks. Maybe even more..." And now that they had the riddle situation? She'd realized Nathan had been right—it could help clear his dad's name, and just might help with her love letter research, too. "When is the interview scheduled for?"

"9 a.m. Monday."

"In four days?"

"This hiring committee likes to move things along."

Ruby shifted the phone to her other ear.

"If you get this position, Ruby, it could really make your career. It's tenure-track."

Ruby's stomach clenched. "But I think there's more here than I originally thought."

Dr. Burton gave a shaky laugh. Then sighed. Ruby could

almost see her rub her forehead.

Ruby felt a bead of sweat form between her shoulder blades. She couldn't lose Nathan—couldn't *leave* him. Right. That's what she meant.

She'd come too far to back out now. The only way to find out more would be to take the time to go through things. Study the documents. And help Nathan find the order. "I can't leave yet. I'm uncovering things that might be very valuable for my dissertation defense. But I also want to be considered for the job."

"Well, it's up to you."

Ruby let out the breath she'd held. "I'll do as much as I can here now, then go back for the interview, and see what happens."

For a second, Dr. Burton didn't say anything. Then, she spoke. "You know, Ruby, we've spent so much time together in the department that it practically feels like you're family. So if you need anything, don't hesitate to let me know."

"Thanks." Ruby smiled. "I'll do that."

She hit end and slid the phone back into her purse. She stared up at the cracked ceiling, and blinked rapidly.

Family.

She bit her lip. She'd never known hers. Not her biological one, anyway.

And, if she was honest with herself, that's why she'd become an academic to begin with. She'd felt like maybe one day, if she dug deep enough, far enough, back into someone else's past, she'd find her own.

What was she going to do now that everything had changed? No, she shook her head. She knew exactly what she was going to do. She was going to do what she always did when faced with a challenge.

Get to the bottom of things. She grinned. Yet another reason she loved history and academics. It gave her persistence.

She picked up her pen and notepad and began to jot notes.

AFTER WORK THURSDAY, in his basement spare room, Nathan studied the sketch of the woman in the tricorn hat that he'd now transposed onto the canvas.

His brow furrowed. How did he know how to do all this? He knew more about computers and the latest graphic design program than his way around a boar-bristle paint-brush.

Yet he dipped the brush into the cerulean on the palette he held in his other hand, and brought it to the canvas.

But he paused. The blood pounded in his temples. His fingertips tingled and his heart—almost in his throat.

A low chuckle escaped him. Could he do this with his eyes closed?

On impulse, he did just that.

All at once, the woman's face came back to him; this time clearer, sharper, and more in focus.

Without thinking, he lifted the paintbrush to the canvas. The bristles touched the surface.

And this strange pent-up yearning, longing, and disappointment poured through him. All at once, his brush began to move.

The exact shade of her green eyes: sea foam flicked with bottle-green and emerald.

The way that her hair caught the candlelight and reflected a million little diamond points of light.

The low, soft way she laughed. The rustle of the pale pink silk of her skirts. The crackle of the flames in the grate as he mixed color after color, a frown of concentration between his brows. The scent of wood smoke and pine mixed with the sharp tang of iron-gall ink and the fuller, heavy-bodied scent of oil paints.

Every muscle in his body tightened, strained, as his brush flew across the canvas. Nathan felt his breathing shift: light yet deep. The long, sure strokes of his brush moved almost too fast to be discernible.

Yet still he painted.

He became aware of only the next color, the next shade, the next piece of the puzzle that would finally fit together everything into one complete whole, into one moment, one second, one suspended transcendent place in time where she was his and he was hers and everything was right.

His chest heaved. His heart swelled. His throat tightened and his jaw clenched.

He gasped for breath even as his eyes flew open.

Nathan's jagged breaths finally settled and evened out as he forced himself to stop and look at what he'd done.

He felt strands of his hair stick to his forehead; he wiped a forearm across it. A broad grin spread across his face. He wiped his fingers on the paint-stained rag before tucking it into the back pocket of his ripped and faded jeans now splattered with paint. He'd done it. He'd actually painted a portrait.

He couldn't stop staring.

*There she was. Whole and beautiful and completely his. To have and to hold til death doth part—A heavy leaden weight filled his heart at the sight of her green eyes. No. Anger flickered. She'd let him down. And he hadn't made it to her in time. He reached out, the satiny smoothness of her cheek under his fingertips as he—*Nathan flinched. He'd never seen this woman before in his life. He gazed at her features. Wait a minute...

He sucked in a breath. Yes. Yes he had.

It was Edwina Belliveaux. Why had he painted *her?*

His hands started to tremble. He had no idea about her personal life, who she was, who she loved. Or why he'd given her the vivid hazel of Ruby's eyes.

Damn it. His hands shook and he fisted them into his hair.

Nothing about this made any logical sense. Especially when he saw that he'd painted her holding a red-and-white rosebud.

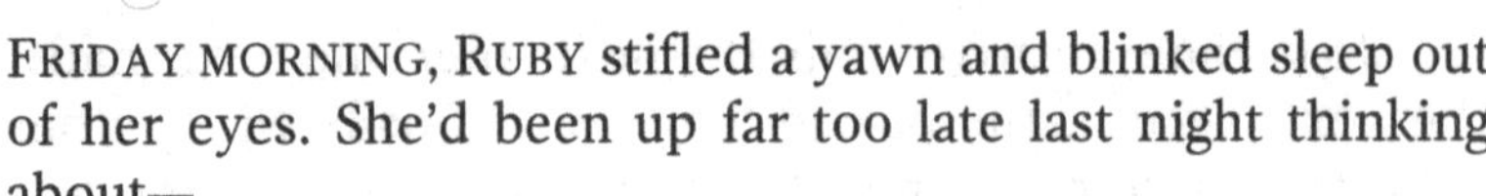

FRIDAY MORNING, RUBY stifled a yawn and blinked sleep out of her eyes. She'd been up far too late last night thinking about—

"Ready to get started on the hunt for Washington's order this morning?" Nathan said as he walked into the room. "I was able to get the day off work today."

"Oh, um, that's great," Ruby jumped, and a blush crept across her cheeks. She smoothed out an imaginary wrinkle from the sleeveless fuchsia polka-dot sundress she wore. Thank goodness he hadn't been able to read her thoughts. Especially since they had, unfortunately, involved him.

He wore a cobalt-blue T-shirt and a pair of faded jeans. His hair was slightly damp from a shower. He smelled like cinnamon and pine needles, Ruby noticed, as he came to stand beside her on the Aubusson rug in the middle of Dr. O'Neil's study.

But after a couple hours, the only thing they'd discovered were out-dated bank statements, a handful of newspaper clippings about colleagues' accomplishments, and copies of Dr. O'Neil's 4000-level course syllabi from last year.

Nathan stood and stretched. Glanced at the grandfather clock against the far wall as it gonged 11 a.m. "Ready for an early lunch?"

Ruby nodded. "We can meet back here in forty-five minutes."

"Oh," Nathan shoved his hands into his pockets, "I meant, maybe we could get some lunch together."

Ruby bit her lip. Looked away from his direct gaze. She'd be gone in a few days.

"Don't worry, I won't bite. I thought we could talk about the riddle and where it might lead next," he added.

She *did* need to eat. "Well," Ruby pushed up her glasses. "All right." Her grip on her legal pad relaxed. "But I'm paying."

Nathan made a sweeping gesture with his hand toward the door. "Of course. After you."

After they grabbed menus at the coffee shop called Kettle Black across the street and placed their orders, they found seats at a table outside. Nathan turned to Ruby. "So. The riddle."

But before Ruby could answer, she heard, "Nathan! How *are* you?" Ruby glanced over her shoulder. A young woman with long curly red hair walked up to the outdoor seating area a few feet from their table. She carried a blue paper shopping bag, and the bright yellow cotton of her sundress fluttered in the breeze.

Ruby saw Nathan shift in his seat. "Zoe. Uh, hi. I'm good. You?" He swallowed. Darted his gaze to Ruby.

"Great," the woman replied. "I haven't seen you in ages."

Nathan tugged at his earlobe. "Uh, yeah. Been awhile."

The red-haired woman laughed. "Listen, I just wanted to say I'm glad it didn't work out between us. Because," she flashed her left hand, "I'm now engaged." She grinned. "So thank you."

Nathan hunched his shoulders. "Um, sure." Rattled the ice in his glass.

The red-haired woman smiled. "Looks like that's all water under the bridge now, anyway." She glanced at Ruby then back to Nathan. "Oh!" She looked at her watch. "Gotta run. Take care, Nathan. Nice to see you again."

Nathan fiddled with the straw in his water glass. "You too, Zoe. And congratulations."

So that was one of Nathan's exes...Or, Ruby's stomach clenched, one of his ex-*fiancées*? She bit her lip. No, it didn't matter.

"You were right." Ruby blurted out.

"I was?"

"This riddle." She twisted a strand of hair around her ponytail. Met Nathan's gaze. "It really got me to thinking." Their food arrived.

"Did it?" Nathan said, after he swallowed a bite of his crab salad.

"There is..." she traced a fingertip along the edge of her plate, "something there."

"So," Nathan leaned forward, "what do you think the next thing to look for is?"

"I don't know. Besides the seal, I mean. Which we don't have."

Nathan frowned.

Ruby sighed.

Nathan shook his head and sat back in his chair.

"Sometimes historical things are like that," she said softly. "You think you'll find something great and it turns out to be nothing. Or only leads to more questions." Ruby took another bite of her battered cod and realized Nathan was watching her. She felt heat surge through her, but forced herself to concentrate on her meal.

"So." Nathan cocked his head and studied her. "Do you have any brothers or sisters?"

"I'm an only child."

"I have an older sister, as you already know." He paused. "That must have been nice having no one to argue with, growing up."

"Not really. I was...adopted. I never knew my real parents." She paused. Fiddled with her napkin. "I don't actually know if I have any siblings." Ruby looked up and met his gaze. Something about the openness of his expression tugged at her and she found herself continue. "I used to have this...recurring daydream, I guess you could call it, starting when I was four or five." She cleared her throat. Glanced at him. He nodded encouragement.

She'd never told anyone this before yet she wanted, suddenly, to tell him every last detail of it. "I would imagine myself sitting on a wooden bench in a tiny stone house, with a huge fire blazing in the hearth, my brothers and sister beside me. Our parents were there, too. I felt..." She lowered her voice. "So safe and warm."

Her gaze darted to, then away from Nathan's. "Like I belonged." She fiddled with her napkin. "I loved that daydream. I'd play it over and over again in my head whenever I was angry at my adoptive parents. Or had a bad day at school."

"Wow, that's pretty specific for a daydream." Nathan leaned forward.

"Yeah, I always thought so too. Made me wonder if maybe it was a past-life memory or something." She ate another fork-full of her battered cod. Then asked, "What about your parents?"

"My mom died when I was seventeen. Hit by a drunk driver when she was coming home from one of my school plays. It was the middle of January. Haven't liked winter since."

"Oh, I'm so sorry."

"Thanks."

Ruby opened her mouth to ask Nathan another question but heard someone calling Nathan's name behind her again.

"Oh, hi there, Nathan."

Ruby took the last few bites of her lunch and looked up in time to see another young woman—a petite blonde—walk by. She waved in Nathan's direction.

Ruby watched Nathan give the blonde woman a quick smile and wave back even while his gaze shifted to Ruby's. He cleared his throat then fiddled with his silverware.

Was that the most recent woman he'd rejected? Maybe there was some truth to what those ladies had said... How many women *had* Nathan dated, anyway?

Ruby wiped her lips with her napkin. Well, really, it shouldn't matter. "Ready to head back?" She pulled out her debit card and, after she paid, quickly checked her account balance. Only $500 left in her savings account. How had that happened? Her student loan payment might have to be deferred this month, too. She worried her bottom lip between her teeth.

Nathan nodded. "Let's go."

They crossed Queen Street and headed up to the condo again.

Ruby picked up the next cardboard box and took off the lid. More jumbled papers. She bit back a groan and started to riffle through them.

Underneath a stack of photocopies was a cloth-bound

book. Its corners had frayed and its spine had cracked. The title, *From Away*, in gold leaf, had mostly flaked off. Ruby picked it up as if she held a newborn kitten.

"What's fascinating you so much there?" Nathan's voice was far too close to her ear. She jumped and spun around in the red leather chair behind Dr. O'Neil's desk.

She hastily set the book down. She hoped he hadn't noticed its back cover had nearly fallen off, thanks to her jerky motion.

Nathan raised his eyebrows. "That looks like one of my father's."

Ruby looked down at the book and traced a finger across its surface.

Nathan frowned. "Don't worry about the back cover. These things are old."

"Right. So," Ruby bent forward and nudged a discarded accordion file with her sandaled toe, then picked it up and threw it in the wastebasket. "I've been doing some cleaning up."

"I can see that," Nathan said, and leaned against the desk top next to the large red leather chair.

She opened the book. Mustiness wafted to her. The flyleaf was warped and the title page was torn in half. She discovered that most of the pages were glued together with age and damp.

But a list of names near the back of the book, in a neatly typed column, caught her eye. It listed all the people who had immigrated to Prince Edward Island before 1800. Half the names were Scottish. The rest, from the looks of it, were Irish, with a smattering of French settlers, too. Acadians, she realized. Belliveaux was listed. Edwina's people?

She had lowered the book halfway to the desktop when the back cover fell completely off. Ruby reached out to pick it up, a hand to her mouth.

But that's when she noticed that the end paper had come loose. And just visible where the end paper and the board of the back cover met, was the edge of a second piece of paper.

Ruby's forehead creased as she used her thumb and forefinger to pull the page free.

She sighed in relief. They'd found it. The signed order from General Washington. Now Dr. O'Neil's name could be cleared.

But wait. She unfolded and skimmed the document. This wasn't an order. It was a letter...

"Nathan," she whispered as she carefully smoothed out the page. "Look at this."

He began to read over her shoulder, aloud. His breath caressed her cheek:

—and how my heart longs but for the taste of your kiss, the feel of your arms around me. Perhaps it goes against propriety to speak of such things so boldly, yet this missive is for your eyes alone.

Nathan's voice was low, soft, deep, in her ear. Ruby felt a thrill go up her spine.

Darling, I did not expect, though I should have guessed, I would be jailed for desertion. On 27 November, only a few days after we arrived in Boston Harbor. But now that I have escaped imprisonment for choosing not to fight in this War, I shall do my damnedest to reach you on St. John's Island. Indeed, I journey there now. But with it being midwinter and with my unfortunate loca-tion at present in the midst of these Rebellious Colonies, I fear these events and circumstances do not afford me much hope that I shall reach you in time.

A sense of longing and desire—for what, Ruby couldn't say—coursed through her. Tears sprang to her eyes and she swallowed, as Nathan continued to read.

Oh, how I so much desire to speak on your behalf against the supposed crimes that these unfeeling Mon-sters seem to think you have engendered! How could Washington fathom you had stolen the Seal for your own ends then send you back to the island?

Nathan's voice had lowered to a whisper, and his breath was warm on her skin.

Thus, I pray this letter be a part of me that shall reach you, give you all the strength, warmth and love you need in order to withstand their cries for blood. I pray it shall not be yours that is spilt.

I am Your most Faithful servant
Alexander

Nathan had stopped speaking. Silence clung to them both, heavy and deep. She didn't want to disturb it, somehow. Didn't want to break the moment, the fragility of whatever-it-was that hung between them, now. Yet her chest felt tight. Hollow. She couldn't leave him. And suddenly, she wanted to turn around, wrap her arms around Nathan, and never let go.

Her heart pounded.

She could feel it, feel all that was unspoken, as it shimmered between them. But it was more than his voice. It was something about the *way* he'd said those words. In that tone. Soft. Low...As if it was a promise. A promise left unfulfilled... Goose bumps broke out on her bare arms and she rubbed them.

"Cold?" Nathan murmured, and placed his warm hands on her exposed skin.

She sucked in a breath as she felt his hands on her. And suddenly, she wanted to stay here, in this moment, with this man, on this island...forever.

Her eyes fluttered closed. Then snapped open.

This island. Washington. The seal. She gasped. "Wait a minute."

Nathan cleared his throat. Dropped his arms from her.

"This is the other half." She spun around. "The other half of the love letter fragment. It was actually *here*. This is huge!"

Nathan crossed his arms and shifted away from Ruby to lean against the desk. "That's great."

She chewed on a cuticle. "Hmm. But Dr. O'Neil said he didn't *have* the other half." She met Nathan's gaze.

"Well," he said, "it was hidden inside a book. I doubt my dad even knew it was there."

Ruby flushed. "Right." She looked up after she re-read the letter to herself. "This means...Alexander was who Edwina had received the letter from. He didn't want to fight in the war." She rummaged around in her notes and pulled out the copy of the first half of the letter fragment.

"Draft dodger?"

Ruby shook her head. Scanned the lines. "The penalty for desertion was death. But only if you got caught. Look at this."

"Well," Nathan said, after he read the letter in whole. "I remember from this lecture one of my ex-girlfriends dragged me to, something about Quakers coming up here in the 1700s because they were pacifists. So maybe that's why he was going up here to begin with? Maybe that's how he met her?"

"That's possible."

The lines from the other half of the letter jumped out at her: *the compass of the heart points in new directions.*

Did this mean that first riddle had something to do with this letter? With the order? The seal?

Nathan glanced at her. "Do you think this has to do with the order? And the seal?"

Ruby laughed. "That's just what I was thinking!"

"Great minds." Nathan grinned. "How about we go to the public library to try to find out?"

Ruby just couldn't snuff out the hopeful look in his blue eyes. The public library was the least likely place to find anything related to the in-depth information they needed. But, who knew? It would be at least a place to start.

"All right," she said. "Let's go."

Somehow she couldn't quite bring herself to tell him she was leaving Sunday for an interview. One that might, if she

got the job, force her to abandon everything she'd started to help with, here.

RUBY AND NATHAN took a left out of Cross Keys Condos and headed up the slight incline toward Great George Street. Ruby noticed three brightly colored row houses on the opposite side of the street. A bronze statue depicted not one but two men dressed in coattails and top hats. They gestured over a document that lay spread out on a barrel. Ruby smiled. She'd have to come back by here and read the plaque.

It had started to drizzle and Ruby pulled up the hood of her purple zippered sweatshirt. Her hair always seemed to frizz in the humidity. She blew away a strand that had fallen across her eyes.

What happened back there in Dr. O'Neil's study? She felt herself cringe. She'd just been overly hopelessly romantic. Or something. Just...too affected by the words of someone long dead. That was all.

She darted a glance at Nathan. He seemed unaffected by their earlier...incident? Encounter?

The drizzle increased.

Up ahead, she noticed a homeless man. The hood of his white windbreaker was cinched around his face. The Tim Horton's paper coffee cup he held was half-full of coins and water as he hunched in the doorway of a three-story red brick building. Nathan reached into his jeans pocket and tossed a few dollars into the man's cup. "Buy yourself some hot coffee."

Ruby's heart swelled in her chest.

But in the next second, a knot formed in her stomach. Based on what had happened when she and Nathan had had lunch together this afternoon, it seemed those ladies on Victoria Row must have been right...

They continued up the block. Ruby paused to glance up at St. Dunstan's tall spires; its golden limestone almost glowed in the late morning sun.

But someone who gave money to the homeless couldn't be all bad, could he?

They reached Richmond Street. After they crossed the brick-paved pedestrian street, they headed up the steps of the Confederation Center of the Arts with its 1960s facade and two-story high plate-glass windows.

But the thin man with steel-rimmed glasses and salt-and-pepper hair who sat behind the reference desk on the second floor shook his head. "There's nothing about a second signed order from General George Washington."

"Oh no," Nathan said and glanced at Ruby.

The reference librarian looked up from his desk. His steel-rimmed glasses caught the fluorescent lights. "We do have a file on the theft of the Great Seal, though. Everything's in it. Typed copies of the original letters that Wright and Callbeck wrote to the Earl of Dartmouth telling him what happened. A copy of the order from General Washington telling Captains Broughton and Selman not to bother any Canadian ships. Even a copy of a pencil sketch some travelling diplomat did of the original Great Silver Seal, as it's sometimes called. The one you're looking for. Er," he chuckled, "I mean, the image you're looking for. But today, I'm sorry. That file has been checked out. And," he referred to his screen, "it's an extended loan. Won't be back for four more weeks."

Ruby bit back a groan. Nathan stuffed his hands in his pockets.

The librarian smiled. "You could always try Googling it. The public archives won't have anything on it. They knew we had the extensive file, so would refer people to us. I'm sorry about that. I'm happy to put you down as the next people to check the file out, once it's returned."

Ruby shook her head. "Thanks anyway but we need it now. Wikipedia isn't very complete. And the Tourism P.E.I. website's PDF brochure about the seal isn't too extensive either. We need the file."

The reference librarian swivelled his rolling chair in

their direction. "You know." He tapped a pencil against the desktop. "If you're looking for things related to Washington, and Edwina Belliveaux, the public archives *do* have all Edwina's personal diaries. They're just across the way in the Coles building. They have a little less straightforward filing system than we do here. But you said you're a librarian yourself, correct?"

Ruby nodded.

"So I'm sure you'll catch on quick." He smiled and scribbled down the details for her before he handed her the yellow Post-it.

"Thanks." She took the sticky note and glanced at her watch. They'd only been there ten minutes. She and Nathan headed out of the building and crossed the lush green lawn to the Honourable George Coles Building, made of reddish island sandstone. Oaks dotted the expanse of lawn—their notched leaves waved in the light breeze.

"Since you like history," Nathan said, and nodded toward a large Neoclassical stone building on their left, "you should take a look inside Province House. It's where talks were held in the 1860s to create Canada as we know it today. And it's where the Legislative Assembly meets. Kind of like the state capitol buildings in the U.S."

A gaggle of tourists snapped photos on the steps of the building Nathan indicated, its Ionic columns bathed in warm summer sun.

"Archives are up on the third floor, miss," the bald security guard said, after Ruby and Nathan had walked inside the Coles building. "How are ya, Nathan?"

"Good, good. You?"

The guard nodded. "Pretty fair." He waved aside Ruby's attempts to show her photo ID, as the sign requested. "I know you two aren't going to steal anything." He chuckled as he turned back to his computer and his game of solitaire on the screen.

They took the rickety elevator. Its doors slid open with a squeak of protest as it arrived on the third floor. Ruby hurried through the doors as if the elevator might change its mind at any moment.

The door on her right read Public Archives and Records Office of Prince Edward Island.

"I'm just going to run to the washroom," Nathan said, and nodded to a door at the end of the hall.

"Okay," Ruby said, "I'll be in the archives office." She stepped through the door into a small, low-ceilinged room. A wall of windows bathed the room in natural light, and a giant philodendron plant sat on the desk by the door.

"Hi, how are ya?" A late 30-something woman with a round face, blue eyes and short curly brown hair sat behind the desk. Ruby cocked her head. Something about her eyes looked familiar.

"Oh, I'm good. I'm Ruby Zalonski. I'm looking for information about a woman named Edwina Belliveaux."

"Ruby, hi!" The woman smiled. "I'm Evie. It's great to meet you in person."

"Oh, hi, Evie! Nice to meet you too." Ruby smiled back at her.

"So. Edwina Belliveaux." Evie tapped her manicured fingernail against her chin for a second, then turned and dug around in a filing cabinet. "We have all her diaries here." She stepped behind a partition and reappeared a few minutes later with a cardboard banker's box.

"You can take a look at these. It should give you everything you need."

"Thanks, Evie." Nathan said, as he came into the room and stood beside Ruby. "We weren't able to find anything on Google about this. Or at the library." Nathan took the box from his sister and headed across the room to a long, low oak table surrounded by wooden office chairs.

"Nathan?" Evie blinked and looked from Ruby over to Nathan. Ruby just nodded.

"He *never* does this," Evie said to Ruby, as she leaned forward in a conspiratorial whisper. "It's like he's allergic to history. He and our dad didn't see eye to eye on that stuff."

"Really?" Ruby said, and blushed, as she glanced at Nathan over her shoulder. Had he taken the time to do this

just for her?

Her heart fluttered. That was sweet of him. But wait. He wasn't doing this for her. He was doing this for his dad. To clear his name.

"So," Evie said, "you're looking for more information about Edwina?"

"Yes, we are. And George Washington. We're trying to find that order."

Evie nodded. "I was there in the lawyer's office too. Dad wouldn't forge anything. But maybe you'll find something about it in Edwina's diaries." She handed Ruby two pairs of white cotton gloves. "Some sort of connection. Anyway, good luck."

"Thanks," Ruby said, before she joined Nathan at the table and handed him a pair of gloves. He slipped his on and she put on hers.

Then they lifted the lid of the box together. Inside, a series of small, squarish sea-green leather bound books were neatly stacked.

She picked up the first one and eased open the cover. The first page was filled with neat, flowing handwriting, with flourishes and the occasional inkblot.

Charlotte Town 1 May, 1775

Found the most exquisite silk for my new gown. Shall stitch it myself. Perfect for Governor's ball two weeks hence. Shall secure an invitation at once.

Ruby turned the page. More of the same. She flipped to the back of the diary. Again, more entries about ribbon and how many cross-stitch samplers Edwina had embroidered. And how many silver coins she'd given to the poor.

Ruby withheld a sigh. There had to be something in here somewhere...

Nathan picked up the next diary. "More of the same."

Ruby rubbed the back of her neck, and raised her head to ease the tension. She shifted in the hard wooden seat but returned her eyes to the faded writing.

She frowned. Flipped more pages. There was nothing here.

Slowly, they made their way through all the diaries.

She checked the time on her phone. Had they been here nearly three hours? She got up. "Might as well copy some of these entries before we go. If nothing else, they'd be good reference material."

Nathan nodded, and began to put the diaries back neatly into the boxes.

After she'd jotted some notes, Nathan stood. Ruby fought back another surge of disappointment. Had this all been a waste of time?

She clutched her jotted notes on their walk back down Great George Street to Cross Keys Condos.

She looked around. "It's so beautiful here. You know, I heard once that people who are drawn to certain places have lived there in past lives."

Nathan made a noncommittal sound.

"So," Ruby said after a beat of silence, "what do *you* know about Edwina?"

"Bits and pieces of what Dad would talk about. Edwina was an important citizen. For a woman. Er, at that time, I mean." He raised his hands. "Uh, I'm all for equality."

"I should hope so." Ruby pushed up her glasses.

Nathan cleared his throat. "Well, there's a story that was passed down through the generations—something about how her father or her mother or someone in her family gave away some priceless heirloom to save themselves from being deported." He shook his head. "Only, it didn't work."

"Oh. I thought she'd just said that one famous quote."

"No. She was deported—well, her family was—after the British signed the Treaty of Paris in 1763 and took over P.E.I."

"But she wasn't?"

"That's the thing. There *is* a record of her death at Fort Amherst, in December of 1775." Nathan paused. "But there's a bit of a gap in the history. That was something my father was trying to figure out. In his spare time when he wasn't too busy ignoring his family and his marriage to go off and chase some obscure reference to something that could mean something to someone. Mostly, to him." Nathan's jaw tightened and his gaze shifted to a faraway look.

"But despite all that," Nathan went on, "pretty much everyone on the island tries to claim some relation to Edwina Belliveaux. Kind of like how they do with Lucy Maude Montgomery." He chuckled.

"They do?"

Nathan nodded. A gleam of pride shone in his eyes.

"And speaking of early island history, did you know that Phillips Callbeck, that guy who got kidnapped when the seal was stolen, has descendants that still live on P.E.I.?"

He paused and laughed to himself. "I don't know why I'm telling you this. Or why, really, I remember all of it." He shrugged. "I don't even care about history, really."

"WHY DON'T YOU?" Ruby said, and blinked once. Then again. Nathan felt heat crawl up his torso. He watched Ruby lift her gaze to his. Noticed the tip of her tongue protruded from between her lips. He wet his own.

His mind flicked back to them standing in the alcove in Dad's study earlier that day. The way she'd felt in his arms.

All at once, he wanted to wrap her up in his embrace, keep her safe and warm and reassure her that nothing, nothing, would ever cause her harm or fear or sadness or pain. That he *would* be there for her.

What the hell?

He stepped backward and banged his heel against the wrought iron bench behind them.

The shock of pain was a welcome relief from the turmoil and tangle of desire and fierce protectiveness that had filled him only moments before.

Was he going crazy?

Nathan swallowed hard and didn't trust himself to speak

for a moment.

"But the history gets in your blood, I guess." Nathan shook his head. "This place isn't really like anywhere else." He held up a hand. "I know, I know, that's clichéd to say. And probably doesn't make any sense. But family legacy and history play a big role here. Even though this is the 21st century." His lips pursed.

"When I got off the plane, I had the oddest sense, that I'd been here before. I'd love to live here. Maybe after I complete my Ph.D., I can come back and see the sights." She sighed. "I wish I wasn't adopted," Ruby blurted, her gaze moving back up to his face. He caught his breath at the sight of tears that glimmered in her eyes.

"Why does that bother you?"

She jerked back. "Bother me? It doesn't—" She bit her lip, averted her gaze. "Okay, maybe it does. But I've never felt like I fit in, somehow." She twirled a lock of hair around her finger then pushed her glasses further up her nose.

Nathan held his breath, careful not to stand too close. He didn't want to scare her.

So he simply waited.

She spoke again. "I don't know why that is. I don't know if everyone who's adopted feels this way. And somehow I feel guilty about it. Because my adoptive parents love me. But I always had this...hunger...deep down, to find out more. To know more. To discover, really, who I am. That's why I went into archival studies. So I could, guilt-free, look into other people's pasts and maybe find the answers to my own." She studied her hands. Nathan had to suppress the urge to place his on top of hers.

"I know what you mean," he said.

She cut her gaze to his.

He nodded to her unasked question. "I never belonged." He rubbed a hand across his jaw. "All my life people judged me, just because of my family name. Just because I didn't know what I wanted to do for the rest of my life. Just because I wasn't like every other goddamn O'Neil on this island."

He hadn't realized Ruby had put her hand on his arm until he felt the gentle squeeze. He looked into her hazel eyes and felt the pull of empathy for her situation, mirrored in his own gaze.

He felt a cord of longing inside his heart stretch to nearly the breaking point as he studied the green, gold and caramel-brown flecks of color in her eyes. Suddenly he wanted to unburden himself to her. To tell her all his dark secrets. As if, in simply speaking them, a light would shine so brightly on the darkness that he'd finally be set free. By the mere act of being witnessed by another human being who cared. His lips parted in wonder.

Someone did care. She cared. At least, she would listen to him. Wanted, it seemed, to hear what he had to say. He felt his heart swell.

The silence grew between them.

He rubbed the back of his neck. Started to walk down the sidewalk again.

They'd arrived at the condo. "Anyway, I'm sure you have things to do. Have a good afternoon."

"No, wait." Ruby reached out and put a hand on his arm. "We haven't figured out anything out about the seal...I could use your thoughts, actually." She twirled a strand of hair around her finger.

"Just my thoughts?" Nathan raised a brow as they headed back upstairs.

"You know what I mean," Ruby said, with a laugh.

BUT BACK IN the study, after a few more hours that turned up nothing, Ruby tugged at the end of her ponytail in frustration. "There has to be something here. But there isn't." She dropped her chin into her upturned palm.

Nathan got up. He strode over to his dad's desk, opened the third drawer from the bottom, and reached inside.

Something crinkled as he pulled his hand back out. "I find a candy bar's always a good excuse to take a break. Do you like white chocolate Hershey bars?"

"They're my favorite."

Nathan laughed. "Mine too." He opened one then handed it to her. Took another one for himself. "These Hershey bars were about the only thing Dad and I could agree on."

"That bad, huh?"

Nathan just nodded, and sat on the floor, then leaned back against the mahogany of his dad's desk. He stretched out his legs and crossed one ankle over the other. He broke off a piece of chocolate and chewed.

Ruby got up and joined him. Neither spoke. The only sound was the ticking of the grandfather clock against the opposite wall. Dust motes floated in a sunbeam.

Finally, Nathan broke the silence. "You know..." He mused. "Someone sketched the seal before it was stolen. Remember what the reference librarian said?"

He jumped up and began pacing. "Now I remember Dad mentioned that too. He even had a copy of it, actually. But God knows where it is."

Nathan stopped his pacing and snapped his fingers. "Wait a minute." He picked up a file on his dad's desk and thumbed through it. "I remember Dad saying something about—getting really excited about it—some museum in London had a duplicate of the seal. Well, not a duplicate exactly...I don't remember."

But Ruby was already typing. She turned her laptop to face him. "Do you mean the University of London Library's Fuller Collection? Says on their website that it's not a duplicate. It's a similar one."

She navigated the site. "Look at this!" She pointed. "Someone in that library decided to note that P.E.I. had a similar seal. So then they uploaded a scan of that 1700s diplomat's sketch showing both sides of P.E.I.'s seal."

He pointed to the image. "On the one side there's a large acorn-bearing oak tree beside a smaller oak, with a trunk that divides into three. Says here that it represents P.E.I.'s relationship to England as a colony. England sort of watched over it like an older sibling. And on the other side of the seal was the king's armorial bearings. Basically, his coat of arms. Plus some Latin inscriptions that I won't attempt to pronounce."

Ruby zoomed in to make the sketch as large as possible. She cocked her head. "What are we looking for, here?"

Nathan started to pace again. "I have no idea. The first clue didn't say much about *what* to look for. Just to look at the seal."

"Hmmm." Ruby scanned the screen, and felt Nathan's breath on her neck as he leaned in to look at the screen too. A shiver slid down her spine.

"Well, logically, it can't be something too complicated. Because the seal isn't very big. The size and shape of a large, heavy coin."

"Right," Ruby said. "And it would have to have been something that could be done quickly. Easily."

"And unobtrusively," Nathan added.

Ruby nodded. "Something that the person leaving the clue and the person picking up on the clue, would both understand."

Nathan didn't respond. He pointed instead to the screen. "What are those marks?" He tilted his head.

"Let's see if I can zoom in a bit more... Oh, around the edge of the seal?" She tapped a finger against her chin. "They just look like strike marks. When they made it."

"No," Nathan said, "they're too regular for that... Too uniform." He leaned even nearer to Ruby. Her heart sped up.

She jumped to her feet. "Here. It seems like you need to sit down. Have my seat."

He glanced at her, held her gaze for a moment longer than necessary, then sat. "You don't need to be afraid of me, you know." He paused. "I don't bite."

Ruby gave a shaky laugh. "Of course not." She tightened her ponytail. "I was just giving you more room."

He caught Ruby's eye and winked. "You know," he said, "the last time I had to sort through documents and do some research was at UPEI. After hours. In the library stacks.

Somehow I ended up making out with my research partner. Got an F on the assignment. But I did enjoy myself." His eyes twinkled.

Ruby gave him a playful shove on the shoulder. "Well, that's not the kind of research we're doing here."

He held her gaze. "You sure about that?" His tone turned serious.

Ruby shifted her weight and crossed her arms. The ticking of the grandfather clock sounded loud to her ears.

She cleared her throat. The man was too perceptive for his own good. How did he *do* that? Interpret her in ways she could barely begin to admit to herself?

She turned back to the screen and ignored the way her heart pounded. She was leaving. In three days. Couldn't get involved. And she wasn't going to just have a fling—she wasn't the type. She cleared her throat. "So what do you think it is?"

"Numbers," he said, and traced a finger along the edge. "But not Arabic numbers. See the repetition of marks? The vertical lines. These are—"

"Roman numerals." Ruby grinned. "Nice job!"

Nathan leaned back in the computer chair and looked up at her over his shoulder. "We make a pretty good team."

Ruby smiled back. Held his gaze as she held her breath. Somehow, she found herself move forward ever so slightly. What would it be like to lean in, reach up, run her fingers along his jawline, press her lips against his—

The ding of an incoming message on Ruby's phone made her jump. She glanced at it.

Maggie wanted to know how the hunt was going. And wondered just where things were at with a certain Nathan O'Neil. Ruby tapped back a 'talk soon' reply, then turned to Nathan. "But what do the Roman numerals mean?"

"Well, assuming we're looking for another riddle, the numbers are obviously some sort of clue. So..." Nathan trailed off.

"Let's think about what we already know," Ruby said. "That first clue referred to the compass. And then General

Washington. And lastly to the seal. But I don't get how the Roman numerals fit in."

Nathan pushed away from the desk suddenly and stood. "Why didn't I see it before? It's a cipher. The numbers are a cipher. But which one?" He ran a hand through his hair.

"There are so many codes and ciphers..." Ruby rubbed her temples. Then stifled a yawn and checked her watch. "I can't believe we've been up here for this long. It's practically 10 p.m." She sighed. "You'd have to memorize whole books to know stuff like that."

"I got a book like that for Christmas once," Nathan said, and glanced at the screen again. "But this points to a specific cipher because the numerals are in sets of three. It's a book cipher. Technically," Nathan tilted his head. "...it's called an Ottendorf cipher."

Ruby laughed softly. "How do you *know* this?"

"I spent time reading that code book—plus a few more—back when I'd been unemployed for months. Dad knew I loved logic and rational thinking. Math. That sort of thing. I think he gave me that code book because he might've been getting a little desperate in hoping I'd get a good job. He joked I should join CSIS." Nathan chuckled. "It's the Canadian version of the FBI," he said, in response to the questioning look in Ruby's gaze.

"Wow, you know something I don't," Ruby couldn't help teasing.

A sparkle gleamed in Nathan's eye. "Maybe more than one thing." He leveled his gaze on her.

She blushed and changed the subject. "Right. So what's an Ottendorf cipher?"

"It's a series of three numbers used to reference a document that contains a code. That's the beauty of it. You can use any written document—even the dictionary—as a way to convey a secret message. So the way the numbers work— the first one refers to a page. The second number refers to a line. And the third number refers to a word on that line in the document."

"Okay. That sounds simple enough. But which document?"

"Hmm, good question." Nathan began pacing. "Well, it needs to be old. In the same era as the seal."

Ruby nodded. "And it needs to be...official, probably. Historically significant."

"Wait. In the first clue... It talked about *Goodhearted General's Orders did put forth—*" Nathan met her gaze.

"You're right," Ruby said. "That means we need to use this Ottendorf cipher on Washington's orders."

Ruby stifled another yawn and glanced at her watch again.

"We can call it a night for now, though. But can we meet back here tomorrow after I'm done with some things at the office, and keep going?"

Ruby nodded. "Sounds good."

AFTER NATHAN LEFT, inside the condo bedroom, Ruby changed into her oversized sleeping shirt. She belted a light robe around her waist and glanced out the door leading to the small balcony overlooking the back of St. Dunstan's cathedral and Gahan House restaurant.

Her hand was on the doorknob before she realized it.

She stepped out onto the small balcony. The amber glow of fairy lights strung across the outdoor patio of the restaurant combined with the scent of bright red potted geraniums and the murmur of the diners. She exhaled softly and closed her eyes. So peaceful. She found herself leaning against the wrought iron railing.

Warm summer air blew across her face and she breathed a sigh of contentment. What was it about this place that had her feeling so at home?

She pursed her lips.

She headed back to the bedroom and fell asleep as soon as her head hit the pillow.

He ran to her down the forest trail. Her heart lifted, the sting of sea salt on her cheeks, the scent of wild roses in her hair.

He neared her. She could see the shine of the brass buckles on the strap of the leather artist's bag slung across his chest, over the forest green wool of his great coat. The coat that her fingers had brushed over many a time in these late summer evenings with the tang of salt in the air and the taste of his skin on her lips.

Oh, how she longed to stroke her fingers along the length of that strong, sturdy leather. To feel the broad width of his shoulders under her palms, the scratchy wool of his jacket, the rough scrape of his stubble against her. Everywhere.

She whispered his name, those well-loved syllables—

"Alexander," the name jerked Ruby awake. Even as she spoke the word, half-awake, half-asleep, she felt as if rust and saltwater coated her throat.

Ruby swallowed, then startled fully awake. Because in the strange manner of dreams, he had had Nathan's face.

Chapter Five

SATURDAY MORNING LIGHT slanted through the large plate-glass windows at Island Design & Tech. Nathan sat at a glass and chrome desk in the southeast corner. A few of his colleagues sat at their desks, too.

He executed the last few keystrokes on his Mac and then sat back in the white office chair, his fingers steepled as he studied the rendering on the screen. Pretty good.

He cocked his head. There was something missing from the design. He narrowed his eyes at the image on the screen.

Hmmm. He tapped his fingers on the chair arm. What was it? No. The lines were fine. And the perspective was good... He tilted his head to the other side.

Of course. He sat forward. The shading. He made a few adjustments with the keyboard. A surge of satisfaction pulsed through him. There. That was exactly right.

Just then, his phone rang. He picked it up. "Nathan," his boss said, "since you're working today, just wanted to check in and ask how the new logo's coming?"

Nathan grinned. "Just finished it." Without thinking, he picked up one of the freshly sharpened No. 2 pencils he kept in one of his mother's glass jam jars at the top right-hand corner of his desk and, out of long habit, began to sketch absently as he talked. "I'll send you a proof in a minute."

"Good." His boss continued. "See you Monday."

"Sure," Nathan said then hung up the phone. He glanced down at the page in front of him. His hand froze as he stared at the sketch.

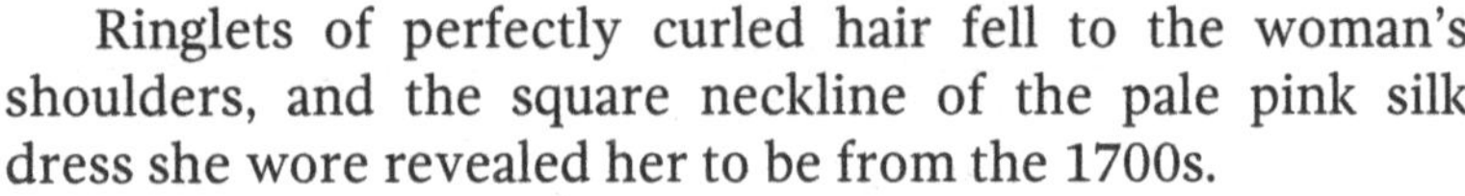

Ringlets of perfectly curled hair fell to the woman's shoulders, and the square neckline of the pale pink silk dress she wore revealed her to be from the 1700s.

And behind her, drawn in hurried strokes, was a waning moon with a wind-blown chestnut tree and the hasty outline of a man astride a horse.

But it was the slight smile that touched the woman's half-formed lips, as she looked up at the man that held Nathan's gaze. Because it was the same woman he'd painted...which meant it was Edwina Belliveaux. Again.

Nathan stared at the pencil in his hand and willed it to stop trembling. But he couldn't make his fingers stop shaking. Or his heart stop pounding.

Because her large green eyes—they seemed...familiar somehow. His mind flitted back to the way Ruby had looked at him yesterday at the archives.

At the eager, excited expression on her face when she'd found that letter fragment. He grinned, but it quickly faded. There was such a sadness and frustration in her gaze when they hadn't found out anything more about Edwina. He sighed. What could he do to help her? He had to do something. Ease her burden.

People who are drawn to places have lived there before. Ruby's words flashed through his mind. Was that true for events, too?

No. These drawings were just some ramblings of his subconscious mind, what with all the talk they'd been doing about Edwina.

That was all. Just doodlings, transferred onto paper.

Besides, Ruby was an academic. He would have thought she'd be more grounded than to believe in those sorts of New Age things.

Looked like she was just as much a romantic as his father had been. He had to keep his distance. Good thing she was leaving soon. His attraction to her would fade when she was gone.

All the more reason to stay away from her. At least as much as he could, what with them still working together to find that damn order. He couldn't afford to be disappointed in love again. So why was he more interested in her than he had been in any other woman he'd met?

He shook his head and glanced down at the sketch again. No. Her eyes weren't green. He hadn't colored them in. And her dress wasn't pink. He hadn't shaded that in, either. He crumpled up the sketch. What the hell was going on?

He'd always loved drawing. But in university, when deciding his degree path, he chose a double degree: business and graphic design. For the simple fact that his parents had agreed to pay for his education if he stayed on P.E.I. But if he'd followed his passion and gone to art school off island, he would've had to pay for it himself.

So he'd done the practical thing. Even if it had broken his heart in the process.

He shook his head at himself. He was perfectly happy in his job. Wasn't he? He wasn't miserable or broke.

He couldn't keep doing this. Keep thinking he'd made some mistake over and over when he had a good job with good pay in a place he loved.

He studied the pencil lines, the shading, the use of light. He frowned. Maybe he should've gone to art school after all. He carefully folded the paper and tucked it into his pants pocket.

Nathan shook off his thoughts and turned his attention back to the logo design in front of him.

RUBY HAD MADE quite a bit of progress on the cataloging that morning, so she decided to head over to the boardwalk along Victoria Park.

She watched the mid-morning sun sparkle off of the bay. The occasional caw of a crow intermingled with the cry of a seagull as they fought over some French fries and half-open wild mussel shells scattered on the rocky shoreline along the winding boardwalk of Charlottetown's waterfront.

She didn't want to leave now. Ruby chewed on a corner of her thumbnail. But who knew when she'd get another interview for a job as perfect as that?

Sailboats bobbed on the calm waters, and the occasional jet-ski buzzed by. But mostly, she had the place to herself. Only a few dog walkers and joggers were out this time of day.

She'd found the other half of the love letter fragment. And that was great. She grinned. She'd already started adding it into her research.

But she still had so many questions. For instance, what had happened to Edwina? What had she been up to? And what else had happened between her and Alexander?

Maybe there weren't any more love letters at all...

Ruby inhaled the scents of sea salt and pine trees as she walked past the long-needle pines whose limbs grew at fantastical angles that reminded her of something out of Dr. Seuss.

She grinned. Those had been some of her favorite books as a child. And she thought she could recite pretty much every sentence from every one of his books.

Her eyes darted to a long outdoor line-up as she passed a small wooden building painted yellow with blue shutters. The words dairy bar were done in block letters above the gingerbread scrollwork of the front porch. She'd have to stop for ice cream another time. She chewed on her other thumbnail.

Was Edwina a spy? And who was this Alexander person? The 'young man whose name has been lost to history' that Dr. O'Neil had mentioned in his emails to her? Not only that, what about that dream she'd had? Did it have anything to do with all of this? Have any basis in reality? Not that she could exactly use it as a primary source...

Ruby kept walking along the wooden boardwalk. She spotted a lighthouse at the far end and couldn't help smiling.

It was painted a bright white with a red stripe near the top. It seemed to watch over the quiet scene, perched there on a pile of red sandstone outcropped against the blue waters of the harbor.

Despite everything, she felt a thrill run through her. She was really here. On Prince Edward Island. She'd make it. She'd prevail, no matter what it took.

Her thoughts flicked to Nathan for a moment. He'd been very helpful. Was Evie right? She'd definitely implied Nathan wanted to spend time with her. Ruby's heart pounded.

But was he just being nice? Just serving his own ends, wanting to find the order so that his dad's name could be cleared? Did he *really* want to spend time with her? Someone that attractive... With that kind of past...

But then she remembered the look in his eyes as he'd given the money to the homeless man. The way her heart had melted, just a little, when he'd asked her if he could come by again. Or that feeling of...what? ...when they'd been together in the alcove. And then again on the street. How she'd opened up to him. The way she'd just wanted to melt into his arms when he'd read that fragment.

She frowned. If she didn't find out exactly what was going on with Edwina, and with the love letter, not to mention finish sorting through the rest of Dr. O'Neil's papers, then not only would her dissertation have to be significantly rewritten, but she'd lose the edge she needed for the job application.

Just then, Ruby's phone rang. She glanced at it. Dr. Burton.

"Listen, Ruby. Are you back in town yet?"

"No, why? I just booked my flight—I get in Sunday."

A pause. "Listen, Ruby. I'm really not supposed to be telling you this." Dr. Burton lowered her voice. "But these are special circumstances, what with the investigation into Dr. O'Neil's research. Someone on the committee who's reviewing your dissertation defense says that your research is suspect. That means you'll need to have rock-solid primary sources prepped for it."

"What? How? But everyone approved it initially."

"I know." Dr. Burton sighed. "Seems one of them read something online about this whole inquest into Dr. O'Neil's research. And since you were corresponding with him, well, it's reflecting badly on you and your research."

Ruby chewed her lip. "But—" If only Dr. O'Neil hadn't left things in such a mess. They hadn't even been able to find that psalm book he'd mentioned in his email to her. Of course, even if they had, he had obviously already taken the order out of it.

"I know, Ruby. I don't like it either. Please, just get back here as soon as you can."

"Okay," Ruby said. "Thanks for telling me." She ended the call.

She reached the lighthouse at the end of the boardwalk. She paused to watch puffy clouds sail across a blue sky. Then she turned around and headed back to the condo and let herself in.

She sank down onto a stool by the door to take off her tennis shoes and then headed to the bathroom and splashed cold water on her face.

After she towelled off, she raised her head. She wouldn't stop until she had the answers she was seeking. There was always an answer. Always a solution.

Even though she had no clue what that was right now.

"HI NATHAN," RUBY said, as he walked into his dad's study Saturday afternoon.

She'd just logged onto her Simmons College email provider and printed out the first order. Her laptop screen flickered. "Okay, so I'll print out the whole thing. Just to be safe. Because even though Washington only refers to Canada in the very last paragraph of this order, who knows? Maybe the rest of the message is in the other part."

"Good thinking."

Ruby waited for the printer to spit out the page. She frowned as the computer's screen flickered again, and the laptop made a choked whirring noise. "So," Ruby said, "this is what we have." She took the page and turned to Nathan.

"Okay," he said. "Let's apply these Roman numerals."

"But how do we know if we're starting in the right place?" Ruby asked.

She set the still-warm sheet down on Dr. O'Neil's desk and she and Nathan looked at it. "Well," he said, "actually, that's simple. There is only one page to this order, so we know that first number would be a one. These other numbers that come after are too high."

"That makes sense."

"The second number is the line..." Nathan counted down the number of lines on the order. "Okay," he tapped a finger. "Here."

"And what's the third number again? Oh right, the word in the line." Ruby counted over. "'Hearts'" is the first word."

She grabbed a yellow legal pad and wrote that in neat block letters.

"Looks like 'of' is the next one." Nathan picked up the pen and wrote that down beside Ruby's word.

"And..." Ruby's eyes scanned the page, "'ink' comes after that."

Nathan picked up the pen again after Ruby had written down *ink* and wrote down three more words.

Ruby glanced at the pad. "You're good at that."

Nathan shrugged. "Practice, I guess. All those months of unemployment I had to do something." He grinned. "So it looks like we have our first sentence."

Ruby read it aloud. *"Hearts of ink/Sealed in highest wooden frame, where—'* That's not the whole thing, though."

"But that's all the numbers for this page. There are other numbers but it must refer to a different page."

"No, not just a different page. A different order. The rest of the message is in the other order. And I bet it's the one that Washington sent about Edwina. That makes the most sense." Ruby grinned. "I have the second order right—"

But when she turned back to her screen, it was completely black. No amount of rebooting would revive it.

"Your computer's dead," Nathan said.

"But you're the computer expert. Can't you just fix it?"

"It's too far gone for that."

Ruby chewed a cuticle. "Now what? We need to look at that second order." She slumped back in her seat. "And my email software client was the only way to get a look at that. That is, unless we somehow stumble upon the original your dad had around here somewhere." She glanced around. Sighed. "This feels impossible all of a sudden."

"Hey," Nathan said softly. Put a hand on her shoulder. "Something's bound to work out. But in the meantime, have you walked along the quay yet?"

Ruby shook her head.

"Come on," Nathan said, "getting some fresh air will maybe give us a new perspective."

A few minutes later, they were walking along the quay. The gray boards creaked and heaved ever so slightly under Ruby's footsteps.

Sailboats bobbed in their moorings, and the blue water sparkled in the afternoon sun. The sounds of an acoustic guitar mixed with the slap of the waves against the pier as a guitarist picked out a melody on the small stage by Peake's Quay.

"Ruby," Nathan said, "don't give up." She looked at him, her eyes wide. Nathan's gaze became serious. "You can't. You've come too far. Literally."

A little girl with blonde braids zipped past their slow amble. A group of tourists, all eating ice cream cones, sat on one of the old-fashioned wooden benches that faced the water.

Ruby gave a shaky laugh. "Well, thanks."

"No," Nathan said, "I mean it. You're determined. Smart. You don't back down. People like that, well, I really..." He cleared his throat. "Admire. Because," he ran a hand through his hair, "I haven't done that. Sure, I'm in graphic design, something I enjoy. But... well, I felt so restricted. By Dad. By expectations." He sighed. Then spotted a bench tucked into a quiet corner and sat.

Ruby sat too and waited for him to continue.

He looked out over the harbor. "Truth is, I feel like I've settled, with my job. And maybe even with my life." He raised his eyes to her.

She found herself leaning forward, wanting to reassure him. Somehow. "Well, what would you like to do? If you could?"

Nathan reached into his jeans pocket and pulled out a neatly folded piece of lined paper and handed it to Ruby. Its edges fluttered in the soft breeze as she unfolded it.

Ruby traced a finger along the pencil lines. "She's so lifelike. The way you've captured her eyes..." Ruby's own eyes widened. "That's the same woman in my locket picture. She looks...wow. For what it's worth, Nathan, you have got talent."

Nathan blinked rapidly a couple of times. "Thank you." He took a breath. "No one's ever said that to me before." He put a hand over Ruby's and squeezed.

"My family situation, well...Dad and I had a huge fight," Nathan continued. His blue eyes were fringed with dark lashes. But as he blinked, Ruby thought for a second that she saw his eyes change color to a caramel brown. And in that instant, she felt a pull of recognition, familiarity. But in the next moment, as he blinked again, his eyes were blue.

She took in a breath. Probably just a trick of the light.

Ruby tried to pay attention to what he was saying. But all she could do was revel in the feelings of desire and open heartedness that welled up in her as he continued to talk. Continued to open up his soul for her. To her.

"I felt terrible about it. And now," he paused, "there's nothing I can do about it. We were never that close. In fact," he laughed, though there wasn't anything funny, "Mom used to say that we were too much alike. She said that was what our problem was. If you can call it a problem. Maybe it wasn't a problem. Maybe it was simply who we were. Who we are...And now who he'll never be." Nathan studied his hands. Then looked back up at Ruby.

"You know, I've always been like this. Ever since I was

little." He rubbed the back of his neck. "I think he thought that I had some sort of predilection for not following the rules. Taking risks and loving it." He gave a quiet laugh. "And if Mom could see me now." He moved his eyes back up to Ruby's. "I don't think she'd be proud of me at all." He swallowed. "Because what am I doing?" His lips twisted. "What am I doing here? I'm 33 and I thought I would've figured that out by now."

He tugged at his earlobe and blinked rapidly a few times.

Ruby held her breath. Let it out slowly. "What is bad, anyway? There are so many shades of gray." And maybe, just maybe, things weren't quite so black and white as she would've liked, about Nathan. "Maybe," she added, "there isn't really bad and good. Maybe everyone has parts of each."

Ruby felt his fingers intertwine with hers.

But the bark of a Scotty dog that trotted by, made Ruby startle and remove her hand. She glanced at her watch, straightened then got up. "Well, I should probably get back. Thanks, though, for...this."

Nathan nodded and stood too. Shoved his hands in his pockets. "Yeah. You're welcome." He sighed. "I guess we have to think of something else, with that order. I need to get home now, but I'll think on it, ok?"

AT HOME THAT night, Nathan flipped through the channels on TV, his mind elsewhere. Ruby was leaving soon. They hadn't found much of anything to do with the order at all. What was he going to do about Dad, then?

His fingers clenched.

He wouldn't give up. Not yet. Not now. He got up and began pacing. His steps led him somehow downstairs to the studio in his basement.

He needed to straighten things up a bit.

He lined up the containers filled with paints and brushes. Then bent down and picked up a drop-sheet he'd haphazardly placed on top of a coffee table nearby.

Underneath, still bundled in its linen wrappings, was that small leather book. How had it gotten here? Oh, right. He must've brought it down here after he'd had it in the lawyer's office.

Nathan picked it up and drew a thumb across the cracked leather-bound surface. How many years had it lain in the wall? Would this, maybe, be some way to help Ruby out? Even if she was leaving, he did want to help her. It was the decent thing to do.

Had someone stolen it from whoever this person was, and hidden it behind the brick?

Nathan watched the overhead light glint against the faintest gold-leaf remnants that still clung to the front cover.

Why was it blank? A crease appeared between his brows as he flipped pages. The faint scent of citrus wafted to him.

Nathan's pulse sped up. Why go to the trouble of hiding something like this if all the pages were blank? There had to be a reason.

He set the journal back down on the coffee table near his battered old couch and reached for his laptop. Typed 'old journals and citrus' into the search box. It seemed, as he scanned the hits, that citrus was used in the old days to make invisible ink. Hmmm.

Which meant that the pages weren't blank after all, but simply disguised...

After a few minutes of research, he came across a website detailing how to make invisible ink visible.

He went upstairs into his ensuite bathroom and rummaged around in the drawer below the sink. Hmmm. He usually just towel-dried his hair but—Yes. Here it was. He pulled out a hairdryer.

He went to the kitchen, hairdryer in hand and set it on the table. Then he went to the kitchen sink and grabbed a couple of kitchen trash bags from the Glad dispenser below the sink, along with the rubber gloves he used to wash

dishes with.

He came back to the kitchen table, spread the new plastic garbage bag out, placed the hairdryer on top, and then pulled on his rubber gloves.

Then he went back down into the basement for the book and went back upstairs into the kitchen. He set it down on the plastic, and opened it to the very first blank page.

He picked up the hairdryer and flicked it onto the lowest setting then held it aloft. Paused. Looked down at the page. Swallowed. Slowly aimed the hairdryer at the surface.

He moved the hair dryer along the antiquated page, in long slow passes. Would this even work? Nothing seemed to be happening.

But he worked his way along the page until the entire surface was heated.

He hoped he wouldn't somehow set it on fire.

He shook his head. What would his father think of him doing this? He chuckled to himself.

He'd probably have a fit. And Ruby? What would she do? She'd thank him, probably. Maybe. If, that is, he found anything in here worthwhile.

He glanced down at the antiquated surface. But the page remained blank.

He frowned. Had he read the instructions wrong? It said to wait for a little while. He pursed his lips and cocked his head. Then again, it was the internet. Maybe the instructions were completely wrong.

He looked up at the clock on the wall. One minute had passed. He looked back down at the page.

Something *was* there.

Nathan's heart pounded. Was this how Ruby and Dad felt every time they discovered something? Nathan grinned. He could see why they kept chasing. Because one thing just might lead to another and if enough time and energy were put in, who knew what might be uncovered.

Nathan studied the page. It looked like... He cocked his head. A date. And two entries. He read the first.

Charlotte Town   3 June 1775

I shall not fail in my second attempt to regain my family's heirloom, as I did when attending Governor Patterson's Ball. He, who bought the compass from Lord Amherst. Oh, how my heart beat when I nearly held its engraved golden surface in my hands in the dark and stillness of Patterson's private offices. I did not count on his fondness for puzzle boxes, else I would have my heirloom even now.

Nor did I believe I would have to explain my uninvited presence to Himself, so I could not gain time to procure my prize. Given I was in the Governor's private offices, it does stand to reason his demanding an explanation. I could not risk the Governor's suspicions, so while I answered him, I took heart in having hidden my precious heirloom in plainest sight.

I fear to say quite where, even betwixt these pages, for this Book may fall into the Wrong hands. I can only pray that hiding my heirloom in plainest sight, alongside the Seal, will keep it safe until Providence affords me the good fortune of retrieving it.

Nathan then turned to the second entry:

Boston   22 Sept. 1775

Though the commissioners from the Continental Congress in the 13 Colonies have failed to win the French-Canadians to the Cause, W. still has hope, as he told me, that some French-Canadians may be sympathetic to the Patriots and provide Aide to the Rebellion. That is why he is allowing me to join Captains Broughton and Selman on their mission to intercept British ships bound for Quebec along the St. Lawrence River, six weeks hence.

Though 'tis not for W. nor any of the Patriot Cause that I take upon myself this sworn duty, but for myself. And most of All, for my Family. The compass shall be restored to our family. 'Tis, after all, my rightful heir-

loom.

I shall see to its safe return, no matter what shall befall me. The British did not honor their Word when they deported my family instead of allowing us to stay. But the British will pay. And the compass shall be mine again.

W. has entreated I come aboard ship as Cook. He assured me of my safety and that none would be the wiser as to the true emissary nature of my mission with the French-Canadians. So he thinks. I pray it be so...

Before we sail, I shall make my way to Mr. Revere the Silversmith at his shop on Clark's Wharf to fetch the locket he has crafted specially.

Nathan pulled out a chair. Was there more? Only one way to find out. He flicked on the hairdryer again and set to work.

He grinned. Ruby would love this. He had to show it to her. He could give it to her. This would definitely help her research about the love letters, which was, apparently, connected to Washington and the order. And to the seal.

Maybe he could trust Ruby not to put her career before...whatever this blossoming connection was between them. And maybe Dad hadn't been so crazy, after all. Which meant Ruby had never been, either...

THAT EVENING, RUBY stepped out of the shower and wrapped herself in her robe. Glasses in hand, she started to thread her way through the chaos of the partially renovated living room, on her way back to the bedroom.

Her heart felt like a helium balloon. As if it would just lift off and float up into the sky. Into the blue, blue sky. The same blue as Nathan's eyes.

She grinned. Nathan.

She hummed as she wove around the haphazard stacks of drywall, buckets of mudding mix, and ladders. She coughed as her footsteps stirred up dust.

As she wiped her eyes after she finished coughing, she tripped over the bucket of drywall mud. She caught her balance, but the glasses she carried went flying.

They landed in a large hole the contractors had made when they'd ripped away the old plaster. She crouched down near the large bucket and studied the hole in the plaster.

She took a deep breath and shoved aside the heavy bucket. Slowly, Ruby put her hand inside the hole to retrieve her glasses. She hoped there weren't any spiders.

Mildew, dust and the faintest hint of wild roses greeted her as she leaned in close to the hole. She sneezed.

Her heart pounded.

But instead of a smooth plastic glasses frame, her fingers encountered something scratchy and warm. It felt like...a wool blanket?

She moved her fingers forward. There were her glasses.

Curious, she drew out a moth-eaten green wool saddle blanket, along with the glasses. She unfolded the blanket. Inside, bound with a frayed pink ribbon, was a single tattered letter. Her heart sped up. Had that Molly person stashed it here?

She flipped over the thick paper. The wax seal was still intact.

She hesitated only a moment before she slid her finger under the wax and lifted.

St. John's Island 14 Dec. 1775

Edwina, my love,

I have received your latest missive and do not know where to begin, so I shall at the heart of the matter.

You voiced your concern over the actions you took on Nov. 17 in Charlotte Town when you absconded with not only the Seal, but also with me.

Yet what other way was there for you to fight back against those who stole your Property than in the man-

ner of your upbringing?

The British, and these so-called Colonists, forced your People out. It was only natural, your desire to stay on that island's shores. After all, 'twas your homeland before the British claimed it.

Do not fret, my darling. We need to trust that the Compass shall reunite us. You have told me of its powers to do just that. Have you not regaled me with tales of its powers working throughout the generations of your family? And that was why it was such a precious Heirloom?

The British knew not what they took from you. But your father, in attempting and failing to barter your family's Freedom, with the sale of the compass to Lord Amherst, did. Yet he only thought he was doing what was Right.

Do not lose hope, beloved. All at last shall be set to rights.

Your Faithful Servant
Alexander

Ruby's eyes widened. The *sale* of the compass? She tapped a finger against her chin. That family heirloom tale Nathan mentioned... So there was truth behind that legend, too. A smile curved Ruby's lips.

She cocked her head.

All those receipts she'd gone through...Wait a second. There'd been a crumbling old bill of exchange for a compass. Hadn't there?

She scrambled to her feet. She headed into Dr. O'Neil's study and plucked up the pile of receipts she'd sorted. Here it was.

Her heart pounded. Nathan could use this to help clear Dr. O'Neil's name. It wasn't the second order, but at least it would help people believe the late professor wasn't a crackpot.

She straightened up and looked back at the letter. She turned it over. Held it up. But as she did, she paused.

It looked as if—she cocked her head and peered more closely.

Underneath the flourishes and ink splatters of the original words, various letters had tiny dots under them. In a random order. No. Not random at all. It was a coded message:

Compass rose sheds its light in the rose-red moonlight —A

OUT OF THE corner of her eye, Ruby saw Nathan walk through the study doorway on Sunday morning. He dusted off his jeans and approached her. Ruby smoothed a stray curl behind her ear. She was leaving tonight. She swallowed down a lump in her throat.

Where had he been? She darted a glance at her watch. He was supposed to have been here more than 30 minutes ago. She tamped down a flicker of irritation.

"Sorry I'm late," he said. "Had to go pay a speeding ticket."

"Oh." She couldn't pretend she wasn't disappointed. The flicker of annoyance grew. She forced it back.

Nathan extended a handful of documents to her. "I'm not quite sure what they all are. But I hope it might give us some hints about where the order might be."

He yawned but tried to hide it behind the fistful of papers. "I found them in Dad's car." He shook his head. "He liked to file things *everywhere*. Kept his mind sharp, so he said."

"Thanks." Ruby took the documents from him. Her stomach dipped. She wouldn't get to see him again, if she went back to Boston and took that job. If the interview went well and they offered it to her, anyway. Her heart hammered. Her palms felt clammy. She couldn't lose him. What? She shook her head and forced herself to take a breath. She wasn't losing him. She was leaving. This was her

choice. Her life. Her career.

Just then she noticed his bloodshot eyes. "Are you hung over?" She bit her lip. *Still acting like a teenager*—the women's words echoed in her ears. Maybe it was a good thing she was going.

But Nathan just chuckled. "Yeah. Friend's bachelor party last night." He yawned again. Shook his head. "Been having strange dreams for about two weeks solid, which hasn't helped either."

He rubbed his chest. "I'm getting too old for that kind of late night. But at least I have my jalepeňo cream cheese bagel to tide me over." He held up a paper bag with the Great Canadian Bagel logo emblazoned across it. "Want one?"

She winced. That bag might've been near some irreplaceable documents. The flicker of annoyance surged again.

"Oh, um, no thank you. I don't do spicy things."

"No?" Nathan glanced at her, eyebrows raised. He reached into the bag, pulled out a bagel half and took a bite.

"I, uh," She reached for the container of paperclips but knocked it over. She cleared her throat. "I found a love letter yesterday." She let out a huff of irritation. "But it just leads to more questions. Not answers." She crossed her arms.

"Well, that should be exactly what you want, right?"

She dropped her chin into her hand and looked around. The piles of junk she'd organized. And the random things she'd arranged. They were no longer scattered across the desk surface, the floor, the windows or the built-in bookcase.

Nathan pulled out a small leather-bound book. "I found something interesting." He switched on the lamp on the mahogany desk.

She caught sight of his eager, hopeful expression as she watched him look at her out of the corner of her eye.

She felt a stab of guilt. How could she be judging him like that? He was only trying to help. It was kind of sweet.

"I think it's Edwina's diary, Ruby," he whispered. His breath stirred her hair and sent a shiver down her spine.

"But we just looked at her diaries a few days ago."

"No, I think this is another one. I found it at Fort Amherst. I know how important these documents are to you, and so..." He met her gaze.

She swallowed. Then reached up and put a hand on his arm. "Thank you. You said Fort Amherst?"

Nathan nodded. "Across the harbor. It's a national historic site. Used to be French. And a jail. Anyway," he grinned. "There's a bunch of entries. But I didn't have time last night to read the whole thing. Used a hair dryer to reveal the invisible ink." He flipped the book open. Leaned forward. "See?"

But Ruby leaned back in the cracked leather wingback and chewed on her bottom lip. She avoided Nathan's gaze. "I have a job interview to go to tomorrow," she blurted.

Nathan frowned.

But she hurried on. "And because my research is connected to your dad's, it's being called into question too." She blinked back tears. Took a breath. She *should* be happy he'd found another journal of Edwina's. But somehow, she just felt...afraid, she realized. Afraid that by looking in the journal, she'd find out—what? That things with Nathan would end? But that didn't make any sense. Yet the feeling persisted.

Why was she feeling so overwhelmed all of a sudden? She clutched the locket. No. She wasn't abandoning Nathan. Wasn't leaving him. She took a deep breath. She'd done what she could, here. That was all.

Beside her, Nathan stiffened. Pushed away from the edge of the desk he had leaned against.

Ruby's heart sank to her toes. "I need to go back to Boston. I...I...don't want more clues, more questions. I have to finish things, not start more." She slid the locket chain through her fingers and watched him turn away. A spasm of panic clutched her chest. No. He couldn't just walk away from her. Not after all they'd shared. What? They hadn't shared that much...

Nathan's shoulders tensed. He clenched his jaw and moved into the center of the room.

"I—I need to substantiate what I've found," she continued. "Not hunt down what could be more dead ends."

Nathan's gaze bored into hers.

"So," he said slowly. "You only want that position. Want to further your career." Nathan crossed his arms. "You're leaving me here to fend for myself."

Ruby pushed back from the desk. Looked up at him. "That's not true."

"No?" He raised his eyebrows. "I should have seen it coming. I thought you were...different. But no. You're just like my dad." Nathan shook his head. "That's all you really care about, isn't it—your career."

"No, Nathan," she said. "It's not. I just—"

Nathan started pacing. "We haven't found the order." He shoved a hand through his hair. "My dad's name is about to be mud if we don't, and you're... You're..." He clenched his jaw and his voice rose "—leaving for some damn interview."

"I need to prep for it. Go back to Boston." Ruby fought to keep her voice steady even as the flicker of annoyance came back, hovered just above a sense of panic. Grew.

"Well, maybe you should."

Ruby lifted her chin. "I need to figure out what I'm going to do about my research." She narrowed her eyes. Fought down the panic. "Finish my dissertation. Prep for my defence." She knew she was repeating herself but she couldn't help it.

"No," Nathan said. He paced faster. "You're giving up. Selling out. When all I tried to do was help you. When all I wanted to do was the right thing."

Ruby jumped up. "And you're being completely irrational. You knew I'd be leaving. I knew I'd be leaving. The cataloging is basically done." She tore her gaze away from his icy stare.

"Well, where I come from," he said, voice tight, "a

promise to help is a promise. Loyalty means something."

"Oh, don't go pulling that Island heritage crap on me. You're blowing this all out of proportion."

Nathan merely raised his chin.

Ruby gave a huff of irritation. "Fine, Nathan. You want the truth? Here it is. I've come across more than I'd dreamed. Not only that, I've gone through these things. Done my job here. After all, that's what I came here to do." And yet...Her eyes flicked to Nathan. Then back to the last pile of papers. Guilt tore at her. She was leaving him...

"And yet you're still leaving." Nathan ground his teeth. "You know what?" He shoved the diary at Ruby. "Take the journal. Maybe it'll remind you of what you should've done."

Then he turned and left the room. The door rattled as he slammed it.

Chapter Six

OUTSIDE THE CONDO early that evening, Ruby tugged her battered purple suitcase behind her on the sidewalk.

She turned the corner, where the cab was supposed to pick her up, and caught her breath. Golds and pinks of sunset shimmered along the harbor, just visible from her vantage point at the intersection of Queen and Dorchester streets. The evening light touched the red brick facades. Seagulls soared overhead against the background of a few wispy clouds in an otherwise blue sky.

And then she saw Nathan. He leaned against the rough brick wall of the building, his expression impossible to read. Her heart plummeted.

He pushed away from the wall, his jaw clenched. "Thank you for organizing the papers."

"You're welcome," she said in a tight voice. She sought his gaze, as if it might tell her something. But it was unreadable. Yet a ripple of déja vù passed through her and she gripped the handle of her suitcase as sudden images flashed through her mind.

It couldn't be much longer now. She paced back and forth in the tiny cell, the hem of her skirts heavy with rainwater and the tears that seemed endless. She clutched the locket to her heart. The two miniatures of herself and Alexander that he had painted that far-away August day, were tucked inside.

Still she paced.

She glanced toward the horizon and saw the faintest pinkish glow as the moonlight faded and the rays of sun tinged the blue gulf to gold.

She swallowed and stared at the brick walls of the tiny cell.

She had to be strong in the face of death.

At least they couldn't take away her hopes, her dreams, her wishes. She closed her eyes, as she imagined:

...the heavy gold compass lay in her palm, filling her with warmth that made her heed neither the wet nor the cold.

She stroked a finger on the ornately carved faceplate of the compass then scanned the horizon again. She raised the spyglass to her eye.

There.

Her heart pounded.

There he was.

But her heart climbed into her throat. A long jagged crack ran down the three-masted schooner's hull from stem to stern. And it listed badly.

Those blasted colonists.

She gripped the compass more tightly then clutched it to her heart.

Seconds ticked by like centuries as the ship limped into the harbor. As it breached the low water mark and began to head toward shore and the docks, she lifted her skirts and raced down the winding iron staircase and out into the wide rolling lawn, then down the street.

At this early hour, fortunately, no one was around to see such unladylike behavior as her churning arms and legs as she raced to the quay.

The scent of fish and tar stung her nose as she clattered onto the weathered dock. Her chest heaved as she finally came to a stop at the very farthest edge of the wooden moorings.

The ship slowly inched its way up to the dock then threw anchor and put down the gang plank.

"Miss, Miss, you can't be coming up here."

She ignored the man's voice.

She plunged up the narrow gangway and onto the wooden deck, its surface stained with God knew what. But she ignored that, too. Her eyes darted left and right.

"Miss," said a voice behind her, "I'm afraid you'll have to leave. I might be forced to walk the plank if I allow a lady aboard."

She spun around, a laugh of pure joy bubbling up within her. She threw her arms around Alexander's neck. "You always joke when you have good news. What is it this time?"

His brown eyes twinkled. "Why, it's that I've returned home to you, of course." He cupped her face gently in his hands and kissed her. He tasted of rum and salt and himself.

He pulled back a fraction and stroked her cheek. "If it wasn't for the compass, I would've never found my way back to you. Never known you were my one and only," he whispered. "But that compass is truly magical."

"I know," she said, and raised up on her tiptoes and kissed him again. "That's why we must guard it with our lives, and pass it down to our children when the time is right..."

She opened her eyes. A single tear slipped down her cheek. Dawn. It was time.

Ruby took a jagged breath as if she had been running hard, squeezed her eyes shut then opened them wide. She forced herself to take more lungfuls of air as her heartbeat returned to normal.

"What is it?" Nathan said, reaching for her arm.

She fought down a flutter of residual panic. The compass? Her eyes widened. Edwina had been in jail—about to die. But she had the compass? No, she was imagining she had the compass again, imagining her reunion with Alexander...

Ruby's fingers trembled. "I don't—I don't know. Like a vision. Memory?"

Nathan swallowed. Clenched his jaw. "I've been having...visions...too."

Just then the cab pulled to the curb.

Ruby's fingers trembled and her throat felt raw. "You have?" She looked at Nathan and opened her mouth. But no words came out. How could she tell him about her dreams, or visions, or...whatever they were, *now*? She couldn't risk being that vulnerable. Not now.

But Nathan didn't reply to her question. Simply reached around her to open the cab door. "So this is really it then? You're giving up."

Ruby clenched her jaw. "I'm not giving up. I'm going to the job interview. Sometimes, when you don't find what you're looking for, you need to do something else. Formulate a new theory." She clenched her teeth. She had to get away from here. From him. Go back to Boston and get some perspective.

Why had she allowed him to affect her this much? Her chest tightened. To let him into her life, into her heart, when she'd known all along that it would be a dead end? That she'd lose everything. She forced herself to take a calming breath. No, that was irrational. She hadn't lost anything.

Ruby shifted her purse to her other shoulder. "I have to go. Need to go. My work is done here. I cataloged all the papers. They're being shipped down to Simmons. This position, if I get it, will open up all sorts of doors for me. I need to get on with my life. I can't chase after something that isn't there. We didn't find the order."

"But we still could," Nathan said.

"Nathan, it's a dead end. Sometimes you have to walk away." Her palms felt damp. She looked into his blue eyes. She didn't want to go. Couldn't just leave him here... Yes. Yes, she could. She would leave. She had to leave.

"Walk away." Nathan clenched his jaw. "Like you're doing."

"It's not like that. I just *told* you."

The cab honked. Ruby got inside.

Nathan opened his mouth to say something else but then closed it, his expression shuttered. He rubbed the back of his neck and then raised a hand in farewell.

"Goodbye," she whispered, as the cab sped off. She took a breath. She didn't have time for this. Didn't have time to connect with him, only to have that connection disappear... So she had to be the first to let go. Just like she had with all those other men. This was just like that third-date cliff.

Yes. That was exactly what it was. And now she was ending things before he got a chance to. Safer that way.

NATHAN TAPPED THE pen against the thick manila folder on his desk at the office Monday morning. He startled, as he realized he'd been staring off into space for quite awhile. Ruby had gone. Chosen her career instead of him. No, no. He had no say in her life. Not really. Why did he feel so rejected? Deserted?

He opened the folder and glanced down at the sketches. Paged through them. God.

He raked a hand through his hair. There were five of them in total. And they were all different.

He turned to the very first one. Edwina.

Nathan remembered the wild, free feeling of his brush loaded with color. The heavy weight of the oils on the fine boar-hair bristles of the paintbrush. The sheer joy he'd felt as he'd put color after color and shade after shade onto the thick heavy canvas as he'd painted her portrait.

And, most peculiarly, the way that the textures and colors, and even emotions, had seemed real. Not only real, but...familiar.

He inhaled. Did that mean there actually was something to this past-life stuff Ruby had mentioned?

He shook his head. He didn't want to believe it. He leafed through the other pages one by one.

A tall ship with its snow-white sails unfurled, headed toward Charlottetown harbor. A tiny cabin in the woods with smoke that uncurled from its chimney. Nighttime. Only the soft white glow of the moon as it shone down on a beach, deserted except for the faint trace of two sets of footprints.

He set the last one aside. Cocked his head.

The evidence was literally looking back at him. If you could call it that. It was just a bunch of pictures. Things that he could've, very easily, plucked from not his own memories but from some TV show he'd watched or book he'd read.

Besides, if the whole past-life thing was real, then what

was the point if you forgot everything anyway when you were born again?

That familiar tug of longing he felt every time he held a pencil in his hands, welled up within him. He sighed and ran a hand through his hair. But he couldn't push that feeling aside any longer.

It wouldn't just go away if he kept shoving it down. It needed to be acknowledged. It needed to be acted upon. It needed to be validated.

So he turned to his computer and registered for a painting class at Murphy's Community Centre.

THE SHORT, GRAY haired woman smiled at Ruby as she approached the desk. "Hi there. I'm Ruby Zalonski. I have an interview at 9 o'clock this morning for the special collections position."

"Right," she said. "Have a seat."

Ruby sat and tried not to chew on her cuticles. She rummaged around in her purse for a stick of gum instead. She'd left half a pack in here the other day.

Her hand brushed the cool leather journal cover. Almost reflexively, her fingers closed around the small book. It fit comfortably in her hand. As if it was made for her. She'd tucked it in here even though a valuable document like this shouldn't just be thrown in a purse. Yet somehow it brought her reassurance.

She turned the small book over in her hands. A sense of rightness—ownership—swelled within her. No. She tried to shake off the feeling. But it persisted. This couldn't be *her* journal. It was hundreds of years old.

Her heart squeezed.

She glanced at the clock then back at the journal. And risked opening the small volume.

Port-la-Joye 5 Dec. 1775

I've escaped my cell. I pray Alexander has avoided

capture on Loyalist ground and brought the Compass as he swore he would do. I do not know if the rose-red moonlight will guide me to our forest rendezvous.

I pray that I am not too late, that Alexander remains unharmed and has stayed well-hidden. That the British, who patrol the fort, Which is perilously near our cabin, do not discover us there.

'Twas I, after all, who laid eyes on him at Cross Keys Tavern that November day. 'Twas I who made him board the ship. If only I'd left him in Charlotte Town, instead of bringing him aboard, then we would've had a chance to be happy together. But now, I fear, we never will. And it is all my own fault.

Ruby frowned. She paged to the end of the journal, but there was nothing there. She flipped back to the beginning.

Charlotte Town 7 Apr. 1774

The British will rue the day they deported my family. Just because the Treaty of Paris was signed eleven years ago doesn't mean that we Acadians agree with our mother country to cede this land to the British. One day, I will strike back. My family is gone. My family heirloom is gone. Bartered away for a freedom that never came. But they will not take me. No. They have taken what is not rightfully theirs. 'Tis a shameful confession but my attempt to regain my heirloom has failed. But I will get it back.

"Ruby?" the receptionist said. "Go on back. They're ready for you now."

Ruby startled. Slipped the book back into her purse. Stood. "Uh, sure. Right." She'd figure it all out later. She strode into the meeting room set up for the interview.

The members of the hiring committee stood and shook hands with her.

"Good morning, Ruby. You had a good trip up to the Maritimes? Beautiful country up there," one of the committee members said.

"Yes, I, uh, did." Nathan had said Edwina had been executed in December of 1775...

"So tell us," another committee member said, "what you've been working on and how your researching and cataloging skills fit this position."

...which meant Edwina must have hidden the journal in her cell. Ruby opened her mouth, but nothing came out for a moment. She took a breath. Forced her thoughts back to the question.

"Uh, well, I love research and academics." Ruby paused. "Um, when I was working on cataloging the letters in Dr. O'Neil's collection, I discovered it's important to not only pay attention to what is cataloged, but also to the way things are cataloged."

She shifted in her seat. "I'll defend my doctorate soon. Even though I don't have my Ph.D. yet, I feel that cataloging all of the professor's papers..." She felt a stab of guilt. Nathan had looked so hopeful, so happy, when he'd shown her the journal—"...which he'd donated to this university's archives collection, shows my willingness and abilities in not only cataloging but also in understanding just what..."

Ruby cleared her throat. "Uh, just what goes into big research opportunities." She winced. She could explain things better than this.

But the interviewers just nodded and jotted notes. As the questions continued, Ruby's fists clenched. She had to focus...

"Did you have any more questions for us? Is there anything else you'd like to add?"

"Dr. O'Neil's work is valid and worthy of consideration," she blurted. "And I believe mine is, too." She stood. Straightened her spine. "Because he believed in his work and I believe in my own work. And if you're going to judge me, or my work, based on the hearsay of others in this department, then, well, I believe that's your loss. Because my research speaks for itself. And that should be enough to satisfy anyone." Ruby pushed up her glasses.

The committee members exchanged glances then scribbled something down on their notepads.

Ruby fought a sinking feeling. There went her chance at the job.

All the members of the hiring committee stood up. Shook Ruby's hand again. "Well, Miss Zalonski, that will be all. Thank you for coming in. We'll be in touch."

THAT EVENING AFTER work, Nathan ran a hand across his face and headed down to his basement studio. He picked up his laptop that lay on the coffee table and absently clicked onto Google. In one corner of the room, he'd propped the almost-complete painting of Edwina.

Ruby's hazel eyes flitted through Nathan's memory. She wasn't from around here, that was sure. Not with a name like...what was it again? Zamboni? No. That was an ice-cleaning machine used for skating rinks. Oh, Zalonski. That was it. What origin was it? It sounded Slavic. Or maybe Russian. Polish? He typed her name into the search box and hit enter.

Hmmm. No Facebook or Twitter account. He scrolled down. His eyes landed on the link to her page from Simmons College.

But he sat back, his finger poised mid-click. Uh-oh. He'd done it again, hadn't he? He shook his head. Thinking about her. Looking her up online... He sighed. This wasn't a good sign.

But he clicked on the link to her CV anyway. And then on her dissertation abstract. As he scanned it, he realized it must have been written long before she'd come up to P.E.I. to sort his dad's papers, because some of her research questions had now been answered.

Archival Studies

In Love & War: A Discourse on Women's Love Letters During The American Revolution

Ruby Zalonski

Dissertation under the direction of Professor Jill Burton

Abstract:

Women's love letters were important documents not only for historical referencing and archival research, but also as a vital means of expression and communication between lovers in times of war.

These letters also gave women voice and outlet for their emotions. An outlet and means that they would not have otherwise been able to have, in polite society, in the latter half of the 18th century. I argue that love letters were an essential and vital means of expression to women in times of war. The numerous love letters collected—in particular, the love letter fragment found by Ruby Zalonski and written to a woman named Edwina Belliveaux—supports this idea. Further postulation holds that there are additional love letters to and from Edwina.

This dissertation also puts forth that Edwina may have been a spy for General George Washington, as evidenced by the cross-reference of the love letter fragment addressed to 'My Darling Edwina' and George Washington's signed order, dated Nov. 23, 1775.

Supporting documents:

(1) love letter fragment, to an 'Edwina,' dated Dec. 2, 1775, given to Ruby Zalonski from an antique book dealer in Boston who found it in an old family bible in their collection

(2) signed orders from Gen. George Washington dated
   Oct. 15, 1775 and Nov. 23, 1775

(29) love letters from Smithsonian Institute between
   prominent patriot and his betrothed

(12) love letters from the collection of a Mrs. H.
   Robinson, as addressed to her ancestor while he
   fought at the Battle of King's Mountain during the
   Revolutionary War

(18) love letters between prominent Bostonian socialite
   and her betrothed in France

Ruby's face swirled through Nathan's head again. She'd come here to do a job, he reminded himself. And that's what had happened. It was simply the facts she'd collected. And now she was gone.

His eyes flicked up to his painting. His brows drew together and he crossed his arms, suddenly cold despite the warm room.

A frisson of longing passed through him and he realized it was because of the painting. He stared at it. Blinked. Looked again.

Nathan froze.

There was something about Edwina's eyes that reminded him of Ruby. Not...directly. But somehow, her eyes helped him to *remember* Ruby. Why was that?

It was as if she was...somehow...inside Ruby or...Ruby was inside her. He shook his head. It didn't make any sense. And yet...it did. Well, they did say the eyes were the windows to the soul...

RUBY RUBBED HER eyes. She forced them wide open and didn't bother to stifle a yawn. She'd been back in Boston a week now. She could continue to look at this tomorrow.

Yet the cramped, faded handwriting kept her reading anyway. She tapped her finger against her chin. What was the connection between the compass and the seal?

She turned another page.

Edwina hadn't written down anything that explained Alexander's coded message about a compass rose in that letter he'd written, either.

Hmmm. A compass was a tool for finding out what direction you were going in. And a compass rose was used on a compass to display the cardinal directions.... Wait a second. *Cardinal directions of the heart...*

There must be some connection. But she was too tired now to think about it. Ruby reached up and switched off the lamp. She'd figure it out tomorrow.

THAT SAME NIGHT, Nathan walked back up the basement stairs and into his bedroom. He flicked on the lamp on the nightstand and remembered his argument with Ruby in the study. She was right. He had been irrational.

He sat down on the dark blue bedspread. Sighed. Had he been naive enough to allow himself to let Ruby in? To entertain the thought that maybe, just maybe, she could've been...special?

No. He shook his head. It went far deeper than that.

She had awakened something within him that he hadn't known existed, before he met her. Yet some part of him—part of who he was, part of what he was—shouted: 'this is it!' But *that* couldn't be.

Could it?

Was she—this feeling—the whole reason he'd always felt so empty inside with other women? Always wanted to put on the brakes, say no, end things, break up, cut off engagements?

Because of this tiny piece of dissatisfaction that gnawed at him, that wouldn't allow him to fully give his heart wholly to anyone. No matter how much he'd want to, no matter how much the other women had loved him. He just couldn't return their love. To any of them.

Any of them before now, that is?

He swallowed, his throat suddenly dry.

But he didn't, couldn't, have feelings for Ruby. He'd only just met her, for Chrissakes.

This...this thing that he couldn't even begin to describe. And this thing that had made him push her away.

He sat up. Sudden anger coursed through him. If that were true, if she was more than special to him, and if there was something—just maybe—to that reincarnation thing, then why hadn't they been able to overcome their differences and be together?

He shoved those thoughts aside and the anger faded. He had no one to blame but himself. What was he going to do? Dad's hearing was tomorrow. Ruby wasn't here. She couldn't add credibility to the hearing on his dad's behalf.

He rolled over onto his back. Sighed. Then folded his arms over his bare chest and, after what seemed like hours, finally fell asleep.

His hands, though slippery with sweat, nonetheless gripped the reins with the tightness and conviction of a condemned criminal, though his travel and duties were not that of any sort of prisoner. His heart pounded. He was still a wanted man, down in the 13 colonies. But was he safe up here?

No matter. If endangering his own life would bring him even one step closer to his Edwina, it would be worth it. He didn't care if he had to fight off the entire British navy to get her back.

He saw the pink light of dawn filter through the pine trees near Fort Amherst. And the prison.

Edwina.

His heart squeezed and his fingers clutched the box to his chest. He'd returned to the island with it safely. Now he just had to get to her. Had to rescue her. Save her from a fate she didn't deserve. She couldn't die. She was only trying to get back what was rightfully hers. The compass.

Because when he'd been accosted by his brother, there in Boston, he'd had to hand over the seal. He'd managed to keep the compass. But only just. Simply because the Americans believed he only carried an empty box.

The horse's hooves churned up sand on the moonlit beach. He kept the cloak's hood drawn up around his face. He'd come this far. He clutched the box tighter. He saw the lights of Fort Amherst in the distance. If he delivered it to her there then she'd be safe. And they could be together again. At last.

But first he would see if, perchance, Edwina had somehow gotten away from her captors and was about to meet him at their rendezvous. On their six-day journey together from Charlotte Town to Boston, the cabin was the place that he and Edwina had promised they'd meet, if trouble arose.

He'd managed to smuggle a coded letter to Molly at the tavern, in case Edwina was able to make her way there and ask for him.

The brim of his tricorn hat slipped low over his eyes with the frenzied gallop across the sand and into an open moonlit meadow full of wild roses. Flecks of sweat from the stallion, coupled with the rhythmic pounding of its hooves, did nothing to still the pounding of his own heart as he remembered that November night aboard the ship bound for Boston...

"I've made a mistake. I never should have involved you in this raid. I'm sorry," she said to him. Her green eyes studied him with uncertainty.

"I should not have known one such as yourself if you hadn't. Regret nothing." He stroked a finger down the satiny contour of her cheek. His skin wiped away the trail of moisture that had accumulated there.

"We'll be together. Somehow. When all of this is over," he whispered. "When we first met that day in August, I had no idea—and neither did you—of what would happen. No one did."

He clenched the fingers of his free hand together into a fist. "You know I cannot stay away from you. I love you."

The cabin lights were lit. His heart leapt. She was there.

His thoughts flitted back to that night in the moonlight, the love in her large green eyes. The way she'd tasted when he'd kissed her.

The scent of wild roses that clung to her skin as they'd lain on the beach together. The roar of the surf at least as loud as the blood pounding in his veins each time he looked at her.

And now, if he didn't get to her in time, she was going to be executed for being a traitor. All because she'd wanted her compass back, and stolen the seal, instead.

He squeezed his hands into fists. She didn't deserve to be treated like that. It didn't make her a traitor. The Crown, in fact, had been a traitor to her and her family when they'd deported her loved ones despite their payment in solid gold.

The light in the cabin flickered. He pulled the reins up short and dismounted. He led the bay stallion over to the low-hanging branch of a chestnut tree, its branches mere silhouettes in the light of the waning moon.

His footsteps light and anticipatory, her name on his lips, he stepped into the cabin. "My love," he whispered.

"Good evening. I trust you had a pleasant ride." The muzzle of a musket instead of his lady's open arms, greeted him. And that uniform—it could be none other than a British officer's.

"Now hand over your precious cargo. Stolen property of the Crown."

When he didn't move, the officer nudged him with the weapon. "The seal," he hissed. "I know you have it."

"I swear to you, I do not."

"Lying Patriot." The officer spat. "For that, you shall die."

Nathan awoke with a start. His heart pounded and his hands clenched so tightly into fists that his fingers began to cramp. He took a deep breath then let it out slowly.

But his heart still pounded.

It was just a dream. But it felt so real. He sat up. Dreams always felt real to him. Ever since he'd had that nightmare as a 7-year-old. Where people in funny hats with strange accents were trying to stab him.

He shuddered at the memory.

Dreams felt especially real when he was under stress.

All right. Breathe in. He felt his shoulders relax, his heart rate drop. Breathe out. He continued to breathe slowly through his nose.

Just a dream.

That was all. No, no it wasn't. Was it? He rolled to the

side of his bed. Now, he couldn't sleep.

He got out of bed to splash some water on his face and almost tripped over the trash can on his way to the bathroom. He swore and went into the bathroom. The dim light from the streetlights outside made shadows jump out.

Nathan scraped a hand across his unshaven cheeks. He tossed the towel onto the faux-marble countertop but forgot to dry off his face.

He returned to his bedroom and propped himself up against the blond wood headboard. Then he brought his knees up to his bare chest.

He glanced at the clock. 1:45 a.m.

He couldn't deny it any more. These dreams...there was something to them. Something unfinished—restless—in his soul, that was trying to communicate to his consciousness. And it all started with Ruby. And that journal. He couldn't rationalize this away any more. He could still smell the wood smoke. Taste the memory of her kiss. Feel the weight of that gold object... Gold object? The compass. He held his breath. Let it out. Yes... The compass, as crazy as it sounded, *was* real.

He blinked. Took a breath. Why did he care?

His thoughts went back to Ruby's Simmons College webpage. It wasn't his own secrets she'd posted online. It was one of the love letters from Alexander to Edwina, that she'd put up, along with her CV.

He shook himself. He stood up and began pacing. *He* wasn't the one who'd written the letter. Goose bumps broke out on his skin.

Was he?

Damn it. He was in love with Ruby. He exhaled and stared out the window at the pouring rain. He crossed his arms. He'd told her everything. Completely let her in.

He rubbed his temples. He'd never felt like this before. Hoping... No, not hoping. Knowing. Beyond the shadow of a doubt. That he was right for her. And that she was right for him.

But did she feel it too? Or was this just lust and loneliness talking?

He shivered.

The rain fell harder. It pounded on the roof. Nathan's thoughts drifted back to his last conversation with Ruby.

Growing up, he used to have these vivid dreams in which he was wearing clothing from different eras and speaking in funny ways. He used to tell his mom about them but as time had gone on, they'd come less and less, until finally, they'd stopped.

But that was before a few weeks ago. Those dreams had been so vivid, felt so...real...that he'd almost sworn he had actually been there. Back in the 1700s. Living someone else's life...someone else's life that felt much like his own.

But that wasn't possible. Everything ended after you died. Didn't it? He picked up the glass of water on his nightstand and his thoughts shifted back to Ruby. Why did he think she was so different from all the other women he'd known?

What if this was just his ego telling him this time things were different? This time she was The One? This time—he drained the glass's contents—this time she'd left.

He got back in bed and fell into a deep, dreamless sleep.

RUBY SAT UP all at once. The digital readout on her alarm clock said 1:45 a.m.

She blinked and fumbled with the bedspread then disentangled herself. She rolled over. Half-remembered images tumbled through her mind. No, not just images. She sat up. Her nightgown clung to her. Memories. Intense memories. She blushed in the dark.

She brought a hand up to her throat and felt her pulse pound beneath her fingertips.

Oh... Moonlight. His lips, warm and tender, and hers, seeking and urgent. Their embrace, a promise made to be broken. The sharp sea spray and the taste of salt on his kiss.

Her fingers clutched the solid oak ship's railing. Her

heart, heavy as lead, as she watched the shoreline fade into the distance.

The safe security of his arms around her as they slid to the sand. Her pressing against the firm solidness of his chest, heat spreading through her.

The rough scrape of his stubble against her fingertips. She cradled his face between her hands. A deep knowingness and rightness welled within her. As if he was made for her, and she, for him. As if she could tell him her every secret, reveal every flaw, and still be adored. Honored. Beloved.

She'd tried to save him. Tried...and failed.

Ruby pressed a hand to her heart. She turned the dream memories over in her mind as the image of a compass, reflecting the moonlight, came to her consciousness.

Ruby took a ragged breath and finally felt her hammering heart slow to a more normal rhythm.

She took another breath and reached for the glass of water on her bedside table. She drained the contents. Then she swung her legs over the edge of the bed and got up. She walked to the window. Looked out.

She didn't even realize she was looking for the moon until she saw it, framed between the branches of a chestnut tree in the yard outside.

She blinked.

There was no chestnut tree in the yard. She took a step back. She shut the blinds with a snap, microwaved herself some hot milk and then crawled back into bed.

But all she could think about was the way Nathan's blue eyes had pierced her as she'd said goodbye to him. How words had stuck in her throat as she'd longed to say more.

Finally she fell back into sleep.

The next time Ruby opened her eyes, sunlight streamed through the thick slats of the blinds, which created a striped pattern across her pale green duvet.

She sat up. Memories of last night faded into the background. She bit her lip and then got up out of bed. Made herself some breakfast and then began unpacking her carry-

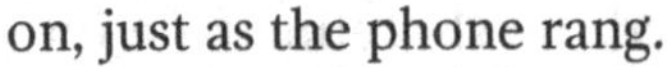

on, just as the phone rang.

"Hello?" She didn't recognize the caller ID.

"Good morning, Ruby. This is the dean's office calling. You've been offered the position."

NATHAN'S ALARM WENT off at 7 a.m. He yawned, stretched, got out of bed and rummaged around for a T-shirt. He picked up the one from last night that he'd flung next to the clothes hamper. He pulled it on. Clean enough.

Then he put on a pair of pants and ambled into the kitchen. Making breakfast would kill some time until it was a decent hour for him to go over there and take another stab at looking for the order.

He switched on the coffee pot. Plopped a slice of bread into the toaster.

He rummaged in the fridge and poured himself some orange juice. The toast popped up out of the toaster and he reached for a butter knife to load the golden brown slice with a generous slathering of gooseberry jam. His favorite.

The coffee pot began percolating, so he reached for a mug from the dishwasher he'd forgotten to empty yesterday.

He poured himself a cup of coffee, black, and went to the table to sit and eat.

But he burned his tongue on the coffee and discovered that the underside of the toast had burnt.

He muttered under his breath. Just when he felt he'd started to figure things out, it all shifted and this was what happened. Stubbed toes. Burnt toast. And, he grimaced, bitter coffee grounds.

He dumped the coffee out in the sink and tossed the partially eaten toast into the compost bin. Well, he glanced at the clock, at least now he could reasonably go over and talk to Ruby.

No, he remembered. He couldn't. She was gone. Suddenly he wasn't hungry.

Damn it. He shoved back his chair. Where was all of this coming from? Before she came along, his life had been just fine.

He clenched his jaw. That was irrational. It wasn't *her* fault.

Shit. He really did have feelings for her, didn't he? He threw a sideways glance out the window in the direction of downtown.

No. He ground his teeth. He couldn't have feelings for her. Not now. When it was too late.

Chapter Seven

INSTEAD OF THE relief and happiness Ruby expected to feel, she bit her lip and gripped the phone tighter. "I—" She swallowed. Finished unpacking her small carry-on case and zipped it shut. But the zipper stuck. It caught on a piece of crumpled paper.

She pulled it out.

A photocopy of the second of Washington's orders. Ruby sighed and put it on the dresser. She had to find it *now*?

She set that aside and looked down again at the letter she'd found only yesterday tucked between the journal's pages. The connection between the compass and Edwina and Alexander.

Port-la-Joye 2 Dec. 1775

Darling Alexander,

It has Lately come to my attention—and my heart—just how much the compass has its own set of Powers. If some mishap should befall us, I have devised a plan of safekeeping for the Compass. Mistress McDuff knows of it.

When I touched its surface, a thousand feelings and memories touched not only my mind but also my heart. I knew in an instant that your and my meeting that moonlit August night 'twas no accident.

I await Word of my Fate this day. I had heard of your narrow escape of imprisonment for desertion from sailors' talk on my shipboard journey northward, and prayed for Word from you. How happy I am to have received your encoded missive even in this wretched cell. Once I decoded the letter, it Pained me to read your words. How you believed that I betrayed your trust in choosing to not reveal my spying to you while we were aboard ship to Boston.

I am gladder still of your foresight, upon hearing of W's Order for my forced exit of Boston, in securing the Seal and Compass. But it gladdens me most of all to know you chose to forgive me for withholding my spying from you, in those last few lines of secret postscript.

Even if your brother implored you to give up the Seal at musket-point for the value in silver Coinage it would fetch him, I applaud your Brave heart in holding fast to your convictions and not letting the Compass fall into the Wrong hands. Your Loyalty and Love in volunteering to bring it back to the island, and risking your own life to do so, fills me with such admiration and gratitude.

Oh how I long to feel those hands of yours along my blushing cheeks. But I trust that with Good faith I shall be in your arms once more, before the new moon reaches its zenith.

Always your True Love,
Edwina

"I'll accept the position," Ruby heard herself say even as she glanced back at the letter. Then she found herself reach for the copy of the order.

"Well, Ruby, that's great."

She fiddled with the pencil in her hand. Found herself counting lines and spaces. She sank her teeth into her bottom lip. She'd painted Nathan in black and white, assumed he was just like what everyone said about him, when the reality was...She cocked her head.

Ruby put the order back down on the dresser. She had to find a way to accept him for who he was, not just assume he was one way or the other. She had to forgive him his faults and focus on his good qualities. She glanced down at the order again. Was the rest of the message there? And if it was, would it help her make up with Nathan?

She felt her heart expand and a blush color her cheeks as soft and gentle warmth spread through her. Try and deny it though she might, she did care about him.

She picked up the page from the dresser.

Memories washed over her. Him giving the change to the homeless man in the rain. Him taking the time to help her with the research—and taking time away from his own job to do it. The look of...tenderness...in his blue eyes as he watched her in the alcove.

No, Nathan wasn't the bad guy she'd mistaken him for. But would he even care if the rest of the message was deciphered?

"We'll get all the paperwork together and then set up a time for you to come and sign it."

"Okay," she murmured into the phone.

"We'll be in touch."

"Great," Ruby said, and ended the call. She reached for the pad of paper on her dresser to scribble the rest of the decoded message from the second order.

Where good sirs gather
Under the sign of the Keys

Her heart pounded. Did that mean Cross Keys Condos was involved in this riddle? She chewed on the end of the pencil. Her phone buzzed again. Dr. Burton.

"Hi," Ruby said, and heard the rustle of papers on Dr. Burton's end of the line.

"Congratulations, Ruby! You got the job."

"Thanks. That was a quick decision on their part." Ruby blurted.

"The thing is," Dr. Burton said, "what with your corresponding with Dr. O'Neil, and his research being investigated, well, the hiring committee decided to push things along so word doesn't spread too far into the academic community."

"Oh." Ruby said. "Right. That makes sense."

"So. Are you going in over the next few days to sign the paperwork and make it official before your dissertation defense?"

"Not quite. There's somewhere I have to go, first."

"Oh?"

"Prince Edward Island. I have to...wrap up my research there." Find out where this riddle led.

Dr. Burton sighed. "That's why I called." Ruby could imagine her advisor's perfectly plucked brows drawing together in a frown. "Your funding for the love letter research grant's been cut."

Ruby sank onto the bed. "What?" She chewed on a cuticle. "How is that even possible?"

"Well, you remember when they built the new stadium awhile back? Turns out they went over-budget. So they're having to reallocate funds from other departments to cover the costs."

Ruby's stomach knotted. She was so close to figuring all of this out. Now that she had Edwina's journal, and figured out what the rest of the riddle was, she couldn't just walk away. Nathan's face rose in her mind.

She was going to be true to herself, to her own feelings, her own heart.

"Ruby? I know what that silence means. You're thinking. What are you thinking?"

Ruby sighed. "I have to go back up there. I need to. Not just for my research, but for... Well, I just do."

"But there's no more money. You can't."

Ruby pushed up her glasses. She logged onto her online bank account. Only $400 left in her savings account now. Well, if it used up the last of her savings, it would be worth it. She needed to talk to Nathan. Needed to help him. Because he was right. A promise to help was a promise.

She felt a strength surge through her. She had to be willing to trust her own feelings, her own emotions and her own mind, in order to risk making that real connection with him. The one she craved. The one she deserved. And the one that she hoped she hadn't completely destroyed.

NATHAN SHRUGGED INTO his dark blue suit jacket and adjusted his tie. He stepped out of his car at the UPEI campus and headed into the meeting room.

He tucked the folder under his arm and went up the stairs to meet his lawyer, who was standing outside the door of the meeting room.

"Right on time, Nathan," she said. "Let's do this."

Nathan nodded. Tightened his jaw.

"We'll do the best we can. I know you've tried your hardest to find the order. And I have all the evidence you could gather, right here with me." She patted a fat leather briefcase.

Nathan gave her a tight smile. It was time to get this done and over with. "I have to speak on Dad's behalf, even though we never found anything. Even though I looked everywhere." He adjusted his cufflinks then held the door open for her.

"Welcome, everyone." The chair for the committee on academic misconduct cleared his throat as the door swung shut silently behind Nathan.

The man continued. "We're here to discuss the series of allegations made against Dr. Gordon O'Neil's research."

Nathan sat.

"Shall we begin?"

After awhile, Nathan glanced at the clock on the wall. Fifty minutes had passed. He shifted in the hard oak chair. Cleared his throat.

"And now, the committee will recommend to the university senate that Dr. Gordon O'Neil's title of emeritus will be removed, effective immediately." The committee chairman surveyed the room. "Does anyone have any final remarks?" He adjusted his half-glasses.

"Yes," Nathan said. "I'd like to go on record as saying that the credit for working to clear my father's name, goes in part to Ruby Zalonski."

The chairman nodded. "Then—"

But suddenly the door opened. Nathan swivelled in his seat.

Ruby stood in the doorway.

"THAT SECOND SIGNED order from General Washington. That's why I came back." Ruby paused to take a deep breath as she stood on the threshold of the meeting room.

It didn't matter what Nathan or anyone else thought. Or said. Or even did. What she had to do was tell him what she knew. She owed it to Edwina. And Dr. O'Neil. So she continued.

"Your famous historical figure, Edwina Belliveaux?" Ruby stepped fully into the room. "Washington knew she was a spy. But what he didn't know was *why*. But I do. The charges against Dr. O'Neil should be dropped. Edwina led the raid on Charlottetown. I have the proof right here, if that's what you're looking for." She held up an antique letter and the journal.

Ruby saw Nathan's knuckles turn white as he gripped the arms of his chair. She moved to stand beside him then raised her voice to address everyone in the room. "Washington knew she was a turncoat. She was helping him. But what he didn't know was why she was actually loyal to her *own* people. The Acadians. Not the British. That's why she'd—"

The dean looked at Ruby. "Edwina Belliveaux did not do all those things. She was an upstanding citizen. She told the Americans to leave the seal alone. She—"

"She was a spy, sir. Not a privateer. Not a saint. But a spy."

The dean opened his mouth to protest.

"Dr. O'Neil seemed to think she was." Ruby waved the

article she held in her left hand. "That's what his own journal says. And I have the original journal of Edwina Belliveaux's here, too."

"It will, of course, have to be authenticated," the dean said.

"Yes," Ruby straightened her shoulders. Pushed up her glasses. "It will. But I assure you, you will find it to be one hundred percent real. Edwina was responsible for the schooners coming up to P.E.I. And she was responsible for the raid on Charlottetown. And she was responsible for kidnapping not only Callbeck and Wright but also a man named Alexander McEachern."

"WHO?" BUT ALL the blood had drained from Nathan's face. Alexander. *He* was Alexander. And she—Nathan caught his breath—was Edwina.

"It sounds like you already know him." Ruby tapped a foot on the polished floorboards, and Nathan noticed her toenail polish, underneath the peep-toes of her pumps, was that same pale pink he'd seen the first time he'd met her.

Nathan closed his eyes but couldn't shut out Ruby's hazel ones. He opened his eyes and looked down at the page in her hand.

"That's why she came up to Charlottetown with Captain Selman and Captain Broughton in the first place."

"But how do you *know* this?" the dean demanded.

Ruby held up the cracked leather-bound volume. Tiny pieces of leather flaked off its gold-embossed cover and fell onto the floor.

Nathan reached a hand out and stroked a fingertip along the journal's surface and addressed the dean. "I found that at Fort Amherst."

"Also known as Port-la-Joye—that's what Edwina called it in her journal," Ruby added. "That's where she was executed."

The dean held up his hands. "This case is on hold. Based

on examination of the new evidence presented today, in light of the forgery charges, your lawyers will be notified regarding further proceedings."

Everyone filed out of the room.

Beside him, Nathan heard his lawyer breathe a sigh of relief as they stepped out of the building and into the sunshine.

"Thank you, Ruby," she said. "I'll let you both know when things re-convene. We'll be in touch," she said to Nathan, and gave him a maternal smile. "In the meantime, it looks like you two have some things to discuss." The lawyer winked, waved and headed to her Mercedes.

Nathan turned to Ruby. He swallowed and angled his head to look at her. "You know who Edwina hoped would came back for her." It wasn't a question.

In the near-empty parking lot, Nathan realized, he and Ruby stood only inches apart. "Yes," she breathed. "Alexander."

Nathan's gaze bored into hers. "And why did *you* come back, Ruby?"

His voice trailed to a whisper, and he saw her eyes dart from his gaze to the pavement and back up again.

His breath stirred a stray curl that had come loose from the messy ponytail she seemed to always have her hair done up in.

He wondered how she'd react if he reached up and slid that pencil out from its secure place in her thick brunette waves and buried his fingers in her silky strands.

He could feel the soft warmth of her breath on his cheek. Saw the questioning look in her hazel eyes. He slowly reached up and tucked the stray curl behind her ear. He saw her eyelids flutter, and a faint pink color her cheeks. Held his breath. He turned his palm so that his fingers now brushed the side of her face, and watched her lips part as he slowly, gently, stroked the pad of his thumb across her cheekbone.

He leaned closer. The scent of wild roses filled his head. He saw the pulse jump in her throat and felt her body stiffen, saw her lips tremble.

"I would never hurt you," he whispered.

"I know," she whispered back, as a tear slid down her cheek. "But I've accepted that job. I start Monday."

His gut tightened and he dropped his hand from her face. "Oh." He took a step back. Fiddled with the button on his suit jacket. He buttoned it, glad for something to distract himself from the clench of anxiety that had suddenly formed in his chest. She'd deserted him. Just like she had before. Suddenly he couldn't breathe.

But he forced his lungs to expand. So that was it, was it? She hadn't really come back because of him, at all. Only to do her duty. For her career. He frowned.

Ruby must have seen the look in his eyes because she crossed her arms then said, "Nathan. I don't want to fight with you. Does it matter?"

"It does to me."

"Fine. I'm sorry. Is that what you want? An apology?"

Nathan didn't reply. Just clenched his jaw.

Ruby held out a lined sheet torn from her yellow legal pad. "This is the other half of the clue. From the second order. I found a copy in Boston that I'd printed out. *'Good Sirs gather/under the sign of the Keys'*"

"You—" Nathan swallowed hard, "—deserted me." He ignored the piece of paper. "You expect me to just jump right back in and help you with this now that you've figured it out?" He crossed his arms. "Now that you've gone to your interview? Now that you've just happened to come in and miraculously produce evidence that may save my dad's reputation? That may lead to the compass? Well, no thank you. I'm not going to help you. Go find it yourself if you want it so badly. You obviously don't care about anything but how it'll look on your academic record."

Ruby's hands tightened into fists. "Fine. Looks like I won't be needing this anymore, either." Ruby shoved the small leather-bound book at Nathan, who automatically reached out to prevent the book from falling. But as he did so, their fingers collided and the book fell onto the ground.

Ruby let out a cry of dismay and knelt to pick up the book. But as she reached out and picked it back up, she froze. Raised her eyes up to Nathan's. "Do you see what I see?"

Nathan crouched down beside Ruby and angled his head. He could see the pulse flutter at her throat.

She swallowed and pointed to the pressed-together pages. On the flat surface created by the pages being pressed together, were faint ink markings.

"It's a sketch of a wild rose. And a compass."

Chapter Eight

LATER THAT SAME evening, Nathan raked a hand through his hair. His thoughts kept turning round and round about what Ruby had done. *She came back,* a voice in his head whispered.

Her hazel eyes flashed through his mind as he took a handful of salt and vinegar Covered Bridge chips from the bag on the counter after his art class. A smile that Nathan couldn't quash rested on his lips as he spotted his sketchpad and pencils in a tote bag slung over a kitchen chair.

He pulled the instructor's business card out of his pocket. It was just like P.E.I. that she'd been Dad's neighbor. He smiled.

Even better was that the instructor had mentioned that their company was looking for a new intern, since theirs had just graduated. She didn't seem to mind that Nathan was older than the average student.

Nathan shook his head. He wouldn't have had this opportunity to actually pursue his passion if it hadn't been for that sketch....

But the thought of his drawing made him think of Ruby. Why was he always feeling this sadness whenever he was around her? It was as if the sadness came from—he squinted and took another chip—a memory associated with her.

He frowned and took another chip. Flipped on a comedy show and tried to forget about it. But it was only when the presenter had told his fourth joke that Nathan realized he couldn't forget about it at all.

He took another chip and turned off the TV. Might as well go to bed. But just as he entered his bedroom, his phone rang.

"Nathan, sorry to bother you this late at night. But I've just gotten a call from the committee chair," the lawyer said. "Seems that someone on the committee wasn't satisfied with how things turned out today. One of the members still insists your dad's findings are all bunk. Even with the new evidence. So they've all stayed late and pushed through a vote. And, well, your dad's research, along with all his work, has been declared completely invalid."

Nathan caught his breath. Sank onto the edge of his bed. "But—but the original letter? The journal?" He blinked, his throat tight. "None of it was good enough?"

"No."

"But—"

"I know, Nathan. I'm sorry. We tried."

Nathan jumped up and started to pace. "That's not good enough." He resisted the urge to put his fist through the wall. "All that time." He raked his hands through his hair. "All that energy." He ground his teeth. "All that *work*. That I did. That Ruby did. That my d—dad did..." His throat tightened. "That can't be the end of things." He narrowed his eyes. "That won't be the end of things. I'll see to it. Justice has to be served. The wrongs have to be righted. I'm going to *find* that order. Find the seal, if it's still out there. And find the compass. Put it all to rights." Nathan said, and ended the call. Tossed the phone onto the nightstand. His mind flicked back to Ruby.

What if she disappeared on him? And what if that was entirely his fault? His pulse sped up. What if he couldn't prevent her from leaving? His mouth had gone dry. What if he couldn't prevent her from being hurt, from being forever taken away from him?

He stood and rubbed his temples. He was getting carried away. He'd take a hot shower. Relax. Then he'd finally maybe be able to fall asleep tonight without disturbing dreams.

After he finished his shower, he tucked a blue paisley-print towel around his waist then towel-dried his hair.

On impulse, Nathan padded barefoot down the base-

ment stairs. Gave a frustrated sigh. He'd lost his cool—again. Acted completely irrationally there in the parking lot. He flicked on the light.

He wandered over to the painting, which he'd now completed. He'd looked at the picture a thousand times before. He cocked his head.

Edwina's honey-blonde hair was windblown, though she stood inside a room next to a window that was firmly shut.

In one hand, she held a half-open rosebud, its petals a swirl of blood-red and white. Her other hand was splayed against the slippery peacock-blue silk of her ruffled gown with ruched stomacher and square neckline.

Nathan followed Edwina's gaze out the window to a moonlit, storm-tossed ship half-visible through the lacy curtain that fluttered at the six-pane window.

And though Nathan had captured her smiling, it was her eyes—filled with reflections of guilt and sadness—that made his heart squeeze.

Just then, the doorbell rang.

RUBY STOOD ON Nathan's doorstep. The doorbell glowed, a small amber dot against the dark paint of the doorframe. She heard the soft chirps of crickets in Charlottetown's East Royalty subdivision.

Ruby shifted her weight from one foot to the other and studied the way the light caught the leaded panes of frosted glass set into the panelled door. Maybe she should have waited till morning.

But this was important. She knew he'd want to know that his dad had been on the right track all along, that there *was* a connection between the compass and the Great Seal.

She pressed her finger against the doorbell again and a series of chimes rang out in the stillness.

Crickets chirped.

A car went by.

And no one answered the door.

Well, she'd tried. She hiked her purse up onto her shoulder and started to turn away from the door when it opened.

In the half-light from the hallway, Ruby swallowed. Nathan's face was partially in shadow and the scent of Irish Spring soap drifted to her. He wore only a terrycloth towel wrapped around his waist.

Their eyes met.

He didn't say anything. Neither did she.

She didn't move, and her throat tightened. She could see a single water droplet fall from his damp hair and slide down his neck.

It landed on his bare shoulder. Ruby blinked, her heart pounded, her breath caught. She watched as the drop slid over his collarbone, his skin soft and smooth in the golden light.

But as the water drop slid down onto the smooth, flat plane of his chest, Ruby gasped. She moved forward. Closed the space between them. "You're hurt," she said. The wound puckered angry and red at the midpoint of his chest.

The cabin walls spun around her. He was bleeding. She had to stop the bleeding. He was bleeding so much. She bit her bottom lip so hard she tasted the salty sharp tang of her own blood. Better hers than his.

She pressed her already-soaked handkerchief more firmly to his chest but it only grew darker with his blood. The delicate edging of lace she'd spent hours stitching onto the soft white cotton, now bright red.

Her heart pounded and she clenched her jaw. He would not die. He could not. She fought back a sob but the tears fell anyway, and mingled with the scent of gunpowder, pine and wood smoke. She pressed his cold fingers to her warm cheek.

The tromp of boots on the threshold told her she'd come too late. For both of them.

Her fingers grazed his bare skin, warm to her touch. She heard his intake of breath. She looked up at him, her gaze caught and held there by the depths of his blue eyes. Slowly, ever so slowly, his gaze still locked on hers, he inclined his head toward her.

Her eyes widened even as his briefly closed. He reached up and placed his warm, strong fingers around hers. She felt herself lean forward. She tilted her head up.

"It's not..." Nathan whispered.

She could feel his heart beating under her palm. His skin, not ragged, not torn. But smooth. Soft. Whole. Underneath her fingertips. Her fingers trembled and her lips parted. "Oh God," she murmured, blinked. Her heartbeat sped up.

His lips were only millimeters from hers...

But the honk of a horn, accompanied by catcalls, as a car passed on the street behind them, shattered the silence. Nathan startled and jerked his head back.

"That's not," he opened his eyes, "a wound." He cleared his throat. "That's a birthmark."

"But—" She looked again at the place and blinked. It wasn't swollen or puckered. She grazed her fingertips across it, which caused goose bumps on his damp skin.

"Oh," she said. She dropped her hand from his chest and wrapped her arms around herself.

Nathan shifted his weight. Stepped away from her. "Is everything all right? I was about to go to bed."

"I, uh, sorry. I know it's late. But I couldn't sleep if I didn't come and apologize. I'm sorry. And," she cleared her throat and stepped into the foyer. "I wanted to explain more about what I discovered. I found a letter from Edwina to Alexander about the Great Seal and the compass." She paused. Held Nathan's gaze. "I also deciphered the other order. Then put both halves of the clue together. But I don't know what the riddle means and..." She bit her lip. "I need your help."

Nathan didn't move for a moment. She could feel him look at her, study her, from the semi-darkness of the foyer.

She shifted her weight. Wet her lips.

He let out a breath, and flicked on the overhead light. "I got a call earlier tonight from my lawyer. All my dad's findings, all his research, all his work, was declared invalid.

Every. Last. Thing." Nathan ground his teeth. "The journal and the antique letter weren't enough." Nathan's jaw clenched. "So I told her we'd figure it all out. So what's the whole clue again, now, from the orders?"

Ruby read it aloud: "'*Hearts of ink/Sealed in highest wooden frame/where good Sirs gather/under the sign of the Keys'*"

Nathan tapped a finger against the wall. "Let me get dressed. Have a seat in the living room."

Ruby sank onto the black leather couch and waited for Nathan to come back.

"So, *hearts of ink*," Nathan said, after he returned. "Ink could be tattoos. But I doubt it was meant in that way in the 1700s."

"Hmmm...what do you do with ink? You can draw with it. Write with it," Ruby said. "Write.... Wait a minute. Hearts of ink. Hearts of writing..." She paused. "Could it be something about hearts? A story or a letter or a—"

"A poem." Nathan said. "*The Fair Isle Lovers*. Why didn't I see that before? It contains that legend about the compass of true love. And all these clues have been pointing to the compass, in one way or another, all along." Nathan nodded. "It's about that poem."

Ruby shot him an exasperated look. "But what about the rest? I was thinking 'sealed' could be a reference to the seal itself. Or it could mean literally sealed up."

"Well, we don't have the seal. So we'll have to assume it means something else."

"Okay. So how about the next line? *In highest wooden frame*...What has wooden frames?" Ruby glanced at Nathan.

"Lots of things. Doors, windows. Scaffolds. Houses..." he said.

"Houses. Doors. Windows. I think it could be a house," she said.

"Yeah, but which one?" Nathan asked.

"That doesn't mean—Oh." Ruby paused. "*Highest* frame. On a top floor, maybe? What houses had high floors in 1700s Charlottetown?"

"Well, none of them, really," Nathan said. "They were all just log cabins basically. The only place with multiple stories was...the tavern. Cross Keys Condos used to be Cross Keys Tavern. That's why they kept the name 'cross keys.'"

Ruby grinned at him. "*Under the sign of the keys.* That makes perfect sense. And also fits with 'where good sirs gather.' But what about a wooden frame?"

"Well, I guess we'll just have to check all the windows and doors on the fourth floor. First thing tomorrow morning," Nathan said.

A pause.

Ruby got up off the couch. "Okay, well, um, thanks. I'll just...let you get to bed, then." She tucked a strand of hair behind her ear and headed for the front door.

Nathan cleared his throat. "Right." He followed her to the entryway. "Have a good night, then, Ruby." He closed the door behind her.

RUBY'S MIND WAS still reeling as she got into her bed. She kept seeing the expression on Nathan's face as she'd touched him in the foyer. She rolled over onto her side. Her stomach tightened. And the *way* she'd touched him. What she'd seen as her fingers had brushed his skin...

Finally, her eyelids fluttered closed and she fell asleep.

Branches and brambles snagged at her long skirts as she stumbled through the darkness. The day was lost. But she was free from the prison and the night might still have hope. That only made her heart pound faster as she continued to run. She was almost there. Almost to him. Alexander.

Her breath came in ragged gasps as she made her way to the tiny pin-prink of light she could see in the distance. Their cabin rendezvous. Where everything was safe and they were together. Warm. Happy.

Tree branches scraped against her skin as she continued to run, the only light coming from the sliver of red harvest moon that scrabbled between clouds in the December darkness. She shivered and watched the ice crystals form in the air as she breathed his name.

Her lungs burned. She was almost there. She had to make it. She would make it. She put on a final burst of speed.

As she approached the clearing, her body sagged with re-lief. No redcoats. No glint of muskets in the moonlight.

She slowed. Finally came to a halt in front of the rough hand-hewn cabin door. She cocked her head.

She could see the glow of the lamp in the window. She opened the door.

Goose bumps broke out on her skin.

She stepped over the threshold that she had, for so many years, imagined her true love would carry her across on their wedding day.

The room was warm; she shivered. The scent of roasted meat lingered in the air. She turned around and shut the door behind her then rubbed her arms to ward off the chill.

As her eyes adjusted to the soft firelight, she glanced at the hearth.

Then she fell to her knees and pulled out her handkerchief. All the breath left her lungs. She looked down at his face, at the blood on the lace at his throat. Bright crimson seeped through the snowy white fabric. She pressed her handkerchief futilely to his wound.

"No. No, no, no."

She stroked a hand down his cheek. Her own hand still held the letter he'd written her. His skin, cold. She swallowed. Saw the governor's puzzle box and a letter clutched in his unmoving hand.

He was dead. And she was too late.

They'd killed him. Her hands tightened into fists. They'd pay for this. But not before she hid the box, with the compass secreted inside. No one would get that. She'd see to it.

"Alexander," she whispered, before she buried her face in his velvet jacket and sobbed.

Ruby's eyes flew open. Her heart pounded. Alexander was gone. She shivered in the predawn darkness. Gone.

Alexander?

That was no dream. The colors were too vivid. The smells were too strong.

Alexander.

She wiped a tear from her eye and felt another shiver run through her. Even though he'd been dead, she knew it was *him*. Could feel his very essence as she looked at his face, because he spoke to her soul.

Alexander...

She wiped away more tears. The sadness seemed to move out of her very being, as if all the memories were somehow just under the surface of her skin.

But wait. Alexander...

She stiffened. Lifted her head. Blinked. And then blinked again. The person from the dream in the 1700s clothes with the blood on his shirt—that was the same person that she'd seen in flip-flops and an un-tucked dress shirt.

God. She put a hand to her throat. It all made *sense* now. All those other dreams. Those visions. Those intense emotions when she'd first met him. Of course.

Nathan O'Neil. Nathan...Alexander...*was* Nathan. They were the same soul. Just different lifetimes.

Which meant only one thing. That she was...Edwina.

Chapter Nine

BUT EARLY THE next morning, back at Cross Keys Condos, Ruby and Nathan didn't find anything.

"Damn it." Nathan brought his hand down hard against the window ledge in his dad's study. "We've searched everywhere—"

Ruby pointed to a tiny carving of a heart on the ledge. "Do you think that means we should look there?"

Nathan traced a fingertip on the wooden carving. "All those centuries..." He shook his head. "Well, let's find out what's underneath."

They examined the window ledge. On the underside was a hidden hinge. Nathan crouched down and lifted up the ledge.

Ruby kneeled down beside him. "I think there's something in there," she said.

He reached for a folded piece of yellowed paper tucked into the small cavity created where the window met the wall. Nathan handed the page to her.

She cupped it in her palm. "Looks like it's from the mid-to-late 1700s."

"Really? Wow. How do you know all this stuff?" Ruby noticed he was lightly running his fingers along his jawline.

"Oh, uh, it has to do with the weight of the paper and the materials used." She frowned to cover the way her heart raced. "I should really go get my cotton preservation gloves." But she didn't move. She could feel the warmth of him as he crouched beside her in the tiny alcove created by the dormer window.

She unfolded the antique page. "Oh!" She scanned the

flowing script. "It's a poem." She held it up.

Nathan's eyes widened and he gave a short laugh. "What? Is that the *original* version of *The Fair Isle Lovers*?" He shook his head slightly. "And it looks like it's even signed by Molly McDuff. Everyone on the island who knows their history, knows that Molly was the first barmaid at Cross Keys Tavern."

"So that was in addition to her being the first postmistress?"

Nathan nodded.

"You keep referring to that poem," Ruby said.

"Every school kid on the island had to memorize it. We'd all recite it during our grade six graduation ceremony. Island tradition." As he met and held her gaze, he began to speak from memory:

Though the sea 'twas bottle-green
A love like theirs has n'er been seen
Except on stormy, windy nights
When the moon is high & bright
You can still hear her true love call
The best and most handsome of them all
But when tragedy did befall
That fateful December night
'Tis said if one but wait for the light
Of the waning moon
Their hearts shall once more unite
Under glittering stars, black satin night
When the compass rose sheds its light
And all is, at last, set to rights

Ruby looked at Nathan with wide eyes. "This poem," a smile broke out on her face, "is *about* the compass. And if we find the compass, then we may find the seal, too."

"How do you know that?"

"The..." She blinked. "A dream," she said softly. Slowly.

"That I had last night...it was about—" her eyes darted everywhere but Nathan's face, "—two lovers who weren't meant to be kept apart. And it's a clue. I see it all so clearly now. And this poem, it's a clue trail that will lead to the whereabouts of the compass. Because that's what your dad was onto. The treasure he referred to that the British wanted, must have been the compass. And the legend... He knew they were connected. And that memory, it's in the poem. It's all in the poem. It's real, Nathan." Her eyes widened. "And it's up to us to find the compass so we can restore history as it was meant to be written. As Edwina and Alexander would have wanted it."

"Wait," Nathan said. "The poem isn't referring to the compass... But to the compass rose." He tapped his finger against his chin. "My painting... Edwina was holding a rose bud."

Ruby cocked her head. "So we're not looking for a literal compass rose... We're looking for a rose. A rosebush, I think. Maybe. Could that be why I've been smelling wild roses...?"

"Wait, you've been smelling wild roses too?"

Ruby nodded.

"And I don't think it's just any rosebush," Nathan murmured. "I think it needs to be a rosebush with red-and-white blooms. Like the one in the painting I did."

"So you're saying if we look for a rosebush, we'll find the compass?"

"Exactly," Nathan said. "And maybe even the seal, too. Hmmm. That rosebush... The poem mentions rose-red moonlight."

"One of Alexander's letters had a secret message that referred to rose-red moonlight, too," Ruby added.

Nathan nodded and glanced down at the page Ruby held. "That's strange. There are different ending lines. I mean, more of them..."

"Oh, you mean this?" She pointed to a stanza at the bottom:

The tale does not end
If you take the roses' path
To where it all began

"Another clue," Nathan said. "Sounds pretty literal."

Ruby nodded. "But where?" She glanced at the page again and pointed. "What's that?"

"Looks like a sketch of a canon."

"So that would mean some sort of military reference. Where were canons here in the 1700s?"

"Well, it wasn't the battery along the boardwalk. That was built in the1800s. So the only other place that would've been defended was Fort Amherst."

"Looks like that's where we're headed." Ruby got up.

"Come on," Nathan said, "Let's go."

RUBY GLANCED OVER at Nathan as he drove along the South Shore Route—Highway 19—toward the fort. "There's so much to think about."

"Maybe that's the problem." Nathan tousled his hair. "We're both thinking too hard."

Nathan's thoughts flicked back to the previous evening. What had happened there on the porch last night? All those thoughts swirled around in his head...

Thoughts that were memories. Memories of another time and place...memories of love and desire and heart-ache...as he'd watched Ruby. As he'd felt her fingers on his bare skin.

He took a deep breath and the racing thoughts faded.

Ruby had been affected too. His breath caught. He'd seen it as he'd looked into her eyes. How those same expressions had flitted, one after the other, across her face, too. Love. Desire. Heartache.

He and Ruby were...connected. Yes.

Nathan pressed his foot harder to the accelerator. The Lexus's engine screamed in protest as morning light crept across the rolling hills and pine forest.

He gripped the wheel. His stomach swooped as the car descended the hill and rounded the curve. The dusky green pine trees, brighter green potato fields and yellow-green of pastureland whipped by in a blur.

He barely glanced in the rear view mirror. He fumbled as he rolled down the driver's side window, but kept one eye on the road and one hand on the wheel.

He inhaled deeply. Felt his whole body relax: his attention sharper, clearer, as the fresh cool morning air entered his lungs. As a sense of exhilaration zipped through him.

Sunlight sparkled off the Northumberland Strait. Nathan adjusted his sunglasses.

As the red car wound along the gray ribbon of road, Nathan noticed Ruby clutched the seat cushion but she said nothing.

He eased his foot off the gas pedal and slowed the car. He topped a hill. The merest hint of a rutted red dirt track curved off to his right.

The light of dawn strengthened to golden morning as he turned the wheel and eased the car into the deeply rutted route just off of Highway 19. Dirt scraped the undercarriage as he inched along the familiar road.

Moments later, he turned off the engine and they both got out. The wind carried the scent of salt and the cry of seagulls.

Nathan looked out over the ridge as the sun began to glint off the calm waters of the strait. His eyes finally came to rest on the wrought iron fence that surrounded the small graveyard. Gnarled oaks and twisted paper birches guarded the entrance.

"This isn't Fort Amherst," Ruby said.

"No," Nathan said. "I just need to do something first. You'll be okay for a sec?"

Ruby nodded, and Nathan set off.

He walked down the grassy path and his attention turned to the gravestones in front of him. The dirt had settled some since he'd been here last, but the bouquet of carnations still leaned against one specific red granite headstone.

He sank to his knees in the soft earth and traced a fingertip along the carved words. "Hi Mom," he said in a low voice. "Well," he sighed and a half-smile tugged at his lips, "I'm in love. She's not even from here. And she's American, on top of that. But, well, her name's Ruby and she's so sweet. Beautiful." He gave a soft laugh. Shifted to a crouch. "I'm beginning to think I've known her, before." He shook his head. "Crazy, right? But I had to come out here and tell you. I know, I know. It's not logical or rational or any sort of left-brain thing. But I'm beginning to think that doesn't matter. That that's not how love works."

As Nathan continued the drive over to Fort Amherst, Ruby sat in the passenger seat. Her fingers brushed the surface of the locket and her eyelids fluttered. Suddenly she was standing in a drawing room.

She saw green-and-white striped wallpaper. Heavy green velvet curtains with gold tassels at the windows.

And a man.

He stood with his back to her. She moved her gaze upward. Took in his tailcoat and the way the lightweight navy blue wool fell away to reveal long lean legs. The shiny brass buttons at the small of his back. The lace at his cuffs. The neatly tied cravat. And that glossy black hair tied in a queue at the nap of his neck.

Alexander.

He turned around, but his gaze slid right through hers. She was the ghost. Not him. She followed his gaze as the study door opened.

Ruby gasped. Because she was looking at herself.

She knew it the second she saw those green eyes. Green eyes that held the reflection of her own soul.

Ruby studied the cobalt blue silk dress, the pale skin, the blonde hair curled into neat ringlets. "Alexander," the woman whispered, a red-and-white rosebud in her hand.

"Edwina," he said. He took a step toward her, kissed the back of her hand. "Edwina," he repeated, and Ruby felt her toes curl at the loving caress of his voice, his tone. "Let me paint you."

She smiled up at him, stroked his cheek, then reached up and wound her arms around his neck. He put his arms around her waist. "Yes, Alexander," she whispered, just as their lips met. "For you, I will."

Ruby blinked and the images faded. She rubbed her arms to dispel the goose bumps. She turned to Nathan, her eyes wide, her lips parted.

He met her gaze. "So you saw them too," he whispered.

She saw his knuckles tighten on the wheel. He gave a shaky laugh. "So either we're both going crazy...or..." He glanced over at her.

Ruby licked her suddenly dry lips and nodded. "...Or I'm the reincarnation of Edwina."

"And I'm the reincarnation of Alexander."

Chapter Ten

THEY ARRIVED AT the national historic site. No cars were in the lot and all the lights were off in the interpretive center. And when they got out to look at the grounds, long yellow strips of caution tape criss-crossed the entrance. A couple of small bulldozers and a backhoe were parked along the perimeter beside a cement truck.

"Now what?" Ruby muttered under her breath.

"Looks like they're re-paving the sidewalks and part of the lot." Nathan said. He turned off the engine and got out of the car. "We didn't come this far to stop now." He popped open his truck and pulled out a small folding shovel. "Never know when we might need this. Normally I keep it in here in case I get stuck in snow drifts in the winter."

"But..." Ruby said.

"I know the head maintenance guy. And the main desk guy. Besides, we're going, most likely, in the opposite direction of where they're working."

Ruby put her hands on her hips. "But we can't harm the historical or structural integrity of anything." She threw him a long, rather speculative look.

Nathan hoisted the shovel over his shoulder. "Of course not."

"Then all right."

Ruby had tucked the poem into a manila folder that she now had under her arm. She frowned. "Where did you say the rose bushes were?"

Nathan pointed toward the cliffs. "Over there. Through the pines. There's a whole row of them. Might as well start there."

Ruby followed him through a winding gravel path that led through towering pines, their dark green shapes somehow comforting to her.

The gravel crunched under their shoes and Ruby could smell the salty air.

"So, the stanza's led us here," Nathan said, and came to stand by Ruby. She could smell his aftershave—a woodsy pine scent.

She glanced up at him. Nodded. "But we don't know where to go at this point. There aren't any other clues." She plucked the sheaf of paper out from the folder and held it in her hands. Dawn filtered through the antique yellowed page.

"Hey," Nathan said, and pointed at the blank space just below the last stanza. "What's that?"

Ruby twisted the chain of the locket around her fingers. "What's what?"

"There's more to this clue." Nathan's voice lifted. "Do you see that, right below the last stanza? It looks like...Here, can I take a look for a second?"

"Uh, sure." Ruby handed him the page.

He held it up to the morning light and angled the page so that she could now see what he meant. "It's another line of text," she said.

"Not just one," Nathan said. "Several..." He peered closer. "Whoever wrote it must have pressed the quill point hard enough that it left an indentation on the next sheet of paper. And then they used the sheet two or three sheets beneath the one originally written on, as the means to convey the message." Then he began to read.

Chained up hearts
To set them free
Use the lock
As the key

"Hmmm." Ruby frowned and fiddled with her locket. "Maybe it'd make more sense if we read the whole thing together. I mean the two stanzas that are clues."

The tale does not end
If you take the roses' path
To where it all began
Chained up hearts
To set them free
Use the lock
As the key

"So we've followed the roses' path," Ruby said, gesturing to the pale pink blossoms. They clung to the profusion of wild rose bushes that grew with abandon along the cliff's edge.

"But it ends here," Nathan said. He raked a hand through his hair and gestured to the rose bushes that petered out.

"What's beyond there?" Ruby asked as she pointed to the edge of the property.

"Just the woods. It's owned by Parks Canada but they haven't really done anything with it. There's some old foundations and stuff out there, apparently, but they haven't had the budget to develop them just yet."

"Foundations of what?"

"Houses, outbuildings, that sort of thing," Nathan said.

"We have to keep going."

"Look!" Nathan pointed to a faint red dirt footpath barely visible through the dense green undergrowth dotted with the occasional wild strawberry plant.

Purple asters poked through the foliage. Tall pines stretched to the sky as if they created a tunnel.

Nathan and Ruby walked along the faint trace of path for several minutes until Ruby spotted an area of the woods that looked as if it had once been cleared of its trees. New-growth forest poked its way through the dense underbrush.

Neither of them said anything as they both got closer.

Ruby met Nathan's gaze. "I was wrong," she whispered, and shook her head. "About so many things." She sighed. "But there's nothing here."

Nathan glanced around too. "Except for that." He pointed to the far corner of what looked like a huge mound of earth, but what, Ruby realized, as she stepped closer, was a pile of stones. But not just any pile of stones. A foundation. "A cabin," she breathed.

She followed Nathan as he approached the ruins. A gnarled, bent and crooked chestnut tree nearly five feet wide grew nearby. Its roots pushed the stones away from the remains of a rotting wooden doorframe.

"Look!" She pointed at the lintel. "There's that same heart carving as at Cross Keys! Just on the corner there. This has to be the right place."

"Nice work," Nathan smiled at Ruby. "And look here." He nodded at a rosebush, which grew near what was once the doorway, its last few red-and-white blooms nearly spent.

They knelt on the ground beside it. Nathan carefully began to spade over red dirt.

But as the sun continued to rise and the pink streaks of dawn gave way to bright daylight, each shovelful resulted in nothing.

After long minutes, she looked up at him. "I'm sorry."

"I know," he said. His voice caught over the breeze that gusted through the birch and oak trees that surrounded the small clearing. Ruby got up and went around the perimeter of the ruins, Nathan close behind.

As she made her way back to the chestnut tree, Ruby gasped. "I didn't see it from the other side of this tree, but look. Next to the rosebush? The chestnut tree's roots made what must have been the interior wall heave. I think there's something there."

Nathan crouched down beside her.

"I think if we just pull here..." She pressed her fingers into the small exposed crevice and tucked them under the tiny lip. As their fingers interlaced, and the stone shifted, he felt a jolt pass between them.

Nathan shone his light in the dark cavity. "It's some sort of handmade box." He reached in and picked it up. It weighed next to nothing. Intricate marquetry work in floral designs decorated the lid.

"Here. I don't want to spoil the surprise for you. You do it."

Ruby smiled up at him and took the box. It opened easily.

But there was nothing inside.

She scrubbed at the red dirt on her hands and under her nails then sat back on her heels and sighed. The morning sun filtered through the trees and she glanced at Nathan. "We've come all this way..."

Nathan met her gaze. "Not for nothing, Ruby. At least we've made it this far. The legend was real. The compass, well, at one point anyway, had been real. Before someone else solved the clues and found it. Or who knows, maybe even Molly decided to keep it herself. We just don't know. But at least we tried."

"Yeah, I guess you're right." She fiddled with the locket around her neck. She twined her fingers through the fine silver chain. Stroked a thumb along the heart-shaped surface. "Chained up hearts," she murmured to herself.

"That's referring to Edwina and Alexander. They were chained up. Well, probably not literally. But they were prisoners," Nathan said.

"Right," Ruby muttered as she looked down at the locket in her hands. She looked up at Nathan, her eyes wide. "What if...?" She reached up to unfasten the locket from around her neck.

As she cradled it in the palm of her hand, she said, "Chained up hearts. It's the *locket*. Something about the locket has to do with the seal. The compass. I mean, that's where the first clue was."

"True," Nathan said as he looked at the locket. "If you're right, then 'use the lock as the key' means...the locket itself is the key."

"Yes but we've already opened the box. There's nothing inside."

"Unless..." Nathan cocked his head. "It's one of those

puzzle boxes? Sometimes they used special inlaid wood designs to disguise hidden compartments."

Ruby fumbled with the locket a second before she snapped it open. "But I don't see how—"

"Here," Nathan said, "on the inside of the box. Do you see that design?" He angled the box to catch the morning sun. "Yes... There?" He indicated a starburst shape on the underside of the box's lid. There's a tiny indentation where the sides and top of the box meet. It's the exact shape of—"

"This?" Ruby said, as she held up the locket. "There's a tiny groove in the back of the locket here. Don't know how I'd missed it before. Guess I just wasn't looking for it, so I didn't see it." She held Nathan's gaze a moment, paused, then put her fingernail into the groove. A small popping sound followed, and the whole back of the locket rose up. "I think you're supposed to twist this around..."

She put action to words and flipped the back around so that the pointed part of the heart now faced up, as if it was a key. "This must have been what that one diary entry of Edwina's meant. She had Revere craft the locket for her with this mechanism."

Ruby's fingers trembled slightly. Nathan placed his hand on top of hers. "Here," he said, "let's do this together."

With both of their hands on the locket-key, they fit it into the slot. There was an audible click. The top of the box popped open.

"Edwina must have concealed it in here after she realized she had to hide it when the governor discovered her in his private office." Ruby reached out and touched a fingertip to its shiny gold surface as it lay nestled among layers of rotted muslin.

"The compass of true love," Nathan said. He looked up and met her gaze. "We've found it at last."

"Yes," she breathed, as a smile spread across her face. "We have," she whispered, then gently picked it up. Nathan reached out and closed his fingers around hers.

"Their hearts shall once more unite
Under glittering stars, black satin night
When the compass rose sheds its light
And all is, at last, set to rights"

"God, Ruby." He reached up and stroked a fingertip down her cheek, then cupped his fingers under her chin and tilted his head. *"...how my heart longs but for the taste of your kiss, the feel of your arms around me,"* he whispered, as a slow blush spread across Ruby's cheeks and her eyes widened.

"You knew?"

"Yes," he whispered, "I finally figured it out." He brought his other hand up to stroke the nape of her neck. She shivered as his fingers caressed her skin.

He trailed his hand back down her arm. Stroked his thumb across the back of her hand before he picked it up and pressed his lips to the thin skin there.

"I was so afraid of losing you," she whispered. "That's why I ran away all the time, from all those men. I wasn't afraid of commitment. They just weren't you, so I couldn't commit to them. That's why I left that afternoon. I'm sorry. It was Edwina's fears and worries I was carrying around into this lifetime. She was afraid of losing Alexander. She'd gotten there too late."

"And he had thought she'd abandoned him. Deserted him. Chose her own heritage, her own people, over him." Nathan held Ruby's gaze then withdrew his lips from her hand and interlaced their fingers together.

"I think part of me knew it all along but I was just resisting. I clung so long to logic and rationality that I forgot what it felt like to feel with my heart. I'd closed off that part of myself. But it wasn't really closing myself off, being emotionally unavailable to all those other women. I was simply waiting—to be with you, my love..." He skimmed his lips along her wrist and up her arm.

"Because with you, I already knew the truth. That you

and I were meant to be together. That's why we came together in this lifetime. So we could finally realize that." He intertwined their fingers together and ran a thumb across her palm.

She reached up and placed a hand on his chest.

"Yes," she whispered, and leaned into him. She cupped the compass in her hands and looked up at Nathan.

He watched as the needle spun crazily for a moment and then came to rest, pointed directly at him. Then she handed the compass to him.

He held it up. Sunlight glinted off its polished face as the needle swung around and pointed in Ruby's direction.

Nathan brushed a strand of hair out of her eyes. "Dad was right."

She smiled up at him. "I'm not going to say I told you so, because there were times when I doubted it too. But yes he was." She grinned, leaned in, wrapped her arms around his neck and pressed her cheek against his chest.

But the buzz of Nathan's cell phone in his pocket made her jump back.

Nathan dug out his phone. "Evie? What's up?"

"Nathan, you'll never believe it! When I was cleaning the twins' room this morning, I found a wrinkled, folded up piece of paper in their dollhouse. I thought it was just trash so I was about to throw it out but the feel and color of the page made me stop and unfold it. From what I understand from their disjointed story, Dad somehow had shown them the order. Guess he wanted to give them an appreciation for history. Anyway, one of the girls—they both tell me it was the other—kept it. They were playing post office with it all these months." Evie gave a incredulous laugh. "So Dad's name can now be cleared of the forgery charges."

Nathan let out a long, slow sigh and closed his eyes for a moment. "Thank God. We'll all go out to dinner tonight to celebrate."

Nathan ended the call and relayed the news to Ruby. "Now we can clear up this whole business with the UPEI Board of Governors and that committee, too."

"But we haven't found the seal."

"No, we haven't." He paused and cocked his head. "Hmmm. But I do know what happened to it now. Because in one of the dreams I had, I remember Alexander's brother took the seal from him when he was in Massachusetts. Said he was going to melt the seal down for coinage."

Ruby nodded. "That letter I found in Edwina's journal mentioned the same thing."

"The compass was really the treasure," Nathan added. "And the poem points to the compass, and the compass is clearly real, so now they'll *have* to validate Dad's research, even though the seal no longer exists. I'll talk to my lawyer tomorrow about this. She'll be able to get everything arranged. My dad," Nathan's arms tightened around Ruby's waist, "wasn't the crackpot everyone thought he was. Thanks to you."

She reached up and put a hand on Nathan's cheek. "I'm so glad. And thank you," she said softly, "for everything that *you* did for me. Because if it wasn't for you, I wouldn't have found out the truth."

Nathan grinned. "And you know what the first thing I'm going to do is, after talking with the governors and lawyer tomorrow?"

"What's that?" Ruby asked.

"Design a website for Edwina Belliveaux and Alexander McEachern. Edwina mentioned his last name in one of the journal entries. So everyone knows exactly what happened. They—we—deserve it."

"With what we've found," Ruby said, "I can finish my research now. And then I'll contribute that to your site." She paused. "I want to stay here on the island. That's why it felt so familiar when I stepped off the plane that first time. And why I couldn't stay away. Because it'd been home for me—and for Edwina—all those years ago. And now I'm free to stay here." She looked into Nathan's eyes. "I know why I've been yearning for a place to belong. I thought it was because I was adopted. And that was part of it. But it was also because of my past life as Edwina. She, as me, knew all along that P.E.I. was home. I just had to discover it, too."

"And Edwina and Alexander's story would've remained hidden from history...forever." Nathan reached up and brushed back a strand of hair that had blown into Ruby's eyes. "Until you came along. And until I realized that she and you were one and the same."

Ruby felt a thrill of happiness shoot up her spine. "You mean...?"

"I mean," Nathan said, as he smiled at her, "that now I'm convinced past lives do exist. They're as real as...well, you and me."

He leaned in, and she could smell his woodsy aftershave again. She tilted her head up, and threaded her fingers through his thick silky black hair.

"You know what else?" he whispered. "I'm going to paint a picture of Alexander and Edwina together." He pulled back a fraction to look at her. "But what about your job offer? And your doctorate?"

"Well, after everything we've uncovered, I'll have to make a few tweaks to the dissertation after I defend it early next month, but after that, I'll finally be able to graduate with my degree. I've also been talking to your sister at the Public Archives," Ruby said. "They want to hire me, after all I've done to contribute to the history of the island."

"Are you sure? It's not the big city, and it's not tenure-track."

"I know," she said. "That's what I thought I wanted. But I discovered what I needed is right here. A sense of belonging. Home... You."

"Yes," he murmured. He stroked her cheek and then closed the small space between them as he pressed his lips against hers.

And suddenly, everything felt right. All that they'd been through. As if no time or distance or longing or yearning had ever existed. Because in that moment, there by the cliff tops in the sparkling August sunshine, all that mattered was that they were together. Again.

"You know what?" Nathan said, after a few minutes.

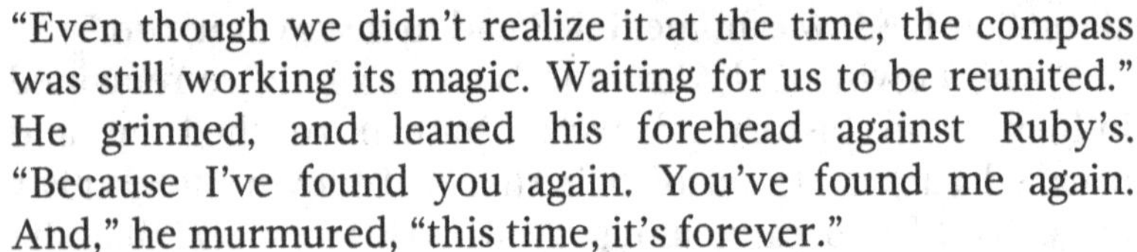

"Even though we didn't realize it at the time, the compass was still working its magic. Waiting for us to be reunited." He grinned, and leaned his forehead against Ruby's. "Because I've found you again. You've found me again. And," he murmured, "this time, it's forever."

Acknowledgments

Karen Dale Harris—developmental editor, whose excellent insights and suggestions helped me shape this story into its final form

Shannon Page—copyeditor/proof reader, who had a great eye for detail

Dr. Graham Lea—academic consultant, who patiently and kindly read and provided feedback on all the academic-related content

Sabrina Volman and J. Esmee McAskill—beta readers, who were awesome and read and encouraged this story from manuscript to publication

Jane Dixon-Smith—graphic designer, who gave me a beautiful cover for the story

Author's Note

I'd always loved the movie *National Treasure*, but wished it had a bit more romance in the plot. When I came across the intriguing historical tidbit about the Great Seal of P.E.I. being stolen in 1775 by American privateers, my imagination took off. I knew I had enough historical facts to create a piece of fiction that could intertwine three things I love: history, romance and treasure hunts. I hope you've enjoyed it!

There are a few places in this story where I tweaked the historical events and the historical timeline to suit the plot.

According to real historical events, the French left Fort Amherst in 1768, not in 1775, as I have had it occur in the story. Cross Keys Tavern was torn down in the 1800s but the red brick building that was built in its place does house Cross Keys Condo.

And the seal, truly, has never been found...so you might want to keep your eyes open. Who knows what's in your attic!

PRINCE EDWARD ISLAND LOVE LETTERS & LEGENDS
JESSICA EISSFELDT
Now it's for always
Book 2

Now it's for always

A Novel

**Book 2 in the
Prince Edward Island Love Letters & Legends Trilogy**

JESSICA EISSFELDT

Now It's For Always: A novel
Jessica Eissfeldt

Chapter One

MAGGIE KILHOUGHERY SHOVED her still-blank sketchpad to the side of her desk and looked down at the flash of gold in her palm—the charm bracelet she'd designed and made herself.

Cobalt-blue grosgrain ribbon had been woven in between heavy links in a half-inch wide gold chain. Seven gold coins—designed to look like Spanish doubloons—dangled along the chain's length beside several other treasure-inspired charms: a tiny treasure chest, a pirate ship, and a spyglass.

Such a little thing, and yet...

Her lips curved upward. And yet...it had been the start of everything. Her heart fluttered. She still couldn't quite believe her bracelet had gotten so much attention.

Attention she should be giving to her follow-up piece. Her stomach knotted.

Maggie glanced at *The New York Times* crossword she had almost solved. Just one more word to go. She chewed on the end of her pencil and ignored the sketchpad and the pile of jewelry supply catalogs that she should be going through. On top of the stack was the latest Courtney Jewelers brochure she'd skimmed earlier today. They'd been around since 1815 and rivalled Tiffany & Co. in prestige and quality.

She bit her lip and neatly penciled in the final crossword answer.

She turned her attention to the crypt-o-quote beneath the crossword and was about to start on it when she heard a tentative knock at her half-open door. She looked up to see Nicky, her assistant.

Nicky adjusted her pencil skirt. "We just hit 500,000 followers on all the social media accounts. On the website, too. And, well, our sales are up. Way up. Musta been that social media campaign of yours, hey?"

Nicky beamed and continued. "Oh, and I've had tons of emails and calls—people are wanting to know what you're going to do next." Nicky paused. "You really inspire me, you know? Even with all those failed pitches to style editors and fashion influencers, you've never given up. And now your bracelet's the hottest thing on the market."

Maggie smiled. "Thanks, Nicky." But guilt surged through Maggie. Nicky didn't know the half of it.

When Maggie had decided to launch her own jewelry line, she'd known she wanted each piece to be based on real treasure.

Just like the Tiffany-designed antique bracelet Zak Stuart, her ex almost-fiancé, had given her for her birthday one year.

But when they'd broken up, he hadn't asked for the bracelet back, so she figured she could keep it. She loved to wear it.

So much so that she'd used the antique bracelet as the inspiration to create her charm bracelet. In fact, she brought the antique piece with her to work regularly as a reminder of the quality, history and workmanship she wanted to put into her own jewelry.

She'd launched her charm bracelet as the first piece in her *Treasured Oceans of Love* series.

Since the antique had directly inspired her own creation, she'd taken artistic license and used Zak's family story about the antique bracelet in the social media campaign she'd undertaken for her charm bracelet. All without Zak's permission.

Maggie fidgeted with one of her pearl earrings. Half a million followers? She swallowed. "It takes inspiration, yes. But hard work is the other half they don't tell you about in school. Designing something inspired by real treasure was a huge risk."

"Real treasure." A light came into Nicky's eyes. "Wow." She hurried off, oblivious to Maggie's inner turmoil.

Before this bracelet, she'd thought her career was over before it began. There'd been only a smattering of sales. Pretty much no one but her friends and family had ever bought anything she'd designed and made. Major design houses kept rejecting her work. The people at Harry Winston said she shouldn't have even bothered approaching them.

She winced. Zak *really* wouldn't like it if he knew she'd implied he was in any way a treasure hunter or involved with treasure hunting.

Maggie tapped a French-manicured fingernail against the charm bracelet.

The next piece in the series had to not only be as beautiful as this one but also make a statement. She doodled in the margin of the sketchpad. It was all about risk.

That's why she'd decided to look up female pirates. She wanted to convey female power in overcoming obstacles.

But somehow, Anne Bonny, Mary Read and Grace O'Malley had all taken a back seat in her imagination when she'd discovered Eleanor. Her gaze travelled to the tattered, gray-blue clothbound book on the edge of her desk.

She reached for the book, *Petticoats & Pistols: Legends of Female Pirates in Piracy's Golden Age*, published in the 1940s. Eleanor had been a pirate. So she had to have hoarded some sort of treasure, right?

Maggie flipped to water-stained, yellowed page 88. She'd found the beat-up volume on top of an Art Deco dressing table crammed into the back of a dusty antique shop in Greenwich Village.

He saw coming toward him, through the billowing smoke, a tall silhouette. She wore a tricorn hat and a captain's jacket; its brass buttons gleamed in the moonlight despite the cloud cover overhead. He nearly dropped the bucket as he fumbled for the hilt of his sword. But the woman in the tricorn hat merely laughed. He could see, as the clouds parted for a moment, her sea-green eyes flash emerald in the starlight. She was the most beautiful woman he'd ever laid eyes on. The flames danced and twisted around her, with her raven-dark hair coiled into a tight braid that formed a crown around her head. A jagged scar marred her left cheek. Though his lungs filled with the burning, acrid smoke, he managed to choke out, "Who are you?" The woman touched a necklace at her throat, diamond and emerald rings flashing on her fingers as she did so. She finally spoke—in a whisper-soft voice that commanded his attention with its sweet chiming sound. "Though my eye color and manner in which I dress my hair give cause for others to call me an emerald queen, my name is Eleanor."

Not a very long legend, as these things went. Which was somewhat strange, come to think. The story read more like a first-hand account. Still.

This was something to latch onto. And the tale made Maggie smile every time she read it.

The problem was, she didn't know enough about this pirate named Eleanor. Maggie needed to find out more. She needed to immerse herself in the history of this woman. Know what it felt like to *be* her. Because the more Maggie found out about Eleanor, the more her jewelry would come to life. For 500,000 people who were expecting another great piece.

Her shoulders tensed. The next design had to be something... phenomenal.

Stunning.

Mysterious.

Romantic.

She crumpled up the piece of sketch paper with the half-drawn doodles and tossed it into the trash with the ten other balled-up pages already there.

She sighed. Picked up a fresh sheet of paper and re-sharpened her pencil. Stared at the blank page.

Maggie looked away from her blank page to the pen-and-ink drawing on the book's facing page. The woman's raven-black hair was braided into a crown.

Some wisps escaped from the tightly woven coif. Strands framed her high cheekbones and highlighted a scar underneath her left eye.

The most arresting feature, however, was not the necklace at Eleanor's throat, but the gleam in Eleanor's eyes, captured by the sketch artist. As if she was daring the viewer to have the courage to seek the truth, to follow her heart.

Maggie shook her head. That was her own artistic imagination filling in the blanks. Who knew if the picture was even an accurate portrait?

The drawing, she noticed, had no artist signature. According to the entry, the portrait was done circa 1698.

Maggie was a designer, not a scholar or a historian. She didn't know anyone she could ask about this pirate. Not any more.

She glanced out the window of her tiny office she'd just started to rent. Now that she was becoming successful, she had to have this office, right? The rosy glow of the setting sun touched the skyscrapers. Off in the distance, if she craned her neck and stood in exactly the right spot, she could *almost* see the Empire State Building.

She uncrossed her arms and the contours of her second-hand white silk Armani suit jacket flowed with her movement.

She picked up the antique jewelry piece beside her charm bracelet and carefully placed the antique back in its original leather pouch. She studied the scuff marks on the leather, the cracked edges. This pouch had to be at least 150 years old, if not more...

Her charm bracelet was this season's must-have. The gold flashed in the fading afternoon light. But all she could think was: what would Zak say?

No, it didn't matter.

But her heart clenched, just the tiniest bit.

Because Zak, after all, was the man she'd fallen in love with all those years ago on Prince Edward Island. And the man who never wanted to see her again.

Because, according to him, the last time she'd seen him—the evening they'd broken up—she'd not only stolen his heart, but also smashed it to bits.

DR. ZAK STUART'S grip tightened on the railing of the boat. He inhaled the scent of salt air as the research vessel bobbed ever so slightly off the shore of Bay Fortune, Prince Edward Island. Calm July day. Perfect conditions for exploring underwater here on the Northumberland Strait.

He rubbed the back of his neck and smothered a yawn. He was still adjusting from the jet lag. That conference in Turkey had been great but it felt good to be back in Canada—even if his research grant deadline now loomed.

He glanced down at his Hublot Oceanographic 4000 divers' watch and frowned. He'd gotten it three years ago to celebrate his success in helping to find Captain William Kidd's ship *Adventure Galley*.

And, he shifted his weight, if he was totally honest with himself, he'd also gotten the watch as a way to ease the pain of Maggie breaking up with him.

The watch had certainly lived up to its craftsmanship and advertising—it'd been a trustworthy companion and never failed him once. His frown deepened. Unlike Maggie. Who'd refused his proposal three years ago.

But their relationship was ancient history now, so why had she come to mind after all this time? He adjusted the elapsed time bezel on the watch's face and took a breath. He had to focus on the dive. They just might find the wreck of *Lady's Revenge* today.

And if they did find it, well, he'd be able to finally prove there was a real ship behind the legendary Ghost Ship of the Northumberland Strait. Some of his colleagues wondered how a scientist like him could chase after something as unscientific-sounding as a ghost ship. But Zak had grown up with the stories. Something inside him longed to prove its existence. Its realness. To connect with that part of what he saw as his Island heritage.

The phantom vessel had sailed these waters for over 200 years, but was first sighted in 1786. Down through the centuries, the ship had been seen over and over. By the young. By the old. By disbelievers and devotees. By his granddad, even. But never by him.

Zak's lips quirked.

No one knew why, or where, the ship had originated. And everyone had different theories about its origins. Some had seen it in Nova Scotia. Others, in New Brunswick. But most often, it had been sighted off the shores of Prince Edward Island.

Canada Post had featured the ghost ship on one of its Haunted Canada stamps. U-Haul had even painted it on the side of their vans—#130 in their Ventures Across Canada series.

Some people said a ghostly Captain Kidd piloted the doomed vessel to pay for some piratical debt.

Others swore the real story was that a P.E.I. Acadian girl fell in love with a sailor whose ship accidentally caught fire.

But no one knew with absolute surety.

Zak's eyes returned to the horizon just off the starboard side of the vessel he'd secured for the project. Not a cloud in sight. Sunlight glinted off the calm waters of the strait.

A porpoise surfaced and Zak felt himself relax. Always a sign of good luck. Not that he was superstitious. But he could use a little luck.

Even though his mentor, Dr. Woods, was along to help out, this was the first time Zak had led a survey project like this since he'd gotten his PhD three years ago. Zak sighed and stuffed his hands in the pockets of his tan cargo shorts. He had only four weeks left in his year-long deadline to find the shipwreck. He had to find something soon. No wreck meant no more grant funding for the project.

Suddenly his cell phone rang. It was his agent.

"Zak, you must not be diving for gold bars yet since you answered your phone."

"Just about to get into my dry suit." He laughed. "But this isn't a treasure ship. It's a ghost ship. Sure, I mean, some of the local lore says Kidd had something to do with the vessel. But his name pops up all the time when you're talking about this type of thing. The treasure I'm seeking is the shipwreck itself."

"Sure, sure. I bet all nautical archaeologists say that," his agent joked. "Well, I won't keep you, but I just wanted to give you some good news. The acquisitions team at Simon & Schuster loved the on-spec pitch. They were especially intrigued by the ghost ship."

Zak's heart beat a little faster. If he could publish his book, *Legendary Shipwrecks of the North Atlantic: Real Facts Behind the Fiction*, it would solve everything.

Well, maybe that was a stretch. But publishing about this find would help open doors to more money to continue the project. Because, once he found the ship, he'd need more funds to actually excavate it. A big-name publisher would mean excellent exposure, too.

If he could prove that the phantom ship had existed as a real vessel, he'd have the scientific answers to a legend over 200 years old.

"Really?" Zak cleared his throat and hoped that the excitement wasn't too evident in his voice. He had to remain professional.

"What you're doing, it's like a real life Clive Cussler novel."

Zak chewed his lip. He'd conjectured the latitude and longitude from the travel journal of explorer and fur trader Henry Davies. But what if he didn't find the wreck?

"You find that wreck, Zak, and the publisher's willing to not only sign you, but also give you a big advance. Five figures."

Zak scrubbed a hand across his jawline.

"You've submitted all the other chapters on all the other shipwrecks. When can you have that last chapter on the ghost ship to me so I can pass it along?"

"I'll have it to you as soon as I can. I have a good feeling about things today. Once we find the ship, I can write up that final chapter."

"Sounds good. Talk soon," his agent said.

Zak ended the call and took a big breath. Five figures. Zak ruffled his hair with a free hand and shifted his weight.

The university would get a chunk of that amount, but he'd get a pretty big piece of it, too, which he could then use to help with the project's future expenses.

Memorial University provided a modest amount but they weren't set up to handle really big projects. And this was a pretty big project.

But he'd gotten lucky. The project was deemed not only culturally exciting but also significant historically, so he'd been given a grant and the go-ahead for the year-long project.

Which meant, if they actually found the wreck, it would be worthy of mounting a full-scale excavation and all the funding that came with it.

If they didn't... He winced. It'd be hard to get future funding and he'd lose professional credibility, too.

Not only that, while he'd grown up, he'd seen his father, and his grandfather, fail time and again at what they held so dear. So, deep down, he felt he owed it to his family to succeed with this. He tightened his jaw. He wasn't going to give up on something that he'd believed for so long was real.

He'd taken a chance, persuaded everyone on the committee that this shipwreck was not only real but also could be found.

Which was pretty miraculous, given that, according to his research, *Lady's Revenge* had gone down after being set ablaze.

Which meant it would've been in pieces as it sank. As a result, there might be little left to find on the sea floor now.

"Dr. Stuart?" His graduate assistant approached. "The side-scan sonar's completed its search of this section of the sea floor."

"Great, let's take a look."

They headed to the cabin, where the three other members of Zak's team were assembled. Zak took a seat at the main computer next to the other scanning equipment.

"The sonar's scanned this area for significant bumps or shadows." The assistant pointed to the computer screen. "It found four potential places we can dive."

"Well, this is a morale boost." Zak studied the screen. "Let's drop buoys at each of those four spots the sonar picked up and see what we can find." He paused and addressed everyone. "But remember, because of the red silt and clay that make up the strait bottom, we have to expect some sinking, especially in shallow waters like these with a bit of turbulence. So let's not expect to go down and see something immediately just lying on the sea floor. Evidence of the ship will at least be partially buried."

The others nodded.

A few minutes later, Zak zipped up his dry suit and adjusted his goggles. He glanced over at Dr. Woods, his dive partner. If they didn't find anything in this section of sea floor at the first target, they would've wasted another few days of their rapidly dwindling four-week period.

And they'd have to move the boat and send down the sonar again to scan a new section of the larger search area.

He stepped off the back of the boat.

MAGGIE GLANCED AT the clock. Almost time to go. Just then, the phone on her desk rang.

"Maggie Kilhoughery speaking. How can I help you?"

"Maggie, I'm with the *Sun*. Just a few quick questions. To confirm, your site just hit half a million followers. And your sales are through the roof. Tell me, how did you do it, coming out of nowhere like that? What's the secret behind your success?"

Maggie's stomach churned. "Yes, I can confirm we've hit half a million followers and nearly double that in sales. It's great." She paused. "Sorry, but I'm not doing any interviews at the moment."

"Oh, come on, now, Maggie. Don't be coy. Everyone wants to know the real story."

Maggie swallowed. "Everyone?"

The reporter laughed. "All of your fans."

The real story... Memory washed over Maggie.

"Back in the 1880s, my great-great grandfather Samuel Stuart commissioned Charles Lewis Tiffany to design this bracelet as a gift for his new bride." Zak said, as he held out the gold bracelet. It caught the moonlight. "And now I want you to have it."

Maggie's eyes widened. "But Zak, why are you giving this to me? You don't even like treasure hunting."

Zak grinned. "You're right. I don't." He stroked her cheek. "But I want you to have this piece of my family history, this piece of me... so you can remember me even when I'm not here."

They gazed at each other for a silent moment. Maggie touched a fingertip to the gold coin that dangled from the delicate chain. "Since treasure hunting runs in your family, Samuel must've had this coin, then?"

"Yep," Zak said. "You remember I told you he'd been running around looking for that lost treasure? Well, his friend named Robert Morriss had gotten it from a treasure hunter named Thomas Jefferson Beale. But Morriss didn't have time to go off treasure hunting, so he gave Samuel the coin."

Then Zak continued. "Tiffany made this bracelet. He attached that single gold doubloon to this delicate chain that he hand-etched with a design of flowers and vines." Zak tucked a loose strand of hair behind her ear. "The coin was rumored to be from Kidd's hoard."

Maggie looked down at the bracelet that Zak had unclasped.

"I know how much you love all these romantic stories connected to lost treasure. So," Zak whispered, "that's why I'm giving it to you." He fastened the gold chain around her wrist. "Happy birthday."

"Oh, Zak," Maggie said, voice husky.

Maggie shook off the memory. "I'm not in a position to answer any more questions right now. I'm sorry."

"Are you sure about that?"

Maggie's hand clenched around the phone. "Yes."

"Just five minutes."

"No," Maggie said.

"Well, I'm sure I'll find out one way or the other."

"I'm sorry but I'm not doing any interviews right now. Good bye." She hung up then grimaced. Zak would truly hate her forever if she let the press find out it was *his* family story behind that social media campaign.

Why did she care what Zak thought of her any more? It'd been three years...

Besides, he was off in Turkey on some nautical archaeological summit, last she'd heard. He'd be more inclined to read an issue of *Archaeology* than *Vogue* or *Vanity Fair*— both of which had mentioned her bracelet on their own social media platforms.

Besides, she didn't care what anyone thought of her. She hadn't gotten this far by being nice.

She got up and put the small leather pouch into her sample-sale red leather Hermes bag, slung the purse over her shoulder, locked her office door, and headed home to her rented brownstone.

Her cell phone buzzed. She glanced at the text from Nicky. *You just missed a call from Courtney.* Maggie replied: *Did you get a last name?* A second later, her phone buzzed again. *Uh, it was Courtney Jewelers.*

THE BLUE WATERS of the Northumberland Strait closed over Zak. The water was clear and warm. P.E.I. had the warmest water north of the Carolinas because of the Gulf currents that flowed up here.

As Zak's senses adjusted to the watery environment, he focused on the sea floor.

Sand and silt. Nothing else.

He swam further. Watched the fluorescent-yellow swim fins of his dive partner move off to the side.

Lobsters and crabs scuttled around clumps of mermaid's purse, yellow-green seaweed and tufts of sea grass.

His eyes scanned the sea floor. Still nothing but sand and silt.

His jaw tightened. There had to be something here. The sonar had picked it up.

He glanced up from his close study of the sea bed. A dark shape loomed in front of him. His heart pounded. This must have been what the sonar picked up. As he stretched out a hand, he realized it was nothing more than solid sandstone.

Technology was great. But sometimes it couldn't tell the difference between wreck-shaped rocks and rock-shaped wrecks.

They'd have to search elsewhere. He gestured to his dive partner and they headed to the surface.

But hours later, when Zak clambered up onto the deck for the fourth time without results, he fought down the bitter disappointment that clawed at the back of his throat.

Sunset streaked the water pink. Looked like tomorrow they'd have to move the boat and send down the sonar again to scan a new section of the larger search area, after all.

He'd triple-checked everything.

But maybe he'd miscalculated the margin of error he'd set for the ocean currents. Or the tides. Or the weight of whatever cargo might've been in the hold of the wreck.

Or maybe so much silt covered the ship on the sea floor that the equipment was thrown off. Hell, it could even be that centuries of sea creatures had eaten away the entire thing...

He gave a frustrated sigh.

But that was the risk he'd taken, he supposed, when he'd decided to hunt for this thing. He wasn't going to give up the search. Especially not now. But he did have to head in for the night.

He stripped out of his dry suit and grabbed his cargo shorts and put them on. Then he reached for his favorite T-shirt, the one with the logo of Memorial University of Newfoundland Sea-Hawks.

Maggie had always hated this shirt. Too old and holey, she'd said. She had always been pretty opinionated. He

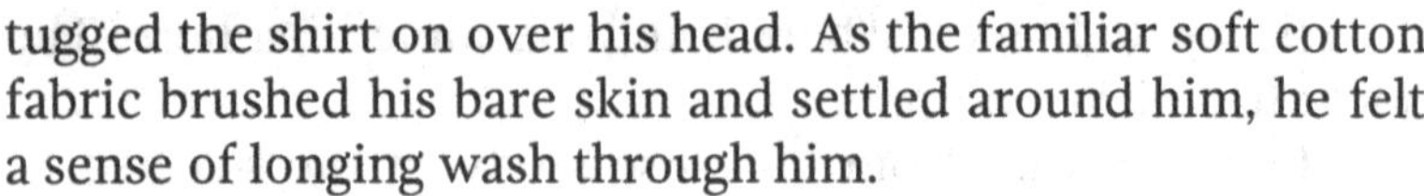

tugged the shirt on over his head. As the familiar soft cotton fabric brushed his bare skin and settled around him, he felt a sense of longing wash through him.

Maggie.

That's why he kept this shirt, if he was completely honest with himself. Because it reminded him of her. And because it reminded him that at least he hadn't failed at his career... yet.

He'd gotten his undergrad at UPEI. Then he'd gotten his master's in archaeology from Memorial University in Newfoundland and his doctorate from Texas A & M in nautical archaeology. After he'd graduated at the top of his class, he'd snagged a prime position back at Memorial in nautical archaeology. If only he could bring the sense of comfort and familiarity from his work into his personal life.

He wished for a second that things had worked out between him and Maggie. Then shoved that thought forcefully away as he stepped sockless into his Top-Sider boat shoes.

Zak gestured to two of his other team members—Dr. Woods had decided to stay on the water a bit longer—and headed over to the dinghy that would take the three of them to shore.

No. She'd betrayed his trust in her.

His mouth tightened as he piloted the dinghy. He'd trusted her—twice with his heart and once with his heirloom. She'd never given that damn bracelet back, either.

His grip tightened on the wheel. That was a piece of his family's history she'd stolen. She'd probably sold it so she could buy a new pair of designer heels.

He frowned. Seems that he'd had more failures than successes. His almost-engagement to Maggie. And now, his inability—yet again—to find the phantom ship.

He swore under his breath. Thinking like this wasn't going to get him anywhere. He took a breath. He had to remain positive.

But a trickle of weariness slipped into his system anyway. The dinghy nudged up against the pier. How many more times was he going to be wrong?

Zak payed out the lines. This was the best damn chance they'd had to find the wreck, what with Davies' journal practically stating where the ship had caught fire.

Well, he'd just have to try harder. He stepped onto the pier and used two half-hitches to make fast the dinghy to the moorings.

After his two other team members had stepped ashore, Zak double-checked that the knots were tight.

"Dr. Stuart," Zak's assistant said, "once we finish these errands, we'll take the dinghy back out to pick up Dr. Woods."

Zak nodded then headed toward his navy blue four-door Dodge pickup truck.

He got in and turned the key. The engine came to life with a rumble and the radio came on too. He turned up the volume on the CBC news as he drove down Fortune Wharf North Road.

"—*storms start earlier than ever. Though Prince Edward Island usually only gets tropical storms and not full-fledged hurricanes, experts predict that this season is going to have hurricanes sweeping through the province, so Islanders need to be extra-prepared.*"

Zak pursed his lips as he turned on to Route 310. Forecasting the intensity of storms could be a bit tricky, he knew from experience. Because where the storms went depended on the weather of the day, not just on what meteorologists said.

He flicked the channels until he found the local pop station, Ocean 100, and followed Route 310 back along the bay.

Supposedly, Bay Fortune had been originally called that because Captain Kidd had buried a fortune somewhere around the area.

Zak had never believed it. There were too many long hard winters with too little for Islanders to do other than entertain themselves with lore like that. His frown deepened. Tales that only encouraged fortune hunters like his great-grandfather, James P. Stuart.

Zak shook that thought away and rolled down his window.

Pine trees flashed by. He took a deep breath of the pine-scented air that still held the tang of salt and turned on to Howe Point Road.

Though he was originally from the north shore of the island—Dalvay by the Sea, up Covehead way—he'd rented a rambling old Victorian house near Bay Fortune for the summer while he worked on the project. He pulled into the drive and went up to the house.

After he grabbed the latest edition of Charlottetown's local paper, *The Guardian,* off the porch, he ate a quick dinner of cold pasta. Then he headed over to the box of research books he'd brought with him and aimlessly began to go through the pile.

He glanced at the small leather-bound book that should, he mused, actually be in a museum instead of in his possession. Yet Davies' journal, which sat in its own container, was the only solid piece of evidence he had.

Because the journal mentioned a real ship that not only matched the phantom vessel's description but also went down in flames—87 years before the first alleged ghost ship sighting.

But Zak didn't pick up the journal. Instead, his fingers closed around a cheap pasteboard kids' book titled *Secret Codes, Secret Ciphers.* Despite himself, a small smile flicked across his face. He wouldn't hear the end of it if his colleagues knew he kept this around. He picked up the familiar volume and flipped to the flyleaf. *For Zak, on your eighth birthday. Happy treasure hunting, son! Love, Granddad*

Zak turned to battered, dog-eared page 58 without thinking. His eyes scanned the familiar lines.

The Beale Papers: Hoax or Fact?

Thomas Jefferson Beale stayed for several months at the Washington Hotel located in Lynchburg, Virginia, back in 1822. The innkeeper, Robert Morriss, didn't know it at the time but Beale was on the trail of a treasure.

Before Beale left, he gave Morriss a locked box for safekeeping. Beale told Morriss that if he didn't return in ten years, Morriss should open the locked iron box and read the enciphered information inside.

Beale never returned. And, though Beale had promised to send a cipher key to Morriss so he could decipher the box's contents, that didn't show up either.

Morriss was left with a dilemma. Should he wait for Beale or open the box? But after more than 20 years, Morriss decided to open the box.

Inside, Morriss found a note—written by Beale—that was wrapped around a single Spanish doubloon. But there were also three other pages there, enciphered in some sort of number code. In the note, Beale explained that he and his partners had found a vast treasure in New Mexico that they'd dug up and carted back to Virginia.

Once back in Virginia, one of Beale's partners, John MacDonald, revealed that, according to his grandfather, Nicholas MacDonald, a portion of the treasure they'd found, specifically a collection of Spanish gold doubloons, had belonged to Captain Kidd. Beale's note went on to say he'd enclosed a single coin, now in Morriss's possession, as proof of this.

Beale also mentioned that John had hinted even more treasure was to be found. But John didn't know any more about it. John said his only clue came from his grandfather Nicholas, one of Kidd's crewmen, who had confessed on his deathbed that some treasure was hidden on "an island east of Boston."

Morriss couldn't decipher the three pages and had

no time for treasure hunting. So, in 1862 Morriss passed those pages—and the single coin—on to a friend. That friend would become the anonymous author of the Beale Papers. The Beale Papers, published as a twenty-three page pamphlet in 1885, contained the three enciphered pages and the story about the treasure.

Zak traced a finger along the crude childish printing that spelled out his great-great grandfather's name: Samuel Stuart.

Zak had scrawled the name in blue ballpoint pen above and across the words 'anonymous author of the Beale Papers.' He had such faith in Granddad's stories when he was a kid. When he was in grade school, he daydreamed all the time about how he'd discover piles of gold coins under every tree.

Zak shut the book, shook his head and sighed.

Samuel Stuart wrote the Beale Papers, and Zak's dad also knew that Beale and MacDonald claimed more of Kidd's treasure was out there. So Zak's father concluded that the crewman's deathbed confession meant he'd be able to find more of Kidd's treasure on P.E.I.

But Dad had paid for treasure hunting with his life. Just like Samuel had.

Thanks to a bad accident at a dig site, Dad had died just before Zak went into his last year of high school. Zak's lips compressed into a line and he put away the children's book.

Dad's death was when and why Zak had vowed to never become a treasure hunter.

Zak turned his attention back to his research. After he slipped on white cotton preservation gloves, he picked up the slim leather-bound travel journal. Then he sat down at the kitchen table.

He placed the book on a clean kitchen towel and flicked on the table lamp he'd moved for the purpose.

There had to be something else in here that he'd missed the first time. The question was, what?

MAGGIE STOPPED ON the sidewalk and stared at her phone. Courtney Jewelers? She blinked. Straightened her shoulders. She'd call the jewelry company back first thing tomorrow morning.

She opened the elegant wrought iron gate and unlocked the door of the converted brownstone. She pushed open the door to what once had been a grand foyer but was now the entry to her small studio apartment.

The evening light caught the leaded cut-glass fanlight and sent a shimmer of rainbows onto the worn red and blue Oriental runner in the hall.

Maggie smiled as she inhaled the scent of vanilla and oleander from her favourite Crate & Barrel candle. It sat on the reproduction Louis XVI hall table she'd found at a rummage sale.

She stepped out of her black faux Gucci pumps and sighed in relief as she rotated her ankles and stretched her toes. She hung up her purse in the hall closet. She put her house keys and the leather pouch that contained the antique bracelet onto the side table. She'd have to put the bracelet away in the bedroom safe later this evening.

A slight scuffling sound on polished hardwood made her grin. Pierniki, her big Maine Coon cat, just over a year old, trotted up to her.

He wound himself around her ankles. His loud purr rumbled a soft vibration against her legs.

She leaned down and stroked his head, and his bright yellow eyes watched her. She smiled. Pierniki still thought he was a kitten. He loved to get into mischief.

"All right there, big boy. Come on, let's look in the kitchen cabinet. I never feed you at all, now, do I?" she teased.

Pierniki just blinked then turned and trotted toward the kitchen counter.

Maggie laughed ruefully to herself. What was this saying about her social life, that she enjoyed talking to her cat

sometimes more than her own friends?

Never mind that Pierniki was the only male companionship she'd entertained in longer than she cared to remember.

Maggie made a face at her mopey thoughts then padded barefoot to the kitchen, where she placed a portion of Fancy Feast into Pierniki's dish. She crouched down and petted him while he ate.

"How about it, Pier? Do you think I should stop making up fantasy men in my head? Get out there more and go on some dates?"

Pierniki just kept eating.

"Well, you're right." She sighed as she blinked back sudden tears. "I guess I'm just a little..." she cleared her throat. "Some companionship would be nice."

Maggie rubbed the cat behind his ears. She tucked a strand of her own shoulder-length dark hair behind her ear and then grabbed the leftover Mexican takeout from last night out of the fridge. She heated it up in the microwave, rummaged around for a fork in the silverware drawer and then took the food and settled onto the creamy white leather sofa. She pulled a pale blue cashmere throw over her. Then she took a few bites of the leftovers with the fork she wielded.

See? She was just fine by herself. Maybe it didn't matter that she hadn't seriously dated anyone since Zak.

She winced. And that was three years ago. Not that she hadn't gone on dates since then. She had. They'd just all been first dates that had headed nowhere.

Her phone buzzed. She glanced at the text from her friend Sarah. *Hey! The girls are going to that new place that just opened in Tribeca. Join us for a drink?*

Thanks for the offer, Maggie texted back, *but I just need some alone time tonight. Feel like I've been running a million miles an hour for the last month. Maybe next week?*

But before she could put the phone aside, it dinged with another incoming message along with a photo. *Having a great time with Nathan in Ireland!* Maggie smiled at the picture of her friend Ruby with her new husband Nathan. Married life seemed to suit Ruby. Maggie sent a smile emoticon back and a note that said they'd have to chat when Ruby got back from her honeymoon.

Maggie laid the phone down beside her as her thoughts went back to her work. If she was honest with herself, a lot of the stress was from her least favorite part of the business—overseeing the day-to-day administrative details. Going in to the office. She just wanted to create jewelry and didn't want to have to worry about spreadsheets and inventory numbers and staff... But, she supposed, that was part of the deal, wasn't it?

She frowned and her thoughts drifted back to Zak. Why did she always use him as the yardstick for any other man she came into contact with? It wasn't fair to those other men, or to him, or to herself.

Besides all that, it wasn't healthy. That wasn't what she needed or wanted in her life—to be hung up on someone with whom things had long since finished.

No. She wasn't hung up on Zak. She just hadn't found anyone else as compatible as she'd felt, thought, *known*, they'd been. She shook her head. Dislodged the negative thought spiral. She was happy. Really. She was doing what she loved. Had great friends. Loved this city. She took another bite of burrito.

Was she a fraud? After all, she'd basically stolen the story of the bracelet. She shifted on the couch cushions. But it was a story that needed to be told. And obviously it had resonated with her target audience. Even if she hadn't told Zak she'd "borrowed" his family story for the social media campaign.

If that ever got out... everything she'd worked so hard for would disappear. And what a relief that would be.

Maggie sat up straight at the thought. No. She hadn't meant that.

She gave new life to priceless, historic objects—pieces that would otherwise molder in museum back rooms—and used them as inspiration for her art. That was *not* fraud.

To pass those feelings of freedom and enjoyment to her customers, that was her true passion in life. It gave the everyday woman a chance to have a little piece of treasure for herself.

She shook her head. Remembered the excitement she'd felt when Zak had first given her the bracelet. She sighed. Had she made the right choice to refuse Zak's proposal? She'd kept the bracelet because it reminded her of Zak, of their time together, of their connection. Over the years, she'd thought about sending the bracelet back to him. But she somehow couldn't quite bring herself to do it. That would've been like trying to send him back a piece of her own heart—

A loud clunk from the hallway broke into her revere. The sound of glass shattering made her leap up from the couch and head toward the foyer. Her heart pounded.

She flicked on the hall light and made herself walk carefully down the short hall in the direction of the sound. No one had broken the front door open. There was nothing out of place—

The side table.

The unlit Crate & Barrel candle had fallen. The crystal candle holder she'd placed the candle in had also fallen to the floor and shattered into a million sparkling shards. She noticed the strands of cat hair amongst the mess.

The corners of her lips tugged up into a smile. Pierniki liked to keep her on her toes. In this case, literally.

She grabbed the broom and dustpan out of the hall closet and started to sweep up the mess. As she crouched down with the dustpan, she spotted the leather pouch that contained the antique bracelet.

As she reached under the table for the pouch, she noticed the tooth marks along the edge of the leather. Pierniki thought everything was a toy.

As she closed her fingers around the ancient pouch, the bracelet fell out the bottom. The cat must have chewed all the way through the stitching. Crap.

At least the bracelet hadn't been damaged. Unlike her

modern charm bracelet, this antique had a very simple design: a single Spanish doubloon on a delicate one-fourth inch gold chain.

She put the bracelet back on the side table but the recent mauling was too much for the ancient pouch's stitching. The whole piece of leather fell apart at its seams.

Maggie winced. Something else Zak wouldn't like if he knew about it. When he'd given her the bracelet, it'd been inside that leather pouch.

Zak had told her that originally, the pouch had contained only the single gold doubloon. Then somewhere along the line, the coin had been fastened to the chain to make the bracelet.

She placed the pouch, now a flat rectangle, onto the side table and then turned on the table lamp. She'd have to put it into a plastic bag to protect it.

As she returned to the side table with a Ziploc baggie, a dark blot on the exposed leather interior caught her eye. Must be a stain from the leather dye—

But no. She looked again. It was—she frowned—not an ink stain. She peered closer. It was whole sentences. She held her breath as she read it.

Emerald queen of the North Atlantic deep,
Jewelled heart of stone that does not sleep.
An earl, a Speaker; a Captain's unheard plea.
Twenty-three cryptic pages,
Nearly All lost to a treasure's ravages.

Maggie felt goose bumps rise on her arms, and the sudden brush of soft fur against her legs made her startle.

She glanced down at her cat, who looked up at her with his round golden eyes. Pierniki blinked and she scratched him under the chin.

Where had this come from? Zak hadn't mentioned anything about this...verse?...poem? in the story he'd told her about the bracelet.

She bit her lip as guilt nudged at her. She sighed. For a

second, she wished she could just call him up and ask...

The lines almost seemed—she shook her head—like a riddle. But that was impossible. That sort of thing only happened in novels. Didn't it?

ZAK GAVE A huff of irritation. Even if he continued to stare down at the leather-bound book, it wasn't going to make any new information suddenly appear. He needed some fresh air.

He headed out to his pickup. Crickets chirped.

A drive would clear his head. Maybe give him some ideas for what damn step to take next now that he'd run into yet another dead end.

With his mind on autopilot, he took a left out of the driveway and headed to the TransCanada.

After driving for about forty minutes, he found himself approaching the capital city of Charlottetown.

Instead of heading downtown and stopping for a drink at the Churchill Arms on Queen Street like he might've usually done, he kept going along Capital Drive.

On impulse, he took the roundabout toward Argyle Shores and drove through the twilight.

God. He hadn't been out this way in years... Not since he and Maggie had been together.

He drove in silence for awhile before he flicked on the radio to Ocean 100. Tapped his fingers against the steering wheel to the latest pop hit.

He'd never admit to any of his buddies but he actually liked pop music. He cranked up the volume, cranked down the window and began to sing along.

A little while later, the beam from his headlights cut across the grove of rather windblown pines and his tires crunched on the gravel of the parking lot at Argyle Shores Provincial Park.

He got out and took a deep breath. The wind picked up and buffeted his hair. He headed across the grass. Felt the wind blow harder against him the closer he got to the cliff's edge. Moonlight spread across the Northumberland Strait.

A bit of chop out there tonight, he noticed. He headed for the wooden stairs that hugged the craggy cliff face. The stairs creaked as he descended. Tide was out.

After he reached the bottom step, his scuffed up, brown leather Wolverine work boots crunched slightly on the reddish sand and rocks. He took another deep breath. Out here, he could actually breathe. Could actually feel alive again. He tilted his head back and looked up.

A million pin-pricks of light winked back at him.

Yes. Out here, he could actually feel free from career pressures. The wind picked up again, and he welcomed the salt spray of the incoming waves.

Freedom to explore and have adventures.

That was all he really wanted.

Maggie hadn't understood that. It was such an integral part of who he was.

He absently picked up a small piece of sandstone that had flaked off the cliff face. He flicked his wrist. The stone skipped six or eight times across the water before it sank beneath the surface.

He reached down and picked up another sandy stone. The toes of his boots scuffled against the damp seaweed and greenish lichen that covered the sandstone rocks.

He walked a bit farther. His shoes squelched on the damp sand. But he didn't care.

That freedom to have adventures was why he needed to explore. Where he got the urge to dive. Why he'd become a nautical archaeologist in the first place.

Because there in the peace and silence of the deep, he could get in touch with a deeper part of himself. Explore the connection to the history left behind on the sea floor...

He noticed the wind had brought in some clouds and the moonlight had begun to wane. As his eyes followed the scuttle and rush of the clouds, a shiver climbed up his spine. He rubbed his arms against goosebumps and shoved his hands deeper into his jeans pockets, but the slight chill remained.

He scanned the horizon and wondered whether he should grab his hoodie from the truck. But then his eyes caught a flicker of light on the far, far horizon, out in the darkest part of the strait.

As he watched, the flicker of light seemed to get bigger and brighter. It appeared simultaneously to move toward him yet pull away.

His breath caught in his throat and he swallowed hard and blinked rapidly.

But the light remained.

In fact, it had quadrupled in size and substance in the few moments he'd watched it. And it began to head, he now realized, as the slight chill continued to persist, straight toward him. It was now no longer just a flicker of pale yellow light. It was now a distinct bright orange. The same bright orange he knew to be that of fire.

Flames, to be more precise.

They licked at the darkness, at the blackness, as if it were paper. The orange glow grew bigger. And closer. And bigger still. Until he could see the flames had taken on a distinct shape. A certain outline. One that Islanders the whole province over knew. That of a ship.

A burning ship.

Zak couldn't move even if he wanted to. The sight froze him to the spot as the flames licked higher and higher still.

The shape drew even closer, so that now, he could see flames consume the yardarm, the keel and the bow of a four-masted tall ship.

Over the rush of the surf and the howl of the wind, he heard the crackle of the fire as it continued to burn, bright and hot.

He held his breath.

He could even hear the shouted orders, the muffled thuds and the coarse oaths, as the crew fought for not only their lives but also for their ship. Water splashed as some sailors jumped overboard.

Another splash sounded, and his attention went to a small rowboat that came around the bow of the burning ship.

He cocked his head. He hadn't heard that happen in any of the reports he'd read for his research. The shouts of the sailors and crackle of the flames grew louder.

His fingers closed reflexively around his cell phone. But he knew that a call would do no good.

That this particular crew, and this particular ship, could not, would not, be saved.

Because this—he blinked quickly and his heart pounded even as he watched the last of the sails become engulfed in flame, and the shouts of the crew turn to screams—was an apparition.

"The ghost ship," Zak whispered. He'd spent his career wondering if he'd ever see it.

Until now.

Chapter Two

WEDNESDAY MORNING, MAGGIE chewed on a cuticle for a second as she stared at the phone on her desk. But she pushed aside the fragments of guilt along with the charm bracelet, and picked up the receiver to call back Courtney Jewelers.

"This is Maggie Kilhoughery. What can I do for you?"

"Well, Maggie," the woman on the other end of the line said, "My name is Jia Rathod. I'm from Courtney Jewelers."

Maggie felt her palms begin to sweat.

"To get straight to the point, Maggie, Courtney Jewelers wants your talent."

"Oh?" Maggie swallowed.

"This charm bracelet you've designed has been selling like crazy on your website—you've had such big numbers that we couldn't help but notice. We keep an eye out for up and coming designers like you."

Maggie's pulse pounded.

"We'd like you to design a new piece for us." A pause. "We especially loved the story behind the bracelet."

Maggie's stomach clenched.

But the woman continued. "Because of that social media campaign you did, everyone wants to feel like they're part of the romance. Part of the history. Part of the legend. And your bracelet, thanks not only to the exquisite design, but also to the story behind it, does exactly that. So, we want your next piece to have just as compelling of a story behind it."

Maggie felt her mouth go dry. "Well, I know of a certain female pirate who has a very compelling story." She winced.

If she could find anything else out about her, that is.

"Great. If things go well, we'd like to pick up your whole *Treasured Oceans of Love* line."

"That'd be—" Maggie cleared her throat "—fantastic." She chuckled. "Er, I mean, I'd be open to that possibility."

"Wonderful," the woman said. "We need the preliminary drawings for this new piece by the end of next week."

"The end of...next week?" Maggie echoed. Today was Wednesday. Her stomach dipped. That gave her only nine days.

"Exactly," the woman confirmed. "If things go well, we'll be in touch again to set up a meeting and draw up the contract and all the other paperwork."

"Okay," Maggie said. "Sounds great." She hung up the phone.

Oh God. What if she couldn't come up with anything? What if she didn't have any more good ideas? What if that bracelet was her only success—No. She shook her head. She'd think of something. She just needed to expand on an idea.

That meant more research. And more research meant help. Yes. That was the answer. She felt the panic begin to ease. She didn't have to do this alone.

She picked up the tattered blue hardcover, got up from her desk and went over to Nicky's workspace. "I need you to find out everything and anything you can about this woman named Eleanor." She handed Nicky the book. "It's for the next piece in the line."

"Okay." Nicky scribbled down notes. "I'll look for whatever I can find associated with her."

"I haven't found much about her online, so you may need to call people. Use this book as a place to start. Page 88 has some about her. Then look through libraries, that sort of thing. I need to find out as much as possible so I can figure out where I'm coming from with this next design. And if you can, set up a few meetings for me to talk with any experts you may find. By Friday, please."

This was legitimate research. It might take a bit more

time away from her actual sketching. But it would be worth it when the design was perfect.

And it *had* to be perfect. This was for Courtney Jewelers, after all.

"Experts." Nicky nodded. Scribbled more notes. "I'll dig up whoever I can."

EARLY FRIDAY AFTERNOON, Maggie sat at her desk, a clean piece of sketch paper in front of her. But her mind was as blank as the page.

When the knock sounded at her door, she welcomed the distraction. "Nicky. Find anything?"

"I spent a lot of time at the library and on the phone yesterday and this morning. All I found was this one reference in *From Maids to Matriarchs: Unconventional Women Through the Ages*. Got it in a second-hand bookstore in Brooklyn." Nicky handed Maggie a photocopied page.

Eleanor Webster: (c.1660-?) An American woman, born about 1660 near what is now Plymouth, Massachusetts, Eleanor was the daughter of a successful merchant. While from a prominent Puritan family and relatively well off, she was nonetheless accused of witchcraft. She narrowly escaped being burned at the stake. Soon after, she stole one of her father's merchant ships and took to the high seas. Then she sailed for the East Indies, intent to captain her own fleet. What happened to her after that, is, however, lost to history. Scholars debate whether she was a real person or simply a fictional character.

"Great job, Nicky. Thanks so much. You deserve a promotion!"

Nicky laughed. "Don't worry, I won't hold you to that. Oh, and I finally tracked down an expert—sort of. His assistant said he and his research team are working on some shipwreck project in the North Atlantic in the era you're interested in. His assistant also said this guy wasn't exactly an expert on Eleanor but that he had heard of her and had some primary sources, apparently, that talk about her."

"Thanks so much, Nicky. Go ahead and set up a meeting with him."

"I thought you might say that, so I've already done it. He's okayed it. His assistant said you could even come on board, ask questions, observe for awhile if you like. Maybe for an afternoon or even a full day."

"Oh?" Well, the more in-depth, the better. She needed all the inspiration she could get. If spending some time out on a boat would help, she'd do it. "Great. Go ahead and set that up for me, please. You can take care of all the details. Where is it?"

"On Prince Edward Island."

Maggie bit her lip and fidgeted with a button on her blue pinstripe blouse. She hadn't been back there in... three years.

"They'll be ready to meet you Sunday at 7 a.m."

"Okay. I guess I can wrap things up on the island in a day or two, then come back here and actually create the piece."

"Didn't you grow up on Prince Edward Island?"

Maggie nodded. But she, her parents and her siblings now all lived off-island.

"Well that'll be nice for you to be back there for a bit," Nicky said as she turned to go. "When should I book your flight for?"

What Nicky didn't know was that P.E.I. was where she and Zak had fallen in love in high school then called it quits. Where she and Zak had *almost* gotten engaged. And the one place she hoped she'd never have to go back to.

"As soon as possible. Oh, and Nicky? I didn't catch a name. Who's the expert I'll be working with?"

"Dr. Zak Stuart."

❧

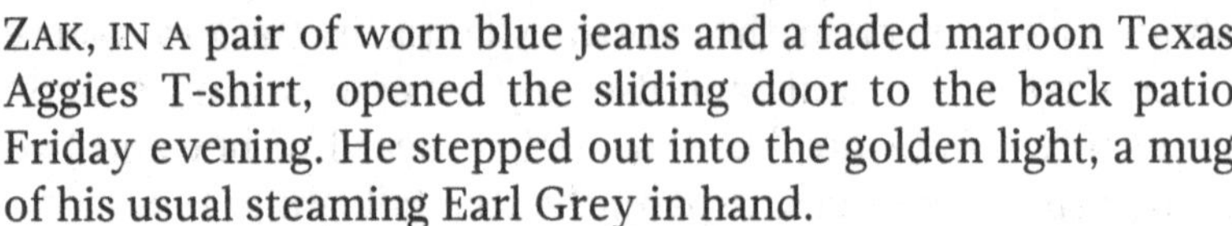

ZAK, IN A pair of worn blue jeans and a faded maroon Texas Aggies T-shirt, opened the sliding door to the back patio Friday evening. He stepped out into the golden light, a mug of his usual steaming Earl Grey in hand.

The ship sighting flashed through his mind again. That rowboat wasn't in any of the other hundreds of accounts he'd studied—only in Davies' journal.

He took a sip of tea. But maybe he should check again.

He headed back inside and took a seat on the beat-up suede couch. He reached for the thick binder on the side table.

He propped his bare feet up on the brown leather ottoman and then began to flip through the pages.

Always the same thing, though. People described a tall ship with three or four masts.

Sometimes it was already burning when they saw it. Other times, it burst into flames as they watched.

He turned another page but he knew the material so well that he didn't have to really read it. Sightings were mostly at night. Or dusk. And usually between September and November. Though some had seen it in the summer months.

He rubbed his temples. Everyone saw it in different places. Along the South Shore. The western side of the island. The sand dunes along the North Shore.

Which essentially meant the wreck could be anywhere. He put aside the binder. Picked up his cotton gloves beside the slim volume written by Davies.

That's why he'd been so excited to find Davies' journal last month before he'd headed to Turkey for the summit.

He'd found the leather-bound book at an estate sale near Georgetown, P.E.I.

Some lobster fisherman's great-great grandmother had found it, the old lady had said. It had been in the family ever since.

Until they'd sold it at the estate sale, anyway.

He put on the gloves and carefully opened the cracked leather volume.

He paged through it until he found the entry that mentioned Davies' campsite—the location Zak conjectured the wreck to be near.

2 July 1701

My journey with the Hudson's Bay Company ends at last. Have set up camp and await my Beloved.

But my worry grows great, as here, along the mouth of Bay Fortune, Eleanor assured me she would dock. Though neither she nor Lady's Revenge *have shown themselves to be in evidence. I fear Kidd's Quartermaster may be the cause.*

The entry ended abruptly. Zak turned the abnormally thick page. The next few pages had only faded ink sketches of Mi'kmaq dwellings and various wildlife. Notes about paddle routes dotted the margins alongside tallies of beaver and fox pelts.

Zak found the next entry. The penmanship was unsteady and the ink marred in several places.

15 July 1701

No moon tonight. An ill omen, mayhap. The black waters of the strait seem to sit in ominous silence. Though the lens of my spyglass, I saw Lady's Revenge *slip over the horizon at last.*

The next part of the entry had faded badly, and the ink had run. That part of the page was hopelessly indecipherable. Zak could make out the handwriting a bit further down.

—doused the deck in what I suspect was kerosene, he set the mess alight. By the time the crew noticed, 'twas far too late.

Eleanor lowered the sole remaining dinghy and had just loosened its ropes and almost managed to heave herself inside when he attacked her.

My hand shakes much.

The entry ended there and it appeared as if someone had ripped out the next few pages. He'd noticed that had been done earlier in the journal, too.

Zak heaved a frustrated sigh. Seeing that dinghy didn't fit the pattern of the other sightings. Which, in a way, made this journal entry even more legitimate. He closed his eyes and brought to mind the apparition he'd seen.

His brow furrowed. He seemed to recall two figures in the dinghy but then again, he could've just made that up now.

The ping of an incoming text message on his phone made him open his eyes. He glanced down. Granddad. *Zak. Emergency family meeting. I need you to come up to Dalvay as soon as you can.* His granddad, Ian Stuart, always did have a flair for the dramatic. When he said emergency family meeting, it usually meant he couldn't find his reading glasses.

Ever since Granddad had retired from active treasure hunting, Zak had gotten these messages more frequently. Probably just needed a sense of excitement in his life. *Sure, Granddad. You OK?*

Zak got up off the couch. He was the only family Granddad had now. He'd better head up to the Dalvay estate on the north shore right away. *Right as rain, son. No need to race up here. I'm not dying.*

Zak exhaled in relief. *I need to meet with my team tomorrow so if you're OK with it, I could come up Sunday afternoon?* After a second, his phone dinged. *Sunday's fine. See you then.*

Zak rubbed his eyes. Long days of searching and diving was making his brain foggy. But he thought he remembered one of his team members had said something about some New Yorker coming aboard for research Sunday morning.

Chapter Three

On Sunday morning, Maggie drove her rental car along the winding highway that hugged P.E.I.'s south shore. Morning light gleamed off the water and filtered through the pines.

Crap. What had she gotten herself into?

She straightened her shoulders. She wasn't going to feel intimidated to see Zak again. He'd approved it, which meant he was totally fine with this. She was worried for nothing.

Besides, she wasn't going to let her one chance at more success than she'd dreamed of slip away from her just because the person she needed help from happened to be her ex almost-fiancé. Who had ignored her artistic dreams in favor of his own career.

Her hands tightened on the wheel.

She'd stick this out. See it to the end. Her jewelry design, and her career goals, were worth it. Yes. She'd stay professional. Calm.

Everything would be fine.

She stepped out of her rental car and onto the tiny pier as the wind buffeted her blue striped cotton sundress. A smile formed on her lips.

Even though she hadn't been back here since she'd helped her parents move off-island for retirement, nothing had changed. The scent of pine still lingered in the air. And the cry of gulls still sounded overhead. As the water sparkled in the sunlight, Maggie's heart lifted. Her fingers closed briefly around the antique bracelet, which she'd put in a zippered interior pocket of her purse. Maybe, since she was here anyway, she could try to ask Zak about that verse

or stanza or whatever it was...?

Way down at the end of the pier, a dinghy bobbed on the water's surface. And a man in a pale yellow button-down shirt began to walk up the pier. His wavy brown hair ruffled in the breeze.

Maggie adjusted her over-large tortoiseshell sunglasses and wished the glasses hid more of her face. She pulled the wide brim of her straw hat lower. She could do this. Her toes curled in her white Keds as he got closer. Even as she watched him approach, she held her breath.

Oh no. No. No. She couldn't do this.

But before she could turn and run-walk away, Zak stood in front of her. She hadn't seen him since the night she'd refused his proposal and broken his heart for the second time.

The wind gusted and she put one hand on her hat. She swallowed. Her mouth went dry and her palms suddenly felt sweaty. Crap.

"Thanks for agreeing to help me," she finally managed, "with my research for this next piece in my jewelry line," she finished in a rush.

"Maggie." His eyes narrowed. "It was *you* my grad assistant meant." He crossed his arms over his chest. His hazel eyes were cold.

She opened her mouth to reply but no words came out. How did he even know who she was in these giant sunglasses and wide-brimmed hat? Not to mention the hideously wrinkled dress she was wearing. He must have remembered the sound of her voice. She cleared her throat and went to slide her hands into her pockets. Hide at least some part of herself from his gaze.

But her dress didn't have any pockets. So she fisted her hands at her sides, instead.

Her pulse pounded in her throat and she willed him not to notice. His eyes, however, remained firmly engaged on her face.

Her chest tightened. "So—" she forced the word past the sudden lump in her throat "—where are we going?"

He leaned against one of the pilings but a muscle in his jaw ticked.

He uncrossed his arms and stuffed them into the front pockets of his neatly pressed navy blue Dockers.

She felt like she might throw up. Were those the same pair of pants he'd worn on their second date in university? She thought she recognized the torn left belt loop.

He jerked a thumb to indicate the boat behind them. "As you should already know—" he paused, his tone measured and formal "—the project's out here on the Northumberland Strait."

God, had it been three years, really?

Her lips compressed in a line.

Three years since he'd ignored her artistic dreams in favor of what was probably yet another dead-end in his tireless hunt for shipwrecks.

A slice of anger surged through her, and she clung to it as if it were a life preserver. She straightened her spine. "Right." Her heart pounded. She held her hands up, palms out. "Believe me, if I'd known I'd receive this kind of...welcome... from you—" she tapped her foot "—I would've never come up here."

Zak shifted his weight. Studied her for one long minute. Then two.

Maggie put her hands on her hips.

Just then, an older man came up behind Zak. Probably his assistant. "Everything's ready to go, Dr. Stuart. This the person we were waiting for?"

Zak gave a curt nod and turned away from Maggie without saying anything else.

Maggie lifted her chin and followed behind the two men.

AFTER THEY BOARDED the research vessel, Zak glanced at her as they crossed the deck. It dipped slightly under Maggie's feet but she kept her balance as she dug out a pen and notepad from her purse.

She had to at least make an attempt to ask him some of the research questions she'd come here for. She straightened her shoulders. Best to start with a broad open-ended one. "So what do you know about female pirates?"

"I'm a scientist, not a historian."

He walked on without waiting for her.

Maggie forced herself to take a slow breath and speak in a calm tone. "The thing is, this ship you're looking for is in the same era as a female pirate I'm interested in learning more about."

"Try Wikipedia."

She fought down a wave of frustration and followed him across the deck. "But my assistant said that you knew something about a female pirate named Eleanor Webster."

"Listen, you're wasting your time. That's not my field."

Her lips compressed. "But surely you have some story about her—" She stopped talking. She'd been naive to think she'd be able to ask him about much of anything, let alone that verse. She shook her head and shoved her pen and notepad back into her purse.

"You think some big, romantic story can stand in for serious research?" He lifted his brows.

Maggie lifted her chin and glared at him.

Zak glared back.

Overhead, a seagull wheeled and called.

Zak blinked. He rubbed the back of his neck then turned to the rail and studied the water for a long moment. "Since you're here," he said at last, "you might as well come take a look at the monitors so you know what it is we're looking for."

"Thank you." She followed him, her back straight, into a small low-ceilinged room where monitors and switches and lights flashed and beeped.

Despite herself, Maggie noticed Zak's scuffed Top-Siders with frayed white laces. A traitorous smile tugged at her lips. He always had loved beat-up old shoes. More comfortable, he said.

When Zak tapped the screen directly in front of him, she dragged her eyes from his shoes and lifted her chin. "So, what are we looking at, here?"

"Frankly, just sandy sea bottom," Zak said. In the blue glow of the monitor, Maggie saw the worry lines around his eyes. She tamped down a surge of annoyance at herself. His worries were none of her business.

"We're moving the boat a few inches at a time," he explained, "and using robotics and computers to map out the bottom. But until we get the big, clear picture of what we're looking at, we don't know exactly where to search."

Maggie's heart squeezed. He sounded so...formal. Distant. No. Of course he would. He had nothing to do with her personal life any more.

"That was the mistake I made before," Zak muttered under his breath, so softly at first that she didn't think she'd heard right.

But she knew better than to ask him about mistakes. Her gaze traveled to the stacks of files and charts and papers next to the monitors.

"So," Maggie said, "what's the name of the ship? Is there anything I can do here to, uh, help?" Why was she offering her help? Zak didn't need it. Or want it.

"*Lady's Revenge*." Zak slid a glance in her direction that she couldn't quite read. "I thought you were the one who needed an expert's help."

An awkward silence ensued.

One of the research assistants poked her head in the doorway. "Zak? We need your input on where to drop the sea floor scanner next."

"Okay." Zak headed out the door.

Fine. If he was going to be uncooperative, the least she could do was get some work done on the drawing. Maggie returned to the deck and the bright wind-tossed sunshine.

But as she did, chatter from some of Zak's team members drifted to her. "Did you hear them arguing?"

A pause. Then, "Seems like there's *something* between them, eh?" the other person said. Maggie paused mid-stride.

"Yeah. I wonder how long they've known each other?"

Maggie's heart lurched as she recalled standing at the railing of Zak's sailboat, his warm embrace warding off the damp sea air.

"They looked kinda cute together, didn't they?" the first person added.

And the way that her heart had leapt to her throat as they'd talked about the future. *Their* future. Sadness rippled through her.

"Maybe there's more going on there...?" The second said.

Maggie took a deep breath. Nothing was going on here. He didn't *get* her. Had never gotten her. Hadn't been supportive of her art, her dreams...

She clenched her jaw and made her way back to the table she'd spotted in the corner of the deck by a pile of ropes and the life jacket storage unit.

She got out her sketchpad and pencil and took a seat.

After twenty minutes with no progress, she looked down at the blank page and sighed. She was not going to acknowledge the way that his memory lingered in her mind the same way that his cologne now lingered on the breeze.

Besides all that, thinking about him wasn't getting anything useful down on paper.

She started at the sketchpad. She'd drawn some sort of half-circle that was supposed to be a pendant but looked more like something a four-year-old had done at daycare.

She ran a hand through her windblown hair. Tapped her pencil against the sketchpad and looked out at the horizon.

The water lapped at the boat and made her wonder if there was actually any point. What did she want to convey? Feminine power. Passion. Strength. And beauty.

She chewed on the end of the pencil and frowned. Why was this so hard? Maybe she couldn't create something entirely of her own imagination.

Maybe she couldn't be successful unless she had some pattern to follow, some guaranteed sure thing. Her mind strayed back to her charm bracelet tucked into her purse alongside the antique bracelet.

She worried her bottom lip. Maybe she couldn't be successful completely on her own. She had to have someone hold her hand, point her in the direction she should go, rather than follow her own heart.

Her pulse pounded in her ears and she tried to push the negative voices, the negative thoughts, down. But they only grew louder and louder until they were all she could hear.

She threw down her pencil and jumped up from the plastic deck chair. It nearly toppled over as she went to the railing with the sketchpad still clutched in her hand.

She felt the tiniest dip in her stomach as she recalled Zak's avoidance of her—and her questions. But then again, she was the one who'd done it to him. Made him afraid to get close. Afraid to actually *trust* her.

She sighed. She didn't know why she'd bothered. Besides, she had more important things to think about.

She sat down again and picked up her pencil.

Suddenly her phone buzzed. She looked at it. Zak's granddad? She grinned. She'd always liked him. They'd occasionally kept in touch. She answered the call.

ZAK KEPT HIS shoulders straight as he crossed the deck. They'd been out here the whole morning and found nothing. Some archaeologist he was.

His lips twisted into a wry smile. Now Maggie could see how close they were to not finding anything... He forced his thoughts away from that. From her.

He clenched his teeth. Maggie. He hadn't seen her since she'd refused his proposal. His hands fisted at his sides. The ding of an incoming text made him glance at his phone. *So how many gold bars can I tell the publisher you picked up on your dive? (Kidding, kidding! But I hope you have good news for me about the boat.)*

He rubbed the back of his neck. How was he going to tell his agent that he hadn't made any progress on finding the ship? That the last chapter still hadn't been written?

He glanced at his Hublot. Just about time to head to Dalvay to meet with Granddad. He texted his research assistant to make sure the dinghy would be brought back to the boat.

"Listen," he said as he found Maggie near the back of the boat, "I have somewhere to be. But feel free to spend the rest of the day out here if you like. Take notes, whatnot." He made an expansive gesture.

Maggie put her hands on her hips. "Notes on what? I'm researching Eleanor Webster, not nautical archaeology."

Zak shifted his weight. "I don't know much about her."

Maggie narrowed her eyes at him. "You could at least tell me what you *do* know instead of avoiding me."

"I'm not avoiding you. I'm trying to find a damn ship-wreck. Why do you want to know about this female pirate anyway?"

"She's going to be the inspiration for a new piece of jewelry I'm, uh," Maggie bit her lip, "supposed to be designing."

Zak glanced at his watch.

"Well, fine then," Maggie tapped her foot. "Go on and do...whatever you need to. I'll see if one of your colleagues is more forthcoming." She wheeled around and walked away.

Zak bit back a retort and headed to the dinghy. His research assistant helped him undo its moorings. He wasn't avoiding—He sighed. Okay. He *was* avoiding her. But how could he bring himself to admit he knew so little about Eleanor?

He shook his head and piloted the dinghy back to the pier. After he handed off the boat to his assistant to take back to the research vessel, he headed to his pickup and up the highway to Dalvay.

At the Dalvay estate, he made his way across the lush expanse of lawn. The big sandstone-and-timber Victorian home that sat on the property faced the Gulf of St. Lawrence.

Alexander MacDonald had built the huge house in 1897 on 120 acres and had named it Dalvay-by-the-Sea.

Zak chuckled. MacDonald had intended the place as a summer cottage. A plaque now designated MacDonald's home as a Canadian National Historic Site.

Dormer windows with graceful white-painted eaves dominated the roofline and English Tudor-style beams framed the gable ends. Clusters of tourists sat in the Adirondack chairs and wicker settees on the wide white-pillared verandah. Zak went around the back of the wide wrap-around porch.

A little way off, smaller cottages dotted the property. They'd been added in the 1950s when the MacDonald family couldn't afford to keep the estate and it had been converted into a resort.

Granddad liked to rent one of the small cottages during the summertime. He'd been doing that for years and this summer was no different.

"Hi Granddad."

"Zak, you made it!"

Sunshine streamed past the heavy wood girding. The older man, with once-jet-black hair now nearly silver, sat on a wicker chair with yellow chintz cushions. He wore cheap plastic reading glasses and a silk bowtie emblazoned with navy blue anchors.

"Good to see you." Zak hugged him then raised his eyebrows. "But what's with all the theatrics? And the bowtie?"

"A tribute to the occasion, son."

"You didn't lose your reading glasses again, did you?"

Zak's grandfather chuckled and adjusted his glasses. "Went to Shopper's Drug Mart and got myself a new pair this time." He glanced around and lowered his voice. "But seriously, Zak, you might want to sit down for this."

Zak threw his grandfather a rather speculative look and sat down in a matching wicker chair across from him. Zak opened his mouth, but Granddad raised a hand before he could speak. "Please. Just listen this time, okay? And if you could set aside your, shall we say... healthy skepticism, I'd appreciate it."

MAGGIE BREATHED A sigh of relief as she drove her rented sedan down the highway. It'd been a good idea to get off the boat—she'd left not long after Zak.

Zak's colleagues hadn't known too many details about Eleanor. They'd told her Eleanor had been mentioned in some travel journal Zak had. Aside from that, they'd all said to talk to Zak.

Zak's grandfather, on the other hand, had asked her to come up to see him this afternoon; after he'd heard what she was working on, he'd said he had something to tell her about Eleanor. What kind of information *would* he have about her? She felt a tingle of excitement.

She glanced at her folder full of supposedly-inspiring pictures—some ripped from magazines, some taken with her own Nikon—on the seat beside her and smiled.

It felt good to be back on the island. Something about the salt air revived her. No, restored her...soul.

ZAK SHIFTED IN the wicker chair.

His grandfather leaned forward. "I didn't think what I'm about to say was relevant to your work. But, well, I recently learned that ship you're looking for is called *Lady's Revenge*. Not only that, after talking with a certain young woman we both know, I've come to realize a few things and I hope that means you've come around."

"Granddad," Zak frowned, "you're not going to tell me that story again about—"

"My father and the original owner of this place? Yes, I am. Because you see, there are a few details I never shared."

"If you think I'm suddenly going to believe you and go off on some wild treasure hunt, then you can think again." Zak crossed his arms. "That's why I went into nautical archaeology. Science and facts, not here-say and pipe dreams."

"Oh, so nautical archaeologists don't have theories or speculations?" A twinkle gleamed in Ian's eyes. "Wreck diving seems an awful lot like treasure hunting to me. You *were* the assistant to the nautical archaeologist who found Captain Kidd's ship *Adventure Galley* three years ago."

"I was a PhD student back then." Zak's jaw tightened. "And that was based on years of research, time and effort."

"And treasure hunting isn't? Besides, aren't you, right now, looking for the shipwreck that's supposed to be the Ghost Ship of the Northumberland Strait?"

Zak gave a huff of irritation. "Treasure hunters aren't the same as archaeologists. If the treasure hunters aren't trained, they risk damaging the historical and cultural significance of a site, of an artifact. They're looking for gold, valuables. They want money, fame... Glory." A muscle in his jaw twitched. "I care about the history, the science, the stories of the people behind the objects and the sites. Treasure hunters—" Zak shook his head "—their emphasis is completely skewed." He crossed his arms and frowned.

Zak's grandfather set his jaw. "Listen, Zak, I didn't ask you here to debate viewpoints and perspectives. I asked you here to listen to me." He cleared his throat and his tone became somewhat stern. "Can you please do me the favor of that much?"

Zak tugged on his earlobe. "Yes, Granddad." He scuffed the toe of one shoe against the wide oak floorboards.

"Thank you." The older man reached into the breast pocket of his faded gingham shirt and pulled out a small white envelope folded and refolded so many times that its edges had creased and frayed.

He put it on the small table between the two chairs but kept his fingers on its edge.

"When my father, your great-grandfather, James P. Stuart, was a young man in his twenties, he worked for the man who built this place—Alexander MacDonald, once president of Standard Oil alongside John D. Rockefeller. Your great-grandfather became MacDonald's most trusted employee. Over the ten years Dad worked here at Dalvay,

MacDonald saw how much he loved the area, and they developed a great friendship—"

Zak drummed his fingers on the chair's arm. He'd heard this before too many times to count. "That's when you mention the part where Samuel Stuart wrote the Beale Papers, which supposedly." Zak made air quotes, "leads to some sort of vast treas—"

The older man shot Zak a piercing look. "Son, just hold on a minute longer will you?"

Zak inhaled then exhaled slowly. Nodded.

"One summer evening," Ian continued, "when Rockefeller came up to Dalvay to visit MacDonald, Dad overheard MacDonald tell Rockefeller about a letter in his possession written by the famous pirate Captain Kidd."

Zak stopped drumming his fingers.

"Unfortunately, the letter was only a fragment."

Zak leaned forward.

Ian went on. "Nicholas MacDonald, Alexander's great-grandfather, received that letter from Kidd when Kidd was in jail."

Zak's brows rose. "He did?"

"Before Kidd was executed in 1701 for piracy," Ian added.

"Really?"

"It turns out—" the older man cleared his throat again "—that Nicholas served aboard two ships. One, Captain Kidd's ship *Adventure Galley*. The other ship—" Zak's grandfather held Zak's gaze "—*Lady's Revenge*."

Despite himself, Zak drew in a sharp breath.

"So Alexander inherited that letter," the older man continued, "or what was left of it. But it ended up in my father's possession after Dad told Alexander of his own connection to the Beale Papers, through my grandfather, your great-great-grandfather, Samuel Stuart."

The older man tapped his fingers against the worn envelope. Picked it up. Carefully opened it. A small Ziploc bag lay in his palm. Two fragments were encased in the protective plastic.

The pieces were old. Zak cocked his head. *Really* old.

On the first fragment, which looked deliberately torn, was a faded, yet still discernible, signature.

Wm Kidd

Zak's eyes widened then darted to the other piece of the antique letter. The second segment was larger. Zak silently read the faded penmanship:

Newgate Prison London, England

20 May 1701 Nicholas MacDonald

My loyal Friend,

Your Aide is the last and only to which I now appeal. Neither Bellomont nor Harley believed nor heeded my requests for clemency and so I turn to you. 'Tis too late, I fear, for my own life to be spared, but I pray I may count on you to honor one last Request of mine.

I feel I owe Eleanor. As you are already in Eleanor's employ on Lady's Revenge, *I trust that you make way in the North Atlantic. Mayhap even toward that fair land the French call St. John's Island.*

If that is indeed the Case, though she is no longer under my command, I swore I would give Eleanor no more do—

Zak's eyes traced the torn edge. Another mention of *Lady's Revenge*? By Kidd himself? His pulse sped up but his frown deepened.

"Seems to me," Ian said, "this letter indicates Nicholas's deathbed confession about 'an island east of Boston' meant P.E.I."

"So this letter is why Dad thought he'd be able to find more of Kidd's treasure on P.E.I.," Zak said.

Ian sighed and nodded. "But the question is, Zak, what do *you* think about the letter?

Zak threw his granddad a look. "It seems like a lot of conjecture to me. I mean, Kidd doesn't directly *say* there's some sort of treasure. Kidd doesn't even know for sure that Nicholas was headed for St. John's Island—what's now P.E.I. But what would Eleanor have to do with all of that anyway?"

And yet...

Could this lead somewhere? Zak's heart began to race. But he clenched his jaw and shifted in his seat. Zak cocked his head. "Why are you telling me all this?"

"Because I want you to have it." Ian held out the plastic bag but Zak didn't take it. "I want to pass this piece of my legacy on to you before I kick the bucket. And I thought you'd appreciate it—heck, it might even help you—what with this very serious ghost ship research you're doing." He chuckled then punched some buttons on his cell phone.

He held out the bag again to Zak. "It's our legacy."

"It's not a legacy, Granddad. It's a hoax." He scuffed the toe of his shoe against the floorboards again. "Besides, this letter wasn't mentioned in anything published about the Beale Papers."

"Of course it wasn't." Ian wiggled his eyebrows. "They didn't know about it. You know what else they didn't know? That Samuel wrote the Beale Papers—anonymously—so that people wouldn't bust down his door looking for treasure."

Zak stood abruptly. "People—like our relatives—have searched unsuccessfully for years for Kidd's supposed treasure and have sunk millions of dollars into it." He shoved his hands into his pockets. "I'm sorry, Granddad. I love you but I have, as you say, this very serious shipwreck I'm looking for and a book to finish writing. I'm not getting involved in this."

"Well," the older man replied, "fifteen years, I'm sorry to see, hasn't changed your mind any. In fact," he rubbed his forehead, "it's only made things worse." He got up out of his chair too and walked over to the edge of the porch. "But I thought—" he beckoned to someone across the lawn "—at the very least, since Maggie told me she's doing research on Eleanor Webster, the two of you might want to look at the letter together."

MAGGIE LIFTED HER fingers in a half-wave at Ian and smiled—a genuine one. "Mr. Stuart! It's great to see you. I'm so glad you said you could help me out." She avoided looking at Zak and shifted her folder to her other arm.

"So, what do you have there?" Ian asked. "All your information about Eleanor?"

She laughed. "Oh! No, this is for my jewelry ideas and inspirations." She held up the folder.

"Good for you." The older man sat down again at the same time that Maggie walked up onto the porch.

Zak leaned stiffly against the porch railing as Maggie settled into the chair opposite Ian. She ignored Zak.

Ian glanced between Maggie and Zak. "You sure finding out more about Eleanor's the only reason for your visit to the island?" Ian gave Maggie a wink.

"Oh, well, I'm—" Maggie looked down and tugged at her skirt.

"She's spending some time on my boat doing research for some jewelry project she's working on." The deep, rich timbre of Zak's voice cut into Maggie's heart.

Maggie crossed her arms.

Zak shifted his weight and stared out across the lawn.

Maggie pulled out a pen and notepad from her purse. "So, what's this about Eleanor, Mr. Stuart?"

"Well, Maggie..." He drew in a deep breath. "I was trying to give Zak a family heirloom of sorts, but he isn't having it."

Maggie peered down at the plastic bag in Zak's grand-dad's weathered hands.

"Don't go getting her involved in this," Zak said and crossed his arms too. "She'll just use it against us later."

"I'm not getting her involved," the older man said. "I'm only asking her if she wants to join us." He held up the plastic baggie and offered it to her.

"I told you *I* don't want to get involved." Zak said. "She shouldn't, either. Complete waste of time."

"What is?" Maggie repeated as she took the Ziploc bag.

"No, don't—" Zak began.

"—A fragment of a letter from Captain Kidd." The older man threw an impatient look at his grandson. "Involving some lost treasure on P.E.I. that our family's been searching for, and a woman named Eleanor."

"Really?" Maggie's eyes widened as she read the fragment. What did Kidd owe Eleanor? And how had she ended up on or near P.E.I.?

"Wow!" She looked up at Ian after she'd finished reading. "This is...an amazing piece of information." She jotted down some notes. "Thank you, Mr. Stuart, for showing me."

She darted a glance at Zak and fiddled with the folder in her lap. One of the glossy pictures slipped out and onto the floor.

As Maggie leaned down to pick up the fallen photo, Ian eyed the picture—an emerald-studded cuff. "Emeralds..." Ian looked intrigued. "Like the Pendant of the Pure Hearted. Another missing Island treasure." He chuckled. "Never know, it might even be part of Kidd's haul."

Zak tsked. "That's just another ridiculous Island legend. There is no pendant, just like there's no treasure."

"And no ghost ship?" Ian raised his eyebrows at Zak and continued. "The pendant's said to be a large emerald. It's also supposed to tell the wearer whether the love they have for someone is true and lasting. Pure hearted, shall we say."

"Well," Mr. Stuart added, "I've never read the story myself but I've heard there is an article about this particular gem somewhere in an early issue of *The Prince Edward Island Magazine*..."

"There is?" Maggie said. But the two men weren't listening to her.

"You know that's all made up, Granddad. They wrote those things in that magazine for entertainment. And—"

"How do you know unless you've read it, Zak?" Mr. Stuart retorted.

"Listen, Mr. Stuart," Maggie broke in. "I'd love to help. But this seems like it's between you and Zak." She bit her lip and stood up. "I'm sorry. I have a big deadline this week and I need to focus on that."

She pivoted on her heel and walked back the way she'd come.

As she slid behind the wheel of her rental car, guilt knotted in her stomach. She'd already done too much when she'd used the Stuart family story for her bracelet. She couldn't get involved with some treasure hunt. Especially not with Zak.

Maggie sighed. Zak wasn't being any help with her research about Eleanor. And while this letter fragment had shown her Eleanor was mentioned elsewhere, it wasn't exactly conclusive. It didn't give much in the way of additional information she needed about the pirate, either. So why was she even here on the island now? Maybe she should just go back to New York.

She put the key in the ignition and started the car.

No. She couldn't leave. She wouldn't give up that easily. There had to be more information out there somewhere about Eleanor. This letter fragment proved that, at least. But maybe she should put Eleanor aside, for awhile anyway, and look into other options? It wouldn't hurt anything.

Like that emerald? She didn't want to hop from one thing to the next but the gem sounded like it had a story behind it that might work really well for the second piece in the line. Hmmm. Maybe if she looked into that, it might turn up something? She tapped a finger against her chin.

Yes.

She put the car into drive. It would be a place to start.

Chapter Four

ZAK SIGHED AND rubbed his neck. He opened one of the windows in the living room then rested his head against the cool leather of the couch and squeezed his eyes shut.

He blew out a breath. Seeing Maggie today on the boat and then at Dalvay had been harder than he'd expected.

His cell phone dinged with a new text message. His gut churned but he ignored the phone. Zak hadn't replied to his agent's earlier text. So it was probably another prod from the guy about Zak's progress on the last chapter of this damn book.

His hands tightened into fists even as his mind wandered back to earlier in the day. The way that Maggie's dark brown hair blew across her forehead. The way his fingers had itched, for one tiny moment, to tuck her hair behind her ear. And the way she'd broken his heart.

He shook his head. He might as well do something useful like get things down on paper for this last chapter instead of wallowing in memories. Question was, what?

A light breeze blew in through the window as he put on his pair of white cotton gloves. He picked up Davies' journal and opened it at random. He frowned and set it down again, still open. His lips pursed. At the very least, he could do an outline of the research he'd done.

He returned his attention to the blinking cursor on his blank document screen. This final chapter wasn't going to write itself.

The breeze rustled the journal pages.

He fisted his hands into his hair. But where the hell was

he going to begin?

He glanced at Davies' journal again. A sudden wind gust caused a single page to turn over and reveal an earlier entry.

3 Jan 1698

Reached the Malabar Coast nigh three days ago.

I must confess, I have not seen more compelling a creature than Miss Eleanor Webster, now that I've come aboard Adventure Galley.

Though she avoids all my forays into discerning her home and origins, I cannot help but ruminate on such matters, as the rather hunted look in her eyes bespoke volumes to me during our chance encounter last eventide on the quarter-deck.

Though she did not hold her consul this day when she spoke to our captain, one William Kidd, of her need for procuring a new ship of her own—

But the entry ended there, thanks to seawater damage, and Zak could see, it had been hastily blotted, as if the writer had been interrupted in his task.

He stared at the last line: *...a new ship...* His mind raced back to the letter fragment: *As you are already under Eleanor's employ...*

"Of course," Zak muttered under his breath.

He should've paid attention to this entry in connection with his search for the ghost ship when he'd read the journal initially. He didn't like to miss details. He shifted his weight. But maybe he'd become so focused on *Lady's Revenge*, that he hadn't seen the value of Eleanor's personal story... Because this entry spelled out that Eleanor wanted her *own* ship. That ship must have been *Lady's Revenge*. Which meant that Eleanor wasn't just a crew member on *Lady's Revenge*. She was the captain. Kidd's letter fragment cross-referenced this perfectly.

He turned the page over. Hmm. This was that one that seemed oddly thick. He rubbed the paper between thumb and forefinger and lifted up the journal. But before he could

investigate further, his cell phone rang. He grabbed it up without glancing at the caller ID.

"Zak here."

For a second, there was no response. But then he heard the sound of a throat being cleared and a very familiar voice.

His heart sped up and his jaw clenched.

"Zak, please don't hang up on me. I know we've had some...opposing views in the past but—"

"How did you get my number, Maggie?" He fought to keep his voice calm.

"Your granddad was—"

"—Always too forgiving." Zak swore under his breath.

"Zak," Maggie said. Her voice sounded strained. Zak felt a twinge of guilt. Why was he acting like this? He took a centering breath. Forced his tone to be formal. Professionally distant. "I'm sorry. That was unfair. What can I help you with?"

"Well, I debated whether to call you, seeing as how we're, uh... But it kept niggling at me. I can't leave without at least trying to look into this as much as I can. Your colleagues said, in your research on the ship, you'd come across some travel journals with Eleanor Webster mentioned in them. They weren't able to tell me much. So. What do *you* know about her? And don't think about avoiding me this time."

Zak rubbed a hand across his jaw. He wasn't being fair to her. He winced. What would it hurt to share what he'd found about Eleanor? Eleanor wasn't his focus, after all; the ship was.

"In around 1701, she was apparently the love interest of a fur trader and explorer named Henry Davies. Before I found his journal at an estate sale up in Georgetown, the crew manifests of *Adventure Galley* were key to my making the connection between Eleanor and Kidd."

"Okay," Maggie said. "But I thought you didn't care about Eleanor."

Zak shoved his free hand in his pocket and bit back a

retort. Instead, he said. "Davies mentions in his journal that Eleanor talked to Kidd about a new ship for herself. That new ship? Was *Lady's Revenge*."

"Wow. What else?"

"Well," Zak added, unable to help the excited note that crept into his voice, "My original theory was that Eleanor, after she parted ways with Kidd, became a crew member on *Lady's Revenge*. I didn't think too much about her. But it turns out she was the captain." He didn't have to tell Maggie he'd *just* made that discovery.

"I could've told you that."

"Wait, what?"

"You never asked me what *I* knew about Eleanor."

Zak shifted his weight.

Maggie cleared her throat.

"No," Zak admitted at last, "I didn't." After a moment, he added, almost to himself, "I pretty much made educated guesses about things that could've used a little more education. Maybe if I hadn't done that, I wouldn't be up a creek now." He lowered his voice. Ashamed to admit it?

"That's tough," she said.

"Especially when you haven't finished the last chapter for a book that could be worth a five figure advance..."

"Oh?"

Zak shrugged. "I'm sure I'll get it done. I just need to find the damn wreck by the start of next month."

"Well, if you need any, uh, help..." She trailed off and then rushed on before he could say anything else. "By the way, you know anything more about the Pendant of the Pure Hearted?"

Zak crossed his arms. "I'm a serious nautical archaeologist. I don't do research on local legends."

Maggie snorted. "Right. How else would you find out about the ghost ship?"

A strained chuckle escaped Zak. "Always perceptive, Maggie." A long time ago, he'd liked that about her. The way she cut to the heart of the matter. Zak winced. Focus. Deep breaths. He could do this.

"I'm sorry." There. That was civil. Pleasant, even. "I don't know anything else about it. And I'd take Granddad's treasure story—along with his mention of that article in *The Prince Edward Island Magazine*—with a grain of salt."

MONDAY AT NOON, Maggie took the last bite of her deviled ham sandwich, brushed the crumbs off her denim capris then tossed the empty bag into the trashcan by the biography section in Charlottetown's Confederation Centre public library.

She rolled her shoulders. As she waited for the librarian to return, her mind wandered back to yesterday. The look in Zak's eyes as his granddad had talked about the treasure and the letter fragment. *Pendant of the Pure Hearted.* The words kept rolling through her mind. But she hadn't gotten hold of Mr. Stuart to ask him anything more about it.

Which is why she'd ended up here.

Maggie chewed her lip. She hadn't wanted to impose. He wasn't almost-family any more. She had no business asking him for anything. Even though when he'd called her on the boat, he'd insisted she take Zak's cell phone number, too... She twirled a lock of hair around her finger. For strictly professional purposes, of course. But Zak hadn't been much help about the pendant, either. She glanced at the clock. Ten minutes had gone by.

The elevator dinged at last.

A tall, thin man in his late sixties, with wire-rimmed glasses and a green-checked shirt, reappeared. He held a cloth-bound volume with frayed corners. A red sticker read *non-circulating* on the book's spine.

"So that pendant story appears in *The Prince Edward Island Magazine, Volume I.* These volumes—" he tapped the cover "—are great resources because they are collections of every article published from that magazine in the early days of Island life."

He paused. "What's more, no one really references these books. You can't check them out, either. Hardly anyone—including some of the younger staff members—knows the library has these volumes because they're so rarely requested. I'm pretty much the only one left on staff who knows." The reference librarian flipped through the age-spotted pages until he reached page 277. "Now, this pendant tale is one few Islanders know about but—"

Maggie's cell phone dinged. She ignored it.

"—it's one they should *all* know about. Because, well..." He handed her the book. "I'll let you read it yourself."

As Maggie took the book, a faint mustiness wafted to her. She glanced down at the reprinted article.

April 1848   A Missing Pendant   Vol. I, No. 1

It was well nigh some seventy-odd years ago that this happened. I myself was just a young lad no taller than my grand-pap's knee. But oh, I have a keen memory and a sharp mind. I still remember, clear as day, that cold winter night.

Grand-pap told the tale of himself being a young man no more than 21, and a sailor in the days when tall ships still ruled the seas.

"I solemnly swear this is the full and honest truth, now, lad," my grand-pap said to me. He looked at me with his clear blue eyes and the crackle of the flames in the hearth seemed to jump along with his words:

"See, I was a captain in the Royal Navy and had many strange happenings occur. When I served on a ship called The Patagonia in the year 1701, a huge storm blew up one evening out of a clear, star-filled sky. Off in the distance, as the rain lashed down, I could see an orange-ish glow. A shade of orange that strikes fear into the heart of every sailor. A fire ship. And 'twas heading straight for us.

So I get the idea to set up a sort of bucket brigade. As the flaming ship drew nearer—it came almost stem to stern with The Patagonia—I jumped aboard the flaming ship, buckets in hand, and began to douse the flames.

That's when I saw, through the billowing smoke, a tall silhouette. The figure wore a tricorn hat and a captain's jacket with brass buttons that gleamed in the moonlight despite the cloud cover. I nearly dropped the buckets.

I fumbled for the hilt of my sword. But the woman in the tricorn hat merely laughed. I could see, as the clouds parted for a moment, her sea-green eyes flash emerald in the starlight. She was the most beautiful woman I'd ever seen.

The flames danced and twisted around her. Her raven-dark hair was coiled into a tight braid that formed a crown around her head. And a jagged scar ran down her left cheek.

Though my lungs began to fill with the burning, acrid smoke, I managed to choke out, "Who are you?" The woman touched a necklace at her throat. Diamond and emerald rings flashed on her fingers as she did.

Finally, she spoke, in a whisper-soft voice that commanded my attention with its sweet chiming sound. "Though my eye color and manner in which I dress my hair give cause for others to call me an emerald queen, my name is Eleanor Webster. Do not try to save us, foolish man. We are in far graver danger than some leather buckets filled with seawater could ever douse."

I began to cough at that point, as the flames crackled even higher. "But," Eleanor said—her voice reached my ears despite the wind, waves and flames—"your heart is pure. For that, you shall be rewarded. Though you are not the first man who has been taken by my beauty."

I did not know what to answer. My eyes came to rest on the necklace around her throat. "Ah," she said, "You admire the piece? I met a wise woman—once a maharani—who gifted me the central pendant. She told of its power to discern true love. She saw within me what others did not, could not; that I had a pure heart. Here," she said, and raised her hands to the sparkling necklace at her throat. Her expression saddened as her fingers brushed the heart-shaped gap in the necklace.

"Take the remaining gem—I need it not. Though 'tis not the central pendant, may it still serve you as reminder: do not allow your course of true love to be thwarted, as I did. Perhaps you, then, shall not be forced to pay for your mistakes in such a manner thus."

She waved one hand at the flames while the other twisted the final gem from the necklace and handed it to me. "Do not forget," she called as the smoke closed in around her. Well, I wasted no time.

I leapt across the rail to my own ship and caught onto the yardarm just as billows of smoke obscured the strange, doomed vessel. And in the last moments before my feet touched The Patagonia's decking, I thought I heard her voice on the wind. "For I became more concerned about the trappings of love than with being with my dearest."

When I looked again, as I blinked against the sting of smoke and sea spray, I saw that the flaming ship had completely...disappeared. Yet somehow I still clutched the gem in my hand.

"And so, my dear boy," my grand-pap said to me, as he gazed into the dancing flames, "that is the tale of a missing pendant, a phantom ship and a pirate queen."

My mouth hung open, and as I looked up at him I recall that I said, "But Grand-pap, what happened to the queen? And the missing pendant?" But my grand-pap just shook his head. "Lad, if I knew that, I'd be a richer man than most. No one knows what happened to either. Not even I."

Maggie looked up from the aged pages, her eyes wide. So Eleanor was a ghost, just like her ship, *Lady's Revenge*. And at one point, she'd also had the pendant.

Maggie's heart pounded. This was... She scrambled for her notebook and a pen. Exactly the inspiration she needed. Hmmm. Eleanor seemed to like jewelry. She'd had the necklace. Did that mean maybe she'd had something to do with the antique bracelet, or at least, that coin on the bracelet, at one point, too?

But then she frowned. Glanced at the passage again. Why did part of the passage seem familiar?

She paused. Re-read it.

Right. That *Petticoats & Pistols* book. But that had only been a small section. A sort of modified excerpt, she realized. Surely they would've listed this in the bibliography?

The bibliography. She rubbed her temples.

In all the excitement, she'd completely forgotten to check the back of that book. Well, it didn't matter now. She'd found the original source. She grinned and took photos of the pages with her phone.

Then she gently closed the musty book and handed it back to the reference librarian. "That's quite the story." This would be the perfect jumping-off point for the story behind the second piece. "Can I make a photocopy of this?" She'd add the paper copy to her inspiration folder.

The librarian took the book from her. "I can do that for you here, actually." He ran the copier and then handed the still-warm pages to her. "Are you working on some research then?"

"Oh," Maggie answered. "Yes..." There had to be more about Eleanor here... "Do you know anything more about this pendant that's mentioned?"

The reference librarian adjusted his glasses. "In the thirty years I've been on staff here, that's the only reference to it that I've ever heard of." He frowned. "But let me make a call."

He punched some numbers on his desk phone. "Hi Beth, it's Jerry at the Confed Centre library. How are ya? Mmm-hmmm. Oh, did she now? That's great. Congratulations!"

Maggie tapped her foot.

"Listen, I have someone here asking about that pendant story in *The Prince Edward Island Magazine, Volume I*."

A pause. Then, "No, no. I didn't think so." He shook his

head. "Right. Thanks anyway."

Jerry hung up the phone and turned to Maggie. "I just called the public archives. Unfortunately, that's the only piece of information we have about the pendant. And they don't know anyone who might know anything else."

"Oh." Maggie tried to ignore the ping of disappointment in her stomach. "Well, thanks anyway."

"Sure. Glad to help," the reference librarian said, before he turned back to his computer.

Maggie pulled out her phone and scanned the message that had come in earlier. It was from Jia at the Courtney Jewelers. *How's the sketch coming? We're looking forward to seeing the preliminaries on Friday.*

Maggie's mouth went dry. Was she relying too much on waiting for inspiration to strike? No. No. This was legitimate research. This would give her what she needed in order to create the drawing.

She couldn't draw just anything. This was Courtney Jewelers. It had to be perfect.

ZAK'S PHONE RANG. He answered it without thinking.

"I just forwarded an article to you," Maggie said.

"Article?"

"That article your granddad mentioned."

"About what?"

"Do you want to help me find it?"

"Find what?"

"The pendant."

Zak fisted a hand in his hair. "Even if I believed it was real—which I don't—" he smiled despite himself "—I'm too busy."

"And," Maggie continued as if she hadn't heard him, "if we found it, I'd be willing to split the proceeds fifty-fifty."

"Right." Zak frowned. "I'm not a treasure hunter. The answer is no."

"But—"

He hung up. Then glanced at the text he hadn't looked at earlier. It was from his agent.

Just got out of a meeting with the publisher. Sorry, but they've changed their minds about buying the manuscript, Zak. No hard feelings? Remember, no contract was signed. It was only in talks, after all. Publishing's cutthroat—they can't wait around forever on an incomplete book. I could try to shop your nearly-complete manuscript around somewhere else but to be honest, I'm not sure it's worth my time. So we'll need to part ways.

Zak resisted the urge to punch something. Instead, he stood up and stalked out to the deck. He gripped the railing. Now what was he going to do about future funding?

He sighed and turned his attention to his phone.

Absently, he opened the photos he'd received from Maggie and read the pages. He knew exactly why he hadn't seen the story about the pendant before. And why he wouldn't have paid attention, if he had.

Because it was just another lost-treasure legend. With no basis in fact...

He exhaled. A pirate queen on a burning ship. He shook his head. A burning ship...that had vanished? And Eleanor? As he finished the passage, his pulse began to race. There was no way—

He re-read the date of the sighting. The year 1701?

He flipped back through his notebooks on the earliest phantom ship sightings. No. This one wasn't listed. Which meant, this was the very first sighting.

How had he missed this account in all the time he'd spent doing research? Probably because it had mainly to do with that supposed pendant.

He looked up from his notebooks. Maybe he could use some of *The Patagonia*'s logbooks—if any still existed—to pinpoint the location of the wreck?

He glanced down at the coffee table. Eyed the worn leather of Davies' travel journal.

Hmmm.

Davies had seen the real ship that became the legendary

phantom, too... So this piece in *The Prince Edward Island Magazine* was more proof that *Lady's Revenge*, which burned in 1701, was the Ghost Ship of the Northumberland Strait.

He drew in a sharp breath. Davies had mentioned Kidd, too. And Kidd had mentioned Eleanor. Not that he was going to believe Granddad's treasure stories, but...

He tapped a finger against his chin.

Could he help Maggie look for this supposed pendant? Would that help him to find the wreck?

But if he did help Maggie, he might, at the very least, gather more evidence about the ship, since the pendant was connected to Eleanor. And Eleanor was connected to *Lady's Revenge*. And in the best case, he could uncover the wreck.

Which would prove completely that the ghost ship was real. If he did that, he could finish the book. Sell it to some other publisher, even? Gain back that wider exposure and funding he was looking for.

Because if one had been interested, that surely meant another would be, agent or no agent. Hell, he might even publish it himself.

Yes.

Helping out Maggie—and perhaps indirectly, his grandfather—was the answer he was looking for, after all.

TUESDAY MORNING, MAGGIE sat at the back of the boat with her hands in the pockets of her white shorts as she looked to the horizon.

She couldn't help but remember the way the glow of firelight had danced over Zak's bare chest as they'd come out to Bay Fortune on his boat one August night...

A splash and the sound of climbing pulled Maggie's thoughts to the present.

"Find anything?" one of the assistants called as Zak climbed aboard. His dry suit dripped water onto the white deck.

Maggie's breath hitched as Zak's fingers moved to the diagonal zipper pull on the front of the suit.

But she couldn't look away as he tugged the zipper downward.

The slow slide of the zipper brought to mind the taste of chocolate and marshmallow as they'd kissed on that sand bar. Ate so many s'mores by the driftwood fire that their hands were covered in sticky marshmallow...

Zak stepped out of the neoprene dry suit.

Heat rose to Maggie's cheeks.

Oh, those kisses... her eyes fluttered closed. The tenderness beneath each touch. The soft promise of care, of *love*, behind each—

"Maggie, look."

Her eyes flew open. Found Zak's hazel gaze regarded her with curiosity.

She hastily sat more upright. But instantly regretted it. Because now she felt far too close to the strong lines of his chest outlined against the thin white polyester under-suit he had worn beneath the dry suit.

She swallowed. "Uh..." Wet her lips. Blinked. "Oh, what am I looking at?" Her gaze flicked over his chest, at the way his collarbone dipped in at the base of his throat where his pulse beat. At the way his shirt perfectly set off his slight tan.

Zak held out a tiny misshapen object encrusted in barnacles and silt. As he leaned toward her, she inhaled the scent of fresh laundry and saltwater that clung to him.

"Musket ball from the 17th century," he said. Grinned. And the flash of excitement, joy and...something else... in his eyes, tugged at her.

Reminded her how carefree he'd been when they'd been growing up together. The way the wind buffeted his hair as he stood at the helm of his sailboat, a boyish grin on his face.

The way he'd always given her the first slice of lemon cake he baked even though it was his favorite flavor.

Or the way he'd share an idea with her, then lean back

and close his eyes so he could shut out all other distractions in order to take the time to listen—really listen—to her response.

She always could share openly with him. A lump rose in her throat as she studied the flecks of gold combined with the moss-green in his hazel eyes. Wished she could do something, say something that would bring it all back.

Bring *him* back to her.

Her breath hitched again and she swallowed hard.

This wasn't the past. This was now.

"What, uh, does that mean? How does a single musket ball signify finding *Lady's Revenge*?"

"It doesn't, in and of itself. But it does mean there just might be a debris trail, which could lead us straight to the ship. We find more artifacts like this, we just might be one step closer to finding the wreck." Zak grinned at her. "Join me tonight for a bit of a celebratory meal?"

THE PINKS, PURPLES and golds of sunset glinted on the water just visible from the table at Sheltered Harbour Cafe. Zak fidgeted with the band of his Hublot and finished the last of his fresh-caught clams. Was he actually going to admit to Maggie that he'd decided to help her out?

He rolled up the sleeves of his dark green polished cotton dress shirt then pushed aside his plate and glanced across the table at her. Yes. It would help out both of them. It was the logical thing to do. Her chocolate-brown hair framed her face and set off the lavender scoop-neck lace-edged sundress she wore.

He forced himself to look away, the sight not just filling him with a tug of attraction but also with a morsel of...regret that had somehow pushed aside his anger.

He took a sip of his lemonade. "Tide's out. Evenings like this are perfect for digging clams," he said, almost to himself.

"Remember the time we went to Tea Hill beach and that

group of tourists thought we were an actual clam digging company?"

Zak allowed himself a smile. "I think it was because of the logo on my T-shirt."

"Or that brand new shovel I had." Maggie smiled too.

Zak held Maggie's gaze.

"Oh!" Maggie said, "remember that story your half-crazy uncle told us our second year of high school?"

Zak nodded. "About the cache of pearls that went down on the *Molly Mae* in 1769, the year after Charlottetown was founded. We spent that entire summer with a metal detector and a shovel digging on practically every beach along the South Shore."

Maggie laughed. "We really didn't know what we were doing, did we?"

Zak joined in, and shook his head. "We didn't. And we weren't even dating then. We were—"

"—Just friends." Maggie finished for him.

He met Maggie's eyes and felt his heart lurch. That gleam of joy was because of him. Well, at least, because of the happy memories they'd created together. "Funny," he murmured, "it doesn't seem that long ago."

"No," Maggie said softly, "it doesn't."

"But that was two years before Dad died," Zak added, almost to himself. "So." He cleared his throat. "I've come to a decision."

"Oh?"

He picked up his glass and ran a fingertip around its rim. "I, uh..."

Maggie cocked her head.

Zak shifted in his seat. "What I mean to say is that, well, there's—" He glanced away from Maggie then back to her. "I'm guessing that you're wanting to find out more about Eleanor, right?"

Maggie nodded. "I'm wanting to find out how Eleanor and the pendant are connected."

"And I'm wanting to know where the hell *Lady's Revenge* is now."

"Okay…" Maggie said.

Zak rubbed a hand across his jaw. "The pendant's tied to Eleanor. And Eleanor's tied to the wreck I'm looking for…so it makes sense for everyone if we join forces, I think."

Maggie gave an involuntary laugh. "Wait, what?"

"Just to be clear: I'm not treasure hunting, I'm uncovering evidence about the ship," he added quickly. "I was thinking that what we discover about Eleanor and the pendant will tell me more details about the fate of *Lady's Revenge,* and by extension, the ship's location now."

"This is a switch," Maggie studied him as she took a sip of her drink.

"Yeah, well…" Zak trailed off. "I read that article you sent me. It got me thinking."

Maggie looked down as she swirled the contents of her glass then glanced back up at him. "All right," she said. "It's a deal."

Zak nodded and leaned back in his seat. "We can meet at Granddad's cottage at Dalvay tomorrow mid-morning."

Suddenly, Maggie drew in a sharp breath. "If we find out what happened to the pendant—" her eyes widened and she leaned forward "—then we'll also find out what happened to Eleanor and the ship. It must all fit together somehow."

"Mmm," Zak tugged on his earlobe. "I don't know if that's one hundred percent accurate, exactly. We don't want to go jumping to conclusions, so we'll need to formulate some theories."

"Well…" Maggie tapped her fingernail against her chin. "in that letter, Kidd said he owed Eleanor. So maybe Kidd took the pendant from her, intended to give it back, but couldn't before he, er, died?"

"That's a possibility. I mean, Kidd was in India at one point."

A gleam came into Maggie's eyes. "Your granddad said there's lost treasure here on the island. Maybe since your ancestors were searching for it, they had something to do with all this, too?"

Zak frowned. "There's not a direct connection between

the treasure and our family—we were given the letter fragment. It wasn't in our family originally." Zak fiddled with his napkin. "We'll have to do some digging on all of this." The murmur of other diners mixed with the soft rustle of the breeze. "Speaking of," he added, after a moment, "have you dug any clams lately?"

Maggie glanced down at her plate then back up at Zak. She took a sip of her water and shook her head. As she did, a stray strand fell into her eyes. She brushed it away. "I haven't had time."

Was that a trace of sadness in her tone? She took the last few bites of her battered cod.

He leaned forward. "Why not?"

Maggie gave a half-laugh. "Too busy chasing success, I guess." Her hand froze on the water glass. "Wow. That blatant honesty just slipped out. Usually I'd say something that—" she bit her lip and met Zak's gaze "—would have you believing that everything was great and that I was totally fine."

She swirled the contents of the glass. "But maybe that's because we've known each other so long. It feels like I can be completely honest with you. At least, right now." She paused. "I can open up to you and," she whispered, "that's something that I've learned is really valuable... I've missed that."

She averted her gaze, her voice low. "Missed...this." She gestured to the open water, the colors glinting golden, the sea breeze and the sense of freedom. "Missed...us talking like this, you know?"

On impulse, Zak reached across the table and placed his hand on top of hers. He stroked the thin skin above her wrist with the pad of his thumb. Her eyes flutter closed.

"Oh Zak," she whispered.

His heart pounded. He imagined he could reach across the table and wrap his arms around her. She turned her palm up, so that their fingers now intertwined. A small smile flitted across his face in answer to hers. He wanted to keep her safe and tell her everything was going to be all right. Give her anything she'd ever want and—No.

Anger surged through him. What the hell was he doing?

She'd smashed his heart into a thousand pieces—twice. His stomach clenched. She'd only come back into his life by mistake. And he wasn't going to just mistakenly start to feel something for her again. He clenched his jaw. She'd made him too vulnerable before. She'd made a fool out of him, before. He wasn't going to be that stupid again.

He disentangled their clasped hands and then shoved back his chair. "I'll see you tomorrow."

Maggie's eyes flew open and a small frown line appeared between her brows. She opened her mouth, then closed it and set her jaw as she stood up too. "Right," she said in a clipped tone. "At your granddad's place."

MID-MORNING ON WEDNESDAY, Maggie pulled into the lot at Dalvay and got out. She crossed the lawn and headed for one of the cottages nestled amongst some pines.

Zak, in a pair of torn jeans and a tan T-shirt, leaned against one of the square white columns on the porch of the small bungalow.

Maggie took a deep breath and felt her heart stutter under her turquoise blouse. She was doing this for her jewelry line. For her customers. That was all.

As she walked up the porch steps, her wedge heels clicked on the wide wooden boards. She couldn't help but remember one long-ago summer morning when she'd climbed these steps. Her feet had been bare and dusted with red sand. Saltwater drops had clung to her skin...

She swallowed. Lifted her chin. This was a professional alliance. Nothing more.

"Let's get things straight." Zak's tone was distant. When he met Maggie's gaze, she couldn't help but flinch ever so slightly. Had his eyes always been that deep shade of hazel? That blend of gold and emerald?

She shook off the thought.

"This," he said, and crossed his arms, "is strictly professional. Our past history has no bearing on this. And we work together as a team. Equally."

"Of course," Maggie said as she came to a stop in front of him. "I wouldn't expect anything less."

"Oh, good, Maggie, you're here." Ian Stuart's voice floated to them. The screen door squeaked as he opened it and gestured for them to come inside.

"Make yourselves comfortable," Mr. Stuart said, as he glanced at the clock on the wall and then turned to a serving plate on a nearby table.

Maggie crossed into the house. The scent of fresh-baked banana bread wafted to her. She smiled. The last time she'd tasted that was—Her lips compressed into a thin line.

She had to get this over with. Find the pendant. Use it for inspiration. Get back to New York. She had no time for nostalgia. And no time to be affected by Zak Stuart.

She sure as hell wasn't going to stick around long enough to do anything crazy—like develop feelings for him again...

She followed Zak into the living room and sat down on the love seat. A red-and-white granny-square afghan was thrown across the back. He sank onto the matching couch across from her.

She eyed him for a second. "So." She rummaged around in her purse. "After dinner last night, I remembered something I'd found that might help us."

Zak raised his eyebrows. "I'm listening."

Her fingers closed around smooth plastic. She drew out the dry, cracked leather pouch, now in a clear protective sleeve. "This," she said as she placed it on the glass-topped coffee table, "is the—"

"—Original leather pouch that came with that gold coin," Mr. Stuart said. "Piece of banana bread?" He offered a plate of the fragrant treat in Maggie's direction.

She took a slice and then a big bite. She carefully wiped her fingers and then slid her hands into a pair of cotton preservation gloves afterward.

"Delicious. Thank you," Maggie said.

Mr. Stuart grinned. He offered Zak a piece then looked up at the clock again. "Well, it's about time for my daily walk—gotta get some fresh air. But you two stay here as long as you like. I'll be back in a bit."

"Sure, Granddad," Zak said.

"Thanks, Mr. Stuart," Maggie added. The screen door creaked as he left. Maggie continued, "There was something written on the inside. I feel like it might have to do with Eleanor and our research." She turned the bag over so that the faded writing was displayed:

> *Emerald queen of the North Atlantic deep.*
> *Jewelled heart of stone that does not sleep.*
> *An earl, a Speaker; a Captain's unheard plea;*
> *Twenty-three cryptic pages,*
> *Nearly All lost to a treasure's ravages.*

"Hmm." Zak jumped up and strode to the window that overlooked the Gulf of St. Lawrence.

"See any connections?" Maggie said.

"Well, it's a riddle of some sort."

Maggie nodded. "I figured that part."

"Okay." Zak rubbed his jaw. "As far as connections, we break things down piece by piece. That's how we do it in the field."

"That makes sense. So the first line..."

"Emerald queen—we know that's Eleanor Webster," Zak said. His gaze slid to Maggie's.

"Right." Maggie grinned at him. "That article in *The Prince Edward Island Magazine* confirms it."

Zak dropped his eyes to the verse and scanned the first line again. "We've also got a place—the North Atlantic."

"The North Atlantic," Maggie muttered under her breath.

"Mmm," Zak said. "Lots of battles. Lots of shipwrecks. Lots of pirates and privateers marauding along the coast..."

Maggie straightened suddenly. "Of course. In the letter

fragment, Kidd mentioned that *Lady's Revenge* was sailing in the North Atlantic."

"Eleanor's ship." Zak swallowed then shook his head.

"It's a lot to take in, isn't it?" Maggie said softly.

Zak tugged at his earlobe. "Yeah." He cleared his throat. "What about the next line? *Jewelled heart of stone that does not sleep*? It could mean figuratively..."

"No. I don't think so," Maggie said. "It means literally. A piece of jewelry in the shape of a heart. Because again in the magazine piece, Eleanor herself referred to a missing pendant... *Her* pendant."

Zak shoved his hands in his pockets. "The Pendant of the Pure Hearted."

He flipped through a small notebook that he pulled out of his shirt pocket and scribbled some notes. "But the next line: an earl, a speaker, and a captain. That's pretty specific. What would that have to do with Eleanor and the pendant?"

"Hmmm," Maggie said, "And why is the word *speaker* capitalized?"

Zak tapped a finger against his chin. "They capitalized all sorts of things randomly back then."

"But these are three very specific people. Maybe the speaker was an important person?"

"You're right." Zak cocked his head. "Wait a minute." His eyes widened. "Not just an important person..." He stalked to the window again. "An earl... and a captain..."

Maggie followed him to the window.

Zak nodded to himself. "He was *the* speaker."

"What?"

"Yes." Zak said. "The Speaker of the House of Commons."

"House of Commons...over in Britain?"

"Yep."

"Okay. So the next one: *captain*," Maggie said. "Well, Eleanor was the captain of *Lady's Revenge*..."

"True," Zak said. "So maybe the plea has to do with the pendant?" He frowned and looked out the window again. The clock ticked. Maggie tapped her fingers on her leg.

"But the captain... *an unheard plea*... That's it." He snapped his fingers. "Granddad's letter fragments pointed to it. Shortly before Kidd was executed, he wrote a letter to the Speaker of the House of Commons in May of 1701. He basically pleaded for help. He also wrote a letter in April of 1700 to the Earl of Orford, and asked for his help, too. But both of them ignored his letters."

Maggie's eyes widened. "And then Kidd wrote that third letter. To uh, his crewman named Nicholas, right? Nicholas also served with Eleanor on her ship."

Zak swore under his breath. "Right."

They both stared in silence at the riddle for a moment.

Finally, Zak said, "What happened to this?" He nodded to the pouch that once held the bracelet.

"Uh," Maggie averted her gaze from his inquisitive glance. "I, uh...er, my cat wrecked it, actually." She bit her lip.

The screen door squeaked. Mr. Stuart must be back.

"So the unheard plea was from Captain Kidd to Nicholas... But what about the last part?" she went on hastily. "*Nearly All lost to a treasure's ravages...*What do you think it refers to?"

Ian poked his head around the corner. "Likely it's referring to that deathbed confession Nicholas gave," he interjected as he came into the room.

"Deathbed confession?" Maggie said.

Mr. Stuart went over to the coffee table and started to read the verse to himself.

"Well, not exactly." Zak glanced at his grandfather then said, "Yes, when Nicholas was dying, he talked about some treasure on "an island east of Boston." But let's not get carried away." He crossed his arms. "We're not looking for treasure, we're doing research."

"But you can't deny, Zak," Mr. Stuart fixed his grandson with a look, "that this pouch," he pointed a finger at it, "originally held the gold coin your great-great-grandfather Samuel received from John MacDonald, one of Thomas Jefferson Beale's treasure hunting partners."

"The gold coin that became part of the antique bracelet," Maggie whispered, as her eyes widened. "But who was John?" She turned to Zak.

"Mmm." Zak rubbed the back of his neck and murmured. "John MacDonald was Nicholas's grandson. And Nicholas was Kidd's crewman and then Eleanor's..."

"You don't like the fact that this could really *be* something, do you?" Maggie crossed her arms and fixed him with a level gaze.

Zak hunched his shoulders.

"I'm sorry," Maggie said. "That wasn't very professional."

Zak cleared his throat. "But we skipped a part." He turned his attention back to the riddle. "The first part of the last line: *Twenty-three cryptic pages...*"

"More specifics," Maggie murmured. "*Cryptic...*" She frowned. "That could mean mysterious. Or it could mean encoded. What would be twenty-three pages long *and* either mysterious or encoded?"

"I can think of one thing," Ian said. "The Beale Papers."

"Except," Zak said, "there were only three pages of the Beale Papers that were encrypted." He paused. "But those three encrypted pages are supposed to reveal a treasure buried in Virginia, not on Prince Edward Island." Zak glanced at Maggie. Did he remember that she could still recall the stories he'd once shared with her, beside crackling beach bonfire, about his family connection to the papers?

She nodded at him. "Right. The rest wasn't encrypted."

"Nope, it wasn't. It was written in plain English." Zak's gaze slid to Maggie's and she saw the approval in his eyes. She felt her cheeks flush.

Then Maggie gasped. "And the whole thing *was* twenty-three pages long."

"But remember: a part of the treasure buried in Virginia was, according to John, partially Kidd's. And they did mention there was more of it out there." Ian interjected.

"Down through the years," he added, "I've done a bit of

reading on Thomas Jefferson Beale. I'd always heard," he said, "that Beale was a Mason. So was your great-great grandfather, you know," Ian said and glanced at Zak with a note of pride in his voice.

Zak shifted his weight.

Ian cleared his throat. "Beale loved to create puzzles and encryptions. Like how he did with that innkeeper. So he must have written this riddle, too. Which means he probably made the pouch to conceal it, as well..."

"That makes sense," Maggie said.

"I bet Beale heard about Eleanor from John, since John probably listened to stories from his grandfather Nicholas." Zak added. He stood up and blew out a sharp breath. "Which means *Lady's Revenge*, the pendant and this possible supposed treasure *are* connected. So." Zak steepled his fingers and sat down on the couch. "In order to continue gathering evidence for our research, we need to look at—"

"—The Beale Papers," Maggie and Zak said in unison.

Gulls called outside the window, and the occasional car rumbled by on the road. "Well, let's go." Maggie said to Zak.

"I'd say you could look at the Beale Papers online right here," Ian said, "but with the riddle being that old, it'd be smart to look at the originals." He threw Zak a pointed glance. Zak shifted in his seat. Tugged at his earlobe.

Maggie watched Zak. "You know where the papers are?" She got up and began to walk to the door. "Let's go get them."

Zak stayed seated. Maggie's steps slowed. She glanced back at Zak with her brows lifted.

"The original Beale Papers are at Eddie's place now," Zak said.

Maggie winced. "Not your half-crazy uncle's?"

"Unfortunately, yes."

Chapter Five

ATER WEDNESDAY EVENING, Maggie sat at the desk in her
hotel room. Tried to ignore the blank sketchpad that sat
beside her.

Her phone buzzed and she glanced at it. Nicky had sent
a text: *Great news! The* Sun *just called. They were looking for
you. I told them you weren't available but they really wanted to
write up a piece about you and the new project, so I told them
all about it.*

Maggie chewed her lip as she texted back: *Good work!*
She didn't have to worry. This was about her new piece, not
the bracelet. That would help create some more publicity
for her brand and for the new piece when it came out. She
tapped the pencil idly against her chin. Just then, her phone
rang.

"Hi Maggie." Her stomach churned at the sound of Jia's
voice. "What do you have for us?"

"I..." She swallowed. She couldn't lie to Courtney Jewelers. "I'm still working on things," she said at last.

Jia laughed. "Not avoiding us, are you?"

"Of course not." Maggie said, too quickly.

"Good," Jia said. "Unfortunately, if you don't meet the
deadline, we're going to find someone else this time. We
need something by the start of the day Friday."

Maggie's palms began to sweat. "Yes, of course. I'll have
something right away."

"Great," Jia said, voice cheery. "We look forward to
reviewing it."

Maggie ended the call.

She took the pencil and closed her eyes. The pencil lead,

freshly sharpened, pressed against the page and seemed to cut into it. Deep. As if it were breaking in two. Breaking apart. Breaking into a million pieces.

Like a shattered heart. Perhaps that had been how Eleanor had felt when she'd lost the pendant.

Maggie sucked in a breath. Felt the hairs on the back of her neck stand up. All at once, her pencil began to move along the page. Slowly at first, but then gaining more speed as she gave in to her emotions.

All those days and nights spent alone after she'd left Zak. Too afraid to really face her own lies and the deeper truth within her heart when she looked at him, looked into his heart.

She felt a sob build in her chest but she didn't stifle it like she'd done so many times before.

Her pencil continued to move, almost of its own volition. She fed every tiny piece of herself and her jagged, pent-up feelings down through the pencil and out onto the page.

The lines blurred as she blinked.

Blurred and seemed to take on a new shape, a new form even as she continued to sketch.

At last, she put the pencil down and took a slow, deep breath. Her eyes closed and she sat still. Felt the rhythm of her heart rate begin to slow.

In. Out. She took another deep breath as she slowly opened her eyes and looked down at the page.

She blinked once. Twice. The image on the page came into focus.

Beautiful and tragic were the first words that came to mind as she gazed at it. As if the heart had only now begun to bleed for what was left behind. Just like Eleanor, in a way... What deeper tragedies had Eleanor experienced?

Maggie pursed her lips. This design was pretty much the exact opposite of the bracelet. But her customers would surely love it? She knew they'd love the romantic story of Eleanor that she'd begun to uncover.

Yes. This would be perfect. She took a picture of it with

her phone and then emailed it to Jia.

She sat back and slowly exhaled.

So was this it, then? She chewed her lip and her stomach dipped. Now that she'd completed her submission, she could just go home, back to Pierniki, to her apartment and...

But no. She hadn't found out all she could about Eleanor. And it'd been so satisfying, discovering the secrets behind the riddle. She couldn't stop now. She had to find out exactly how Eleanor and the pendant were connected. It would be more background for her jewelry line. Besides, as someone who had experienced a broken heart, Maggie felt, in a way, that she owed it to Eleanor to find out the rest of her story.

Not only that, Zak had said he wanted to help her. She couldn't just walk away—again. He needed her help. And she needed to help him.

So she'd stay.

THE NEXT MORNING, Zak shut the driver's door of his pickup as Maggie, in a pair of jeans and an aqua-colored T-shirt, climbed up into the cab beside him.

He merged onto the TransCanada highway and headed down east to Eddie's place.

He reached over to the dash to flick on the radio and his fingers collided with Maggie's. A jolt passed through him. "Old habits die hard?" But Maggie was a habit he couldn't quite break.

Why was he even thinking this? Was he trying to test his limits? Purposely make himself angry at her?

No, a small voice inside said, he was trying to push her away. Push away the old feelings he thought he'd buried. Push away any trace of vulnerability that might show in his eyes. He couldn't risk Maggie thinking she'd gotten to him.

Maggie glanced at him and smoothed down the non-existent wrinkles in her T-shirt. "Something like that. Looks like we both still can't stand silence in the car." She fiddled with the hem of her top. "Where's your uncle's, again?"

But the radio announcer came on before Zak could reply. "*The first of the monster storms hit the New England coast yesterday, which caused millions of dollars in damage. Crops in the area have been decimated. The storms are expected to hit hard as they work their way up the Eastern Seaboard toward Canada.*"

"Damn it," Zak said. His hands tightened on the wheel.

"Not good for your dives if the storms come up this far, is it?" Maggie said.

Zak shook his head. "Nope." He slid a glance toward Maggie. "I really thought I'd figure out the location of the wreck by now…" He felt something loosen in his chest. It felt good to unburden himself to her. No, not her specifically. Just another person. She was merely a listening ear. "I combed Davies' journal and rechecked all my calculations."

"Maybe you're thinking too hard," Maggie said.

"Maybe I am." He paused. Glanced at her. "But thanks to that article you found, I've looked up *The Patagonia's* logbooks. What was left of them. I *think* I've got some possible new coordinates to try out along the South Shore here. But if a storm hits like it's predicted to, it won't be safe to dive. Even if it was, sand and debris would get kicked up from the shifting currents and make it hard to see."

Zak pursed his lips. "I need to find it," he muttered as he shoved his free hand through his hair.

"I'm sure you'll think of something. You always have before."

"Well, thanks." Warmth curled through his chest. No. He clenched his jaw. She was just being nice. Just saying that. He swallowed. "We're almost there."

"Hopefully," Maggie added, "Eddie'll be having one of his good days."

The wind picked up as Zak pulled the truck onto a long rutted red-dirt driveway. He darted a glance at Maggie. But if she remembered another, similar dirt road they'd gone down that one summer evening, she didn't give any indication.

He shook off the thought and steered the Dodge around a sharp curve then came to a stop amid long grass and gnarled oak and maple trees. He got out.

But when Maggie's door slammed behind him, he paused mid-stride as a jolt of memory passed through him. That one summer evening, her passenger door had slammed just like that—He shook off the memory.

A dog barked.

He felt Maggie next to him as he started up the path that led to the small postwar house. Paint peeled from the narrow eaves. The porch roof sagged ever so slightly. That old lighthouse had been ramshackle like this, too, Zak couldn't help but recall.

Zak frowned at himself as he walked up the front steps and went into the enclosed sun porch. He noticed a shaft of sunlight that beamed through a smudged, dirty window. The dust motes danced on the sunbeam, just like they had inside the lighthouse on that summer evening...

Zak got out of his silver Honda. The early evening light spilled across the bright yellow of the canola field. Maggie slammed the passenger door behind him. The breeze carried the scent of fresh-cut hay.

She came to stand beside him as he looked up at the cherry-red trim around the windows and door of the three-story white clapboard lighthouse.

"So they actually put a road in to this place?" she asked.

Zak nodded. "A few years ago. Not much of a road, really. More like a rutted track. But it serves its purpose." He stared at her a minute.

"Thanks again for coming back to the island to help me and Mom and Dad with loading all their stuff into that U-Haul. I know you have so much to do now that you've finished your doctorate and got that job at Memorial."

"Hey, what are long-distance boyfriends for?" Zak teased, and kissed the top of her head. "Of course. I was happy to help, Maggie. You mean a lot to me."

She smiled at him but it faltered and she quickly averted her gaze. "They're really looking forward to retirement in warmer temperatures." She cleared her throat. "God, the last time we were out here was high school graduation night," she said as she threw a glance over her shoulder at him.

Zak studied her. "I remember." That night, she'd broken up with him. Said she'd decided to go to college in New York while he'd stayed here and gone to UPEI for his undergrad. But that was in the past. They'd started dating again, long-distance, a little more than year ago, while he finished up his PhD.

"Do they still call it the secret lighthouse?"

He nodded. Grinned. "And the door's still unlocked."

Maggie headed around the opposite side of the structure. The yellow blooms of canola brushed against her denim capris.

And all at once, he was far too aware of the swing of her hips as she climbed the two steps to the door. She pushed it open—its paint peeled, its weathered boards warped. A stark contrast to the bright new coat of paint on its octagonal sides.

The musty smell of dusty neglect hit him as she headed for the far corner behind the set of stairs.

Maggie reached a hand out and traced their initials inside a heart scrawled with Bic pen. A half-smile lifted her lips for a fraction of a second. "We were only together for our last year in high school weren't we? Seems like a hundred years ago." She swallowed, blinked back tears.

"I know," he said, so close his breath tickled her ear.

She tensed, as if she wanted to jump, pull away.

"Want to see if the view from the top's still the same?"

Maggie must have heard the knowing smile in his voice. She blushed. Turned away. "Sure."

Zak gestured to the stairs. "Ladies first." His gaze locked with hers.

She put a hand on the almost-vertical rail of the staircase. "If I fall, I know I'll have somewhere soft to land."

He raised his eyebrows.

She started to climb.

Flies droned amid dusty cobwebs at the window she passed. She stepped out onto the first story platform. The walls slanted slightly inward as she stood and waited for him to climb to her level.

She glanced up. Two more stories.

The next ladder was even steeper, and she gripped the handrail a bit more tightly as it wobbled under their combined weight. He saw her swallow but she kept climbing. They stepped out onto the final platform together.

Both of them stooped slightly as the walls narrowed even more on the third floor. The tiny space seemed airless, as if it floated on the tides of memory.

Zak looked out the small pane of glass.

Above their heads, the fixture for the heavy glass lighthouse beacon had rusted into place. The grate, which let the heat from the kerosene out, now let dusky twilight filter in over both of them.

"Think that'll hold us?" Zak gestured to a small crawlspace, open to the elements, that led to a railed walkway.

Without a second thought, Maggie dropped to her knees and crawled out onto the walkway. Then she straightened and leaned against the rail.

Zak joined her at the rail. Put one arm so that it rested deliberately casually against the rail. And the other...his heart jumped...was around her on the other side. When had that happened?

"Remember this?" he murmured, with his lips next to her ear. His breath stirred the dark strands around the nape of her neck and she shivered. He saw goose bumps rise on her bare arms. She swallowed. He remembered that evening all too well...

How the starlight had reflected in her eyes. The long mournful call of the foghorn. The warmth of her cotton shirt as she'd curled her fingers around his. How he'd wrapped his arms around her and pulled her close.

Memory and reality collided as Zak realized he had done the exact same thing again.

Maggie stared up at him, her lips parted, as he watched her.

The breeze ruffled his hair, still a shade too long. She reached up and smoothed a strand across his forehead.

She leaned into his warmth. As if she was letting it surround her.

His arms tightened around her waist.

"How can you be so sure?" she said, her lips inches from his. "About us now that we've gotten back together again?"

"Because, deep down, I always have been," he replied. He tucked a strand of wind-blown hair behind her ear. "And," he whispered, "I always will be."

Zak reached up and traced a finger along the outline of her lips. "Shhh," he said as she started to open her mouth to protest. "It's okay. I forgive you." He moved his caress to her cheek, and she licked her lips. Swallowed hard. "But I was so awful to you. I-I broke your heart. And now you're offering it up again to me on a silver platter?"

Zak chuckled. "I wouldn't say a silver platter exactly. More like a slightly scarred cutting board."

Maggie buried her face in his shirt and mumbled, "You know what I mean."

"Hey, there's nothing to forgive," Zak whispered. "Things happen. Time heals. Besides, we've been dating for over a year now. My heart has had plenty of time to decide that—"

"Don't do this," Maggie said, her voice sharp. "You can't just play the martyr and say everything's all right when it's not. You can't just throw your heart fully into this again and expect me to pick it up and put it on a shelf somewhere safe." Her jaw clenched. "How can you give yourself away so easily?"

Zak sighed and suddenly felt old. "When I was dating other people, I only thought about you. And I guess... I guess," he tucked his chin into his chest, and a strand of hair fell across his forehead again. "I want you to know that 'us' feels so real and true that I'm willing to give it my all." He captured her fingers in his. "Willing to go all in." Zak traced the veins on the back of Maggie's hand. "And maybe," he said, as he met her gaze, "it will all be worth it. Because I love you."

He dropped to one knee.

The bark and growl of a dog behind the screen door jerked Zak back to the present.

The dog growled again, low in its throat, and launched itself at the screen door. As the screen door burst open, Zak threw himself in front of Maggie.

Before the dog could lunge onto Zak, a deep voice boomed, "Carl!" The dog immediately stopped and turned back toward the voice.

Floorboards creaked. A rail-thin man in a bright orange baseball cap with grease spots stood in the shadow of the doorway. He held a 12-gauge shotgun.

"How the hell are ya, Zak? Gone and got yourself married, then, did ya?"

Maggie saw Zak shift his weight away from her. She took a deep breath to calm the flutter of her heart. He was just protecting her from danger. Anyone would've done the same in his position.

Zak cleared his throat. Rubbed at his elbow in a gesture she recognized as discomfort.

"God, no," she answered for him. "We're not married." But for a second, she remembered that one summer evening...

She looked at him, down on one knee, there in the golden evening light. Her heart squeezed and she felt like she might throw up.

"Will you marry me?" he asked.

She had to stop this. Had to stop it now before it got any worse. A knife of guilt and shame twisted in her gut. He'd been unfair to her when he'd asked her to stay on the island and go to college here instead of in New York. And now? They were in different places in their lives, in their careers. If she said yes, she'd be treating him unfairly. It wouldn't be fair to the marriage, either. It would be like they weren't even married if they weren't living in the same place...

Her chin trembled. She couldn't just walk away from her career in New York, not after she'd put so much time and effort into it. Sure, none of the jewelry companies were buying her designs, but that was bound to change. It had to. And she couldn't let him give up this great job opportunity at Memorial, either. His career was too important to him, too. They'd talked about that so many times...

She needed to set him free. She couldn't love him like this. He should be with someone else. Someone who had time to be with him, to live where he lived.

All her hesitation, all her hanging back, she couldn't ignore it any more. She had to follow her own heart and let him go. So they could be free to go in the directions they both needed to now.

"I know you've put your heart on the line here. I know you've opened up to me, let me in, shown me all your secret hiding places. And that's very sweet of you."

"Then say yes," he whispered. His eyes held hers.

She looked at him without blinking as she disentangled her fingers from his. She took a step back, her heart lighter but her shoulders tense as she studied his expression.

He swallowed and blinked rapidly.

"Don't cry," she whispered, "please don't cry. I just...I don't love you."

Zak crossed his arms.

"Why the hell not?" Eddie shoved the brim of his ball cap up with the shotgun barrel. "You're perfect for each other."

Zak shifted his weight. "I didn't realize you got a dog, Eddie."

The old man shrugged his thin shoulders. "Can never be too careful in these parts. Government cover-ups all over out here. Last week I saw a tube ship fly by—glowing red. Weird as hell. Hours later, a cluster of men in all-black suits show up at my door 'n tell me I've seen nothin' 'n can tell no one."

"But you just did," Zak said.

Eddie shrugged. "You're family, Zak. I know you won't say anything." He grinned, and Maggie saw a gold tooth flash.

"Well," Zak said, "we're not UFO hunting today."

"We're looking for some documents," Maggie added.

A gleam came into Eddie's eyes. "So you've finally decided to believe the tales, boy?"

Maggie answered for him again. "We're just..."

The old man burst into laughter. "Sure, tell yourselves whichever ya like." He leaned the shotgun against the doorframe, raised a stiff, arthritic hand, and gestured for them to come inside.

The scent of chocolate chip cookies wafted to Maggie. "Have a seat." Eddie waved a hand at a dusty green velvet Victorian settee. "Don't mind my filing system. You can move that." He nodded at Zak. "Just working on my memoir."

An old Remington typewriter balanced on one corner of the faded couch. A neatly typed page protruded from it.

Maggie leaned down and picked up an old empty Rice Krispies cereal box stuffed with more typed pages. She looked around for a place on the floor to set it, but only saw more boxes and piles of trinkets.

She carefully set down the cereal box. Zak swept off the thick layer of dust before he took a seat. The springs creaked under him. Maggie carefully sat beside him. The settee wobbled slightly.

Eddie reappeared with a plate of cookies. "I just bake for something to do. How many cookies do youse want?" He patted his round belly. "They came fresh from the oven."

"What's with your family and baking?" Maggie muttered around a mouthful of cookie.

Zak shrugged. He took a cookie.

Eddie took two and dunked them in his coffee. He sat down across from them on a weathered church pew.

Zak leaned forward, his tone serious. "Eddie, we need to look at the Beale Papers. It's kind of time sensitive."

Maggie couldn't help but smile. The faintest trace of Maritime accent had crept back into Zak's voice as he spoke to Eddie.

Eddie scratched his head. "'Fraid that's not possible."

"What do you mean?" Maggie's fingers gripped the soft velvet fabric.

"Sold 'em." Eddie propped his feet up on a small wooden chest about the size of a microwave. Its top was slightly rounded and it had wide bands of metal that ran vertically up the sides and across the top.

Maggie noticed its leather handles had partially been

eaten away by either mice or seawater. Or possibly both.

"You sold them?" Zak's eyes widened. "But those are part of our family history. Great-Great-Granddad wrote them."

"So now you decide to care?" Eddie's voice held no trace of bitterness, though. He sounded more amused than anything.

Zak said nothing.

"I needed the money," Eddie sighed. Gave Zak a side-long look. "Bank was gonna foreclose on my property here. You know how money gets tight on the island in winter. I didn't qualify for Employment Insurance last few years."

Maggie saw Zak's knuckles whiten as his hands tightened into fists at his sides. He stood abruptly.

Maggie followed suit. "Well, thanks for the cookies anyway, Eddie," she said.

"Any time, any time. You come by and visit again soon, will ya?"

"Sure," Zak called without looking back. Maggie saw the tension in his shoulders.

Zak was just about to the screen door when Eddie suddenly jumped up. The dog, who'd gone to sleep on the porch, snapped to attention and began to bark again.

"Carl!" Eddie shouted. The dog fell silent. "The Voynich manuscript. Sold a rare medieval copy of *that*. Made a pretty penny on it, too." He grinned. "Nope, nope."

Zak turned slowly around. Maggie took a deep steadying breath.

"Still got 'em..." A twinkle came into Eddie's eyes. "Just wanted to make sure you were serious about our family's heritage, Zak." He slapped Zak on the shoulder. "No hard feelings, eh?"

Zak muttered something under his breath that Maggie couldn't hear.

"So," Eddie continued, "they're around here...somewhere." He gestured to the living room, which was a maze of piled boxes, filing cabinets and enough furniture to stock an antique store.

Maggie's heart fell to her shoes.

The old man stared into space for a minute, his head cocked, a frown on his face. Suddenly he closed his eyes. Inhaled then exhaled slowly three times. "Now," he said to himself, "where would they be?" He passed a hand over his closed eyes.

"He does this every time he loses something," Zak whispered in Maggie's ear. "Says it helps him clear his mind and remember."

"Why," Maggie whispered, "does Eddie even *have* the Beale Papers? They should be in a museum."

Zak lips twitched. "Let's just say my dad lost a bet with Eddie years ago."

Maggie felt a shiver slide down her spine as Zak's warm breath caressed her cheek.

The minutes ticked by. The only sound was the occasional thump of the dog's tail and the sudden loud call of the cuckoo clock in the corner. Maggie jumped at the sound.

Eddie's eyes snapped open. "Of course," he muttered to himself. Then he grinned over at Zak and Maggie and tapped his temple. "Best filing system is up here."

He pointed a gnarled finger down at the floor in front of him. "The Beale Papers are right here. In my safest filing system to date." He chuckled and started to crouch down in front of the battered wooden box. But the old man suddenly stopped, an expression of pain on his face.

Zak rushed over. "Uncle Eddie," He placed a hand on Eddie's shoulder. "Here, let me do that. I know how your arthritis acts up."

Eddie sighed and lifted his eyes to Zak. "Mighty kind of ya, Zak—always were a good 'un." Zak helped Eddie to the more comfortable stuffed wingback near the couch. The old man nodded in the direction of the worn, beat-up box. Eddie chuckled. "No one would think of looking in that rust bucket."

"Where did you get it anyway, Eddie?" Maggie said.

"Funny thing, that." Eddie scratched the back of his neck. "Went out 'n bought myself a metal detector way back. Very first day I had it I was bound and determined to strike it rich." He paused. "Was on a beach near here no one goes to, low tide; sure enough, she started makin' a crackly noise and flashed all sorts of lights at me. I got my shovel out." He grinned and his gold tooth flashed.

"But I didn't hardly needed it, 'cause the top corner was pokin' just at the surface. Well, I cleared away the rest of the sand and uncovered this here chest. No gold inside—it was completely empty. But I kept it as a souvenir of my first find. Good for storing papers and that." He paused. "Did ya see the initials on the front?" He nodded at the rusted keyhole. "*J. F.* Also noticed somethin' odd with it. Scorch marks—you can still see 'em if you look." He shrugged. "Maybe someone tried to get rid of it. Threw it overboard. And it washed ashore."

Maggie's eyes widened. "Wow."

"Tell you what," Eddie said. "After you look in there, you can keep it. I've seen how you were eyeing it, Maggie. Well, take it. It's yours."

MAGGIE PEERED INSIDE the old sea chest. Scraps of watered silk, stained and ragged-edged, were piled on top of wallpaper samples, all thrown haphazardly into the shrunken wooden tray that acted as a shelf in the chest.

Maggie reached in and helped Zak remove the scraps of fabric and paper. But as they sifted through the material to the bottom, they found nothing.

Zak lifted the small wooden tray out and set it down on the floor.

A pile of yellowed newspapers lay underneath. Mustiness wafted to Maggie as she glanced at the date—1892.

Eddie grinned. "Had to have a place to stick 'em. Never know when you might need somethin'."

Maggie carefully lifted out the yellowed pages. Underneath there was a leather pouch about the size of a letter. Her breath caught.

Zak rummaged around in his jeans pocket and pulled out a pair of wrinkled white cotton gloves.

"Like a boy scout, aren't you?" Maggie couldn't help teasing him.

"Never hurts," Zak said, a glint in his eye that Maggie couldn't quite read.

"So," she said to cover up the swoop in her stomach, "let's have a look."

She watched Zak's long, strong fingers close around the old leather. He met Maggie's gaze. "Here," he said, his hazel eyes serious, "you open it."

Maggie's heart skipped a beat as he handed her the gloves.

She slipped them on then reached out and began to unwind the strap that wound around the leather pouch.

After the last of the binding fell away, a sheaf of neatly stacked, though yellowed and brittle, pages was revealed. Zak stood. So did Maggie. He strode over to the kitchen table and placed the leather pouch on the neatly pressed and spotless tablecloth.

Eddie followed behind.

Zak put the pages on the table.

"You know," Maggie said, "since the riddle said twenty-three cryptic pages, maybe it'd be useful to lay each page out side by side just so we can pick up on any patterns or anything."

"Good idea," Zak said. He put action to Maggie's words.

Maggie helped him. The faded ink and swooping, curled letters of each line made Maggie smile. She leaned forward to examine the text.

They scanned the first few pages in silence. "I don't see anything here—" Zak began.

"Wait a minute." Maggie cocked her head and narrowed her eyes. "What's that?"

"What?" Zak said.

Maggie pointed to the very first line. "That capital letter *T*." She tapped a finger on the page. "There's two lines..."

Zak frowned. "You're right," he said. "They both start

beside the *T*. It forms what basically looks like a greater-than sign beside the *T*."

T >

"That has to be what *cryptic* meant in the riddle." Maggie felt her heart speed up. Could this actually be real? The evidence, it seemed, was staring her right in the face.

"So," Zak said, "we have to look for more letters with marks somewhere around them..."

They scanned the rest of the page in silence. "I don't see anything else."

"Well, since it said twenty-three pages, maybe there's just one per page?"

"Good thinking," Zak said.

"But," Eddie interjected, "there are twenty-six letters in the alphabet."

"True," Zak said.

"Look," Maggie said. "There's another one. But it's not the first line and first capital letter. It varies. Whoever did this wanted to be as subtle as possible."

They searched each page. Maggie had pulled a pad of neon pink Post-Its from her purse and began to write down each letter they discovered.

After reaching twenty-three, she frowned. "The last page must have...three letters."

"You're right," Zak said. "Here's *X*."

"There's *Y*," Maggie pointed to a sentence a third of the way down.

"And there's *Z*," Eddie said, a note of triumph in his voice.

Maggie continued to jot down the letters on the sticky note. "Okay. Here's what I've found."

She showed Zak the pad.

He frowned. "That looks just like a jumble of strangely marked letters."

"Until," Maggie said, "you rearrange them." She took a clean sticky note and began rearranging the letters. "If my hunch is right about this, it'll form a grid."

"Still love codes and puzzles, looks like," Zak said, his voice low in her ear.

Maggie's breath caught. "I do the *New York Times* crossword every day. And," she managed, "the crypt-o-quote." She forced herself to meet his direct gaze.

"That's impressive," Zak said.

"Keeps my mind sharp," she replied.

"Now," she said, "judging from my rearrangement of letters, it looks like this is a pigpen cipher key." She held up the Post-It. "See?"

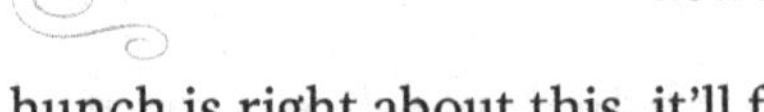

"A pigpen what?" Zak's brows furrowed.

"The pigpen cipher was used by the Masons to encode their documents," Maggie explained. "Also known as the Masonic cipher or tic-tac-toe cipher. It's a simple substitution cipher."

"Okay," Zak said. He tapped his fingers against the tabletop. "So... this cipher key must have been written by my great-great grandfather, since he's the one who wrote the Beale Papers." He chuckled and glanced at Eddie. "Beale must have sworn Samuel to secrecy, because I never heard anything about this pigpen cipher key from any of my relatives. Did you?"

Eddie shook his head.

Maggie's eyes widened. "Ian did say they were both Masons, so Beale and Samuel must've made some sort of secret agreement about the whole thing." She waved a hand at the Post-It. "The grid exchanges letters for symbols. Take away these letters here—" she tapped a finger on the neon pink sticky note "—and you have just the symbols." She drew lines on another Post-It. "For example, the symbol for *T* would be that greater-than sign. *C* uses two lines like a right angle for its symbol. *Q* uses a square without a bottom and a dot at the top for its symbol, and so on. Like this."

$$\llcorner C \quad \boxed{\dot{Q}}$$

"So." Maggie took a breath. "Since these grids include letters, not just the symbols with lines and dots, this is a pigpen cipher key."

"A key to what?" Zak frowned and looked out the window.

"A secret message written in some other document," Maggie said.

"I can't resist—" Zak said, as he met her gaze.

Maggie's pulse thudded. For a second, she imagined he was going to say "you."

"—asking why it's called a pigpen cipher?" Zak's lips quirked upward.

Maggie fought a nudge of disappointment in her stomach then grinned back at him. "The lines look a bit like pens. And the dots could be pigs."

They shared a laugh.

"So." Zak cleared his throat. He got up and headed to the window. Scraped a hand across his stubble. "We need to figure out which document this is referring to."

"Well," Maggie said, "based on the riddle, the document, or documents, must have something to do with either Kidd or Eleanor."

The cuckoo clock chimed in the living room.

"Wait a second." Zak shoved his hands into his pockets then pulled them out again and ran a hand through his hair. *"An earl, a Speaker; a Captain's unheard plea..."*

Maggie raised her eyebrows. "What are you not saying?"

"Captain Kidd's *unheard plea*," Zak said. "His letters to the Speaker of the House of Commons and the Earl of

Orford—I have scans of the originals."

"Then what are we waiting for?" Maggie neatly stacked the Beale Papers, along with the other odds and ends that had been in the chest, and handed them to Eddie. "Thank you so much. This chest is great, and your help has been, too," she said, as she picked up the chest and then turned to Zak. "We have to take a look at those letters."

Chapter Six

"KIDD'S LETTERS SHOULD be in here somewhere," Zak said, more for something to say—and to hide his awareness of Maggie—than because he needed to explain.

"Right," Maggie said.

Zak slid a key into the lock in the drawer of a gray metal desk. He tensed, careful to avoid bumping into Maggie, who stood less than a foot away. As he pulled open the drawer, birds chirped outside the half-open living room window of his rented house.

His heart ached as he looked at her face in profile. Her brow was smooth, and she stared out the window at the calm water of the bay. She seemed so unconcerned.

His jaw clenched.

Despite that, he handled each document and artifact gently. His breath caught in his throat as he sensed Maggie's eyes on him.

"I got scans of these when I went to the Historical Manuscripts Commission over in England," Zak said. "They keep pretty much everything." He chuckled even though it wasn't really a joke. Why was he rambling? He mentally shook his head. "After I helped find that wreck of Kidd's, it's amazing who wants to give you grant money for other, similar projects."

"Right," Maggie said again.

What was he doing? Trying to impress her? Of course not. "Okay," he said, "they're in here."

He pulled out a red file folder and opened it. "Yep. Right on top." He picked up the two sheets. "Kidd was pretty desperate when he wrote these, you know. Edward Russell, the Earl of Orford, who was basically his boss, wasn't known for being a nice person." Zak glanced at Maggie. "Kidd wrote the second letter three days after he was sentenced to death."

Maggie leaned toward him. She still used that honeysuckle-and-vanilla body lotion? He'd gotten her that for Christmas one year—He cleared his throat. "If you read the last lines on the second letter, Kidd's basically warning other seamen to be wary of people in authority."

"Good advice," Maggie said as she glanced at Zak then down at the folder. "So let's take a look at both of these side by side." She picked up the letters and placed them on the desk top, seemingly unaware of her affect on him. "To further confuse people, this pigpen cipher may be arranged across both letters, since it's an easy cipher to break if you have the key."

"If it's so easy, why did they use it?"

Maggie shrugged. "Human nature. Even though this was done something like three hundred years ago, some things don't change. They wanted something quick and easy. Probably wanted to spend more time digging up gold bars on the beach than deciphering complex clues."

Zak nodded. He picked up the first letter and began to read it.

"I say that, but..." Maggie frowned. "It looks like there's nothing actually written on here."

"These *are* scans of the originals. If it's on here, we'll find it." Zak's tone was more fierce than he intended.

"Hmm." Maggie set down the letter she was studying. She tapped a fingernail against the paper. The bare bulb overhead swayed gently back and forth in the light breeze from the opened window.

He tried to ignore the way the wind flirted with strands of her hair that brushed against her skin and... He couldn't afford to daydream or romanticize her or his old feelings for her. It had led to nothing but heartache. And would lead to the same again. He forced his eyes back to the page. "What about this?" He pointed to the second letter, which was dated 1701. "There's ink spots and quill pen drag marks down at the bottom here."

"Mmm." Her brow furrowed in concentration as she studied the piece of paper. Her head jerked up suddenly. "What if I was wrong?" she whispered and looked straight at him.

"Come on, Maggie. Don't doubt yourself like that. I know that ninety-nine times out of one hundred, you're usually right—" he winced. "Sorry, I didn't mean—"

"It's okay." She waved a hand in his direction. "We have more important things to fight about now than that." The corners of her lips quirked upward.

His own mouth lifted in response.

They looked at each other. Seconds ticked by. One minute. Two. Zak felt himself hold his breath. Then exhale. Shook his head. He didn't have time for this.

He returned his attention to the letter.

MAGGIE LEANED CLOSER to Zak and traced a fingertip along the markings underneath some of the sentences and paragraphs of the second letter. "Ink spots," she murmured. "No, those aren't ink spots." She cocked her head. "They look more deliberate than that...Yes. *That's* the pigpen cipher." She scrambled for the tablet of paper nearby then picked up her pen. "They've disguised the cipher around ink spots to confuse the casual observer."

"So what are we looking for?" Zak asked.

Maggie made a few quick strokes on the tablet of paper then held it up for him. "Anything that might resemble these kinds of markings."

<   ^   >

"You remember," she continued, "what the pigpen cipher key looks like, right? So we want as many of those same type of markings as possible. Some of the marks will have dots beside or around them, too. Although they're gonna look less distinct than what I've done with a ballpoint pen. Here," she said, "check the other letter."

Zak took the scanned page from her and began to skim it. "There aren't any on here." He looked over the page again. "Definitely nothing."

Maggie didn't reply. She continued to jot down the marks, dots and lines from the second letter until the entire page of the yellow legal pad was covered.

Just as Zak was about to open his mouth to comment, Maggie looked up. "Now we apply the key and figure out what this is."

Her cheeks were flushed and her eyes sparkled.

"Right," he managed. He studied the page. Despite himself, answering excitement washed through him. This could be leading to something...big.

He felt the heat of her nearness and imagined it felt very much like the heat of his own blood.

And the sparkle in her eye must have matched a sparkle in his own because she grinned at him like she could read his thoughts.

"The key." He cleared his throat and pulled it out of the file marked *Bay Fortune.*

He picked up a pen and began to help her to decipher the marks. Minutes ticked by in silence until he said, "I think I have something." He began to read. *"Lines of love/Locked in—"*

Maggie's voice sounded soft in his ear as she picked up the rest of the phrase. *"—a prison of glass/Where—"* She stopped reading. "That can't be the whole message," she said as she picked up the letters and checked them thoroughly again. "But there is nothing more here."

She chewed on her lip, glanced at Zak and then looked away. Was that disappointment in her eyes?

"Well," he said, "we need to figure out what this part of the riddle means."

"Maybe then we'll know where to look for the rest? And then be able to figure out where Eleanor's pendant is."

"And the ship." Zak cleared his throat. "So. *Lines of love.*" He cocked his head.

Maggie twirled a strand of hair around her finger. "It was back in the days of sailing ships. Maybe lines means ropes?"

"That doesn't make any sense."

"No, you're right. It doesn't," Maggie said.

"Okay, so what else could lines be referring to?"

"Well, lines are usually straight. Narrow." Maggie chewed on the strand of her hair. "Parallel to each other..."

"But then there's the 'of love' part. So I don't think we're talking about literal lines."

"But this is a riddle," Maggie countered.

"Written by pirates," Zak replied.

"True."

"What do lines and love have to do with each other?" Zak's brow furrowed.

"Well, there's always Shakespeare."

Zak arched a brow.

Maggie grinned. "I miss this," she said all at once.

The smile slipped off Zak's face. "I know," he replied.

Maggie tucked a stray strand of her hair behind her ear and ducked her head.

"*Lines of love,*" he muttered.

"Lines, dots, dashes." Maggie said. "Wait a minute. What do you make lines with?"

"Rulers? Pencils...?"

"Pens," Maggie said, her voice triumphant. "In this case, quill pens. *Lines of love...*I think..."

Zak met Maggie's gaze. "A love letter. That's what this means."

"Okay." Maggie looked out the window. "A love letter *locked in a prison of glass.*"

"Seems to me a glass prison would be pretty easy to break out of," Zak said.

She frowned. "Yes, but this is a piece of paper—we're assuming—so someone put it somewhere."

"Inside something, maybe, where it couldn't get out."

"Or couldn't be gotten out of," Maggie countered.

"So," Zak said, and joined her by the window, "Where are places you can't get in to or out of easily?"

"Jail," Maggie said.

"A prison," Zak murmured. "What else could be a prison?"

"A glass prison..." Maggie said. "Someone put it somewhere..."

"Like in a jar," Zak said.

"Or a bottle." Maggie stopped and stared at him. "That's it. A bottle. A glass bottle. The love letter is inside a bottle."

"Which makes perfect sense, given the time period and the people," Zak said. "The question is, where?"

"Well," Maggie said, "if the first part of the riddle was in *these* letters, then it stands to reason the other part might be in something else that Kidd wrote?"

"That'd be a logical place to start," Zak said, "and if we follow that line of reasoning, we should take a look at that fragmentary third letter."

"Your granddad still has it?" Maggie asked.

Zak nodded. "I left it with him at his cottage."

"Okay," Maggie said. "Let's go look at it."

Zak glanced at his watch. "Let's meet up there tomorrow. I need to check in with my team on their progress and put in some hours on the boat for the remainder of today."

"Right," Maggie said, "tomorrow it is."

THE NEXT MORNING, after Maggie took a shower, she headed to her suitcase on top of the bureau and pulled out a butter-yellow top. But where were her white capris? She glanced at the sea chest, which she'd placed beside her suitcase last night after they'd gotten back from Eddie's. Surely she hadn't put her capris underneath the chest by accident?

She reached out to pick it up and check, just in case. But age and mice had eaten away at the leather handles, and as she moved the chest, they gave way. The chest fell onto the floor with a thud and hit hard on one of the corners, which caused the lid to snap off at the hinges. Maggie looked down at it. Crap.

She crouched down and stared hard at the lining's red pinstripe pattern. She cocked her head. It seemed at odds with the heavy square-headed nails that held the half-rotted box together.

She shook her head. Eddie certainly had an eye for oddities. She touched the lining. The material felt rough, uneven. As if someone hadn't attached it correctly. She frowned as she brushed her fingers along the underside of the lid, near some burn marks. The lining wasn't flush against the top of the lid—as if it concealed a small hiding place.

Very slowly, she peeled away the faded lining. Her fingers encountered...ribbon? And a thick folded page. She slowly pulled the sheet of paper out and undid the bow. The ribbon fell away from her fingertips. She picked up the sheet. No name was written on the folded page. A shiver went through her. She flipped the folded page over and ran a finger across the faded red wax before she gently broke the seal and unfolded the paper.

Coastal waters of Spanish St. Augustine
1 June 1700   Henry Davies

Dearest Henry,

Oh, how my heart beats with gladness at receiving Word that your year-long trek West has successfully begun, as it means your travels come to a close in June next. And that you shall, within six weeks after your journey, return to St. John's Island along the shores of that glorious Bay. I count nigh every moment until we are surely reunited as we have planned.

You may recall what I had written you some months ago. Those who would have me burned as a witch may quiver in fear and small-mindedness; nonetheless, what I have foreseen has come to pass.

I tried to give Kidd aide, as he had so assisted me, yet I fear I was unsuccessful. He has been accused of piracy and travelled to New York in an effort to have the warrant rescinded last June. As he now has been jailed for nigh a year, I fear for his life.

Though, I must confess, I do not fear for my own, as I know how to wield a dagger though I am reluctant to use one on my own Quartermaster, James Fitzhugh.

Yet twice I have seen him skulking about during our journey northward from the jungles of the Amazon, exerting himself in trying to break open my quarters.

In search, no doubt, not only for the doubloons I intend for our wedded life, but also for the necklace I always wear. (Though few know of its Origins—except, mayhap, the wise woman who bequeathed it to me—and fewer still its Foretelling of true Love.)

But that look in his eye leaves me little doubt as to his other intentions, though he knows full well of your & my Understanding. Only the sharpness of my blade has thwarted his unwelcome advances upon my person & my purse.

I should never have agreed to take him aboard. He grows more belligerent daily, and I do wonder if his ill manners and disrespect affect the rest of the crew.

Beloved, I shan't worry you any longer. All shall be well. I shall see to it myself. Now my candle flame gutters, so I must bid you a Good night.

All my love,
Eleanor

She had to tell Zak about this. He'd love to add this new information to his research about the ship. Not only that, the initials *J.F.* that Eddie pointed out must mean that this chest had been owned by James Fitzhugh. He must have kept, and hidden, Eleanor's letter because of his jealousy.

And suddenly, another thought struck her. She could use excerpts from this letter in the story behind the new piece and in the packaging of the jewelry box.

Hmmm. She'd have to run it by Jia once she heard back from her. She could even make the presentation box look like an antique letter with a ribbon around it? Yes. That could definitely work. Maggie's mind churned with possibilities. She hadn't yet heard from Zak about when he wanted her to meet him at Dalvay. So she began to jot notes around the edges of the mood board she'd created for the pendant.

Fabric swatches, bits of shiny foil in delicate designs, glossy pictures of Spanish galleons, and a copy of the pencil sketch of Eleanor, were all pinned to it. She studied the woman's expression again and smiled. They had to find the pendant and find out the rest of her story.

But the ringing of the phone tore Maggie's attention away from her thoughts about Eleanor. She answered it on the first ring. "Maggie speaking."

"Hi Maggie, this is Jia."

Maggie's pulse pounded.

"We received your photo of the sketch."

Maggie pulled out the drawing for reference.

"Yes," a man's voice said. "I'm Mike, the head of the design team."

"Okay, great." Maggie said. She did her best to suppress the tremor of nervousness in her tone.

A pause.

"Well," Jia said, and then cleared her throat. "This is..."

"...certainly creative," Mike said.

"Yes, very," Jia added.

"But," Mike said, "we can't accept it."

"The thing is, it's not in line with the vision of your bracelet." Jia said.

"What else do you have for us?" Mike asked.

Crap. Maggie licked her dry lips and straightened her spine. "I just have the one design at the moment."

"Mmm," Mike said. Maggie could almost hear his frown.

She stared at her mood board and felt hot tears at the edges of her eyes. No. She wasn't going to cry now. She blinked the tears back fiercely.

"Well, if that's all you have for us, that's not what Courtney Jewelers wants to pursue," Jia said.

Maggie's heart fell to her toes.

"So," Jia said, "we won't be using your design."

Maggie swallowed down the lump in her throat and gripped the phone. Her gaze travelled to the copy of Eleanor's picture on the mood board. She couldn't let Eleanor down now.

"Please know it's nothing personal," Jia said, her voice cheery.

"Just business," Mike added.

Maggie took a breath. "Of course." She forced lightness into her tone even as she crumpled the drawing up into a tiny wad and shoved it deep into her purse. "No problem at all."

"But your bracelet's doing so well, we're going to carry that. We'll be in touch about arranging the paperwork for you to come in and sign. Have a great day!" Jia said, just before she ended the call.

Maggie put the phone down with a shaking hand and bit her lip. No. She shook her head. She wasn't going to use their rejection of her design as an excuse to run away or give up. Her gaze strayed back to the mood board and Eleanor's picture. She was going to treat this as a reason to stay, to fight for what she believed in, and to win.

Yes. She lifted her chin. Eleanor probably would've approved of her plan.

Besides, she had to look on the bright side. At least Courtney Jewelers had decided to carry her bracelet. And she and Zak were making definite progress on discovering the deeper connection between Eleanor, the pendant and the ship. And if—no—*when* they found the pendant, it would help both of their careers. Even if Zak *was* too stubborn to admit it. Who knew? Maybe when they found the pendant, that would even change the jewelry company's mind about her new design.

THAT SAME MORNING, Zak, who wore his Memorial University T-shirt and a holey pair of jeans, grabbed the day's *Guardian* off the porch. He'd have to leaf through it later. When he had time. He glanced at his watch, as if just by looking at it, he could give himself more time to find the shipwreck and finish the book.

His cellphone buzzed with a text from Maggie. *Zak, guess what I just found—a letter in the sea chest that mentions Davies AND the pendant! I'll bring it with me when I see you today. By the way, when are we going to go up there? Oh, and apparently, J.F. on the chest stands for James Fitzhugh, the quartermaster on* Lady's Revenge.

Hmmm. This could be really useful.

Great work, Maggie! :) Thanks for letting me know. You can head on up if you want. I'll meet you there in about an hour. I want to check if there's any reference to that kind of thing in Davies' travel journal first. Zak hit send and then went into his temporary office.

Maybe he could find something about a letter in Davies' journal. He hefted the volume and started to leaf through it. But he paused when he got to the thicker-than-normal section. Could this section be concealing something important? Maybe even relating to the letter Maggie had mentioned? He ran his fingers lightly along the edge of the antique paper.

He examined the paper more closely. Then rooted around in a drawer until he found a pair of tweezers.

Very carefully, he peeled away the edges to reveal...a letter.

He looked down at the water-stained and warped sheet.

Port Royal, Jamaica
3 March 1699   Henry Davies

Dearest Henry,

Oh glorious day! My love, I have the happiest of news. Kidd surely made good on his promise of obtaining me a command—and a new and faster ship. Not only that, but I have also begun amassing a crew.

One of Kidd's former crewmen—you know of whom I speak—though I have duly made efforts to dissuade him, has come aboard the Lady's Revenge *as Quartermaster. For what reasons I cannot foretell. I fear they be not entirely pleasant nor good. (Though, with a ship such as mine, not employed in altogether legal activities, perhaps pleasant and good are too generous of words.)*

I fear 'tis too late to undo what has been done.

The other man—Nicholas MacDonald—has joined my ranks as First Mate. 'Tis fortunate indeed, as he, also a former Kidd crewman, I trust entirely.

Oh, but how the lines and sails of this ship remind me of another deck on another sea, with your arms 'round my waist.

I cannot but smile at the memory of your face as you thought me to be a lady among a ship full of cutthroats when you came aboard in the Far East...

It feels an age since I last laid eyes upon your dear countenance. Though I must have faith that we shall again be united, once your western trek with the Hudson's Bay Company has ended. I confess, I shall rest easy once you have safely rejoined that Mi'kmaq settlement on St. John's Island.

I wish you fare well for now, dearest. Though I fear to disclose too much in a missive such as this, I feel I must, nonetheless, unburden myself in your good confidence.

Love, do take care. I await your return to the shores of that Beloved Isle with much anticipation.

Always yours,
Eleanor

Hmm. A primary source would certainly be of interest to his readers. Maybe he could add this to his book.

Zak grinned. He had to tell Maggie. Now they both had letters to show each other. He glanced at his watch. Speaking of which, he had to head over to talk to Granddad.

MAGGIE GLANCED AT the clock on the dash, turned off her rental car and stepped out into the parking lot at Dalvay. She'd gotten here pretty early. Might as well wait for Zak inside the main house. Then they could go to his granddad's together.

She strode into the hotel and looked around. A large sandstone fireplace was adjacent to her, in what was now the lobby but was originally the foyer of the house. Heavy wood panelling lined the space. A wide staircase spanned the opposite end of the room and led to the open second floor.

Some summer cottage. Maggie shook her head. She paused to adjust her car keys, which had started to work their way out of her pocket. Then she texted Zak. *When you get here, I'll be in the main house.* As Maggie wandered across the maroon floral runner, she noticed a couple at the check-in desk. They stood with their backs to her. She cocked her head as their conversation with the front desk clerk caught her ear.

"Where should we put it?" the woman asked the clerk. She waved a hand to indicate the small drop-front writing desk with delicately turned legs next to her.

"My manager told me we should put it in the side parlor over here since it's an original piece owned by Mr. Alexander MacDonald." The clerk came out from behind the counter. "Here, I'll help you guys move it. We want our guests to enjoy the history."

Maggie frowned and looked again at the woman. Was that...Ruby and Nathan? Maggie took a step closer to the pair. Last she'd heard from her friend, they'd still been in Ireland.

The man spoke again. "My mom knew the MacDonalds. And when I discovered that she'd intended to give the desk back after she found out who'd originally owned it, I wanted to donate it here where it belongs. Mom bought it at an auction in North Rustico. For years I thought the desk was Federal style but Ruby here—" he slid an arm around the woman's waist "—told me it's from an earlier period." He grinned at her and Maggie saw the warmth in his gaze.

"Right," Ruby said as she smiled back at Nathan. "It's actually an early Baroque drop-front writing desk. We've done some research on the piece and found out Alexander MacDonald's ancestor Nicholas MacDonald originally owned it. He'd imported it from New York."

Maggie's eyes widened.

Nathan picked up one side of the desk and the clerk picked up the other side. They started to move it to the parlor.

"Ruby!" Maggie called out, before she could follow the two men.

Ruby turned at the sound of her name. "Maggie?" She laughed and they hugged. "What are you doing here?"

"I could ask you the same thing." Maggie smiled. "It's so good to see you."

"We just got back from Dublin yesterday." Ruby beamed.

"I'm so happy for you guys," Maggie said.

"And we're here now because Nathan wanted to drop off the desk before he starts work again in a few days," Ruby said.

Maggie nodded. "I'm on the island here doing some research for a new jewelry piece. I'd love to look at that desk, actually," Maggie said.

"Oh sure," Ruby said, "Come on."

The two women headed into the parlor as the clerk went back to the front desk.

After Maggie said hello to Nathan, she looked at the desk. "It's beautiful." The exterior of the drop-front writing surface was inlaid along the edges with an intricate marquetry pattern. "Can I...?" Maggie reached out a hand.

"Sure," Nathan said. He pulled out his phone and turned to Ruby as Maggie heard him say, "So the realtor thought these would be good options for us."

Out of the corner of her eye, Maggie saw them head to a

couch on the other side of the room. Maggie lowered the writing surface. Inside, tiny compartments and drawers with mother-of-pearl knobs spanned the back of the space. She leaned forward to examine the brightly polished knobs. Oops. Her car keys slipped out of her front jeans pocket and landed on the floor on top of the air conditioning vent.

Maggie bent to retrieve them. But the vent caught the lightweight keychain so that it stuck in the grill, which was partially underneath the desk. As she crouched down, she accidently banged her knee against the front of the desk when she reached farther forward to grab the keys. She started to straighten up. But as she did, the moulding along the bottom of the desk caught her eye. It appeared to have come loose.

Crap.

Had she broken it when she banged her knee? She scooted closer and frowned. No. The moulding had fallen forward at a forty-five degree angle as if it had been hinged to do that. She tucked a strand of hair behind her ear and peered closer. Was that a...lever hidden behind the moulding? She reached out her hand.

Why would—

"Lose something, Maggie?" Zak's voice made the hairs on the back of her neck rise.

She swivelled her head and saw him enter the room. "Oh! Zak. I, uh," she stood up and darted a glance at Ruby and Nathan, who had looked up from their spot on the couch.

"Ruby, Nathan, this is Zak Stuart," Maggie said.

Zak nodded a hello to Ruby and Nathan, who got up from the couch and crossed the room in Maggie and Zak's direction. "Hi, how are ya, Zak?" Nathan said. The two men shook hands.

"Nice to meet you, Zak," Ruby said. He nodded back at her.

"I think I found some sort of lever...here," Maggie said to the three others. "Mind if I show Zak?"

Ruby nudged Nathan and a knowing look passed between them. "You two go ahead. We're gonna keep looking at real estate listings." They headed back to the couch.

A blush heated Maggie's cheeks. To cover for it, she whispered to Zak as she crouched down. "Do you know whose desk this is?"

Zak shook his head and crouched down beside her, so close that his shoulder brushed against hers. She couldn't bring herself to move away.

"Nicholas MacDonald's." Maggie reached up and brushed her fingers against the tiny lever. Yes. Cool metal. "I think there's a hidden compartment here."

Zak gave her a speculative look.

"Only one way to find out." She pressed her fingers against the lever. There was a faint ping but when she examined the front of the desk, nothing seemed to have changed.

Zak leaned first to the left and then the right. "Nothing on either side."

"Which means..." Maggie trailed off. She shifted position at the same time Zak did.

"We need to look underneath," Zak finished.

She lay on her back beside Zak on the plush hand-woven carpet. "Look," Maggie whispered as she pointed at the underside of the desk, near the maker's mark.

"Some sort of panel's been triggered," Zak said. His fingertips brushed against her arm as he reached up to press the panel.

She sucked in a breath as the secret panel popped open to reveal a faded, torn and blackened sheet of paper. Zak's eyes slid to hers and a grin spread across his face. For a second, she was seventeen again. Her heart banged against her ribs. He was so near... If she moved just a fraction, she could close the space between them, taste his—No. She moved her hand toward the page instead and closed her fingers around it. But her eyes remained fastened on Zak's.

A sudden burst of staccato German near the entrance to the room made them both scramble out from under the desk and jump apart. Zak turned back to hastily close the hidden compartment. Maggie smoothed her hair as he adjusted his T-shirt. The loudly-chattering cluster of tourists walked right by the doorway. Maggie coughed. Zak cleared his throat.

"We found, um, a letter," Maggie held it up for Ruby and Nathan to see.

"Wow," Ruby said. She gestured to Nathan and they walked over.

"Yeah, it's—" Zak stopped mid-sentence. His warm fingers brushed Maggie's as she held the page and his eyes grew round as he pointed at the fragment Maggie held. "I think this might be the missing piece of Kidd's third letter that Granddad has."

"Take it," Nathan said. "If it'll help you find whatever you guys are looking for, then you can have it."

Ruby laughed. "You two must be solving some sort of island mystery. Well, have fun." She shared a look with Nathan. "We know what that's like, don't we?"

Nathan grinned at Ruby and interlaced his fingers with hers. "Sure do—we figured out what happened to the lost Great Seal of Prince Edward Island."

"But that's a long story," Ruby said. "Listen, it was great to see you, Maggie, and meet you, Zak, but we should get going. Lots to do now that we're back from our honeymoon. And we should definitely catch up soon, Maggie."

"That'd be great, Ruby," Maggie said. Ruby and Nathan waved as they left. A few minutes later, Zak and Maggie stood on the small cottage porch.

Zak knocked on the doorframe. "Granddad?" he called.

"Come on in, kids," Ian called. "I'm just watching some TV."

Zak and Maggie went inside. "I think we found the rest of Kidd's third letter," Zak said to his grandfather.

"Did you now?" Ian flicked off the television set. "Let me just go get the fragments and we can take a look." He returned a few minutes later with the Ziploc baggie in hand and handed it to Zak.

Maggie held up the fragment they'd found and Zak

compared it with his. "Yes. This is a definite fit."

—ubloons than what she is due, as I feel I owe her for her kind Assistance in attempting to warn me of my Ordeals with the Crown.

Thus, I ask that you deliver to her the Gold, as I cannot.

I remain, as always, your Loyal friend,

"So Kidd paid Eleanor for her help," Zak said. "That's what she meant in those letters, and that's why everyone thought the treasure was Kidd's. But it wasn't—not really. He'd given some of his gold to Eleanor."

"That makes sense," Maggie said. Her brows rose. "And look." She pointed to the page. "Those same ink blots and quill drag marks."

"More of the cipher," Zak said.

"You were right, Zak." Maggie rummaged around in her purse and got out a pen and paper and began to jot down the ciphered text alongside the key she'd drawn earlier. She pursed her lips. "This is the second half of the riddle, then."

—a N.W. circle of water
Meets the Gulf's embrace.

Zak shook his head. "Some sort of location?"

"Let's go over the whole thing, then." Maggie said. "*Lines of love/locked in a prison of glass/where a N.W. circle of water/meets the Gulf's embrace.*" She tapped her finger against her chin.

"*N.W.* must mean northwest," Zak said.

"And it's near the gulf. Probably the Gulf of the St. Lawrence, given the history of everything else." Maggie added.

"That's a safe bet." Zak nodded.

"So a circle of water. Like a pond."

"Or a lake. Near the gulf."

"Just a second," Ian interjected. "I have a sea chart around here somewhere..." He rooted around on a nearby shelf and then handed Zak a creased and faded chart. Zak unfolded it and began to search the area where the Gulf of St. Lawrence met Prince Edward Island's north shore.

didn't even tell anyone here," Maggie said, "so I don't know how the *Sun* got all this information." She gestured to the page.

"You expect me to believe that? It's P.E.I." His eyes flashed. "People talk! If it's not a neighbor minding your business, it's a cousin of your sister-in-law. Or your neighbor *is* a cousin of your sister-in-law. They all want to mind everyone's business like it's their own." Zak's tone turned bitter. "But that's not even the worst part. You know what is? This article," he jabbed a finger at the headline, "is implying I'm a treasure hunter. Do you know what this'll look like to my colleagues? What it could do to my career?"

He didn't let Maggie respond.

"Worse, there'll be hoards of treasure seekers here—" His voice became brittle. Angry. "—jeopardizing the integrity of the archaeological site. And there's nothing we can do about it."

"Zak, it's not like I did it on purpose." She crossed her arms.

"Then why is CBC covering it? And," he added, "it's on *The New York Times'* website."

"What?" Maggie's eyes widened.

Zak shook his head. "You only thought about yourself, didn't you?"

Her breath hitched. She opened her mouth then closed it.

Zak continued. "You basically steal your *inspiration* from my family's history, come here, take advantage of what my research can give you—" he clenched his hands into fists "—and then leave."

He averted his eyes just as Maggie saw the beginnings of real hurt, vulnerability, in their hazel depths. "I was stupid enough to trust you about our research, our working together."

She couldn't say anything to make him believe her, could she? Her bottom lip trembled but she forced herself to remain calm. Unfeeling. But that was...impossible.

Yet she spoke anyway. "Can't you just trust me on this?"

She forced herself to tamp down her growing irritation at Zak. "I came up here—" she dragged the words out with near super-human effort "—to find out more about Eleanor Webster because I thought it would help me with my next piece. I wasn't...trying to wreck your reputation or steal from you. And I didn't do that with the antique bracelet, either."

"No?" He laughed—an empty sound. "Certainly didn't look like that from where I stood. *Am* standing." His gaze bored into hers.

"Just because you gave me the bracelet for my birthday that one year doesn't mean you can tell me what to do with it. Especially not now." She lifted her chin.

Zak's gaze hardened. "You never gave it back. You should have when we broke up. It was a valuable piece of my family's history that you kept for yourself."

"Oh, so this is all my fault?" she said, as her temper rose. "Come on, Zak. I don't want to hear it. Be reasonable. It was a *gift* you gave me. I shouldn't have to give it back to you just because we broke up. And for your information," she shot back, as hurt threaded through her, "I *did* think about giving it back to you. But I—" she blinked back sudden hot tears "—just couldn't," she whispered. She swallowed down a lump in her throat and her anger rose to the surface again. "All you care about—ever cared about—is your stupid scientific projects and lectures. You never wanted to help me with my jewelry design research, did you? You just used that as an excuse to find out whatever you could about *Lady's Revenge.*" Maggie pressed her lips together. "You're not being fair to me. And I think you know a thing or two about *that.* You asked me to stay on the island here when you knew—you *knew*—" she jabbed a finger at his chest "—that my dream was to go to design school in New York City. It was totally unfair of you to ask me to stay. You expected me to give up my dreams for you."

God. Her fingers flexed. Didn't he care how she felt? Didn't he care... at all? And for one, two...three unreasonable moments, she hated him for it.

"You don't know the first thing about fairness, Maggie. You betrayed my trust in you when you broke my heart in high school then refused my proposal—" Zak broke off and clenched his hands. "I thought everything was great. I thought you'd *want* to say yes. I thought you actually loved me. But the only thing you loved was your damn career." He narrowed his eyes at her. "And I was idiot enough to think you'd changed." He shook his head. "Obviously, three years hasn't changed you at all." Zak glared at her.

Maggie glared back. "Just because we're working together, just because we happen to be solving these riddles, that means you have some license to—"

"—Working together? You think we're still working together? After all this?" He folded his arms across his chest. "We're through. And now, it's for good."

Chapter Seven

ZAK FANNED THE sea floor with his gloved hand. It was the best way to search for anything that might be hiding just under the surface.

He grimaced. Why had he fought with Maggie? Things had been going so well and if he was completely honest, he'd begun to hope—No. There was no point in thinking about what might have been. That's what had gotten him into trouble before.

But he could see her eyes alight, her windblown chocolate-brown hair, and her laughter as they'd eaten dinner at Sheltered Harbour Cafe. He swallowed, tried to push the image aside.

But as soon as he did, another, older memory popped up. This time, he could hear Maggie's voice in his head as she'd said, "Do you think we really have a good chance of finding anything?" Hope had mixed with skepticism in her expression. He'd had to do a fair bit of cajoling, and—his lips quirked upward—had to give more than a kiss or two, to persuade her that the romance of the adventure was almost as exciting as *actually* finding something. He could almost smell her sunscreen again. Taste the salt on her lips as the sea spray had rocked his sail boat and the sun had sparkled on the July waters. Cherry lip gloss. That's what she had always used, wasn't it?

He shook himself. What was he doing?

He rubbed the back of his neck. He'd always been a sentimentalist. But something about this dive, he supposed, had it all rushing back to him. Back when it seemed so easy. So simple. As if gold and jewels lay at the bottom of every craggy ocean outcropping. He opened his eyes and looked down at the sea floor.

No treasure here.

But he had spotted a few boats in the previously empty area where the research vessel had dropped anchor. He scowled. Treasure hunters. Because of that damn *Guardian* reprint. He pushed aside those thoughts and tried to concentrate again. If he moped about Maggie, it wasn't going to help him find the wreck. In fact, it might even make things worse. He could miss the tiniest detail.

Clouds of sand billowed around him as he brushed at the sea floor. He was about to move to another spot when a barnacle-encrusted object caught his eye.

He picked it up.

Small and light with a familiar shape. A dagger? From what was left of the curved blade, he'd guess Spanish. He tucked it into his dive bag and kept up his search. The dagger might mean an actual debris trail this time. And a debris trail—depending on the age of the artifacts—could very possibly lead to the wreck. He hoped.

He gave a mental sigh. They only had two weeks left on the deadline. Besides, if they didn't find a solid lead soon, the morale of everyone involved in the whole project would plummet even further. He wasn't sure he could take that. Work was the only thing left to hold onto. And he wasn't going to allow anything to drown out his love for his career.

He returned his attention to the seabed and moved a few centimeters from where he'd found the dagger. Only sand. Just then he felt a tap on his shoulder. His dive partner held up what looked like, as far as Zak could guess, a spoon. He nodded to the other person and they ascended to examine their findings.

Zak stripped out of his dry suit and shrugged into comfortable clothes.

"Set these in solution and then we can take a look at them," Zak said to his assistant, and headed into the makeshift lab set up next door to their computers.

But after the solution had cleaned away the centuries of

accumulation, Zak's heart fell. The spoon wasn't from the right time period. And, while the dagger was from the 17th century, that didn't prove anything concrete. His lips compressed. He'd have to call a meeting.

Ten minutes later, everyone sat around the small kitchen table in the galley. "You all know how long we've been at this now, and we haven't found anything conclusive or useful. We're going to have to change tactics. Look in a few new places that will help us narrow the search area down even further. That means we'll need to take some time away from the water. Talk to locals. Go through the reports and logs we've already gathered to see if we can find new leads to pinpoint a more specific area. Because this smattering of objects we've found so far—" he held up the spoon, the dagger and the musket ball "—aren't enough to warrant funding for a full-scale excavation. We *need* to find a shipwreck."

AFTER AN AIMLESS day of wandering through the historic streets of downtown Charlottetown, Maggie headed back to her hotel room that night and tried to smooth down her windblown ponytail. Where was her hairbrush? She glanced at her reflection in the mirror above the bureau where the sea chest and suitcase sat. She gave herself a watery smile. "What am I going to do?" she murmured. There had to be a solution. She sighed and slid out of her shoes.

A sense of sadness welled within her. What if Zak had been right all along? That she'd been the bad guy in the whole thing? She winced. No. She couldn't think like that.

Maybe this turn of events was actually a good thing? Maybe this was exactly what she needed? Maybe she was exactly where she needed to be, too?

She glanced at the mood board she'd created. All at once, realization came crashing down.

She'd relied too much on waiting for inspiration to strike. She'd called it legitimate research, when really it had been a smoke screen for her fears. Her fears that, without having a framework, something to guide her—in this case, Eleanor's personal history—she wouldn't be able to really do her art justice or be a real artist.

She tried to shove the feeling aside, so she flipped on the TV. But a sudden wave of deeper emotion made her pause. She pulled out the crumpled up sketch paper with her design from the bottom of her purse.

She caught her breath. Deep sorrow filled her as a long-ago memory surfaced: the feel of Zak's hands, warm against her skin, as they had watched the moon rise over the Northumberland Strait.

She should have done more, been more, tried more, for him—with him. Three years ago. And today... She stared at the sketch. Zak was right. She'd been lying to herself. She'd been clinging to the hope that inspiration would save her. That inspiration—a muse—would give her the design she'd been hoping for. She'd been using the story of Eleanor and all that research as an excuse to stay blocked. An excuse to not dig deeper. She'd been afraid. Afraid to fail. Afraid she wouldn't be able to do it. Couldn't do it. Which is what Zak had meant.

She began to doodle along the edge of the crumpled page. She smoothed a hand over her messy ponytail even as she continued to absently draw on the paper. Anger and frustration welled up within her; the culmination of the last few weeks and months of work, and more work; and stress after stress. She tugged on the end of her ponytail and then pulled it free of the hair elastic.

Maggie needed some time off. Some time to relax, re-cover. She was supposed to be the founder of this company. But wasn't that what owning a company was all about? Working harder and longer than anyone else?

She shook her head, looked out the plate glass window and then down at her page again. Suddenly, she drew in a sharp breath. *That's* what had been lacking before. Why Courtney Jewelers had rejected this. Because this drawing...was incomplete.

ZAK SHOVED HIS hands deep into his jeans pockets as he walked over to his truck at the end of the day. He'd decided to take the dagger with him to study more closely at the house. Maybe it would yield some answers. This evening there had to be at least twice the number of vehicles along the dock here than there had been this morning.

A knot tied itself in his stomach. What if the treasure hunters found something conclusive before he did? Worse, what if they totally destroyed the archaeological integrity of the area? Not only that, he couldn't shake the feeling of disappointment about the search. And, if he was totally honest, about Maggie. His truck bounced down the dirt road toward the old Victorian house. Damn it. She'd walked away. She couldn't just leave him. Except she had. Again.

No. That wasn't true. He'd pushed her away. He sighed and shook his head. Suddenly, he felt exhausted. It looked like Maggie was determined to be his enemy. Not that he'd done nothing. He'd participated in his fair share of less-than-stellar behaviors, after all.

Zak pulled to a stop in the driveway and headed inside with the dagger just as a full red-orange moon began to rise over his rooftop.

He went into the kitchen and made himself a cup of camomile tea then headed for the living room, where he put the dagger on the coffee table by Davies' journal. He stroked a finger along the hilt. A thrill ran through him. Almost as if he could reach out and touch the past. Whose was it? Where had it come from? Could it have belonged to someone on *Lady's Revenge*? Perhaps... or perhaps not.

He yawned and glanced out at the moon again. Its orangish light pooled across the floor. Something about the color reminded him of the dagger. He put the small knife down, scrubbed a hand across his face and sighed. He needed to get some sleep. He could look at his find more closely in the daylight.

After he'd showered, he pulled on his plaid flannel pajama bottoms and got in between the cool clean sheets. He yawned again and drifted off to sleep almost as soon as his head hit the pillow...

The wind whipped the rigging and made the main mast creak and groan as the dark clouds whirled and parted to reveal yellow-green light and flashes of lightning just past Zak's vision.

He frowned. Where was he? And why did it seem so vivid? He looked around. All was in darkness except for the bruised patch of sky above him, with the stars all wheeling around, it seemed, at top speed.

He looked around again. No one was here. What sort of dream was this? All he could see was highly polished decking surrounded by a burnished oak ship's rail. Coils of fat, tar-soaked rope were neatly piled on the deck beside leather buckets. And high above him, the rigging creaked and groaned around the reefed sails.

No crew. And no captain.

He walked up near-vertical steps. Headed toward the ship's wheel.

He felt his mind spin and a wave of dizziness wash over him. He managed to shake it off as he gripped the brass handrails more firmly then hauled himself onto the small raised platform with the ship's wheel and large ship's compass. Next to them was a map pinned to the back of a bench that ran along the side of the railing.

Zak reached a hand out to touch the faded, age-spotted map—in the shape of Prince Edward Island, he realized.

"I wouldn't do that if I were you."

At the sound of a low, feminine voice that sounded like bluebirds and brooks in spring, Zak whirled around.

His eyes met those of a tall woman with deep-set green eyes fringed with heavy dark lashes. Her long black hair was braided into a neat plait that circled her head like a crown. Her milk-white skin showed a long, jagged scar that ran in a delicate line from the top of her left cheekbone to just under her chin.

Zak blinked. Cocked his head.

She had a necklace around her throat. Silver and gold fili-gree rings studded with rubies, emeralds and sapphires sparkled on her long fingers.

Fingers that gripped a jewel-hilted curved dagger. She wore a demure, polite smile; one that would, no doubt, not have been out of place in ballrooms and parlors, but one that now sent a shiver of apprehension down Zak's back. "Why not?" he managed at last, as he tore his gaze away from her sea-green one.

"Because 'tis wrong."

"Wrong? What do you mean?" He shook his head. Dreams had their own sort of logic.

The woman's lips curved upward even more. "Oh," she said, jewels winking in the moonlight, "'tis no dream."

Zak took a step toward her and his heart quickened. "Then tell me what to do. Tell me where the treasure is. Where the shipwreck is"

"Ah, you're a quick one. The others weren't, so much. They had grown fat and lazy, their minds dulled by greed. And..." She reached out and tapped the butt of the dagger against his chest. "Their hearts were not so recently bruised by heartache. I've waited a long time for one such as yourself."

He did a double take as she lowered the dagger. It looked exactly like the one he'd found. "So you're...Eleanor, I imagine."

"I am nothing you imagine, Zachary Stuart. No," she waved a hand, "this place is its own sort of reality. After all, it is the realm in which I reside. Me and my doomed crew aboard the Lady's Revenge." She waved a hand again, and Zak saw once more exactly what he'd seen that night at Argyle Shore. He blinked, and the images faded, leaving only the two of them on the tall ship sailing its way amid the stars.

"My crew only appears when the moon is right," she said as she slid a finger along the curved sharpness of the dagger. "When I relive the pain of heartbreak once again. 'Tis a certain purity in the pain." She reached up and touched the necklace, and that's when Zak noticed that the large central pendant was missing. He blinked. How did he—The legend. In The Prince Edward Island Magazine. His breath quickened. This was real.

And he was here.

The woman nodded. "Yes. It is as you recall. Every word of that so-called legend is not so-called fiction. 'Tis real." The pirate queen looked at Zak. Her eyes were more brilliant than the most brilliant emeralds. "That's why, Zachary, you have to help me. Help me, free my crew, and the treasure will be yours. The treasure of your heart."

"You're telling me that if I help you, I won't get your treasure but I will get Maggie back?"

"She has to come back to you of her own volition. I'm no witch." The pirate queen laughed. "But sometimes, I can see the future." She shook her head. "But I didn't that day. Oh, I could've listened. If I had, I wouldn't linger in this...realm. But I thought I knew. And because of that, you and I have, shall we say, a commonality."

Zak shoved his hands in his pockets. "And if I don't help you?"

The clouds scuttled across the moon, and a chill wind swept through Zak's hair, which caused goose bumps to appear on his skin.

"I think you know the answer to that already." She placed a fingertip on his chest where his heart beat rapidly.

Zak nodded. "Let me guess. There's some sort of curse if I don't help you, that will—"

"Ah, you've been reading many a tall tale, I see," Eleanor said as she fingered the necklace at her throat. "No," she said quietly, "no curse. Just everlasting regret for what could have been, but now never shall be." She shrugged and turned her back to Zak. "I cannot pass on to my Beloved, unless the pendant is reclaimed by those of pure heart. Though 'twas my own choice, not by any curse. You see, I linger here because I desire justice to be served. For the man who stole my life, my pendant—and kept me from rejoining my love on that cold July night." She studied the rapid track of the clouds across the sky. "Oh, they tried to burn me for a witch. But I escaped and became a queen. Ah, it seems but a fortnight ago... I was born into Puritan faith, but when I foolishly took my sister into my confidence in an instance of second sight, she believed I'd

turned to darkest witchcraft. 'Twas a sham of a trial. I slipped my bonds and escaped—with a souvenir." She gestured to her face. "So I took to the seas. I'd sailed to India where I met a wise woman. She gifted me the pendant. She saw what others did not, could not; that I had a pure heart. She told me that when I met my true love, my heart would glow just as the pendant would. By such manner, I would know that I could trust myself; could open my heart to the echoes of love within. As soon as she gifted me the pendant, things began to happen. I met Henry. Then, thanks to Kidd, I procured a new ship of my own, after the one I'd stolen from my father was commandeered by the British Navy." She watched the stars wheel overhead. Stopped speaking so long Zak thought she'd forgotten his presence. "Remember," she said at last, "if you do decide to help me, your heart must be pure."

Zak shifted his weight and shoved his hands deeper into his pockets. "Pure?"

"Purely open to love. Your true love. As 'tis now."

Zak took a breath and opened his mouth to speak, but all at once, his surroundings melted into blackness.

MAGGIE BEGAN TO trace the outline of a single teardrop on the crumpled page she'd dug from her purse. She gulped back another wave of sadness as the sorrow turned into something far deeper, more all-encompassing: regret, pain, remorse.

Her heart felt like a leaden balloon but her fingers continued to sketch. More teardrops blossomed on the page like small pearlescent reminders of—no, not reminders of, but in honor of—her time with, and her feelings for, Zak and their relationship.

And around the cluster of teardrops—tiny seed pearls—she added delicate silver filigree in gentle swooping curlicues. With deft pencil strokes, she added more to the design. She felt her heart lighten, and a bubble of peace and joy rise within her. She almost held her breath as she let her pencil draw more and more. Tiny diamonds, caught between the delicate wisps of silver, shed rainbows of light across the entire design.

She paused. Took a breath.

But as she did so, the smell of burning wood filled her senses. Her pulse sped up, and she looked around. But nothing was on fire. Of course not. As she glanced around the room, she thought she caught a glimpse of emerald-green eyes reflected in the window. She put a hand to her throat. All at once, she could hear the newscaster's voice very clearly. She jumped. She'd forgotten the TV was on.

"...visitor numbers have increased noticeably, thanks to word of a supposed treasure buried on the island. Despite impending storms, hundreds of people have come to tiny Bay Fortune to seek its untold riches. CBC's Jaime MacNeil has more..."

Her fingers tightened on the remote as she grabbed it and turned off the TV. She fished around in her purse. Her hairbrush had to be in here somewhere.

Hundreds of people? Zak would be horrified. If he even bothered to care at all.

She slowly pulled out the brush. But as she did, a page also fell from her purse to the floor in a sudden, inexplicable breeze. A silvery sound of...wind chimes? Or was that laughter? reached her. She frowned. There weren't any wind chimes nearby...

She shrugged. Lifted the brush to her hair.

She had more important things to do than worry about how Zak felt. Or how she'd screwed everything up.

The page fluttered for a moment as it settled onto the floor while she started to move the brush through her hair. But it was too late to fix things. She couldn't just head back over there. She shook her head. That would do no good. Or would it? That was a lot of visitors... She bit her lip then sighed. What was done was done. She pulled her hair back into a tidy ponytail. Wasn't it?

She secured her hair with the elastic and then picked up the piece of paper to toss it in too, when she paused. What?

She slowly turned the page over. Studied the burned edges. She couldn't throw this out. How had it gotten here, anyway? She frowned.

She slowly re-read the fragment of Kidd's letter and thought about the lines of the riddle.

The newscaster's words echoed through her mind again. She couldn't let some strangers get to the treasure or Eleanor's pendant. Or ruin Zak's shipwreck search.

She changed into her nightgown and got ready for bed.

She couldn't give up on her jewelry design, either. Least of all, on the pendant she hoped to create—now that she'd finally drawn something worthwhile. She looked down at the fine pencil strokes again. Tilted her head. Hmmm. It would look stunning if she made all those facets into diamonds...wouldn't it? Though she'd never done anything quite as showy as all that, before.

She tapped her finger against her chin. Perhaps this was yet another reason to hunt up Zak and talk to him face to face. She couldn't just stand by and do nothing. Yes. She had to fix things.

Chapter Eight

IN BETWEEN SIPS of strong hot Earl Gray tea, Zak blinked and stretched. Only 6:05 a.m. He shook his head. Normally he didn't get up nearly this early. A restlessness had seized him and he couldn't sleep.

He picked up the dagger and retrieved Eleanor's love letter but his thoughts turned to Maggie. She still needed that pendant of Eleanor's. He winced. He might've overreacted just a tad about that article. Where was Eleanor's pendant? He shook his head. And *where* was the ship? Did the love letter in a bottle have answers to both? He stood up and started to pace. Huh. He must've had some strange dreams last night. But try as he might, he couldn't remember a single one. Just a sense of seasickness and urgency. The black tea had begun to do its work, because, as he drained his second cup, the unsettled, rather nebulous feeling in his gut began to fade. Until he flicked on the morning news.

MAGGIE AWOKE IN the big queen-sized bed with a start. The blackout curtains only partially obscured the morning light that pooled onto the floor and she realized she still clutched the charred piece of Kidd's letter in her hand. The riddle ran through her mind again and filled her with a vague sense of restlessness.

Her eyes were drawn to the edge of dawn around the window frame, and she jumped up out of bed. The thin jersey knit of her pale pink nightgown brushed against her thighs as she padded barefoot to the window.

She hesitated only a moment before she drew the thick outer curtain aside in one firm movement. The swish of the drapes sounded loud in the quiet and darkness. It looked like the storm had held off so far. A yawn overcame her as a more insistent surge of restlessness washed through her. She tried to push it aside.

As Maggie moved aside the sheer inner curtain, the jewelry sketch caught her eye. She didn't have to change the minds of the people at Courtney Jewelers, after all, did she? No. She didn't. Now that things with them had fallen apart, she had a certain sort of freedom. A freedom to create whatever she liked. Go in whatever direction she wanted, design whatever she wanted.

Maggie didn't have to be restricted by deadlines or expectations. Though she did want to make something beautiful for her customers to enjoy. And that, she realized, was what she loved the most. Designing. Creating. Not all the business-y stuff. She could leave that to other people. She could be a jewelry supplier to retailers. She didn't have to have her own store, her own staff.

Maybe, just maybe, she could even do all the designing and creating from her laptop? She wouldn't have to have a real office. She could go anywhere she wanted, then, with anyone...

She gazed out the window. But it was Zak's face that flitted through her mind. The way he'd stood there, his hazel eyes filled with such anger and betrayal during their recent argument. She bit her lip and began to pace. She'd messed everything up between them. Again.

She glanced over at the digital clock on the nightstand. 6:33 a.m.

The only way to fix this was to help him find the shipwreck and prove to him that she wasn't trying to ruin his career. On impulse, she picked up her cell phone and hit Zak's number but ended the call on the second ring and put the phone down. She had to go to Dalvay by herself. She had to find that love letter in a bottle for him and give it to him because it could be vital to helping him find the shipwreck.

She turned away from the window, grabbed her clothes and ducked into the bathroom, where she pulled on a pair of jeans and a long-sleeve green T-shirt. Then she got her purse, picked up the keys to her rental car and left the room.

"ISLANDERS BETTER KEEP a weather eye to the horizon today. It looks like the monster storms, which have been wreaking havoc all along the eastern seaboard, have decided to pay Canada a visit. An extreme wind warning has been issued for the island today. The hurricane is predicted to hit the island late tomorrow. A rare occurrence, but not outside the realm of possibility. Still, we'd better all batten down the hatches, so to speak."

Zak turned off the TV and ate the last of his President's Choice chocolate chip granola cereal. He poured the rest of his tea down the sink. And with it, the last of his good mood. Damn it.

He didn't have time to waste. He'd have to check in with his team. Might also have to fit in a dive today, too. A storm could stir up the sand and silt on the sea floor and they could lose what ground they'd gained.

Well, not if he could help it.

He crossed the room and grabbed his cell phone off the hall table. He sent a quick text to everyone. *Now that we've had some time to talk with locals and comb over our previous research, let's use the sonar to scan that new area closer in to the bay.*

His fingers tightened around the device as he turned it off silent mode and glanced down at it to see he'd missed a call earlier in the morning—from Maggie.

Did that mean she'd called to apologize? His heart leapt to his throat. He should be the one to call her back and apologize for fighting with her. Then offer to help her out somehow. Yes. That's what he needed to do. He punched in her number. It rang and rang. And rang. No answer.

Well, he'd just have to find out for himself if she'd gone where he guessed she had. Then he'd go straight back to Bay Fortune and his team.

He hopped in his pickup truck and headed for Dalvay.

THE DAWN SEEMED to follow Maggie's winding route to Dalvay as the riddle from Kidd's letters ran through her mind. If she could just find the love letter in the bottle...

She pulled into the lot and then headed for the small circular lake at the northwest corner of the Dalvay estate property.

The only sound in the silence was the call of gulls. She took a deep breath of cool, clean salt air. She had roots here. No, that wasn't true, exactly. She didn't have deep roots to this place; she had deep roots to Zak.

She never should have lied to him that evening at the lighthouse. All along, he'd been what she'd needed, and wanted.

She never should have gone looking for greener pastures. Never should've turned her back on him. She squeezed her eyes shut, rubbed her fingers underneath her eyes.

She took a step forward and took another deep breath.

But what if he didn't see it that way?

The wind whipped Maggie's hair back from her forehead.

Perhaps everything hadn't been lost? Perhaps this had been the only way...Things had to go off course so that she could see she'd been on the right track all along. The right track back to her heart and soul. The right track back to Zak.

She took another step. And the way forward right now was to uncover the letter, to prove to Zak that he could trust her, that she hadn't betrayed him after all, and that they were in fact on the same team. If she had enough time before the storm hit. Maggie shivered and rubbed her arms as the wind gusted. The tang of salt air stung her nose. The wind blew harder and stirred a frisson of apprehension in Maggie's stomach.

"Maggie!"

SHE TURNED AROUND. Zak stood a few feet behind her. She felt as if she'd been punched in the stomach. She folded her arms across her chest and blinked back sudden tears. "What are you doing here?"

"Looking for the next clue." Zak came to stand beside her. "And you."

Chapter Nine

"SO," MAGGIE SAID, "this is northwest."

Zak glanced at her. Strands of hair framed her face, and determination glinted in her eyes. She never looked more beautiful than when she had a gleam like that in her eyes. He gave an inward smile. She never had been one to give up, either.

He looked out at the wind-whipped surface of the small lake in the gray early morning light. He should apologize to her. Now was the perfect opportunity. But as his eyes flicked back to her face, all he saw was her expression as they'd argued. His mind went back to his resolution in the kitchen earlier that morning. How could a simple *I'm sorry* and some sort of fumbled explanation make up for years of hurt between them? He swallowed. It couldn't. Not really. He had to *show* her he'd changed. And the only way to do that was to help her find that pendant she needed. Work could wait for a little while.

Zak studied the horizon. It could be a pretty big storm. They had to get going. He took a step, and his foot scrabbled against something hard. He looked down, about to nudge whatever it was out of his way, but then he stopped.

"What is it?" Maggie came to stand by him. A hint of her perfume drifted to him. He reached down and picked up the bottle and turned it over in his hands. A faded label read 7Up.

Maggie threw her hands up into the air. "Well, I'm sure that wasn't around 300 years ago."

They continued to scan the sand. "This is pretty impossible. There's no way anything's left here now—" Zak almost tripped over a large gnarled pine tree root. The wind-ravaged tree was so bent and twisted that its age was impossible to tell. At the end of one of the tree roots, he noticed a large oddly shaped stone pitted with age and nearly filled with lichen. The roots seemed to intertwine themselves around the stone.

He crouched down and brushed his fingertips against the rock. "Hmmm. These look like chisel marks on the surface here." Zak felt Maggie's warmth as she crouched beside him.

"I don't want to jump to any conclusions too quickly." He squinted. "But it looks like they form some sort of...symbol. A crown—with an X underneath."

"You're right," she said. As she reached out and traced the marks, her fingers brushed his and he had a sudden urge to interlace his fingers with hers.

They searched the sand around the rock. A deep shade of green caught Zak's eye. Not a root covered in green lichen but...something cylindrical.

He reached a hand out and felt it. It was, indeed, fuzzy with lichen and moss. And caked with sand. The daylight glinted and Zak picked up the object. It was heavy. A bottle. He turned it over in his hands.

A very old one.

He rubbed his thumb across it, which cleared away a layer of lichen and moss from the sides. Glass. Thick wavy green glass. But what a beautiful shade of green. Like the depths of the ocean mixed with sea foam. He held the bottle up to the daylight, and rubbed more of the moss and lichen away. As more of the glass was revealed, the light streamed more easily through the ancient bottle. His heart sped up. He tilted his head.

There was something inside.

The wind gusted. Zak flipped the bottle end for end so he could look directly down at the bottle's neck. Plugged with cork or wax? He couldn't quite tell, as it was completely blackened.

"Is this it?" Maggie said, a little breathless.

He met her gaze and grinned; he felt his anticipation mirror hers. "Only one way to find out." He reached for the Leatherman multi-tool he always kept in his back pocket but then he stopped. "We can't just open it here. We should take it over to the boat's lab, where we have more of a controlled environment."

"You should probably check in with your team, too, about the shipwreck?" Maggie said.

Zak nodded. But this was also important. He cradled the bottle as they picked their way back across the lawn and then over to their cars. "Come on, get in with me." He held open the Dodge's passenger door for her. "We can pick up your car later."

Maggie nodded and got in the passenger seat of his pickup. As Zak shut the door, he couldn't help but remember all the times he'd held the door for her before. He got in the driver's side and placed the bottle carefully beside him on the seat. He shut his door just as the wind gusted again.

He glanced out at the horizon and his stomach knotted. White cirrus clouds like that showed up before a storm. His pulse pounded. The weather reports looked like they were right. The storm would come soon. Too soon.

Only a matter of about thirty-six hours or so before it would reach here, too.

Forty minutes later, he pulled in at the pier. After he scooped up the bottle, he and Maggie walked down to where the dinghy was moored.

After they took the dinghy out to the research boat and came aboard, Zak briefed his team. A few minutes later, he and Maggie headed to the onboard lab. Zak slipped on a pair of white cotton gloves. Then he used a pair of small needle nose pliers to gently close around the blackened piece of tar or cork or God knew what that was stuck in the bottle's mouth. As he exerted just a bit of pressure, he twisted the pliers to the left.

Nothing.

He inhaled. Held it. Then he twisted the pliers the other way, while at the same time, he exhaled. But the stopper still didn't budge. He set the pliers down. Sighed.

Maggie leaned toward him and said, "So how old is it?" Her breath fanned his cheek. Zak felt warmth fill him. "Probably early-to-mid 1600s, judging from what I can see of the workmanship." He picked up the bottle and looked at its bottom and the edges where the bottom met the sides.

"There has to be a way to open the bottle," Maggie said.

He started to reach for the pliers again, but then he stopped. "You're right." He flashed her a smile as he rummaged around in a drawer until he found a rather battered pale green Bic lighter. After he shoved the drawer shut, he picked up the bottle in one hand and the lighter in the other. He angled the bottle so that it was almost horizontal. He flicked the lighter and an orange-yellow flame burst from its top.

Maggie took a step backward. "Careful with that," she said.

"Yep." He positioned the lighter near the bottle's neck and slowly began to rotate it. The glass began to warm ever so slightly. A pungent, salty, sticky odor began to emanate from the tar or cork or whatever it was.

Maggie wrinkled her nose. "What *is* that?"

"Not really sure what they used to plug it," Zak said.

The glass warmed even more and he felt a bit light-headed from the stench. But he held the lighter with a steady hand and was rewarded with a faint *pop*. He reached up and gripped what was, he could now tell, clearly cork, between his thumb and index finger and slowly pulled upward. At first, the cork remained firmly in place. But as he continued to pull upward, the cork finally gave way with another little *pop*.

"What's inside?" Maggie said.

He angled the bottle so they could both look inside. Maggie put a hand on his arm as she leaned forward to peer in and his breath caught.

"Hmm. What's the best way to get that roll of paper out?" he murmured. Tweezers, he decided.

He took a pair from the drawer underneath the workbench and carefully fitted the tweezers into the bottle's neck. He clamped the tweezers onto the roll of yellowed, brownish paper and began to pull it out a millimeter at a time.

Maggie sucked in a breath. "Let's hope it doesn't crumble or tear."

Zak finally managed to free the rolled-up paper from its ancient prison. His heartbeat sped up as he glanced at Maggie. Her eyes sparkled as he held her gaze before he gently touched the age-darkened, curled page. As he uncurled the edges, pieces of the paper flaked off. Almost-black mottled spots sprinkled the brownish page at various intervals.

Zak winced and held his breath as the creased folds gave way. The paper lay in pieces instead of one full sheet. He focused on the faded cursive and, on an impulse, began to read it aloud.

Coastal waters off St. John's Island
12 July 1701   Henry Davies

Dearest Henry,

The time for our nuptials grows nigh. My heart soars like a bird a-wing. Oh, but for the taste of your kisses and the peace and joy that comes with our reunion. I fairly tremble with gladness to be soon in your arms. I have consulted the charts and believe we shall arrive on the shores of the fair St. John's Island two days hence.

Zak paused and glanced at Maggie. Longing tugged at his heart as she held his gaze for a moment longer than necessary. She cleared her throat and read the next passage.

Even as I write you, I have obtained a gown of finest silk. Though in truth, I should gladly stand by your side as wife in little more than rags if 'twould mean our togetherness sooner.

It gladdens my heart to know that your trading with the Mi'kmaq along the island's north shore Gulf has been so bountiful. I am gladder still that you have arrived unharmed from your voyages with that Company and are awaiting my missive thusly.

Maggie glanced at Zak and he saw an answering longing in her eyes, which was almost immediately replaced with an expectant look. So he took a breath to steady himself and read the final paragraphs, his heartbeat loud in his ears.

Mayhap I shall seal this within a bottle of the Caribbean's finest and, perhaps, toss it overboard? Nay, I jest. Though I have on more than one occasion, entertained such a fanciful notion.

Darling of my heart, though I do not wish to taint such a missive as this with disturbed news, I feel I must. My pendant has gone missing. I have little doubt who may have purloined it, though I shall wait to accuse him of thus until after our day of vow exchange three days hence. For nothing is as important as being with you once again.

Zak's voice grew husky and he stopped, unable to continue or to look up from the page. He blinked rapidly and exhaled in relief as Maggie's voice whispered the last lines.

Your affianced Beloved,
Eleanor

Zak rubbed his jaw and forced himself to look at Maggie. But she quickly averted her gaze and looked down at the desk top. "Zak, look. There's another scrap of paper here that was inside the bottle. With different writing scrawled on it."

Before Zak could respond, his grad assistant came into the room. "The sonar picked up three targets in this new location."

Maggie threw Zak a questioning glance. "Good news?"

Zak explained, "We've gleaned some new bits and piec-

es to go on after talking with locals, which have been helpful to triangulate a narrower search location. So we've used the sonar to scan the new area closer in to the bay."

"Oh?" Maggie said.

"The ship's sails were in flames, so there was no way to control it," Zak said. "So it would've probably drifted toward the rocks near the bay after it had been set ablaze."

Maggie glanced out the window then back at Zak. "Storm looks like it's holding off for now," she said. "You have to take this chance while you have it." She put a hand on Zak's arm. "You should go explore that first target here now."

Zak's eyes widened. Had Maggie seen he'd changed, after all? "Are...you sure about that? I know the pendant's important to you—"

"—and I know how important this is to you." She lifted her chin and crossed her arms.

Zak slowly turned back to his grad assistant. "Looks like it's something fairly large." He glanced at Maggie before he gave a nod to his assistant, "I want two others with me for the dive. We should bring down a lift bag, just in case whatever's down there is worth bringing to the surface."

ZAK GLANCED AT the elapsed time dial on his Hublot and then triple-checked his oxygen. They'd been down here about fifteen minutes already.

He and the two other divers swam toward the large object submerged in the red silt on the sea floor.

As he swam toward it, he spotted several cannon balls strewn around.

The shape was oblong and a good size. He and his dive partners cleared away the excess sand and silt around the object.

He grinned. It looked like...a trunk?

As they continued to investigate, more cannon shot was revealed, along with musket balls, shards of china plates and silverware. Debris.

Zak's heart sped up. If this trunk was well preserved, what was inside just might provide vital clues about life aboard the ship and help him with the goals of this project.

That is, if it belonged to Eleanor's ship. But there was only one way to find that out. They'd have to bring it to the surface. The trunk rested on a gentle slope, sideways and at an angle to him.

They positioned the lift bag near the trunk. After some effort, they carefully extracted it then moved it into the bag. As Zak gave a last-minute check that everything was in order, he glanced back down at the now-exposed area where the trunk had been.

Was that...a ship's bell? His pulse pounded. If it was... He glanced at his Hublot. Not much air left. They had to get to the surface. He gestured to the other divers and they all began to swim upward.

Deck-side a little while later, Zak got out of his dry suit and into his T-shirt and jeans. He scrubbed a hand across his five o'clock shadow. He blew out an excited breath and headed over to the lab. "What do we have?"

"Looks like you were right. Some sort of trunk," his grad assistant said. "I'd say, judging from the construction, Spanish. Mid to late 1600s."

Zak took a step closer as he pulled on his white cotton gloves. "Let's go ahead and carefully take the top off before we start the conservation process."

The assistant nodded. "Wouldn't want to damage anything we might find inside."

The lock mechanism had seized up and must not have been locked when the ship went down because the lid creaked open in Zak's hands. His breath caught. Folded inside the trunk was a swath of material. Aside from a few water stains, perfectly preserved.

Maggie gasped. "It looks like it was packed away yesterday."

Zak grinned. "It's because of the red clay substrate. The trunk was pretty much sealed inside the red clay undisturbed, which kept everything inside it preserved."

He closed his fingers around the material and lifted it out. A gown. He held it up. The style was definitely early 1700s. Which meant, this trunk very well could be from Eleanor's ship.

He cocked his head. It looked like—

"Silk," Maggie whispered. "This has to be Eleanor's wedding dress."

As Zak laid the dress down on the table, a single sheet of paper fell to the floor. It must have been tucked inside the dress's folds. He picked it up carefully. It was a logbook page.

H K F   Courses   Winds   Remarks: 15 July 1701

1 6 4   SSW   S.E.   1/2 past noon. We are in sight of coastal waters off Bay Fortune—62W longitude, 46N latitude. Storm clouds on horizon. —E.W.

2 6 5

3 4 —   SSW

4 5 —   SSW off SW   E

5 6 5   WSW   N.E.   'Tis as I feared. Wind's shifted & weather has turned against us. The Quartermaster, too. His jealousy of my affections for H. has made him touched in the head. —E.W.

6 4 6

7 3 —   SW   N.N.E.   The wheel has been tied and my best men cut down. I have waited too long, been too sure of myself, to realize that I have spent all my efforts in trying to regain the pendant from the Quartermaster, when I should have solely concerned myself with returning to H. Though I fought the Quartermaster blade to blade, I cannot fight the blaze... 'Tis only a matter of time. I espy the lone dinghy and will make

*toward it though I think 'twill do no good now. I can
only set this down and stow it in my trunk, with the
hope that someday my words shall be read and this true
account, if not consumed first by fire, be made
known. —E.W.*

He stared down at the page. This lined everything up: the hour of the day, the speed of the ship in knots, what course they'd charted and the wind direction ... It clearly documented the last known location before Eleanor's ship went down. His pulse pounded. "With these additional points of reference on this logbook page, we can verify the site. Then use that to pinpoint the wreck area even more specifically. With allowances, of course, for time and tides."

Zak's grad assistant nodded. "I'll enter them into the computer and get the sonar to scan this specific region."

"Good. This trunk was Eleanor's, so it's more than likely that the mound of silt it rested on could conceal *Lady's Revenge.*"

AFTER THE ASSISTANT left, and Maggie was alone with Zak, she said, "I've been looking at that scrap of paper while you were underwater. Might have something to do with the shipwreck." She pointed to the scrawled lines she'd noticed earlier.

Do not keep watch for the Highest light,
Where Fortune's fire no more burns bright.

Zak examined it. "It's rhyming." He looked at Maggie and murmured, "This might have something to do with the pendant, too."

"It's like the other riddles," she said.

Zak glanced back at the two lines, which, he noticed, had what looked like tiny squiggle marks underneath each line. "This looks like Davies' handwriting."

"So that means Davies must have gotten Eleanor's letter that was with this at some point," Zak mused.

"But did he receive Eleanor's letter in the bottle, or did he put the letter into the bottle?" Maggie asked.

"Either way, he must've put this extra note inside."

"Why would he do that?" Maggie frowned.

"I have no idea," Zak said. "But I suspect we may find out." He raised his eyebrows at her.

"Well, we're getting closer now," Maggie said. "We just have to figure out what it means."

"We *are* getting closer." His eyes flicked from the faded script back to Maggie's face.

Maggie's pulse jumped at the tone of Zak's voice. "So," she said hurriedly, "this is telling us *not* to keep watch for the highest light. What does that even mean?"

"Highest light...well, back 300 years ago, that could mean stars."

"Or a bonfire on a hill. Or cliff."

"Mmm." Zak repeated the first line. "Who would look for a light?"

"Sailors?" Maggie said.

"Wait a second. Do not keep watch... Keeping watch. What keeps watch?" Zak said.

"Watchtowers," Maggie guessed. "A lighthouse?"

Zak nodded. "But it's telling us not to keep a watch for lighthouses."

"So if we're not supposed to look for a lighthouse, what are we supposed to look for?"

"Look at the next line," he said. "Fortune with a capital *F*. I think it's referring to Bay Fortune, but it also mentions fire. Back then there was no lighthouse here. The British didn't even have the island yet. The French still did."

"So what could it mean?" Maggie asked.

"Well...the Vikings once explored this area. When I was a student, I did a work study on that Viking site at L'Anse aux Meadows in Newfoundland. But I have a friend who found a rune stone here on P.E.I. And Bay Fortune is supposed to have had a Viking watchtower..."

"So I was right about the watchtower in that first guess." Maggie grinned at Zak.

"Funny how your first instincts are usually correct," Zak agreed.

Maggie caught his gaze but couldn't read his expression. Yet something had flashed in the depths of his gaze in the moments before he averted his eyes and looked back down at the page.

"Let's go," Maggie said.

JUST THEN, ZAK'S grad assistant poked her head around the door again. "Dr. Stuart? The sonar's ready." Zak looked at his assistant then back at Maggie.

Damn it.

This was not what he wanted to do. Choose between the wreck that could make his career, and the pendant that could make Maggie's.

Maggie bit her lip and glanced between him and his assistant.

If this were five days ago—hell, five hours ago—he might've let Maggie take her chances with the elements, the pendant.

But something in that look that had flashed between them only moments before, had his heart saying one thing, and his head another.

When would he get this opportunity again? This opportunity to uncover a wreck that had only existed before in legend... Or this opportunity to show Maggie what he truly thought, to make up for three years of not saying anything, not being supportive of her artistic career?

But this, this... would show her, with absolute clarity, what he should've told her long ago. That the history of someone else's life was not as important as the future of his own.

"Let's go," he said, as he headed to the door.

"But Zak." Maggie chewed on her bottom lip and put her

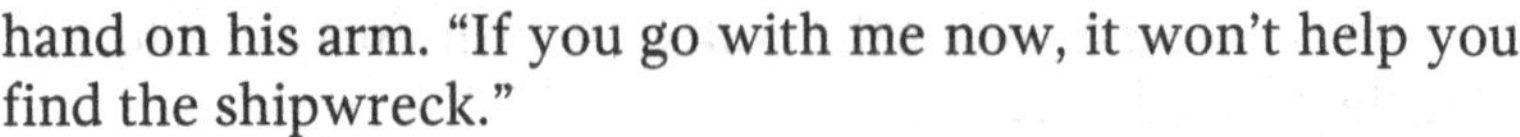

hand on his arm. "If you go with me now, it won't help you find the shipwreck."

"It'll help you find the pendant."

"But I don't need the pendant any more," Maggie said. "I've gotten my inspiration now. So you don't *need* to do it."

"No," Zak said, "I don't need to do it—I want to do it. And that makes all the difference. So come on."

Maggie broke into a smile. "Can I just...?" She indicated a small clear plastic sleeve on the table. At Zak's nod, she tucked the extra piece of paper that had been inside the bottle, into the protective sleeve and then put the whole thing into her jeans pocket.

"Keep me posted. I shouldn't be gone too long," he said to his assistant as he and Maggie walked by on their way to the dinghy. "The moment you find anything more specific, call me."

"Sure thing," Zak's grad assistant said.

"But listen..." Zak scanned the horizon. "I know everyone's gung-ho, but if the storm ends up here, get yourselves ashore."

His assistant nodded, and turned back in the direction of the computers.

Zak picked the ancient bottle up off of the worktop. "Wouldn't hurt to bring this along since I didn't get a chance to look at it very closely yet," he said, as he tucked the bottle into an inner pocket of his windbreaker.

Then he and Maggie headed to shore and over to his pickup.

Rain began to fall.

Zak turned the radio on after he and Maggie jumped into the Dodge. *"Due to the rapid intensification of this storm in the last twenty-four hours, a hurricane watch is in effect for the Maritimes and specifically, Prince Edward Island. Record winds have begun to pound the south shore of the island near Borden-Carlton. The—"*

Zak changed the channel and glanced at Maggie. "Borden-Carlton's a ways from Bay Fortune here, but the storm's close."

"Well," she said, "that should keep the treasure hunters at bay, at least."

"Might make the cliffs around Bay Fortune especially dangerous. Even wash them away entirely."

"But we're too close to stop now," Maggie said.

Chapter Ten

THE RAIN LASHED against the windshield as Zak pulled onto a rutted red dirt track, and the wind flattened the acres of potato plants that grew in glossy green rows on either side of the road.

The truck rumbled further down the lane scored with dozens of recent tire tracks. "People have been here," Zak muttered. "This lighthouse is about the only historic landmark associated with Bay Fortune, so of course some of them would think to look here."

Maggie chewed her lip. "What if they found something?"

"Well," Zak said, "we don't really know what we're looking for, either, so I'd say everyone's on equal ground."

A stand of twisted and gnarled evergreens served as a buffer against the dramatic drop-off of these craggy cliffs along the South Shore.

And there, perched atop the highest, craggiest point, was the lighthouse. Zak leaned forward and looked up at it as the road dipped and wound its way toward what was left of the structure.

He glanced over at Maggie, raised his eyebrows then turned the radio to CBC.

"*—the Confederation Bridge has now been closed and a hurricane warning is in effect for all of P.E.I.—*"

Zak cut the engine.

"You sure this is the right place?" she said.

"Yes," Zak said. "They built this lighthouse in the 1800s. But what most people don't know is that the reason they built it here was because the foundation was the old Viking watchtower. The Vikings had already picked out a good spot and so the Scottish settlers—nothing if not practical—knew a good thing when they saw it. So they just used that foundation and made this lighthouse."

Black clouds boiled above the steel-gray surface of the Northumberland Strait. "You do realize this is kind of insane," Maggie said. But there was a gleam in her eyes.

"Just like that time we got caught in that nor'easter at Annapolis Royal, eh?" Zak said.

Maggie grinned.

Zak glanced out the windshield. "Storm's not that bad here. Yet." Almost as an afterthought, Zak grabbed the first aid kit. "We'll take shelter in the lighthouse if we need to. We'll be safe."

Maggie opened the passenger door as the rain began to pound harder. "Come on," Maggie said. "We'd better hurry or we might get washed away."

Zak got out too and zipped his jacket up just as the wind tried to rip it away from him.

"This way," he shouted over the gathering storm.

Maggie bent her head against a strong wind gust and followed Zak across a grassy field near the edge of the bay. The field was dotted with large and small holes. Shovels and picks lay scattered around, abandoned thanks to the storm. She moved ahead of Zak as they climbed up the narrow cliff-side path that led to the dilapidated lighthouse. Paint peeled off the clapboards. What had once been bright red around the door and window frames now had barely a hint of color.

The wind whipped Maggie's hair around her face as she increased her pace along the narrow path. As Zak hurried to catch up, the glass bottle banged against his ribs. Too bad there wasn't any rum left in it.

THE RAIN PELTED down harder. Another wind gust hit Zak in the chest. Just a little further and they'd be at the lighthouse

door...

He kept one eye on the narrow path as the cliff fell away to his left. He glanced out at the water. The tide was coming in.

Ahead of him, Maggie slipped. Someone had dug a hole right next to the path. She scrambled to regain her feet on the crumbling, uneven ground but she stumbled, inches away from the sheer seven-foot drop off. Just as the wind gusted harder, she pitched forward. Zak lunged forward to snag the fabric of her shirt.

But he was too late.

His heart plunged as he watched her half-slide, half-tumble down the sheer bank. He sank to his knees by the cliff's edge. Pieces of earth broke away underneath his weight as he placed a palm against the cold ground and peered over the edge. His breath caught when he saw she wasn't moving. "Maggie!" he called. Zak's heart wrenched. How badly was she hurt?

But she looked up and grinned.

"I'm fine!" she yelled over the wind and rain. She stood and headed back toward the cliff face as the tide washed over her feet. The wind ripped at his hair and he could taste the saltwater in the air as she reached up toward him. She pointed to something just above her head then shouted something else, but the wind whipped her words away from him. He leaned even closer to the edge. Craned his neck so that he had a better view. His heart jumped as he realized what Maggie pointed at.

Tucked into a small crevice on the cliff face was a badly tarnished something that looked like it could have been, at one time, a brass ring. Or a handle... on a treasure chest?

Maggie scrabbled up to a small ledge and grasped the weathered round brass handle with her free hand. Sea spray splashed against her legs.

Zak held his breath and watched as she tugged on the handle. It didn't move. Was it some sort of marker? Or part of a box?

"Maggie, you don't have time to do that!"

"Now is not a good time to start an argument with me, Zak," she yelled up at him between gritted teeth as she tugged on the ring again.

Bits of earth crumbled and fell away into the roiling waters below as she perched on the tiny outcropping that she'd somehow scrambled up onto. The tide rolled higher.

"I'm going to get you out of here," Zak called. He scooted forward on his stomach and stretched his hand down toward her. He could just brush her shoulder with his fingertips. "Can you move any higher?"

She shook her head.

Suddenly, a huge swell surged and Maggie's legs were submerged. The current sucked at her even as she gripped the ring.

As her grip tightened, more and more red earth crumbled away from her. Another surge swamped her lower body. It tugged at her as if she were a bathtub toy.

Zak, stretched out as far as possible, grasped a piece of her green T-shirt between his fingers at last and held on tight.

Another wave hit.

"You'll have to let go of the ring, Maggie! It's the only way."

"No!" She screamed over the roar of the waves and the lash of the wind. "What if it's the treasure chest?"

"Maggie!" he yelled back, "It's your life or a pile of gold. You have to let it go."

"I-I can't."

Was she crying?

A wave of empathy followed by frustration washed through him as yet another surge of water pummelled her. The force of the wave swept one of Maggie's legs out from under her.

And this time, she couldn't hold on to both the ledge and the ring. As the swell washed over Maggie, she let go and reached up to clasp Zak's arm.

"Damn it." He gritted his teeth and dug his toes into the earth but it did no good. He started to slide. She scrabbled for purchase but her other foot slipped off the ledge. He felt the full force of her body weight add to his as he lay on the bank.

"But I-I didn't get the chest," Maggie said.

Zak's heart lurched. He didn't care about any damn chest. Maggie's life was priceless. He wouldn't trade it for all the gold in the world. He reached down with his other arm and managed to grasp her other shoulder. Then leveraged himself around so that he could try to grip under her arms.

But he knew that he'd never be able to lift her up from this position.

He closed his eyes a second and a flash of those emerald-green eyes came to him. And...what was that sound? He cocked his head. He could've sworn he heard a voice that sounded like bluebirds and brooks in spring, whisper the words *pure hearted* in his ear under the keening of the wind. Yes. *This* was what Eleanor had meant. His eyes welled.

Just then, Maggie called, "I found another toehold! I think I can climb up."

Zak helped her heave herself over the edge of the cliff face. The wind and rain seemed to let up for a few precious moments as she scrambled, at last, to safety.

"God, Maggie." Zak's lips were on her hair, her cheeks, her forehead. "Are you *sure* you're all right?"

She nodded as her breath came in shallow gasps. He traced a finger down her cheek and under her chin. "Are you sure?" Concern filled his eyes.

Maggie sucked in a breath. Nodded. Then took another breath. "I'm okay," she managed then winced. "Besides the fact that my ankle hurts, I think I'm mostly fine." She staggered to her feet. "I had a realization while I was down there. That ring wasn't a box. It was some sort of ancient mooring stuck into the foundation. *Do not keep watch for the highest light...* We need to look at the bottom." She pointed to the foundation as she squinted against the onslaught of wind and rain.

Zak picked up the first aid kit. They reached the dilapidated doorway of the lighthouse as the wind began to howl and the rain turned needle-sharp.

A rusted padlock dangled from the door.

Hell. He didn't think to bring bolt cutters. Zak turned to jog back to his truck to get the pry bar and the toolbox from the bed. But Maggie grabbed his arm. She held up the lock—broken. She grinned and turned the knob. But it still wouldn't budge. He shouldered the door. But it was stuck fast. He felt Maggie shove against the door too.

At last, with their combined efforts, the old door finally gave way. The scent of musty air mixed with old lumber and a whiff of salt air, hit him as they stumbled inside.

MAGGIE FELT ZAK'S hand on her waist as she stumbled a few steps into the small space. She turned to look up at him. He met her gaze. But the shrill of his cell phone cut through the moment. He glanced at the device. "I have to take this. It's from my team."

He put the phone to his ear. Listened. "We can't jump to conclusions." A pause. "Yes. Everyone's all right?" Another pause. "I'm fine. I'm with Maggie." More silence. Then, "I saw that. The bell had letters on it." He nodded. "You're sure? Right, yes. Wait for me to come and verify. We'll stay here til the storm passes. But I think we hit the jackpot." He hung up the phone.

"So," she said, "good news?"

"That debris trail actually led somewhere." He grinned. "The team's all safely ashore and they had time to analyze things. That sandy slope was part of *Lady's Revenge*. Turns out the silt covered the ship's bell—which confirmed it was *Lady's Revenge*."

"Really?" Maggie grinned back at Zak. "That's fantastic!"

Zak laughed. Maggie felt a tug in her chest. He sounded like the Zak she remembered.

"In really rare instances," he said, "in this case, with *Lady's Revenge*—if the silt can cover the wreck quickly enough, it preserves the wooden hull for thousands of years."

"And archaeologists like you live for things like that, don't you?"

Zak's grin widened. "But finding the wreck isn't the whole puzzle..."

"No." Maggie dragged her gaze from Zak and glanced around. "So where do we look now?"

"Under there could be a good place to look first." Zak pointed to a trap door. Maggie crouched down by it. Zak felt around the edges. Fit two fingers into a shallow depression and pulled upward. With a creak and groan, the door raised up on its hinges. Maggie peered over Zak's shoulder. Pitch black. He opened the first aid kit, pulled out a large flashlight and flicked it on. The powerful beam illuminated a series of crude steps carved into the sandstone bedrock that led down to a small hand-dug cellar.

"This had to be here in Davies' time," Zak murmured as his fingertips brushed the stone step. Maggie shivered as a sudden memory of Zak's fingers along her skin flashed through her mind. Zak lay the trapdoor down with a thud. He started down the steps and she followed. Damp sandstone and stale seawater stung her nose as he swung the light back and forth.

"What's that?" She pointed to a shape in the darkest corner.

Zak trained the beam on it and moved toward the corner. "Looks like it's a pile of something...metal?" He nudged it with his boot and peered more closely. "From what I can tell, it was once iron bands. There's some pieces of wood clinging to the metal, too. So maybe it was a barrel? But it's pretty much nothing but rust and rotten wood splinters now." He turned to Maggie. "Can you hold the flashlight a sec?"

She took it from him, set it on the floor and aimed it at the low ceiling. The entire room was bathed in light.

"If my guess is right, those bands would've possibly been about the size and dimensions of a rum barrel—like would've been in here." He pulled out the old rum bottle from his inside pocket.

He idly turned it over in his hands and tapped the base against his palm. As he did so, his brow furrowed. "That's strange."

"What is?"

"The bottom of the bottle—it makes my hand look larger." His frown deepened as he held the bottle upside down, then looked down into the bottle after he turned it right side up again. "It works like a magnification device."

He held the bottle up to the light. "Yeah. It's like a primitive lens... I want to test out how strong the magnification is."

"Here." Maggie handed him the small piece that had been with Eleanor's letter. "This is the only piece of paper I have."

He examined the page through the bottle-lens. "Those squiggles are—"

"—more lines." Maggie's pulse raced.

Zak cleared his throat and read aloud.

For the heart
To finally be unbound,
ReTurn the treasured love
You have found.

"I assume *heart* means the pendant," Zak said, "so we have to *return the treasured love/you have found.*"

"But we haven't found any, uh, love, treasured or otherwise," Maggie said.

"And if we interpret it literally, that makes no sense," Zak added. "Not only that, it's impossible to return something we haven't found."

"Nothing is impossible," she said.

"Well..." Zak paused. "You know what I mean."

"Treasured love..." Maggie cocked her head. "Wait a sec. Eleanor received the gold from Kidd. In one of Eleanor's letters, she said she intended to give some of the gold to

Davies for their life together..."

"So," Zak said, "maybe it literally means treasure."

"Right." Maggie's eyes grew round. "And the treasured love—maybe that means Eleanor gave her doubloons to Davies as a representation of her love for him."

"I thought that was the pendant."

"No. Remember the letters?" Maggie said. "She had the necklace long before she met Davies."

"Hmmm," Zak said.

"But," Maggie said, "doubloons..." She unzipped the interior pocket of her purse and pulled out the antique bracelet. "So your ancestor Samuel had gotten the coin and the pouch both from that innkeeper, Robert Morriss, who'd gotten both items from Beale. Beale got the doubloon and pouch from one of his treasure-hunting partners, John MacDonald, who was the grandson of Nicholas MacDonald. Nicholas, who must've passed on the coin to his grandson John, had served aboard *Lady's Revenge* under Eleanor. So Nicholas must have gotten the coin somehow from Eleanor. I bet she told him to give it to Davies. She did say in one of the letters that she trusted MacDonald completely."

"That's true," Zak said.

"Eleanor wanted the gold to be symbolic of her love for Davies."

"But it says *return*."

"And the *T* is capitalized." Maggie frowned again. Tapped a fingernail against her chin. "Well, maybe that's important. Maybe it's..."

"...also literal?" Zak raised his eyebrows at her.

"*Re-Turn*. Turn again. Turn what again though? I wonder if it means we're supposed to somehow turn the coin around?"

"But it's not attached to anything besides the chain," Zak pointed out.

Maggie sighed and fiddled with the coin on the bracelet.

"Turn can also mean twist. So maybe..." Zak looked at the bottle. Reached for the bracelet in Maggie's hand. "Can I...?"

Maggie held her breath as he picked up the bracelet from her outstretched palm. "I just thought the edges of the coin were showing normal wear and tear since gold is soft," she said.

"But these irregular edges make it look like someone hacked away at it," Zak said. "So how does that connect with the other part...?" He nudged at the pile of iron dust and wood pieces with his boot. "There *was* a barrel sitting here. See how those pieces of wood are clinging to the last iron band? The wood is from the decayed barrel staves." He hefted the bottle in his hands.

"Which means, if there once were bands then *unbound* would fit."

"You're right. The iron bands of this barrel bound the wood together and held it all in place. So that means the treasure must have something to do with the barrel that was here."

He shone the flashlight down among the wreckage.

"Nothing there?" Maggie said.

Zak shook his head and sighed. "I mean, the trap door is right there in plain sight. Someone probably took whatever was down here years ago."

Maggie put a hand on his arm. "But we have recovered some treasure of a sort."

Zak turned to her. "We *are* talking to each other again."

Maggie smiled. "Maybe that's what's important."

She glanced down at the now-exposed flagstone where Zak had brushed aside the pile of iron dust. "That's a funny indentation."

Zak looked where she pointed.

"That indent..." He swore under his breath and leaned closer to examine it. "It's carved out to look like the reverse of the head of a coin. This barrel wasn't put here by accident. Let me see the bracelet again."

Maggie handed it back to him. "It's a perfect fit," he murmured. He pressed the coin down hard into the crudely chiseled receptacle.

"Turn it," Maggie said suddenly. "We need to turn the

coin." She glanced at Zak, a question in her eyes. He nodded.

She laid her fingers on top of his and they both turned the coin clockwise. There was a slight grating sound of stone on stone. The flagstone, which hadn't been mortared into place, shifted slightly to the side to reveal a small iron box.

Maggie caught her breath.

Zak glanced over at her. "You can do the honors."

The hinges stuck, but with Zak's help, the lid finally opened. The glint of gold winked back at them. Nestled in the middle of the pile of gold doubloons was a large emerald. It glowed softly in the dim light.

"The Pendant of the Pure Hearted," Zak said, as he looked into the chest.

"And these coins were Kidd's payment to Eleanor," Maggie added.

"Maybe you're right," Zak murmured as she caught him watching the expression on her face. She knew he didn't mean about the gold.

"I'm sorry," she said. "I've been such an idiot." A small smile appeared at her lips, and she looked up at him through her lashes. "I was lying to myself. About my designs. And about what my heart was telling me."

Maggie came closer to him. Placed a hand on his chest. For a moment, she said nothing and kept her eyes closed. She shook her head. She should've known it from the start. She'd just been trying to keep herself safe.

Fantasies didn't have flaws. Fantasies were safe. Safe and lonely. But she couldn't run to some fantasy. That was just in her head.

But Zak... Zak was here. Zak was warm and real and flesh and blood and he was here. Right here. In front of her.

She swallowed. She was in love with him. Flaws and all. "And Zak? I lied when I said I didn't love you." She moved her hand up to softly touched his cheek. "I'm sorry I said no to you. The truth is, I've never stopped loving you."

"It's okay." Zak shook his head. "I'm sorry for my behavior, too. I couldn't see past my anger. I couldn't see past your supposed betrayal of my trust. But I see now that we just weren't ready to move in the same direction."

Maggie drew in a jagged breath.

"But that's all in the past," Zak murmured.

For a moment, neither of them spoke.

Zak closed his eyes for a moment and whispered, "I've missed you." He opened his eyes, reached out, and laid a hand on her cheek. "So much."

He stroked a thumb down her cheek.

"Me too." She grazed her fingertips along his jawline.

Zak placed one hand over hers. Then reached down and picked up the pendant. The jewel glowed more, as if lit by an internal fire. His eyes briefly closed. When he opened them again and made eye contact with Maggie, she caught her breath at the tenderness in his gaze.

"Eleanor was right," Zak said simply and handed the pendant to her.

It felt warm and...almost alive in Maggie's cupped hands. It glowed even brighter and she felt an answering glow in her heart as she looked at Zak.

"So what are you going to do with that new jewelry design of yours?"

"Well," she said, "I've been thinking. I love designing and creating jewelry the most, and can do a lot of that from my laptop. I'll have more freedom, then. I thought about opening my own jewelry stores. But I've decided I can just be a jewelry supplier to local businesses—here and in New York." She smiled. "I think people are going to fall in love with my new design."

"Just like I'm falling in love with you?" Zak whispered. "Again."

The pounding of the rain on the roof and the lash of wind at the windows were drowned out by the rush of blood in Maggie's veins. "Yes." She laid her cheek against his shoulder. "Just like that. What about you?"

"Well, I'll be able to get the funding to mount a full-scale excavation of the wreck now that the triangulation was successful and we've found it. Not only that—" he grinned "—but I'll also be able to finish that final book chapter. Who knows? Maybe I'll even publish it myself. And now that you'll have more freedom, that means we can travel wherever we want. Together. We don't have to be stuck in different places."

"Yes," Maggie said. "I like that. A lot. So, I think it's time to head back."

Zak maneuvered the small iron box sideways and up and out of its hiding place. But as he did, the lid gapped open and the contents shifted slightly. "What's this?" He paused and picked up a sheaf of papers that lay underneath the gems and gold. One was a neatly folded piece of paper. The others were unfolded, with jagged edges along one side, as if they'd been torn from a book.

H—   Sept 5, 1701

Your plan pleased me greatly, as I, too, felt the burden of guilt from Eleanor's untimely death. As you know, I travelled to England in the first months of this year.

'Tis fortunate Kidd held Eleanor, you, and I, in such esteem, as I availed myself of the opportunity to pay a visit to him in Jail, so as to share with him our Knowledge. He gladly agreed to have me secret the coded message you directed, onto his Letter to the Speaker.

—N.M.

"A note from Nicholas to Davies," Maggie mused. "Which means, since Nicholas served as Eleanor's first mate, he must have been asked by Davies to write the third riddle," she said. "Then passed word on about it to his grandson John, who then must've told Beale..."

"Yeah," Zak said, "And then Beale wrote down the cipher key."

"But if Eleanor intended the gold for Davies, why was he writing clues to hide it?" Maggie asked.

"Hmm," Zak said, "Maybe he couldn't bear to keep it

with him, but didn't want to part with it, either?" They turned their attention back to the uncovered pages.

2 June 1701

Kidd is dead. Eleanor would have been a-grieved, had she known of it. Though I wonder, some nights, if she somehow does...

Maggie read the next entry over Zak's shoulder.

16 July 1701

She is dead. I have wrestled her beloved necklace from the grasp of the Quartermaster, Kidd's former crewman—James Fitzhugh. The gold, as well. Though I longed to drive a blade through his heart for what he has done, I have withheld such urgings. Instead, I trust to Fate that his end shall not be a Pleasant one, to atone for those Sins he has committed.

"So the gold Kidd had given Eleanor had ended up with Davies," Maggie murmured and then continued to read.

22 July 1701

Lately I feel Eleanor's presence, as if she is urging me to do something, though I know not what that may be. I have begun to salvage what is of use that has washed inland from Lady's Revenge.

I have decided I shall stay here amid the Mi'kmaq on this Isle cradled on the waves. 'Tis become my home. Though I could not share it with Eleanor, I do continue to feel her presence. It comforts me greatly.

30 Oct 1701

At last I believe I know what Eleanor has been urging. So, I have taken precautions. I've safely hidden the pendant I retrieved from the Quartermaster, along with the rest of the doubloons and other gems that I gath-ered from Lady's Revenge *when they washed into some shallows.*

'Tis all that's left of her worldly possessions. And that which was freely given her by that Indian wise woman and Kidd. Though it grieves me some, as that treasure trove she and I originally conceived of as the means to our happy life together.

16 April 1702

I have sought and found a way to honor my Beloved, and the memory of our Love. I have written up two riddles, as a testament to our love, our saga. May there be a way for those with strong constitutions—as my Eleanor had; and with pure-hearted love—as our union was to be—to solve the verses.

Whoever so does shall be thusly rewarded with the treasure that I have aforementioned, should they take the time to be diligent and thorough in their quest. After I received Eleanor's letter of 12 July, I decided to place it inside an empty bottle of the Caribbean's finest, as Eleanor had made reference to. I hid one of the riddles inside the bottle, as well. I have also secreted the treasure. I do believe this is what she would have wanted, and I do it solely to honor her memory, to honor our Love. May she rest in peace.

"So these are the missing pages from Davies' journal," Zak said, as he replaced all the papers, closed the lid and tucked the box under his arm.

He took Maggie's hand and went up the cellar stairs, across the scarred wooden floor of the lighthouse, and outside. The clouds began to soften to a dove gray. "Looks like the storm is ebbing." He reached up to stroke Maggie's hair.

Maggie looked up at Zak and smiled. But then she gasped. Pointed out into the harbor. Zak turned to look. Off in the distance, the clouds parted to reveal a rainbow arched across the sky. Underneath the rainbow, white sails billowed in the non-existent breeze. Red, yellow, green and white signal flags flapped all along the mainsail.

A stately four-masted tall ship sailed around the end of the point and disappeared.

"Looks like we broke the curse," Maggie whispered.

Zak reached for her hand and intertwined his fingers with hers. "No curse," he said softly, and looked toward the end of the point. "Just everlasting joy for what was, and now shall always be." He turned his gaze back to her and smiled. "We've found not only the treasure, but also each other." He ran a hand along her cheek and whispered, "And now, it's for always." Zak leaned in and kissed her.

Acknowledgments

Karen Dale Harris—developmental editor, whose excellent insights and suggestions helped me shape this story into its final form

My parents, Sabrina Volman and J. Esmee McAskill—beta readers, who were awesome and read and encouraged this story from manuscript to publication

Jane Dixon-Smith—graphic designer, who gave me a beautiful cover for the story

Kirsten M. Hawley—underwater archaeologist, who very kindly and patiently answered my numerous questions and read through relevant parts of the narrative for archaeological, technical and scientific accuracy

I've always loved the movies *National Treasure* and *Pirates of the Caribbean*. So when I learned about the sightings of the Ghost Ship of the Northumberland Strait on P.E.I., I knew I had the kernel of an idea for the second book in this series, and just *had* to do something to combine romance, treasure hunting, and ghostly ships!

When I wrote this novel, I wanted to be as accurate as possible, and as true-to-reality as the facts would allow. However, there were instances when, because of the time periods of this book, it wasn't possible. So I took artistic license to modify dates, timelines, and such to fit the storyline. For example, the first documented sightings of the ghost ship are really in 1786, not in 1701, as I've written in this novel. (Though perhaps the early P.E.I. settlers did see it but didn't bother to write about it?) Memorial University does indeed have an archaeology department but they don't actually have a nautical archaeology program—I took the liberty of inventing that position for Zak.

When I researched Dalvay and its original owner, Alexander MacDonald, I wasn't able to uncover anything about his ancestors. So I took artistic license and gave him ancestors who sailed with Captain Kidd.

I also made a few timeline tweaks to *The Prince Edward Island Magazine, Volume I*. It was actually published in 1899, but, for the sake of this story's timeline, I've modified its publication date to be 1848.

The Viking settlement in Newfound is real. But the P.E.I. Viking watchtower and Bay Fortune-area lighthouse are purely figments of my imagination, as is the craggy cliff I've placed the fictitious lighthouse atop. And, while there are cliffs along the South Shore, there aren't any around the Bay Fortune area.

The Beale Papers truly exist, but have no ties (that I know of!) to P.E.I.

And remember, if you decide to drive the shoreline of Prince Edward Island, keep your eyes open for the ghostly tall ship... You just might see it!

PRINCE EDWARD ISLAND LOVE LETTERS & LEGENDS

JESSICA EISSFELDT

At last
it's true love

Book 3

At last it's true love

A Novel

**Book 3 in the
Prince Edward Island Love Letters & Legends Trilogy**

JESSICA EISSFELDT

At Last It's True Love: A novel
Jessica Eissfeldt

Copyright © 2020 by Jessica Eissfeldt. All rights reserved.

Chapter One

ICKY STENDAHL'S EYES drifted to the worn and crumpled envelope with its faded, spidery handwriting and vintage stamp.

A few lines from the antique love letter inside echoed through her mind. *I feel that the only thing keeping me sane is thinking of you. Of us. Of being together again. Of kissing in dimly lit hallways with flickering bulbs, closed canteens, and the sounds of swing music floating in from the street while laughter dances in your eyes...*

She picked up the envelope and ran a fingertip across the surface. Inside, she knew, was an antique love letter written from what had been Nazi Germany. She'd found it last summer when she'd flown out to Prince Edward Island for her friend Maggie's wedding.

The ink on the postmark had smeared badly. But she could just make out the word Berlin and the date: March 8, 1948.

The handwritten New York address on the front had been crossed out and a forwarding address had been neatly typed.

```
Vivian Robinson-Leard
General Delivery
Victoria, Prince Edward Island
Canada
```

She frowned. No return address. Odd for a love letter. Even stranger, the letter's postmark was five years after the letter itself was dated.

Nicky reached into the envelope and was about to pull out the pale blue, tissue-thin sheaf of paper when her

phone's alarm buzzed.

She glanced at her watch. Crap. It was ten after. Already late. Maggie didn't like to be kept waiting. She grabbed her purse off the shelf by the door and shrugged into her vintage, plum-colored wool jacket.

Nicky opened her apartment door and rushed out. But as she pulled the door shut behind her, she almost ran into a rail thin balding man.

"Hi Reg," Nicky said, even as her fingers tightened on the doorknob.

"Nicky," he said as he shoved his glasses up on his nose. "Do you know what day it is?"

Nicky chewed the inside of her lip. "Tuesday?"

Reg cleared his throat and crossed his arms across his chest. "That's right."

Nicky said nothing. Maybe he'd forget that it was now October.

But Reg tapped his foot and just looked at her.

"Can I have a few more days? It's only the fifth. I'm still waiting on *Ivory* magazine to send me a payment. They said they'd pay me forty-five days after I submitted, but I still haven't seen the check. I've tried calling and emailing and haven't gotten an answer. But that'll give me what I need to pay you the rent."

Nicky's landlord studied her a minute. She saw sympathy and frustration war on his face.

Nicky held her breath.

He rubbed his jaw and studied the green swirl-patterned hall carpet, then looked back up at her. "All right," he said. "But only because you've never been late on the rent before. I'm giving you fourteen days. By Tuesday the 19th at 9:00 a.m., you'll need to give me the rent money you owe for this month. Otherwise, I'm sorry, but I'll have to give you an eviction notice."

Nicky sighed in relief, then took a breath to speak.

"You're welcome," Reg cut her off. "This is your first warning." He walked away.

"Thank you," Nicky called out, but he'd already disappeared.

She jiggled the doorknob to make sure it was locked, then dashed down the stairs to the subway stop around the corner from her building.

She threaded her way through pedestrians and withheld another sigh. It seemed New York just kept getting more crowded.

With one eye on the busy sidewalk, she got out her phone. Yep, still battery left—it'd been acting up lately and sometimes died. She pulled up her email.

Maybe one of the small magazines or blogs had accepted her pitch? She hoped so.

That was the risk of being a freelancer. But she came by it honestly. Both her parents, now retired, had worked for themselves. They were basically living on Social Security now. No other safety net. Still, she believed the risk was worth it.

She ran down to the platform and darted onto the train car. Out of breath, she squeezed into the last available seat and scanned her inbox. Several new messages.

From: editor@womanslife.com
To: nicky.stendahl@gmail.com
Sent: Oct 5, 7:13 a.m.

Dear Ms. Stendahl,

Thank you for your article pitch about Vivian Robinson. At this time, we are not accepting any new story ideas on women during WWII, as our usual stable of freelancers has filled our needs.

Best wishes,
The editorial team at Woman's Life

Nicky gritted her teeth and opened the second.

From: tina@vintage40sgalblog.com
To: nicky.stendahl@gmail.com
Sent: Oct 4, 5:53 p.m.

Nicky,

Great blog idea about this Vivian woman, but I've already assigned the next few months' guest posts. Sorry about that. Better luck next time!

Tina

Nicky opened the rest of the new messages. All rejections. She propped her chin in her hands and sighed as she fiddled with the ends of her over-long bangs. She needed to trim them.

Now what? She had to pay the rent somehow. She worried her bottom lip between her teeth. But she couldn't just sit here and mope.

She lifted her head. She would keep going. Stay determined. After all, that's how anyone who had gotten anywhere had succeeded.

Yes. She wasn't going to give up. Someone out there had to like her story idea about Vivian enough to run it...

She reached into her purse. Under the World War II spy thriller she'd just finished, she fished out her copy of *Between Silk and Cyanide*, pulled out her bookmark, and started to read.

Twenty minutes later, she squeezed out of the subway car and up onto the busy Manhattan sidewalk near her favorite corner Starbucks. She glanced around for Maggie. No sign of her friend and former boss, a successful jewelry designer.

She chewed on a cuticle as she headed inside.

Nicky saw Maggie wave from a corner table across the crowded coffee shop. She waved back and made her way over to the tiny bistro table.

"Hey! Sorry I'm late. Got waylaid by my landlord." Nicky shrugged out of her coat and draped it across the back of the chair.

"I only just got here, so no problem. Wow, gorgeous jacket. I just love that deep, rich shade. Really sets off your strawberry-blonde hair."

"Thanks! It's vintage forties. Couldn't resist when I saw it in Charlottetown at Linda's Closet on Queen Street. I'm just gonna grab something. You good?" Nicky asked.

Maggie nodded and held up what looked like a mocha latte.

Nicky returned a few minutes later, chai tea in hand.

"So," Maggie said, "I haven't seen you since—"

"—your wedding on P.E.I.," Nicky finished for her. "I bet things are a bit quieter for you and Zak now that you two have figured out the whole mystery behind the legendary ghost ship of the Northumberland Strait."

Maggie grinned. "Yeah. Zak and I had a great time solving those riddles. Funny to think it all started with that gold doubloon..." She took a sip of her latte. "It's good to be back in the city for awhile."

"New York's great." Nicky paused. "I don't mean to complain, but to be honest, I'm getting a bit tired of the wall-to-wall people and all the car fumes."

"Really?"

"Yep. Maybe someday I'll move somewhere quieter." Nicky took another sip of her drink.

"Aww, I can understand that. I've missed all the hustle and bustle. But only a little. Prince Edward Island is definitely where my heart is."

"I can tell," Nicky said. "So you got it finished?"

"I did. I told Zak I was coming here to tie up a few loose ends. Including this." She tapped a small white jewelry box on the tabletop. "Wasn't too hard to resize. Here, take a look." She slid the box across the table to Nicky.

Nicky lifted the lid and peered inside.

QUINTEN LEARD RAN a fingertip across the gold lettering of the words *Princess Royal* written on the front of the antique upright piano. Grandma Viv had always said this one was special.

He started to slide the newly polished cover over the

piano's keys. But as he did so, the mechanism stuck slightly.

Quinten frowned. Hadn't he oiled everything and double-checked it all? Apparently, when he'd put things back together, something had shaken loose. He reversed the lid's direction and that's when he saw it.

A small, now crumpled piece of paper.

He plucked it from its sticking place between the edge of the keyboard and the outer edge of the cover.

His brow furrowed. The yellowish-brown tinge of the faded paper made him think it had to be antique.

It was blank, though.

He moved to throw it into the waste basket near his workbench when he reflexively flipped over the small square.

He cocked his head. Five letters were written across it.

B I O P W

Hmm. Why did that handwriting look kind of familiar?

"Hey Quinten, where are you?" His cousin, Elliot MacEwen, called out from the front of the shop.

On impulse, Quinten shoved the small piece of paper into his faded jeans pocket.

He glanced at his Apple watch.

Damn. He was going to be late for that call with the accountant he'd just hired to straighten out the books. The accounts had gotten pretty mixed up last year in the chaos of Grandma Viv's worsening illness and death. If he didn't get going—

"Quinten?" Elliot called again.

"Be there in a sec. I'm just finishing up in the back here," Quinten called as he put his piano tuning tools down on the workbench nearby and headed to the doorway that divided the private workspace from the public storefront of Leard's Piano Tuning & Restoration.

Elliot had one hand in the pocket of his neatly pressed navy blue chinos while he drummed the fingers of his other hand on the counter. The same counter that their grandmother had sat behind for nearly fifty years. And the counter that Quinten himself had worked behind for the last twelve years.

Quinten stepped out into the storefront space.

"Hiya, Quinten!" A four-year-old girl with blonde curls waved as she leaned against Elliot's leg.

Quinten smiled and crouched down. "Hi there, Rosie. Did you get to go to the chocolate shop today?"

The little girl beamed. "Daddy had chocolate waffles and I got to pick out my favorite jelly beans."

Quinten chuckled. "I'm glad to hear it. My favorite are the yellow ones."

Rose's eyes widened. "Me too."

Quinten straightened back up. "What can I help you with, Elliot?"

"When's my piano going to be finished?"

Quinten resisted the urge to cross his arms. "Well, today's Tuesday... It's nearly done. I just have a couple more adjustments to make."

Quinten held back a sigh of impatience. Elliot had always been a bit pushy. Ever since their grade school days. As a kid, he'd always tried to curry favor with Grandma Viv. She'd never played favorites between the two cousins—Quinten's father and Elliot's mother were brother and sister—but somehow Elliot felt Quinten had gotten the better deal. He'd held a grudge because of it.

In the years since Rose's birth and with Grandma Viv's worsening health, Elliot's sense of entitlement had intensified. Probably because the man felt he needed to secure a bit of family legacy from Grandma Viv.

Elliot glanced around the room. "I see you haven't changed the place much in the three months since she died."

"I like to preserve the character atmosphere for the customers."

Elliot shrugged. "I'm not a fan of quaint and down home. Sleek, modern and trendy is the look I've achieved for all the businesses I own. And acquiring more of those businesses, er, assets is always beneficial. Though I prefer to spend my time golfing, not behind a desk." He fiddled with some change in his pocket. "I'm glad to hear you're making progress on the piano—but I guess when it's something you love, you don't procrastinate much, do you? It needs to be done for my wife's birthday next Tuesday. We're settling into our new house at Dunrovin Estates across the way this week so the piano movers can come by and pick it up next Monday."

Quinten shifted his weight and shoved his hands into his own pockets. Even though this Princess Royal, made in Amherst, Nova Scotia, had been a copy of the one that the princesses had at Buckingham Palace in the 1930s, it hadn't been easy to refurbish.

But that's what his cousin had wanted done. And Quinten was the only piano tuner and restorationist on this side of Prince Edward Island. He'd loved the challenge. Had a chance to put all his music certifications to work.

So he'd done it for Elliot—at half his usual rate. Quinten tightened his jaw. He couldn't really afford to do that, but family was family. He couldn't let them down, even if it meant the business that his grandmother had started might take a hit.

"It tuned up really well," Quinten said.

Elliot smacked a palm against the wooden countertop. "That's great."

Quinten started to head toward the computer. "I'll just print out your invoice now."

Elliot took Rose by the hand and glanced at his watch. "Don't want to keep the boys at the country club waiting, so we'll settle up soon, yeah?" He headed for the door.

Before Quinten could reply, his phone started to buzz. He fished it out of his back jeans pocket. But before he could answer it, Elliot turned in the doorway of the shop. "Don't forgot our lawyer meeting on Thursday."

Quinten nodded. He wasn't planning on forgetting to attend that particular meeting about the family business.

After Grandma Viv's death, no will had been found. So,

due to succession law, the company was, for the moment, equally divided between the two cousins, since they were the only surviving kin. But Elliot had been making noise about getting full control of the company ever since Grandma Viv's death. Quinten's phone buzzed again.

Elliot paused in the doorway. "Don't worry, Quinten, after Thursday's meeting, you'll be able to give me advice on how to run the place once things are sorted out and I take over." His Rolex flashed in the sunlight as he waved and stepped out onto Victoria's main street.

If only there'd been a will...

Quinten took a couple of deep, calming breaths before he pressed the answer button on his phone.

"Quinten. Hope you're good. Listen, you've been doing a great job running the shop since Vivian passed," his accountant said.

"Thanks. I appreciate that."

"So I've begun to straighten things out. From what I've gone through so far, the earnings at the beginning of last year aren't great. We'll get through the rest of the paper-work backlog by the end of this month. But Quinten—"

Quinten's stomach knotted at the grim tone of his accountant's voice.

"—as you know," the other man sighed, "your grandmother's health went downhill over the past five years, especially the last year of her life. I'd be prepared for the possibility that the profits the rest of that year would be dangerously low, if not negative numbers. Now, I have more calculations to do to determine the extent of things, but obviously, if things are in the red, it would have serious repercussions for the business."

Quinten winced. "So you're saying I could be going bankrupt?"

"I can't say that for sure as I haven't done all the math, but things aren't looking good."

Quinten swallowed. He should probably mention this to Elliot. Then again, it would give the man more reason to push for full control. Better to not say anything til things are more clearly sorted out.

"A three-generation business like this doesn't come around every day. But," the accountant sighed again, "they don't always survive the third generation, either."

Quinten's fingers tightened on his phone. His family had lived here for two hundred years. In fact, his branch of the Leards had been one of the first families to settle in Victoria when it was founded in 1819.

"I'm not going to let that happen. I was born and raised here. I'm practically the last piano tuner on the whole island. I'm going to make this work. I won't just let this piece of island history—my family's heritage—slip away without a trace."

"IT'S ALL ORIGINAL to the Middle Ages, you know," Maggie said. "Where did you say you got it?"

Nicky reached into the box and carefully held up the ring. The piece of moss-green amber was set in delicately wrought sterling silver with a pattern of vines and leaves that held the large stone in place.

"At a flea market in Nobo. For five bucks." Nicky said. "I just liked it because I thought it looked neat. And it would go well with my fall wardrobe. The old woman I bought it from said she'd gotten it in an auction lot of assorted World War II stuff from an estate sale up the coast."

"Well, you got really lucky. From the research I did online," Maggie said, "that specific design of leaves and vines is actually Polish."

"Wow," Nicky said. She slipped the ring on her finger. "It fits perfectly now, too."

"I was really careful to make sure the integrity of the piece was maintained. Could be worth a lot. Maybe you could do some research on it. Find out a bit more about it."

Nicky slipped the ring off her finger and put it back into the box. "Good idea. Now I'm kind of nervous to wear it."

"I wouldn't worry about that. 'Cause if you don't wear it,

it's just going to sit there in that box collecting dust. Which would be a shame."

"You're right," Nicky said and tucked the box into her purse.

"So how's your venture as a freelancer?" Maggie said as she took a sip of her coffee.

"I'm not sure that things are really going all that well."

"Oh?"

"Well, you know that after I, uh, stopped working for you, I thought I'd have loads of time to pursue my writing. And I did. But—not to complain here—it took more time and effort than I thought to build up a contact list of editors and magazines who wanted my work, who liked my voice. But I did it."

"Yeah, I remember," Maggie said. "Especially when you got that really great little piece in the *Historical Woman* magazine."

"I know. That was amazing. Especially because they're like the *National Geographic* of women's history." Nicky laughed. "They even paid me a dollar a word."

"Hey," Maggie snapped her fingers. "Have you thought of pitching to them again?"

Nicky straightened. "I didn't even think of that! In fact, that'd be the perfect place to pitch the letter..."

"Letter?"

"Yeah," Nicky said and reached into her jacket pocket. She carefully pulled out the yellowed envelope. "I know, I know. I shouldn't be carrying around an antique letter in my pocket but somehow, it doesn't feel right not to have it together with this jacket."

Nicky eased the tissue-thin sheaf of paper out from the envelope and handed it to Maggie.

June 7, 1943

My dearest Viv,

Funny how war makes you remember the best times and the worst times of your life simultaneously. I can't imagine what would've happened if the canteen had been open that night and we hadn't met. Would we have never climbed up to the roof, a little drunk, with the summer wind in our hair and shared secrets in our eyes?

And I would've never taken up the cause, never learned what it meant to truly fight for what is right, what is good, in this world, in the face of such darkness. Sometimes I think that you are all that's left of that world I once knew. But if Churchill has anything to do with it, that world will exist when this damn war is over.

They've been quite inquisitive. But I shall withstand as I've been trained to do. They cannot know what is in my heart, and they cannot destroy my soul, though undoubtedly, they shall try. Even if my background puts me at greater risk, I am grateful. Grateful that I have a cause to fight for.

I feel that the only thing keeping me sane is thinking of you. Of us. Of being together again. Of kissing in dimly lit hallways with flickering bulbs, closed canteens, and the sounds of swing music floating in from the street while laughter dances in your eyes.

I will think of those times and remember. Remember the future. Remember the past. Remember us.

My heart is with you always,

—A

"Ooo," Maggie handed the page back to Nicky. "A love letter."

"Yep." Nicky grinned.

Maggie's eyes widened. "So where did you find it?"

"In a hidden inside pocket of this jacket, actually. Along with a tiny little key. I think Viv probably owned the coat and kept the letter there."

"Interesting theory." Maggie leaned forward. "Who do you think was writing to her?"

"I'm not sure. I've only just started doing a bit of research about this Viv woman."

"So you're gonna write an article about her?"

"At first it was idle curiosity, you know? I wanted to

find out who this was. But then as I started to do the research, I realized she could be a great candidate for a history piece. Lots of people know about the female codebreakers who worked at Bletchley Park during WWII. Next to no one's heard about other women like Viv who worked with codes, ciphers, and decryption but didn't actually break enemy ones."

"Very cool. I can see why you'd want to write about that." Maggie sipped her drink.

"Right now, I'm just waiting to hear back about an additional records request I made on her work during the war. I'm hoping the record's been declassified." She fiddled with a few strands of her hair. "But I can't figure out who this 'A' is."

"Sounds pretty mysteriously romantic to me." Maggie grinned.

"And tragic," Nicky said. "I think he was captured or something..." Goosebumps rose on her arms and she rubbed them.

"Who knows, it might lead you in a direction you never even imagined."

Nicky laughed. "Maybe so. If I can find the right angle to pitch my idea about Vivian to the *Historical Woman* magazine... They always have such interesting articles about pioneering women doing things in history."

"Like what?" Maggie took a sip of her coffee.

"Well, they did a piece last year on Hedy Lamarr."

"She was that forties actress, right?"

"Yep," Nicky said, "but she was also a brilliant scientist responsible for essentially creating Wi-Fi." Nicky waved her hand. "In simplistic terms."

"Yeah, you should definitely aim high. Pitch it to that magazine."

"You think?" Nicky said.

"Definitely." Her phone buzzed and she glanced at it. "I should run. I'm Skyping Zak for our lunch date together."

"He can't stay away from you a moment longer than he has to, can he?" Nicky teased.

Maggie laughed, a sparkle in her eye. "Nope. Well," she said, and stood up, "it's been great to see you. Come up to the island and visit us sometime. We'd love to show you our new beach cottage. It's up near North Cape."

"That'd be fabulous, Maggie." Nicky hugged the other woman.

"Anytime," Maggie said, and waved goodbye, a spring in her step.

Nicky waved back. But as she turned to gather up her empty coffee cup and her jacket, her smile faded.

If only she could be as lucky in love as Maggie had been with Zak.

Nicky withheld a sigh and pushed down a dart of irritation at herself for feeling the tiniest bit jealous of Maggie's happiness.

Sure, she'd loved the men she'd been with. Enjoyed their company. Enjoyed their attention. The time spent together. But there'd always been something missing... She'd never been in love. Not truly. Nicky pursed her lips.

She was wasting her time feeling like this. She had no man in her life at the moment and there was no point moping about it.

She was better off single anyway. All relationships did was stir up your issues. Then you became so busy fending off the demons in your head you couldn't enjoy the man you were with.

That's what'd happened between her and Ben. He'd been her first long-term relationship. They were together nearly four years. That first year had been great. He was kind, attentive—everything she could've hoped for, and more...

She'd been a romantic, once. Read lots of romance novels. Believed them all.

But when she'd asked him to move in with her the second year they'd been dating, things changed.

He was never a big sharer. At first, she'd liked that. The whole strong and silent thing. But then it had begun to frustrate her. She'd felt shut out, which made her worry about why he wasn't opening up to her more.

So she'd thought moving in together would fix things, and he'd come to live at her apartment; but it didn't last long. There were still a few of his things around she hadn't gotten a chance to give away. Like his second-best micro-scope set. The man had loved science. She loved writing, history, and being creative...

She'd felt, in a way, that he'd never really taken the time to know who she was. He was more by-the-book; she was more willing to take chances.

He was a nice guy. But he just lost interest in her. Lost interest in wanting to be in the relationship.

And he lied to her about it by staying in the relationship when he really wanted to leave. Always covered up his feelings. Never told her what he'd really been thinking...

She'd tried to ask him about it. Shared her own vulnera-bilities in the hopes he'd reciprocate. But that's when he'd really started to pull away—which caused her to hold back; she'd never let him in fully because she'd never felt secure in his love for her. She'd been afraid to open her heart that much, the way that she really wanted to.

Sure, he'd agreed to couples counseling. But that only created more tension than good between them. The relationship had ended not long after that.

It seemed as if everything had been off-kilter between them. The timing. The feelings.

Nicky brushed away a single tear and pushed open the door of Starbucks and headed to the subway stop.

The October air lifted the white silk scarf she'd tied loosely around her neck. She was thirty-one. She wasn't going to drown in all her old issues, her old fears, her old loves.

It was time for something new.

Maggie was right, Nicky realized, as she headed up the steps to her apartment and unlocked the door. She needed to aim higher. What would it hurt? What was that quote about shooting for the moon...?

Nicky rolled her eyes at herself as she sat down at her computer desk. It wasn't like she had delusions of grandeur.

But the more she discovered about Vivian, the more she realized that Vivian's story, well, it deserved to be told. Readers would be interested.

She just wanted Vivian's voice to be heard. Okay, maybe not just that. She wasn't that altruistic. She wanted her own voice to be heard too.

Nicky drummed her fingernails on the desktop, then straightened up. Yes. Why not?

From: nicky.stendahl@gmail.com
To: susanolmsted@historicalwoman.com

Hi Susan,

You might remember last year that I wrote a 100-word article for you about Amelia Earhart when you did that aviation edition.

Well, I have an idea for another piece that I think might fit well with your publication.

I came across a letter from the 1940s—World War II, actually—that was written to a woman whom I've begun to do a little research on.

She apparently worked for an organization called the SOE—the Special Operations Executive, headquartered on Baker Street in London—that sent secret agents to occupied Europe. But she wasn't a spy. At least, not from the declassified records I've started to look through. She worked in the codes department.

If you'd be interested in publishing the article, I'd expect it to be between 1,500 to 2,500 words, perhaps for your upcoming spring issue on pioneering 20th century women in the math and sciences fields.

Thanks so much!

Regards,
Nicky S.

Nicky hit the send button and grinned. If the editor accepted her pitch, since this publication paid very well, she'd be able to put aside money for future rent.

Hmmm. This magazine had also run one of the photos she'd taken for that Earhart article. Which reminded her...she had to empty her photo card so she'd have enough room on it for this new assignment. She didn't want to splurge on a new, bigger card while her rent debt loomed.

So she logged onto Shutterstock then grabbed her Nikon. She hooked up the USB cable to her laptop to upload the latest batch of shots she'd taken over the past month.

Every extra penny of royalties counted. Like last summer when she'd made enough to buy herself that vintage jacket.

Even if sometimes her pictures had nothing to do with the articles she'd written in the past, she just loved taking photos. And apparently, sometimes people actually wanted to buy them.

She checked her royalties tab. Empty today. Well, maybe tomorrow...

"I'M SORRY, QUINTEN, dear, but Al just sold our piano. You know what the economy's been like lately. Down the drain, if you ask me, which you didn't. But believe me, if we still had it, I'd ask you to tune it up good for us right away—this afternoon, even."

Quinten could hear the older woman tsk on the other end of the line. He forced away the sinking feeling in the pit of his stomach. "Okay, well, thank you anyway, Mrs. MacPhail."

"Well, now, don't hang up yet. Let me just get my glasses..."

He heard the sound of the phone being put down and papers being rustled.

"Here we are," Mrs. MacPhail said. "Try Mabel. I heard her playing the piano just yesterday evening."

"Thanks a lot, Mrs. MacPhail. I'll give her a try."

"And from what I hear," the older woman chuckled, "her new next-door neighbor is quite pretty. And around your age, too. You and Sarah broke up, didn't you now? Yes," she continued without waiting for Quinten's reply, "last September, I believe. How long had you two been dating?"

He winced. He'd always been a bit shy around women he found attractive. But he'd also spent too much of his twenties getting an education to have had much time for a love life.

First, he earned an undergrad and then a graduate degree in music at UPEI. But by the time he finished his graduate work, he realized he loved to work on pianos more than play them.

For twelve years, he had worked in the shop. He'd started when he decided to work with Grandma Viv part time while he went back to school again for piano tuning and restoration certification and an apprenticeship.

Then he spent his early thirties working in the piano shop full time as Grandma Viv's health started to go downhill. What with taking care of her as well as running the store for the past five years, he hadn't had too much time to be in any sort of relationship.

As a result, at thirty-five, Sarah had been his first, and only—so far—real relationship. It had failed miserably.

As Mrs. MacPhail chatted on about her new neighbor, Quinten's mind drifted back over the past.

Dating. He withheld a sigh. It was easier being single. No complications. No drama. No demands for professions of love that he couldn't quite make.

His and Sarah's last big fight had been about that, in fact. Just because he never said "I love you" to her during their entire relationship, she'd seemed to think he hadn't loved her. Even though he had. She'd accused him of being too guarded, too closed off from his emotions.

But he'd felt love for her. And he thought he had shown his love for her in his actions toward her. But he never said

"I love you" outright. And that hadn't been enough for Sarah. Maybe she'd been right about his guardedness?

But Quinten wanted to consider things before he spoke, and take the time to know he truly meant them, before he said them out loud. Granted, "I love you" was a pretty big one...

Because Sarah *had* been right. He'd been afraid to say those three little words. Afraid of what might happen if he said how much she'd affected him... Afraid she'd reject him. Like his father had. He much preferred the privacy of his own thoughts.

He made the mistake of sharing his thoughts too many times with his dad growing up, thinking his dad would accept him instead of judge him. Safer to stay quiet. Easier to just say yes and agree with others' opinions instead of stating his own. Less risk of being hurt, blamed, or criticized.

Quinten cleared his throat and opened his mouth, but Mrs. MacPhail spoke first.

"Sorry, sorry, dear. Can't help myself these days. Al canceled our Netflix subscription to save on our oil heat bill for this winter, so now the next best thing to Netflix is being a nosy neighbor."

"Appreciate your suggestion, Mrs. MacPhail. Thanks again."

"Good luck, Quinten. If I hear of anyone needing their piano fixed, I'll let you know."

Quinten hung up the phone. Now what? He'd gone through almost his whole list of contacts and everyone had given some version of the same answer...

He rubbed the back of his neck. Maybe it was time to give up his half of the business? Elliot wanted it, after all. He could get a job at Long & McQuade in Charlottetown and—

Quinten shoved his hands into his pockets. No.

He wasn't going to just roll over and play dead. There was still life in this business, there was still hope; and he wasn't going to let Grandma Viv down...

"How you doing, Grandma?" Quinten said softly as he knocked on the door of her room at Whisperwood Villa in Charlottetown. "I brought you something." He held out a crossword puzzle book and a bouquet of lupins. He put the flowers in a vase by the nightstand. "Your favorite."

She sat on the neatly made bed, her snow-white hair freshly combed, her hands folded in her lap. A box of photos sat beside her on the bed, the lid askew.

"Thank you."

Quinten fought back a sinking feeling at her blank look.

"Do you have time to look at some pictures, young man?"

Quinten eased into the overstuffed chair across from her bed. "Yes, Grandma."

As she handed him a photo, he couldn't help but notice the way the liver spots on the back of her hand stood out against the golden evening sun that streamed through the sheer organza curtains.

Quinten's brow furrowed as he studied the photo. He'd never seen it before in his life.

But even in the black and white of the picture's depths, he saw the sparkle in his grandmother's eyes as she grinned at the camera, the dimple in her left cheek apparent.

She was standing in a busy train station, suitcase in hand, other people in dark coats only blurs in the background. Her figure, in sharp focus, was outlined in bright morning light. Her Victory roll and lipstick were perfectly in place.

"I was very good at crosswords," she said.

He looked up at her. Her voice conveyed confidence, but her face showed only confusion.

He forced himself to swallow the lump in his throat. He had to be stoic. He couldn't show his emotions. That was something she'd taught him.

Must be her British heritage. Or perhaps a product of her times. Or something. But for whatever reason, he'd learned from her that it was best to have a calm exterior. It made things much easier.

He glanced at her. For a moment, a flicker of recognition lit her expression, but it left as suddenly as it had come.

He looked back down at the photo, sudden moisture in his eyes. He blinked hard and flipped the picture over. Pencilled on the top left-hand corner in her neat handwriting were the words "Last day at the Office."

He frowned and murmured, "Was this when you'd been a file clerk in London before you got married?"

She'd married his grandfather right after the war ended. In fact, she'd come to Prince Edward Island as a war bride when she'd met Colonel Wallace Leard in London in the last days of the war. It had been, from all accounts, a whirlwind romance.

"Quinten." His grandmother's voice brought him sharply back to the present.

She'd stretched out a hand as he started to give back the photograph but she batted it away. A steady look came into her eyes and Quinten felt the hairs on the back of his neck stand up.

Never breaking his gaze, she said in a calm, clear tone, "Remember...Amber. You must. Remember. Amber."

AT TEN O'CLOCK that evening, Nicky wrapped her cashmere robe around herself and sank onto the couch in her living room, a mug of steaming vanilla rooibos tea in her hand.

She inhaled the flowery scent and her shoulders relaxed. It always tasted best when it was as hot as possible. She gently blew on the steaming contents and gingerly took a sip. Perfect.

She'd made some progress today. Sent out ten more queries. That article was going to get published if she had anything to say about it.

Her mind drifted back to the conversation she'd had in Starbucks with Maggie. She glanced at the coffee table where the small white ring box sat, the ring itself resting on top.

Too tired to get up off the couch properly, she stretched out a hand and managed to snag the ring with the fingertips of her free hand.

But as she started to lean back, the steaming tea sloshed over the rim and hot rooibos spilled onto her hand.

"Ouch!"

She jumped up off the couch. Reflexively, she dropped the mug and the ring; the tea sloshed out when the mug shattered.

She ran to the sink to run cold water and then rub apple cider vinegar over the burn.

She dabbed it dry with a paper towel, then got the broom and dustpan to sweep up the broken mug. After she tossed the shards in the trash, she went to change her robe and pajamas.

She came back out into the living room, carefully poured herself another, somewhat cooler mug, and sat on the other side of the couch.

She took a sip and felt herself relax again. She closed her eyes. But then they snapped open again. The ring.

It had bounced when it hit the hardwood floor and now lay under the edge of the couch. Swinging her feet carefully back down onto the floor, she leaned down to pick up the ring.

But as she did so, she noticed that the stone was now at a strange angle.

It must have shifted and loosened as it fell. Nicky winced. Maggie wouldn't like that, especially given how old it was.

But as she brought it up to her lap to examine the extent of the damage, the stone fell out.

Nicky swore under her breath. Maggie *really* wouldn't like that.

Nicky picked up the stone to try to wedge it back into place but noticed a slender piece of...what was that...wedged between the prongs that held the stone in place?

How had Maggie missed this? Nicky frowned. She'd resized it. But she probably hadn't had to do anything like remove the stone, as she'd said there hadn't been much resizing needed, just a little tweak.

Using her thumb and forefinger, Nicky plucked the item

from its resting place.

Paper, she realized.

She examined it and saw only a single tiny black dot on the small piece of paper. The dot was the same size as the period at the end of a sentence, maybe a little bigger.

Nicky frowned and held up the small slip of paper to the light. Why would anyone conceal that under a stone? She turned the paper side to side.

She squinted at the tiny dot again. It couldn't be, could it? She'd been reading one too many spy thrillers.

It looked almost like...

She laughed at herself at the thought—a microdot?

Well, she wasn't going to get any sleep unless she found out.

She got up and rummaged around in her junk drawer until her fingers closed around the hard black plastic of the microscope set Ben had left.

She picked it up, shut the drawer, and returned to the couch.

She held her breath as she examined the microdot on the tiny piece of paper. Several lines of type came into view as she peered through the high-powered lens.

```
The secretary marches
To a tune unplayed
But the pianist's journey
Mirrors a plan well-laid
```

Nicky caught her breath. Was this some sort of...riddle? Now she really had been reading too many spy thrillers.

Or had she?

Chapter Two

UINTEN SHOOK OFF the memory as he headed into the workshop. There was no one named Amber. Just another one of Grandma Viv's lapses. Like the time she'd insisted on mailing all her valuable jewelry to the Salvation Army. He shoved his hands in his pockets.

Who had Grandma Viv been, really? Maybe in order to find that out, he should go through all her things. He really needed to sort through it thoroughly. It'd been three months already. But somehow, doing that task felt monumental. Overwhelming. It would mean she was really gone. So he'd put it off. He rubbed the back of his neck as his thoughts returned to her life.

Grandma Viv was his dad's mother but she'd always had a side of herself that Quinten had never really known... even though, growing up, Grandma Viv had been more a mother to Quinten than his own. *She'd* left when he was a toddler.

In fact, he'd spent most of his growing-up years with Grandma Viv, since he and his father hadn't had the best relationship. She'd taught him piano; encouraged his music career choices.

But she'd always refused to talk about her time during the war, or much of her past, actually. If he'd tried to ask, she'd pretend she hadn't heard him, or tell him to take the pie out of the oven. She'd believed in him, though, and listened to him. He should've done more for her in the end. Been there with her more often.

He'd done all he could, he reminded himself, what with running the shop with Grandma Viv part time before she'd gotten dementia, and then full time after. He was an only child. Elliot hadn't helped out. Grandpa Wallace had already passed away.

And after Quinten's dad's death five years ago, Quinten began to notice worrying little signs…Grandma Viv would forget a friend's name. Or go to the hair salon even though she'd just had a trim.

At first, he'd been able to look after her. But he couldn't take care of her twenty-four hours a day when her dementia had worsened. She'd needed professionals for that. So he'd put her in one of the best care homes on the island and had regretted every second of it.

But he'd visited her every day and done everything in his power to make her life there as comfortable as possible.

If he was honest with himself, in some ways he'd been trying to heal his relationship with his father through taking care of his grandmother.

Maybe if he'd shown her more love in all the ways that his dad hadn't shown him love growing up, he would've been able to really know his grandmother, and by extension, connect with his father?

But mulling this over wasn't going to get Mabel's piano tuned. He picked up his tool bag and headed to the door. Most of Grandma Viv's things, he mused, were still all packed away, aside from that box he'd let Mabel have.

Quinten walked across his lawn and then headed across the paved main street. It wasn't far to Mabel's house on Nelson Street.

Autumn sunshine backlit the red maples and yellow oaks as their branches swayed in the light sea-scented breeze.

Leaves in shades of crimson, gold, scarlet, and russet carpeted the road.

Some tourists chatted, and Quinten caught a few words of Japanese. One headed across the street in front of him and took a seat at one of the bistro tables arranged alongside the wrought-iron lampposts in front of the Victoria Playhouse, which was, when originally constructed, the local community hall.

Well, he conceded with a grin, the place *was* pretty cute. A fair number of the heritage homes in the village had been turned into profitable businesses.

He took a right on Howard Street and headed over to Nelson Street.

The scent of seafood chowder and the sound of laughter drifted past him as he walked by the Landmark Oyster House. Its white-shuttered windows were wide open and its flower-filled deck overflowed with happy visitors and even happier locals who traded stories and gossip over glasses of wine and appetizers.

He walked on and waved a hello to the owner as he strode past The Studio Gallery and neared the corner of Nelson and Howard.

The shrieks and giggles of kids playing in the empty green space across the way made him remember the previous summer when that same green space had served as the croquet pitch for Victoria's annual croquet tournament.

He and his teammate Grant had won that year. They'd even had their victory photo taken nearby, next to the rickety old rowboat that served as a gathering spot for bonfires, potlucks, and tournaments.

Quinten headed up the street to a grand old dove-gray Edwardian with a second-floor sunroom. Its wide front porch had a cane-back rocking chair and pots of bright pink geraniums.

A long-haired fluffy gray cat sat on the edge of the porch.

"Hi there, Rainy," he murmured to the cat as he paused to stroke its head. Its rumbling purr vibrated against his fingers.

He continued to the front door.

A woman with short blonde hair, dressed in a rose-pink hoodie and a pair of jeans, answered before he'd even had a chance to knock.

"Quinten!" she said, "Haven't seen you in awhile. And by awhile, I mean since last weekend. How the heck are ya?"

"Doing pretty well, Anna," he said. "How's the food drive going?"

"It's going great. Got lots of donations this week."

"That's good to hear."

"Mom said you might be coming over to take a look at her piano. She loves that thing. Even though she's nearly ninety-eight, she plays it every day—thinks she's younger than I am. Had it for at least sixty-five years, long before I was even thought of." Anna laughed. "It needs tuned up pretty badly. I'm just about to head over to Crapaud to pick up a few groceries from Harvey's, but you know you don't need an invitation. Hang around as long as you need to get that piano back into shape."

"Thanks, Anna."

"Any time, Quinten. Any time."

She made her way out the door.

Quinten stepped out of his shoes and headed to the old upright in the far corner of the living room.

He ran a hand across its slightly warped surface and smiled. He'd come over here so many times growing up.

Anna was practically an aunt; the Leards and the Hendrickses had known each other for generations. Ever since the village was founded, in fact.

He raised the piano top and got to work.

"You know, your grandma had her first piano lessons on that very one."

Mabel's quiet voice made Quinten jump. Not sure what to say, he didn't reply.

But she continued as if he'd encouraged her. "We were fast friends, your grandma and I. But you already knew that."

Quinten did, but he knew she liked to tell the story, so he just nodded and let her talk as he continued to work.

"Met right after she came to town when the war ended. My, that seems like only yesterday." The old woman chuckled. "None of us islanders quite knew what to think of her at first." She clucked her tongue. "But soon enough, she made her way into the hearts of pretty much everyone in this community. I think it helped that her Wallace was from Victoria here, o' course."

"Mmm-hmmm," Quinten murmured as he made some adjustments.

"Viv was whip-smart, too," she continued. "Not like some of these flighty young girls these days. No siree." She rapped her cane against the polished hardwood.

"Uh-huh." He continued with his adjustments and paused to test a few keys. Almost right.

"You know they had U-boats around the island here during the war. All the way up to North Cape lighthouse."

"Oh?" Quinten paused in his work and glanced over his shoulder at Mabel. He hadn't heard anything about that...

"Yes." Mabel paused and inhaled a long breath. She sat on the vast leather sofa, her neatly pressed, pale green cardigan wrapped around her thin shoulders and her glasses perched on top of her head.

"The CBC would make special broadcasts. Tell fishermen to keep a watch out for them. Turn in those Nazi bastards." Mabel chuckled and adjusted the collar of her cardigan. She leaned forward on her cane and narrowed her eyes as she held Quinten's gaze.

"There were strange doings, though, back in '43. Supposed to have been some sort of prison breakout in New Brunswick. A U-boat was gonna try to sneak the German POWs aboard and skedaddle back to the Third Reich. Some even say that U-boat came with a whole hoard of treasure in tow. Hitler's gold and diamonds."

She drew in a breath. "Heard tell it's still out there, in some old rusting trunk, sunk somewhere at the bottom of the St. Lawrence Seaway. But one thing's sure—your grandma musta known something because she was in love with one of them Nazis."

NICKY YAWNED AND stretched and glanced at the clock. Six o'clock on Wednesday morning. She'd been awake, the yellow cotton of her nightgown tangled around her, for what seemed like hours. Unable to think of anything else but that microdot and its contents.

But she'd better start thinking of something else or she'd never get the rent paid on time.

She heaved herself out of bed and into an almost-too-hot shower—the better to wake up with.

She towelled off and pulled on a pair of faded blue yoga pants and a lime-green halter top. Then she made herself some toast in the toaster oven that doubled as a real oven in her tiny suite. Once, she'd crammed half a chicken into it and roasted it. She'd been so proud of herself.

She slathered raspberry jam onto two pieces of Texas toast and took a big bite.

Then she headed over to her laptop and logged onto her email. One new message was waiting.

From: susanolmsted@historicalwoman.com
To: nicky.stendahl@gmail.com
Sent: Tues, October 5, 7:45 p.m.

Dear Nicky,

I remember you! I think your pitch is great. I think it'll fit really well in our spring issue, as you've suggested.

I'd like it to be 3,000 words. Unfortunately, with the publishing business being what it is now, we can only offer you 50 cents/word. If that's acceptable, please let me know by 5:00 p.m. today. We have a few other story slots that need to get filled as soon as possible, and yours might fall by the wayside if you don't reply today.

To formalize everything and make it official, I've attached a copy of your work-for-hire contract. Just email it back to me with your electronic signature and things will be good to go.

—S

Nicky scrolled through the contract. Always good to

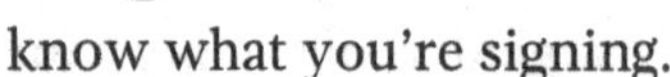

know what you're signing.

Huh. That was interesting. The *Historical Woman* was owned by the same parent company as *Ivory* magazine—the one that was late on its payment to her. Well, the world of magazine publishing was small, and conglomerates were big. So it made sense.

But Nicky's heart sank a little as she reread the email. Work-for-hire contracts meant that you actually didn't own your words. They paid you a flat fee, and you gave away all your rights to the work, forever.

What was worse, if your article, for whatever reason, came under scrutiny, or you got slapped with a libel case, you had to fork over the lawyer fees. For something you didn't even own the rights to anymore.

But Nicky signed the document electronically anyway.

Even if she didn't agree with it, this was the usual type of contract these days for freelancers.

She hit reply and let her now-boss know that her contract was signed and attached.

Hmm. Sometime she should probably shell out some cash for liability insurance. She gnawed the inside of her lower lip for a moment.

It was so expensive, she couldn't really afford it. Besides, the work-for-hire contracts were totally normal.

Her mind strayed back to the piece of paper she'd found inside the ring. She typed *microdot* into the search bar.

Hmmm.

Nicky's heart beat a little faster as she read the first result. They'd come into use during the Franco-Prussian War and then had been used during World War I and World War II to communicate vital information between clandestine operatives. They were also used during the Cold War and even into the present day.

She shook her head.

She couldn't get carried away and just jump on conjecture and assumptions. She'd learned that much from the journalism certificate she'd earned a few summers ago.

She'd always loved reading and writing.

She remembered how she wrote stories in grade school.

It'd been so much fun to interview her classmates.

But then when it came time to pick a college and get a degree, she'd chickened out of applying to journalism schools on the East Coast. Instead, she'd listened to the voice in her head that said business admin close to home was the better way to go.

She'd gone with a generic business admin diploma at a local community college in Michigan not far from her home town and then worked for five years at a law firm in her home state.

It had paid well and had been stable, but she'd hated it. That's where she'd met Ben, actually. They'd dated for such a long time and she'd always hoped he'd ask her to marry him. Settle down together.

But he never had. And she never asked him about that.

And that had been that.

She sighed. She wouldn't make that same mistake again. The next man she fell for, she was *not* going to spend her time guessing what he was thinking or bending over backwards figuring out what he meant. If he couldn't tell her outright, she wasn't going to waste her time with him. She was going to take charge and take her destiny into her own hands.

NICKY TAPPED A fingernail against her stack of research books on the polished oak surface of the table in the New York City Public Library.

She could've just used her own laptop at home. But sometimes she found it useful to get out of the house and go to a place that felt smart and was quiet.

A public space like a library created a certain anonymity that had always felt safe and good to her. A trusted silence was like a trusted friend. Or something like that.

Nicky glanced back through the pages of notes she'd made since her editor had given her the green light for the article.

What, exactly, did she know about Vivian Robinson?

Well, thanks to the SOE file she had received the other day from the National Archives in Kew, England, she knew a bit more about Viv.

It had been useful. The declassified part, at least. She'd put in that request for the additional information, but the other parts of her file were, frustratingly, still classified.

<pre>
            Registry & Archives
             File No. 2666/A
          ROBINSON, Vivian Fern

                                          21.8.40
DF/OR/5234

Dear Miss Fordham,

    I have interviewed Miss Vivian Fern Robin-
son. I am inclined to believe that her previous
experience with mathematics and music makes her
quite suitable for a vacancy in our cipher
department.

    I would, to that end, be grateful to your
agreement of my employment of her.

                                        Yours,
                            (Miss) T. WILLIAMS

Miss Fordham
Ministry of Labour & National Service
Lion House
Red Lion Street, W.C.
</pre>

Vassar College

August 14, 1940

Dear Madam,

With reference to your letter of the 9th of August, I am pleased to provide the following reference for Miss Vivian Fern Robinson. She graduated magna cum laude from this post-secondary institution on December 15, 1939.

Her work during her student years here was exemplary. She has, from my observation, the utmost ability to apply diligence and reliability in any task she performs. I recommend her very highly.

Sincerely,
J. Smith
Dean, Department of Mathematics

Miss T. Williams
Inter-Services Research Bureau
64 Baker Street
W.1.

DF/OR/5234

22nd August, 1940

Dear Miss Robinson,

I am delighted to confirm that your application for a post in this Department has now been approved.

Would you be so good as to report for duty at 9.15 a.m. on September 2nd? In the meantime, if you receive any communications from the Ministry of Labour, please do get in touch with me before making any response.

Yours truly,
(Miss) T. WILLIAMS

Miss V.F.Robinson
Meadows Hotel
Bridge St., W.1.

F O R M   C.R.1.

DATE: 8.1.40   INTERVIEWED BY:(Miss) T. Williams

Surname (in block capitals): *ROBINSON*

Christian names: *Vivian Fern*

Rank or title:

Decorations:

1. <u>FORMER NAMES(IF ANY)</u>

2. <u>PERMANENT ADDRESS</u> *89 Chestnut Lane, Manhattan, New York*
   <u>TEL. NO.</u> *Endicott4 8907*

3. <u>IF SERVING</u> (Regiment)

4. <u>DATE & PLACE OF BIRTH</u> *May 28, 1919, New York, New York, United States*

5. <u>NATIONALITY</u> At birth *American*
   At present *American*

6. <u>EDUCATION</u>
   (a) Schools attended *New York City Public High School*
   (b) Universities *Vassar College*
   Degrees taken *mathematics education, music education*

7. <u>MARRIED OR SINGLE?</u> *single*

9. <u>RELIGION</u> *Methodist*

10. <u>PEACE TIME OCCUPATION</u> *student; part-time piano tutor*

12. <u>OCCUPATION SINCE 3.9.39</u> *piano tutor*

13. <u>LANGUAGES</u>
   What languages do you speak and how fluently?
   French – fluent German – fluent

14. <u>WHAT COUNTRIES HAVE YOU VISITED?</u>
   (other than in passage) *Austria. Germany. Switzerland*

16. <u>HAVE YOU MADE A WILL?</u> *No*

17. <u>NEXT OF KIN</u>
   (a) Name *Lyle Robinson*
   (b) Address *22 Ford St.. Manhattan. New York*
   (c) Relationship *father*

18. <u>APPEARANCE</u>
   (a) Height *5' 4"*
   (b) Weight *120 pounds*
   (c) Colour hair *black*
   (d) Colour of eyes *hazel*
   (e) Complexion *medium*
   (f) Distinguishing Marks *dimple in left cheek*

<u>F O R M   C.R.2.</u>

<u>Office Use Only.</u>

(TOP SECRET)

<u>Former occupation:</u> Student

<u>Current cover occupation:</u> File clerk for Inter-Services Research Bureau (ISRB)

<u>Real occupation:</u> Process agent traffic, codes department, SOE

<u>Employment start date:</u> September 2, 1940

<u>Employment end date:</u> December 31, 1945

<u>Agents assigned to:</u> Oak, Ash, Maple

<u>Country sections assigned:</u> X, F, N

<u>Duties:</u> Decipher incoming coded messages from SOE agents in the field

<u>Notes:</u> Highly intelligent; excellent with crosswords and puzzles; very chatty and chipper; friendly & helpful to the other girls; works well with other codes department girls to decipher indecipherables as they come in (due to Morse mutilation, language mistakes, transposition errors, etc.)

<u>Recruitment:</u> While on holiday after graduation in the spring of 1940, she was seen to be completing a crossword puzzle at a corner table of a pub; she was interviewed by Miss W and accepted the position promptly thereafter; the matter of her citizenship was overlooked, as her skills with both math and music overcame such details.

Nicky pursed her lips. Math and music? Math, she could see. But music—why would that be important? Then again, music had patterns, and if Vivian was deciphering codes, looking for patterns would be an asset.

Nicky drummed her fingers on the tabletop. If Vivian had worked for the U.S. instead of the U.K. during the war, this might be a little easier to research.

Nicky had just finished a great book called *Code Girls* by Liza Mundy, which told all about American women breaking Japanese and German codes during WWII.

That had been a pretty fascinating read, actually. Apparently, the U.S. women had sometimes been recruited by secret letter, which asked them just two questions: did they like crossword puzzles and were they engaged to be married.

A whole ton had been written about the female U.K. codebreakers at Bletchley Park. There had also been a bunch written about the SOE's secret agents and even their female spies.

But only a little bit had been written about women working at the SOE headquarters. And that didn't really mention women in the signals, also known as codes, department.

Then again, the women in the codes department at the SOE weren't breaking Axis codes and ciphers...they were deciphering the incoming enciphered traffic from SOE agents sent into occupied Europe.

Sometimes articles and books lumped together the women codebreakers at Bletchley with the women working at the SOE who deciphered agents' traffic.

Nicky sighed and rubbed her temples. Maybe this wasn't worth her time. Maybe she should just write about something easier. Less complicated to research...?

She laughed softly to herself. Less complicated? That would make it far less interesting. Just because there were a few snarls, a few plot twists, a bit of missing information, didn't mean it was time to quit.

"Far better to roll up your sleeves than wring your hands," Nicky murmured under her breath.

Nicky picked up her pencil and returned her eyes to the screen.

`Agents assigned to: Oak, Ash, Maple`

Wait a minute. Ash? Nicky cocked her head. The letter

had been signed A. Interesting. Could that mean Ash and the A of the letter were the same person? Hmmm. Probably.

But her story was about Vivian, not whoever wrote to her. She turned her attention back to her pages of notes. What had Vivian been like? She wanted to bring her to life, flesh out the bare facts, find out more about the person behind the file. There had to be a way to figure out more...

Was Vivian still alive? Nicky straightened up. It *was* possible...

If that were the case, Nicky would have all her questions answered from the woman herself.

Hmmm. She pulled up ancestry.com.

After about three hours and lots of help from a research librarian, as well as Facebook, Nicky found a few more records for the correct Vivian Robinson.

She scanned the screen.

Apparently, she'd immigrated to Canada as a war bride when she married Wallace Leard from Prince Edward Island. But he was definitely not the A of that love letter...

Nicky's heart sank. Looked like Vivian had passed away three months ago at a care home in Charlottetown, Prince Edward Island. She and her husband had owned and operated a business called Leard's Piano Tuning & Restoration in Victoria, P.E.I.

Hmmm. Maybe that was something to go on? Nicky made a few keystrokes and sat back.

Yes. Nicky grinned. It was still in business.

Question was, had it been sold or was it still in the family? Because if it was still operated by family, chances were, the relatives would know something about Vivian and maybe could answer some of Nicky's questions.

She brought up the search engine and typed in the company name.

It looked like—Nicky leaned forward in her seat—the company was still in the family.

Perfect. She'd no doubt have all her questions answered in no time. She sent an email off to her editor.

AT HOME THAT night, Nicky's phone buzzed and chirped. She glanced at it. A new email from Susan. She opened the message.

From: susanolmsted@historicalwoman.com
To: nicky.stendahl@gmail.com
Sent: Wed Oct 6, 11:58 p.m.

Nicky,

Thank you for sending your contract. Payment will be made to you 45 days after the story has been submitted.

According to the email you just sent me, this Vivian woman ended up living in Canada—Prince Edward Island, I think you said.

Since this is our cover story, if you could go up there and find out more about her, that would really add perspective to the piece. It'd help our readers get a sense of place as well as person, especially since you'll be taking all the photos accompanying this feature, too.

Talk to whatever relatives you can. Get as much in-depth information as possible. I need the completed story by October 19, two weeks from now. Plenty of time to cover it.

Let me know if you need any research assistance.

—S

Nicky brushed her bangs out of her eyes and sat back against the couch. Three thousand words in two weeks? She swallowed. She'd never had to write a cover story before. Never something quite that long, either.

They'd always been short 100-word blog articles, or at the most, 250 words...

The online readerships she'd written for usually didn't have long enough attention spans to warrant quite such long pieces. But print was different. A feature story was different.

Could she actually do it? Would she be able to find out enough information? Would anyone want to read the article when she was done?

She shook off her swirling doubts and focused on the facts. Susan had been willing to take a chance on her. So Nicky needed to believe in her own abilities.

She couldn't let her editor down. She couldn't let the readers down. And she couldn't let herself down. This would be a big step up in her freelance career.

She winced. The plane ticket purchase would pretty much drain the last of her savings... But it would definitely be worth it once the article was published.

She pulled up the Expedia app on her phone and bought a ticket for the next flight to Prince Edward Island.

EARLY THURSDAY MORNING, Quinten glanced at his watch. If he didn't stay too long, he had just enough time to grab an espresso and a couple of chocolates before he headed into Charlottetown for the lawyer meeting.

He walked over to Island Chocolates.

"Hi Quinten. Your usual?" Gemma called out from behind the long wooden counter as Quinten stepped into the heritage space.

"Yeah." He pulled out his wallet to pay. "Thanks. How're the house renos going?" The scents of chocolate and freshly roasted coffee intermingled with the sounds of locals chatting at tables and the excited murmur of tourists examining the bags of brightly colored candy and fresh chocolates on the shelves of the former general store.

"Good, good," Gemma said as she rang up the sale. "Todd really appreciated you loaning him your cordless drill."

"Glad to help you and your boyfriend."

"He's almost done with it, so we'll get it back to you next week."

"Sure, no problem. What are neighbors for?"

Quinten put away his wallet and glanced around. Pretty packed in here this morning. Just one table left—his favorite—near the big picture window by the door.

Quinten took the two chocolates he'd selected and then sat down at the small forest-green metal table and looked out the big picture window.

A wedding party walked by. The bride held the skirt of her billowing white dress in one hand as she laughed at something her new husband said, his slightly lopsided bow tie matching the lopsided grin he gave his bride.

A swell of sadness filled Quinten as he looked at the happy couple. Would he ever have that?

Chapter Three

THE SCENT OF woodsmoke lingered in the cool autumn air as Nicky got out of her rental car in Victoria mid-morning Thursday.

Nicky noticed the tiny shingled visitors' center as she walked from the parking lot by the wharf up to Main Street. Might as well look around a bit to get a feel for the place before she got to work. She slung her Nikon around her neck.

A stray crimson maple leaf drifted down from the branches of the nearby tree. Nicky snapped a few shots.

Such a quaint place—straight out of a picture book. A lot more charming than the small Michigan town she'd grown up in. She smiled and shook her head.

Bright orangey yellow leaves crunched under her feet on the paved road.

She passed a blue character house called Ewe and Dye Weavery & Shop. Cute. She'd have to stop in there later.

As she walked just a bit farther, she noticed a cream-colored clapboard building on her left. The gold-lettered sign above its green antique double doors read Island Chocolates.

"HERE YOU GO, Quinten." Gemma set the steaming cup down in front of him.

"Thanks."

Definitely a gorgeous fall day for photographs—a bright blue sky and a hint of a breeze, Quinten noted. He picked up his cup and saw the bride kiss her new husband as the photographer snapped away in front of the chocolate shop's steps.

All through the summer and fall, wedding parties were a regular sight around here as they posed for photos on the picturesque streets or by the waterfront and its red-and-white lighthouse.

His thoughts circled back to his love life. Would he ever get married? His heart squeezed. Thirty-five was practically forty. And if he was so afraid to open up and share his vulnerabilities to the point that he couldn't give someone what she wanted by telling her how he really felt, things would never work out. A longing filled him. He *wanted* things to work out.

He took a sip of the espresso but it scalded his tongue, so he put the cup down quickly. He tapped his fingers on the table as he waited for it to cool and tried to ignore the lingering wedding party.

Lots of couples did that. Came here to get married. In fact, the old Presbyterian church on the edge of the village had been converted into a full-service wedding venue called the Grand Victorian.

Practically half the locals in the village worked the big weddings there; he'd done it himself more than once. He loved helping out there and enjoyed the feeling of community and togetherness it brought. The place had been doing well these past couple of years, with P.E.I. becoming a haven for destination weddings...

The wedding party started to move on, and Quinten resisted the urge to circle back to thoughts of his nonexistent love life.

He looked at his watch. He should get going soon.

He glanced out the window and noticed a woman with strawberry-blonde hair walk up the steps and open the door of the shop. Must be another tourist.

Right behind her was Mrs. MacPhail.

⚮

NICKY CAUGHT THE scent of chocolate as she stepped inside. The uneven floorboards creaked under her as the low sounds of light jazz floated across the cheerful murmur of the customers seated at round tables that dotted the space.

"Hi there!" A young woman with bangs, light brown hair pulled into a ponytail, and a friendly smile addressed Nicky from behind the long wooden counter.

"Hey," Nicky replied. She eyed the ornate glass case filled with neat piles of handmade chocolates. Colorful, hand-chalked signs declared flavors like Peppy Peppermint and Salted Caramel. Her mouth watered.

"I'll take one salted caramel chocolate and..." Nicky scanned the drink list overhead. "...a hot chocolate, please. No whipped cream though."

"Got it." The girl grinned as she handed Nicky the single chocolate on a small green porcelain saucer. "This is my favorite flavor."

Nicky paid for the drink and the chocolate.

"Your hot chocolate'll just be a sec. I'll bring it out to you. Have a seat anywhere."

Nicky glanced around. It looked like all the tables in the small space were taken.

The woman who'd come in right behind Nicky caught her glance and smiled as she said, "We're not above sharing tables with strangers here. That's how people make new friends."

Nicky's eyes drifted to a man who was seated right by the big storefront window near the door. The chair across from him was the only empty one in the place.

He was looking out the window at a bridal party.

She took the few steps toward the table. "Hey, do you mind if I sit here? I just ordered a hot chocolate and—"

The man turned his head and looked up at her. The beams of bright gold sunlight streaked through his sandy blond hair. Nicky caught her breath as he caught her gaze.

Something in the way the sun streamed through the glass and into his blue-gray eyes made him look both vulnerable and guarded at the same time.

She felt a tug at her heart. Because behind the guarded-ness, something in his posture and body language conveyed a quiet strength. He reminded her of one of the trees she'd seen along the street outside: standing firm with deep roots and strong, solid branches.

He simply nodded once in response to her question and then carefully studied his coffee.

Her heart pounded beneath her ruffled chiffon blouse as she cleared her throat and sat down. "Thanks."

QUINTEN PRETENDED TO study the dregs of coffee in his cup as he studied the woman sitting across from him in his peripheral vision.

Her shoulder-length, strawberry-blonde hair and wispy bangs framed her heart-shaped face. And the ruffled emerald blouse she wore, paired with light-blue ripped jeans, complimented her creamy complexion and hazel eyes.

But it was more than her looks that made Quinten's heart beat faster. She had something about her that was decisive. Certain. She brought to mind a river winding through a canyon. As if she knew exactly where she was going and exactly how to get there.

He swallowed. He hadn't known what to say when she'd approached him. He hoped the nod he gave her didn't come across as rude, but damn if he couldn't talk very well to women he found attractive. Probably because he was afraid of being rejected.

His fingers tightened on the handle of the cup.

"Can I get you a refill, Quinten?" Gemma came up to the table with a coffee pot and a single hot chocolate on her tray.

"Uh, sure, Gemma. Thanks. But just half, please." He avoided looking over at the woman across from him.

Gemma filled his cup halfway and gave the woman her hot chocolate. "Enjoy."

"I'm being rude," the woman across from him said as Gemma left. "I'm Nicky." She stuck out a hand.

"Quinten," he said, as he shook it.

"Hello, dear," Mrs. MacPhail called over to Quinten and waggled her fingers in his direction.

He raised a hand in response.

Maybe Mrs. MacPhail would just go get her tea like she usually did and—

No such luck. She made a beeline for his table. "How are you?" She raised her eyebrows at Quinten and glanced at Nicky across from him. "Don't you two look cozy. I'm glad to see that you're feeling like...entertaining."

Quinten felt heat creep up the back of his neck.

"Hello there, dear. I'm Zella MacPhail." She extended a hand in Nicky's direction.

"I'm Nicky Stendahl."

"Fabulous," Mrs. MacPhail said. "Here for a little holiday? Most people are. Except the locals."

"I'm actually here to cover a story. I'm a freelancer writer."

"And a photographer too, I see." Mrs. MacPhail glanced at the Nikon case on the floor beside Nicky's chair.

How had he missed that detail?

Probably because he was too busy feeling awkward and being worried about what to say to her. He took a breath.

He was perfectly capable of talking with women. He talked with Gemma, with Mrs. MacPhail, with female customers just fine. But this was different.

He glanced at his watch again and ate the second chocolate on his saucer.

"—going to be here for the next five nights, 'til Tuesday. I've booked a room at the Orient Hotel," Nicky finished.

What was it about Mrs. MacPhail that made everyone want to tell her all their secrets? Or at least, all their business. Quinten shook his head and smiled. That was P.E.I. for you. No other place quite like it.

He took the last sips of his coffee. He needed to get to Charlottetown.

She was going to stay here for a few days? He glanced at her again as she took a sip of hot chocolate.

He could deal with this. With her. He just had to think of the right thing to say to her. The perfect thing to say. That way, she wouldn't reject him.

No. He had to think more positively than that. Had to be more confident than that. Victoria was tiny, even with the tourists. He wasn't going to hide from her.

"Quinten here runs a lovely music shop and piano restoration business you have to visit. It's actually on the first floor of his house."

Nope. He'd treat her like he would a customer. Be polite. Professional.

"I love music. Played the flute all through high school and college. Or, uh, university, as you say here, don't you?"

"That's right," Mrs. MacPhail said. "But we knew what you meant, didn't we, Quinten?"

Quinten just nodded. Best to say as little as possible when she was like this.

"And you know, if there's anything I can do for you, please let me know. I consider myself the village ambassador."

"Thanks so much. Actually..." Nicky hesitated and glanced over at Quinten. "I'm looking for information about Vivian Robinson-Leard."

"Well, you're right in luck, you know. Her grandson's sitting across from you."

Quinten shifted in his seat.

Mrs. MacPhail leaned toward Nicky and said in a stage whisper, "Last closest living relative of Viv's, don'tchya know? Well, besides that Elliot MacEwen. But they're only cousins."

"Really? This is great," Nicky said, and sat up a little straighter as she pulled a small notebook and pen from her purse.

Mrs. MacPhail's phone buzzed. "Oh!" She glanced at it. "I really have to run. Minutes to type up and email out to all the board members. By the way, Quinten, thanks so much for helping Al with uploading that video to his crowdfunding page last week. He surely couldn't've done that techy stuff with my knowledge of computers."

"Happy to help," Quinten said.

"Just a second, Mrs. MacPhail," Nicky said. "Do you know anyone else in town here who was close to Vivian?"

Mrs. MacPhail paused a second and tapped a finger against her chin. "Mabel Hendricks," she said in a brisk tone. "One of her closest friends. And Quinten? Don't forget the village council meeting at the end of the month."

"Mmm-hmm."

"Good. I'll see you there, if not before. Nice to meet you, Nicky," she added as she left.

"You too," Nicky replied as she scribbled down the name and then turned her attention back to Quinten. "I'm so glad that we ran into each other like this. But in such a small place, nothing is really coincidence, is it?" She grinned and Quinten could see a dimple in her left cheek.

Like his grandma. A pang filled his heart for a second. But he forced it away.

Quinten shook his head. "Unfortunately, no."

Nicky laughed even though Quinten hadn't intended his comment to be funny.

"Well, this was easy," she continued. "Maybe you have a minute right now?" She handed him her card. "And then we can set up a time to—"

"No." Quinten winced and took a deep breath. That sounded rude. "I'm sorry but I have to go." He pushed back his chair.

Nicky sat back in her chair and he saw her shoulders droop a little.

He cleared his throat and wiped his mouth with his napkin. His heart sank. He'd handled that badly. But what was he supposed to say to her? He stood and glanced at his watch again. He had a lawyer meeting to get to.

"Why not?" Nicky said. "I want to write an article about Vivian. I've been doing a lot of research on her—"

His shoulders tensed and he said simply, "I have other

things to do. Now, if you'll excuse me, I have to be some-where."

He picked up his dirty dishes and headed over to drop them off at the counter.

His jaw tightened. Nosy journalists. Sure, Grandma Viv had worked during the war—but so had everyone else in that time period.

Then again, there were those two reporters who'd showed up at Whisperwood Villa a few months before Grandma Viv's death. They wouldn't stop asking her questions about her time during the war. Had upset her so much she'd begun to shake.

He'd been angry at himself for days afterward because he hadn't taken better care to prevent that. But then why had those journalists come around if Grandma Viv was *just* a file clerk...?

Mabel's words ran through his head. *She was in love with a Nazi...* That just couldn't be true.

He frowned. It was far better to just stay away from drama, from this woman, and move through his life as quietly as possible. Grandma Viv's life was nothing to over-glorify or make a big deal about.

He hated people making big deals about things that actually weren't as significant as they claimed.

His ex-girlfriend had always done that—made a big deal about the tiniest things. Which caused him to retreat even further...

He didn't want attention called to himself, or to his family. Especially not now with all this uncertainty about the business.

He handed his dishes back to Gemma, who was wiping down the counter.

"Have a good morning, Quinten," she said.

"Thanks. You too," he said as he headed out the door.

NICKY WALKED DOWN the steps of the chocolate shop and

headed up the street in the direction of the Orient Hotel. May as well try to start a draft of the article, just to get something down on paper.

She'd be typing it up on her laptop, actually, though she liked to keep a pen and notebook in her purse all the time just in case some great idea occurred to her.

The breeze buffeted a strand of her hair and she tucked it behind her ear.

Nicky's mind drifted back to the chocolate shop. That guy—Quinten Leard—he'd seemed...distant? Preoccupied?

Yet something about him, as he'd sat across from her and had carefully studied his coffee, had made a thread of longing pass through her.

What was she thinking? The man had barely said two words to her. A pretty clear brush-off. She clenched her jaw. If he didn't talk to her about Vivian, who else besides Mabel was she going to interview?

For half a second, she wondered what he'd thought of her and her project. No. Why was she even thinking that? He was a stranger. And she was here in a professional capacity. She wasn't interested in him. She was only here for her story.

But she hadn't really had a chance to fully explain to Quinten what she wanted to do. Was that because someone else had tried to talk to him before about Vivian, and caused some sort of issue?

She needed to interview him; but she hated to bother him again to try and persuade him to tell her what he knew about his grandmother.

She chewed on a hangnail. Quinten was the perfect source. Trouble was, she wasn't a hardened journalist. She wrote for magazines and blogs, for heaven's sake. She recalled that look of vulnerability and guardedness that had flitted across his face.

She didn't have the guts—well, the callousness—of investigative journalists. Some of them would do anything, including make people cry, just to get to the truth for their stories.

Nicky rolled her eyes. She couldn't help but feel that wasn't the point. She believed in the truth, yes. She believed people's voices needed to be heard. But not at the expense of undue pain and unnecessary suffering on the part of the source.

That seemed, in spite of a journalistic code of ethics, well, pretty unethical.

Despite herself, her mind wandered back to Quinten. His eyes were an unusual shade of blue. Didn't that hint of gray in them give him a—

She had no business wondering if his eye color defined his character. Besides, that wasn't even really possible. Another thing you only ever saw in books.

She shoved her hands deeper into the pockets of her jeans and kept walking up the street.

At the corner of—she glanced at the street sign— Howard and Main, she noticed on her left a two-story pale blue clapboard house with white trim.

It sat comfortably on its corner lot, surrounded by a white picket fence, shaded by a large tree. It had a wide porch with pots of bright yellow marigolds on either side of the door. A blue-and-gold hand-lettered wooden sign read Leard's Piano Tuning & Restoration.

Her heart beat a little faster.

She'd have to go in. Maybe if Quinten wouldn't talk, one of the employees would be able to tell her something about Vivian. Or at least, the history of the area so she could get some context for her story.

She paused mid stride. Wait a minute. The visitors' center down on the waterfront might know something about Viv. At least about the village. It was worth a shot. And would allow her to avoid bothering Quinten for a little longer.

She turned around and walked back down the way she came. She passed Island Chocolates again. She couldn't help a glance at the big picture window. An East Indian couple sat inside with their little girl who had chocolate all over her face.

Nicky walked on. She noticed a bright orange house with paler orange trim on her left. Then she passed a few more wooden clapboard homes with woodpiles and white picket fences and big hardwood trees on their lawns.

The seagulls wheeled overhead. The scent of saltwater told her she was getting close to the waterfront. She passed Richard's Fresh Seafood on the corner across from the pier.

She'd heard that place had pretty good fish and chips. She'd have to go there for lunch or maybe dinner.

She took a left and went diagonally through the lot where she'd parked her rental car. She headed over to the small single story one-room building with gray-shingled siding that stood to one side of the lot. A heavy rope fence surrounded the small building.

To her right was a sandy pathway that led down to a small strip of beach beside the wharf.

She passed a bike rack with several bikes. One was a cherry-red retro Schwinn with a woven wicker bike basket. She couldn't help but grin as she pulled out her camera to take a few shots of it. Everywhere you turned, this place had picture-postcard photo ops.

Pots of bright orange and yellow flowers stood on either side of the doorway to the little building.

She went inside.

"Hi there, can I help you?" A woman in a black T-shirt and black jeans, with chin-length, gray-and-white-streaked hair, greeted her. A pair of reading glasses dangled on a chain around her neck.

"Actually, yes. I'm looking for some information about one of the village residents. Vivian Robinson. She married a Leard."

"You're not a relative, are you." The woman's bright blue eyes didn't seem to miss a detail.

Nicky drew out her pen and notepad. "I'm writing an in-depth article about her, actually."

"That's great. I'm working on a book, myself. I have several friends who are Leards. Well, I can tell you that she was from away. Came to Victoria in late fall of '46, I think.

She was a war bride and married a successful local man, Wallace Leard. They met in London. He'd been in the air force and flew a Tiger Moth. Got promoted to colonel. Have you talked with Quinten Leard? He would be your best bet. He's her grandson and would know the most about her."

Nicky bit her lip and felt a blush come to her cheeks. "I just met him at the chocolate shop. He seemed...busy, and I was hoping to get several viewpoints, actually, for the story. I want to give it as much scope as possible."

"Well..." The woman looked speculative for a second. "Elliot MacEwen's her grandson too, but let's just say Elliot's not exactly interested in history. He wouldn't know what I imagine you're needing to find out." She tapped a finger against her chin. "But Mabel Hendricks'll help you out if you talk with her."

"Thanks so much," Nicky said. She couldn't help the smile that came to her lips. People in small towns everywhere, it seemed, liked to share what they knew.

"Oh, and miss?" The woman held Nicky's gaze for another moment. Nicky shifted her weight.

"Don't judge Quinten too harshly. He might be stoic but he has a good heart. Been going through a bit of a rough time lately trying to save the family business, what with his cousin Elliot having designs on it and all."

ALONG SYDNEY STREET in downtown Charlottetown, Quinten opened the brass-handled wooden door of the low red brick building. Originally it had been a warehouse back in the 1800s but now it contained converted office suites.

He headed up the stairs to his lawyer's third-floor office.

He nodded a polite hello to the receptionist. "Just head on back to the conference room, Quinten," she said. "Elliot's already in there."

Elliot, who had taken a seat at the big old oak conference table, watched a video on his phone. It appeared to be about how to improve your golf swing.

Quinten fought an unsettled feeling that only grew in the pit of his stomach as he sat on the hard, oak chair and rested his forearms on the table.

The lawyer walked in a few minutes later with a glass of water. He cleared his throat. "Thank you for coming in, gentlemen. As you know, this meeting is in regards to Vivian Fern Robinson-Leard's business."

The lawyer sat down and pushed his black-framed glasses up on his nose. "Vivian's business was a sole proprietorship. That sole proprietorship ceased upon the owner's, in this case Vivian's, death. After which, the assets went into the estate to be divided evenly between surviving kin."

"Which has already been done via probate," Elliot reminded him. "Quinten and I each own fifty percent of her business now."

Quinten clenched his jaw. "But we both want different things for the business."

"Yes. Therein lies the problem." The lawyer rubbed his temples. "I've seen this before with family businesses. People can take things personally. Egos can get in the way. As things stand now, well, basically either of you could do anything. And with that kind of equal distribution of power between you both, it can lead to feuding, poor business decisions, bad results and, ultimately, failure of the business."

A muscle in Quinten's jaw ticked as he glanced at Elliot. "Isn't there a way to...fix this?"

"Well," the lawyer pushed up his glasses again, "someone needs to be assigned as the sole heir in order for the business to be run smoothly. Otherwise, well, I hope I won't see the two of you in court."

The lawyer glanced from Elliot to Quinten and shuffled papers.

"Quinten could decide to keep on with the sole proprietorship but that would only happen if he was the only heir. The same goes for you, Elliot," the lawyer said.

"But Quinten isn't the sole heir, because there's no will,"

Elliot countered.

"No, not at the moment," the lawyer agreed. "Your grandmother never gave me any documentation. And as I've said, because of that, there was no article, no item that said or clearly indicated, or directly established, who received ownership of Leard's Piano Tuning & Restoration. Sometimes people get so caught up in the daily running of their business that they don't remember to designate a successor. Or write a will."

"So that means I could buy out Quinten's half, now that the probate's gone through," Elliot said.

The lawyer took a sip of water. "At the moment, the business belongs fifty percent to each of you, which is in accordance with intestate succession law. So yes, Elliot, since the probate's gone through, you could buy out Quinten's half."

"But if a will was found and it said I was the heir," Quinten managed to force the words through the tightness in his chest, "then I wouldn't have to sell to Elliot?"

"If a will is found," the lawyer said, "and if it specifically named one of you, then yes, the company would belong to whomever that was, as per the will."

"So then," Quinten said, "that would settle, once and for all, who has the company, legally?"

"Yes," the lawyer said.

Quinten shifted in his seat.

Elliot crossed his arms over his chest.

"Listen, gentlemen, I understand that you may have...differences of opinion about the business. Regardless, in order for this whole mess to be sorted out, a sole successor needs to be designated as quickly as possible." He looked from one man to the other. "This current arrangement isn't doing either of you any favors."

"What do you suggest?" Quinten asked.

"I would advise that the two of you come to some sort of agreement right now."

"On?" Elliot raised his brows.

"On what you both want to do. It looks to me that Quinten, you want some time to look more thoroughly for a will. But Elliot, you want to buy out his half right now. I would propose a compromise."

Elliot shot the lawyer a sidelong glance. "What do you mean?"

"Set a deadline to look for inheritance documentation."

"Fine, fine." Elliot waved a hand.

Quinten's jaw tightened. He should've sorted through his grandmother's papers in detail sometime in the past three months. But somehow, between arranging the memorial service, running the shop, worrying about the financial state of the business, and feuding with Elliot, he'd only had time for a cursory search and had come up empty-handed. But regretting what he couldn't undo wasn't productive. He could only go forward. "That sounds fair."

"Good. I'll get my assistant to draw up some papers for you to sign about this." The lawyer looked back and forth between the two. "Now, do you both then agree on the timeframe of one week—by next Wednesday—in which to find some sort of will?"

Both cousins murmured agreement.

"After which, if said timeframe has passed and nothing is found, then you both agree that one of you will buy out the other?"

Quinten gave a short, sharp nod and stood. He pushed aside growing panic. He wouldn't let himself think about the possibility of the company actually going bankrupt. If that happened, he couldn't afford to buy out Elliot's half. There had to be some sort of documentation in Grandma Viv's things. *Had* to be.

Elliot nodded too, but stayed seated. "There's no will to find. I own half the business now, anyway. So I'll just wait until Quinten comes up empty-handed. A week from now, the business will be completely mine."

NICKY TAPPED HER unpolished fingernails on her jeans-clad

thigh and sighed.

She'd sat on the porch of the music shop for awhile after she'd found it empty but then realized she looked pretty conspicuous, so she headed back up the street to the Orient Hotel.

After she'd played a round of croquet on the back lawn with a couple of other guests and the wife of the owner, she'd headed to her room.

Which was why she was sitting here now staring at her laptop and a blank Word document.

She picked up her smartphone and logged on to her social media account.

Hmmm. Were there any more editors who had mentioned story pitches in their feeds? Nicky scrolled through. Sometimes she'd gotten work that way. Didn't look like it, nope. But Susan from the *Historical Woman* had begun to follow her. That was good news.

Well, she'd update her status anyway.

Working on a new story! she typed. *#amwriting.*

Nicky paused. Speaking of writing, had *Ivory* magazine deposited her money yet?

She tapped her banking app. Hmm. Nope, didn't look like it. She frowned and tried to nudge aside mounting worry mixed with annoyance. When was she going to get that money?

She frowned again as she glanced at her savings account balance. After paying for this plane ticket, she had about one hundred fifty dollars left in it.

Frustration built inside her. That contract had stipulated, much like the one she'd just signed, that she would be paid forty-five days after article submission. And it was well after forty-five days now. She drummed her fingers on her thigh as the frustration grew. What was going on?

She went back to her social media account. This didn't make any sense. The frustration swept through her as she typed *#journalistsneedtogetpaid* and hit refresh. She sighed in satisfaction as her status updated again.

She'd emailed the magazine multiple times but had received no response. And the magazine's receptionist assured her someone would return her calls. No one had.

Maybe they'd respond to a social media post? Doubtful, but worth a try. She clicked onto their page. *#IvoryMagazine, I haven't received my payment from the story I wrote for you. When can I expect it, as it's now overdue. Thanks!*

Maybe she had some money from those photos? She opened Shutterstock. Looked like a few people liked those pictures she'd uploaded on Tuesday. Her royalties tab actually had a couple of dollars in it.

She put her phone down and wished she could set aside her concern as easily.

But she'd better get productive here. After all, there was nothing she could do about that late payment at the moment. She worried her bottom lip between her teeth.

She just had to keep going with the current piece. They'd pay her soon enough. Right? Probably just busy and running behind.

She turned back to the Word document.

What would be the best angle to approach this?

That first paragraph needed to hook her readers and really get them interested.

And it needed to be great. This was her chance to really make an impact, to make a difference. To write about something important. Someone important to history. A voice from the past that touched people's hearts in the present...

She needed to do Vivian justice. Needed to be able to paint a picture of her that would bring her to life, yet be true to her life.

She needed to understand where Vivian had been coming from.

Well, in order to do that, she needed to hear from Vivian herself. Or at least, the closest person to it. She got up and headed outside.

BACK IN VICTORIA, Quinten shut the driver's side door of his silver Acura and got out. He breathed a sigh of relief to find that the journalist—Nicky—wasn't waiting for him on his front porch. He rubbed a hand across his face. He didn't think he could handle anything like that now.

He headed across the porch, opened the screen door, and stepped inside.

Dappled sunlight filtered in through one of the west-facing windows and caught the varnish on the guitars and violins that were on display. A baby grand piano stood at the opposite end of the small space.

He didn't sell too many musical instruments; and those that he did have on hand were stringed ones. The bulk of his income came from piano repair and tuning.

At least, it had.

Maybe he should just focus on instrument sales? But he loved working with the vintage pianos. Bringing new life to old instruments. Bringing smiles to people's faces. Bringing people together around something besides a computer or a television. Uniting them in something that had meaning, importance, emotion, feeling, heart...

He rubbed a hand across his jaw and looked around the store. His grandmother had to have written down some mention of who would get the business. She'd been a tad disorganized but tended to write things down. Usually. That is, until dementia had taken over...

He flipped over the small wooden sign that hung from the screen door so that it read *closed*. He'd been in such a rush that he'd completely forgotten to close up properly earlier in the day.

He needed to start going through her paperwork. Through everything of hers, really. And the attic was probably the best place to start.

A FLUFFY GRAY long-haired cat snoozed on the cane-back rocker as Nicky walked up to the porch of Mabel Hendricks's house. She stroked the cat's head and then rang the doorbell.

It wasn't long before she heard the shuffle of feet. An old woman with perfectly permed, bright white hair answered the door.

"Hello there, dear. Who are you?"

"My name's Nicky Stendahl. I'm sorry to drop by unannounced..." She held up her pen and pad. "But a couple of people—Mrs. MacPhail and the lady down at the visitors' center—told me that you'd be the person to talk to about Vivian Robinson-Leard."

"My reputation precedes me, I can tell."

"I wanted to ask you when it would be convenient for you to talk with me about her?"

The old woman waved a hand. "I'm ninety-seven and a half years old. Got nothing but time these days. Never mind making an appointment. Come on in. I always like a good visit."

She opened the screen door wide and Nicky stepped into the house.

"Come on into the living room. That's where the most comfortable sofas are."

Nicky followed Mabel as she took a sharp left into the living room.

The old woman maneuvered easily around several cat toys and a pile of newspapers beside a large cardboard box that had, from Nicky's quick glance inside, a jumble of odds and ends in it.

Must be donating some items? Or maybe she just needed them close by for who knows what.

Mabel took a seat on the couch. Nicky sat down on an armchair nearby and pulled out her pen and notebook. "I was just wanting to ask you some questions about her life."

"I'm the only one who remembers now. She wasn't well the last few years, you know." Mabel shook her head. "At the very last, poor Quinten had to take care of her all by himself. Only child, that one." She pursed her lips.

"He's a good man, Quinten. Always helping everyone he

can around here. That's what makes this place more than just another small town. It's really one big family."

"I can imagine," Nicky murmured.

"Did you know he stayed up 'til 3:00 a.m. one time just to make sure that my neighbor here—" she pointed a thumb behind her "—got home safe from the pub? Another time, he waded out into the freezing cold water in the dead of January to help my other neighbor up the road find her car keys when she'd lost them. He's always doing stuff like that. A good man," Mabel repeated and looked at Nicky as if she would deny it.

Was it her imagination or was everyone she met here trying to set her up with Quinten?

She couldn't help but wonder what this place was like if you actually lived here. The corners of her lips tugged upward. That might be kind of fun to find out.

"So," Mabel continued, "I think Quinten would really be the best person to talk to. But I've rambled on enough. What do you want to know from me?"

"Well," Nicky said, and glanced through her list of questions, "I understand she worked in the signals department of the SOE during World War II and I—"

"Never heard tell of it." Mabel sat up straight. "Nope. She never mentioned anything like that to me at all."

Nicky's shoulders drooped. "She didn't?"

"Nope," Mabel said. "Never in all the fifty years I knew her."

"Well, what did she say about her time during the war?" Nicky persisted.

"Only that she spent time in London. Mentioned something about being a file clerk."

Nicky bit her lip and tapped her pen on the blank page.

"We never really talked about the war. Our generation, you see," Mabel paused as if gathering her thoughts, "never felt it was right to talk about such things."

Nicky started to put away her notebook.

"Now, just a second. Right after Viv died, my daughter Anna helped Quinten clean out his basement—that house was where Viv and Wallace lived, you know—and Anna found a few things of Viv's she thought I might want, so he let Anna take them for me."

She waved her cane at the cardboard box that Nicky had noticed earlier. "Just there, in fact."

"Oh?"

"Take the whole box," Mabel said, "if it'll be of any use to you."

"Uh...if you're sure?"

"You, well, I think your heart's in the right place. So I don't mind, and I don't think Viv would've, either."

"Wow, thank you so much. I'll bring it all back once I'm done."

"I'm sorry I don't know what you need answering. Quinten really would be the person to answer your questions about Vivian."

"Okay, I'll keep that in mind."

Mabel added, "There was a journal or a diary or something in that box there somewhere. I didn't read it, though. It was locked—all rusted shut—and I didn't have the key and it never seemed right to just pry it open."

She studied Nicky a moment. "I think you're trying to do good. So if you're doing a piece about her life, well, then you'd be the one to look at that little diary. Might need someone to help you open it up, though."

Nicky knelt down by the box. "I'll take a look through it right away." She started to pick up the box.

"If you're looking for a story..."

Nicky paused and looked at Mabel.

"The Nazis were here," the old woman murmured.

Nicky's eyes widened.

Mabel's eyes closed. "It was about 3:00 a.m. ..."

She continued, lost in memory, as if Nicky wasn't even there. "...I'd woken up but I couldn't get back to sleep. The moon was bright, bright and full that night; it shone on the water so that it reflected right into my bedroom window on the second floor. It was early May, I remember. I was lying awake in my bed when I heard rustling downstairs. It was just me and my younger sisters here in the house." She waved a hand to indicate the old Edwardian they were in.

"Being the oldest, I knew I had to see what was going on. So I got up and picked up my flashlight that I always had by my bed. I crept down the stairs, careful to avoid the three that creak. The rustling continued. From the kitchen.

"I pressed against the wall, the flashlight clutched in my hand like a baseball bat. I slowly tiptoed my way down the hall toward the kitchen door. The rustling stopped but the loud pounding of my heart hadn't, and I wondered if whoever it was could hear it.

"I'd gotten to the kitchen by then. Peered into the room. Saw that the pantry light was on. Knew I'd turned it off when I went to bed. The pantry door was open a crack, too.

"I held my breath the whole way across that black-and-white tiled floor. Afraid any second someone was going to jump out and, I don't know, shoot me. Ever so slowly, I nudged the pantry door open with my bare toe. The bulb's pull chain was still swinging back and forth. But no one was in there.

"Oh, I was so relieved. What could've I done with a flashlight?" She chuckled and shook her head.

"But then I saw that the ham we'd planned to have for Sunday dinner—gotten it in trade from a neighbor for some of our potatoes—was gone.

"I'd just reached up to turn off the light when I saw a glint of something silver on the floor."

Mabel opened her eyes suddenly and met Nicky's gaze. "That's why I know Hitler's treasure is here somewhere."

"What do you mean?" Goosebumps rose on Nicky's arms. "And what did you find on the floor?"

Mabel rapped her cane emphatically. "Sit back down, dear. It's time you heard the legend."

QUINTEN HEADED OUT back and grabbed the aluminum ladder down from the loft of the little shingle-sided blue barn painted with white trim around the windows and doors.

Though currently Quinten's storage shed, the small barn had originally been in a different spot in town and was sometimes used for spelling bees back in the twenties and thirties.

Now it sat in his back yard. He'd inherited the corner lot with its 1820s house from Grandpa Wallace.

He put the ladder over one shoulder and wove his way through the neat piles of various items that had collected over the years.

There was the group of four wooden school chalkboards, complete with roll-down maps, that Grandma Viv had gotten from the old schoolhouse up the road after it had been decommissioned.

There was the stack of his neighbor's paddle boats that were in the opposite corner of the shed, waiting for the perfect July day and the gaggle of tourists that would come to rent them.

There were the bags and boxes of his father's things that he'd somehow not had the heart to part with, even in the years since his dad's death.

He shook his head at himself. Sometime he really needed to go through all this. Figure out what he wanted to keep and what he didn't. Elliot was always hounding him to make way for the new, to get rid of the old.

But he couldn't, somehow, just throw it all out. It was his connection to those people, those places, that he wouldn't get back again...

BACK IN HER room at the Orient, Nicky put Mabel's box on the side table. The leather-bound diary was one of the only items in it. A battered shoe box was another.

Nicky lifted the lid on it and saw a jumble of papers. Receipts. Recipe cards. Utility bills. Hmmm. Wouldn't hurt to go through that later.

She picked up the diary and held it in her hand. The place to start would be here. She examined the book and felt a surge of curiosity mixed with a pang of guilt. Going through Viv's personal things...? But it was an opportunity to hear from the woman herself. Mabel had given her permission to take the box, after all. But shouldn't Quinten be the one to look at this? Then again, he'd given the box away to Mabel. The items in the box must not have meant that much to him...

She felt a nudge of regret. Quinten hadn't even seemed interested in helping her out. Or in finding out about his own grandmother.

But maybe that wasn't a fair assessment? He'd seemed pretty stressed out. If what the woman in the visitors' center said was true, well, Nicky supposed she couldn't blame him for being a little...touchy.

She thought again of the way his eyes had caught the sunlight when he'd first looked up at her. That hint of vulnerability...the sense that he had deep roots and solid strength.

Something nudged at her heart but she turned her attention back to the small cream-colored book. She picked it up and tugged the zipper pull.

It slid easily open across the top of the book. But as Nicky pulled it around the corner, it stopped. She frowned. Looked like there was a piece of rust there.

She tugged harder. But now the zipper was stuck fast. She didn't dare pull any harder or the whole thing might fall apart in her hands.

Her brow furrowed more.

Even if she got the zipper all the way open, the diary was still locked. And she certainly didn't have the key.

She withheld a sigh. She had to be patient. This was important; and if she could just get at the information inside, then she'd be able to really do justice to this story, to this woman.

Quinten needed to at least know that. Even if he refused to help her, she at least had to try.

She picked up the small book and her keyring and headed out the door.

TODAY WAS THURSDAY, which meant Quinten needed to sort out the recycling. Usually it got picked up on a weekday. But with the storms they'd had not long ago, things had gotten behind. So pickup was scheduled for this Sunday instead.

With his free hand, he snagged a few clear blue plastic recycling bags from the box on the shelf near the shed door.

He headed outside and back over to the house. He set the ladder down by the porch, then went through the front entrance so he could put the recycle bags on the counter for easy accessibility.

After he started going through things this afternoon in the attic, then he could make some headway on organizing it for the recycling and—

"Good, you're still here."

Quinten's eyes snapped to the front porch. The woman he'd shared a table with at Island Chocolates now stood on his doorstep.

He leaned against the counter in an attempt to feign nonchalance. But his heart thudded in his chest. Right. She was just like a customer. That's all. A customer.

"Sorry, we're closed," he said.

"But you're still here."

"Right. Because I'm the owner." Part owner, anyway...

He crossed his arms. "Can I help you?"

Nicky opened the screen door and stepped just inside the threshold. "Mabel sent me. She insisted that you would know the most about your grandmother."

Quinten felt a nudge of impatience, but hid it in his friendly tone.

"Well, Mabel's a good friend of the family," he admitted. Sometimes too good. "But she can get a little over-enthusiastic."

Nicky fiddled with the straps on her purse.

"Listen," Quinten said, "have you tried the visitors' center?" Maybe she'd read between the lines of the meaning of his suggestion and leave. He continued in case she hadn't. "They might be able to give you what you need. Or even the library in Charlottetown." Far away from here. He mentally crossed his fingers.

Nicky grinned. "Everyone in this town is so helpful. Friendly. It's so refreshing compared to New York." She put her hands on her hips. "The thing is, the lady at the visitors' center told me to come see you, too."

Quinten took a breath. He couldn't agree to this. She'd go poking around, asking questions, creating drama. He didn't have the time for it on top of going through all of Grandma Viv's paperwork... Even though he felt every nerve in him straining to say yes.

Just because that way he'd be liked. He'd be accepted. He'd be—"I'm sorry." He headed over to the screen door and held it open for her. "Nicky, was it? I'm on a tight deadline and have to go through a lot of paperwork." Better to avoid committing.

She stepped back over the threshold on the porch. He moved to latch the screen door shut and caught the flowery scent of her perfume.

He mentally shook his head. He shouldn't be noticing things like her perfume.

But he blinked and came up short when she held up something right in front of him.

"Maybe you'd be interested in this?"

Chapter Four

S HE HELD A small cream-colored book with the words *Five-Year Diary* emblazoned across it in faded gold lettering.

A gold zipper around its edge looked like it'd seen better days and was fastened, Quinten saw, with an oval lock. Where on Earth had that come from? He'd never seen it before.

"Sorry," he repeated, "but I, uh, really have things to do." He turned to the ladder he'd set down by the porch railing.

"It was your grandmother's," she added as she followed him across the porch. He winced. He hoped not too many neighbors were watching this. Lace curtains twitched across the way. Too late.

Despite himself, a thread of curiosity wound through him. What was in his grandma's diary? It would just be a distraction, though. Like Nicky. He picked up the ladder. "I'm sorry to disappoint you, but I'm very busy at the moment with certain obligations and don't have the time to spend to talk about my grandmother."

He had to find the will. He wouldn't be able to focus if Nicky was around. He wouldn't be able to accomplish much if he was distracted by her. He'd be wondering how he came across, worrying about what to say to her...

Nicky bit her lip.

He took a breath. "I don't know that much anyway, okay? Besides, she wouldn't have liked a lot of fuss made about her, let alone some sort of article written up."

Nicky opened her mouth to say something but he continued. "All I can tell you is she was an excellent business-woman—ahead of her time—"

"But—" Nicky started to say.

"Have you tried ancestry.com?" Quinten plowed on. "Maybe other, more distant relatives will be able to help you out. Now if you'll excuse me."

He picked up the ladder, opened the door and made sure to lock it behind him.

QUINTEN HEADED FARTHER inside, careful to maneuver the ladder around the ornately carved newel post at the foot of the stairs.

He sighed. He didn't like to disappoint people. He recalled the way Nicky had bitten her lip. A sliver of guilt niggled at him. He should've said yes. Agreed to help her.

Maybe he'd been too hasty? After all, how long would it take, really, for her to ask him a few questions?

No. He shook his head. He was too busy. He had to find a will, or at least something that would clarify this mess.

He headed up the stairs, mindful the ladder didn't knock into the framed family photos along the stairway.

But those photos, like the piles of stuff in the shed, he couldn't seem to throw away.

He reached the landing on the second floor. After he set up the ladder, he climbed it and pushed open the small hatch to the attic.

He went through the hatch and sat down on the rafter stringers. A cloud of dust caught in a beam of sunlight made him sneeze.

He should probably find a better place to store Christmas and Thanksgiving decorations. Well, while he was up here, maybe he could start going through those things, too.

Grandma Viv had loved Christmas, and there were a lot of extra decorations he didn't need.

He set out the plastic bags he'd brought up with him, and got to work.

A few hours later, he was covered in dust. His stomach rumbled and he glanced at his watch. Getting close to five o'clock. Time flew when sorting junk.

But he'd made progress. One corner of the attic was now neatly organized and he had several bags full of recycling.

He sighed and raked a hand through his hair. But there was nothing about a will. And no paperwork to speak of.

He reached for the last box shoved into the north corner. It looked pretty old. He swiped at the thick layer of dust and coughed.

Hmm. This wasn't a cardboard box. It was a buff-colored suitcase.

A vintage suitcase, from the look of it.

He wiped off more dust and noticed that there was a lock on the case.

Odd. He'd never seen this suitcase up here before. Kind of like that diary...

Could Grandma Viv have been hiding things from him? Or had she just forgotten, thanks to the dementia? His heart twisted.

Granted, this suitcase had been kind of hidden behind all these other cardboard boxes and piles of decorations...

He set it down so it lay flat, then flipped the latches and tugged on the lid.

Nothing.

He put a bit more muscle into it. With a screech of the hinges, the suitcase opened. Huh.

He rummaged through the contents. More Christmas decorations. Really *old* Christmas decorations. Along with Halloween pumpkins and a cardboard cut-out of a turkey colored in with crayon in the shape of a handprint that looked very familiar.

One corner of his mouth lifted as he rubbed a thumb across the faded image. That had been Grade 1 or 2, if he remembered right.

But how did it get in—

Quinten's eyes were drawn to a crumbling yellowed clipping from the Charlottetown newspaper that had somehow attached itself to the bottom of the turkey.

As he tried to carefully loosen and then examine it, the old paper started to crumble under his fingertips.

```
—U-boat was sighted in Charlottetown harbor
early yesterday morning. Two destroyers were
sent out to intercept but the sub slipped away
before a firm lock could be gotten on it.
     This is the first sighting of U-boats this
close to the capital city but not the first
report of German activity in the Northumberland
Strait or the Gulf of St. Lawrence.
     Authorities encourage locals—
```

So Mabel had been right. He clenched his jaw. At least about the Germans. He had thought it was just conjecture and hearsay. Apparently not.

But as for his grandmother being in love with a Nazi, well, that couldn't be true. She'd loved his grandfather, Wallace.

He thumbed the edges of the page, which crumbled off and fell away. Patches of handwriting showed through. He felt his pulse quicken. There was more here?

He nudged aside the crumbling flakes. Yes. It looked like someone had pasted another page underneath...

The yellowed, dried glue simply let go under his touch to reveal a letter, obscured, in some places, by the article. In others, by time and deterioration.

Apri 5, 43

Dear t Viv,

even as my   mind grows grave, my love, fo   future of German   friend Fritz talks   about Socialist Party but I have an uneasy feeling i   That's why I join he cause f things.

time I find myself longing fo   past. For what   ave been my concert   areer.   Thou have not put m s e ivories of any piano in suc   le, I   if I did, all of this unrest w   interfere.

glad I can be certain of our love   I am sure
you   the extent   my feelings for you, and
I   confidently to our future together. I   hope
Germany's future   fare as well!
*   your other question,   a Polish princess,*
not   German queen.
*   You might be surprised to know that though I   Ger-*
man   t name, I am indeed   nt, and can trace my lineage
back to that   line of
*   In fa   ss married the king of France but the*
mi   disappeared until my great-gr
*   found   and now I have   locked*
away — as suc   aluable object   be, along   ith
th   wry—on my family estate.
*   B   was before the SS came knocking*

All my love
—A

Wait a minute. Quinten drew in a sharp breath. Could Mabel be right?

Part of him refused to believe it even though he held this very real piece of history in his hand.

He started to put the fragile page back into the suitcase but it crumbled into tiny pieces with the motion.

His eyes widened. This was more glimpses of a Vivian he never knew. Would this letter give him the answers he was looking for? He cocked his head. Give him a chance to be closer to his grandmother? To get to know the person she was before she'd come to P.E.I., before dementia had robbed her of her memories...

He took out his phone and snapped a few photos of the remains before he continued through the case's contents. He riffled through the long pouch on the underside of the lid and discovered a ream of Christmas music.

He flipped through it idly. He already had a big book of the classic carols sitting on the piano downstairs and didn't needed any more yellowed copies of that. Yep, all the Christmas favorites were here...

Huh. A few other pieces must have gotten mixed in. There was "The White Cliffs of Dover" and something called "Marsch Impromptu" by some German composer he'd never heard of.

Yep, these would be great to add to Sunday's recycling. He shoved the pages into the clear blue plastic bag as well as the crumbled bits of the newspaper article and letter.

His stomach rumbled again and he glanced around the attic. Shadows had lengthened across the floorboards and evening light filtered through the small window. He rubbed his neck. He'd been up here long enough for one day.

Well, he'd made enough progress for the moment. He grabbed up the now-full, clear plastic bags and eased them all through the hatch.

He descended the ladder and put the recycling out in the foyer. Then he headed into the kitchen to make himself a late supper. His mind returned to his grandmother.

Hmmm.

What if the diary Nicky had found helped him find out more about Grandma Viv? Surely, she hadn't really fallen in love with a Nazi...

Perhaps it would also help him figure out the whereabouts of the will? Maybe, somewhere in it, would be a clue?

And what if the letter he'd found could help Nicky in some way? His heart pounded. Could he agree to work with her? But what if she rejected him? He shook his head. No. This wasn't personal. It was strictly business.

She was writing an article about his grandmother, that's all. Maybe she wasn't being a nosy journalist; maybe she was just doing her job well. She'd said she'd done research on the woman, so his grandmother's life would have to be her business. Parts of it, anyway.

He supposed he could talk to her. Working with her wouldn't be a distraction, but a way to bring things into focus. Help him connect with his grandmother.

He straightened his shoulders. It was business. That, he could handle. He took a breath. He'd just be professional. Polite. She didn't need to know he felt a bit attracted to her.

He could easily hide that.

He pulled out his phone again along with the now-crumpled business card Nicky had given him.

NICKY STARTED TO read through the Word document on her laptop. But her phone buzzed with an incoming text message before she could continue. From Quinten?

Why don't we meet at the music shop tomorrow morning? You're right, I'd like to look at her diary.

Without hesitating, she texted back.

Sounds great. See you then.

She put her phone down. Hmm. Battery was getting low again. Needed to charge it.

She turned her attention back to the story. She needed to look in the diary. What was inside? She felt a tingle of excitement go up her spine. And, well, she wanted to know...was Quinten *always* like that? Or was the lady at the visitors' center right?

She glanced back at the page. She'd made a little headway tonight on the story. Transcribed some of her notes on what Mabel had told her. That incident about the stolen ham would be a good one to layer in, somehow. Maybe as a sidebar?

She turned her attention back to the open document. She'd typed about a hundred words when her thoughts strayed again.

If she wasn't careful, she could think of several excuses to stay longer. The scent of the fresh sea breeze, the taste of salted caramel on her tongue... And Quinten Leard agreeing to help her?

No. As much as she needed the information and was grateful to Quinten, she knew she couldn't allow herself to be attracted to him. It would interfere with her carefully laid plans. She only had a few days here, after all.

She lifted her chin. She needed to stick to reading spy thrillers.

The romance genre was one best steered clear of. It wasn't realistic. It didn't do anyone any favors. Least of all for people like her who'd believed in romantic notions and then got them completely smashed when they discovered that real life, real love, wasn't the same as it was in a paperback.

She sighed. If only...

If only, nothing. She had a story to write, and a very good lead to follow now, what with Quinten's agreeing to help her. That was all.

QUINTEN GLANCED OUT the window Friday morning. Golden light spilled through the trees and cast dappled patterns on the pavement of Main Street.

Some tour buses were scheduled to come into the village later this morning, and he needed to be open for that. But he had a little time now.

He noticed Nicky as she walked toward his house. She said hello to a few people who headed up the street.

Sunlight caught the reddish highlights in her hair and burnished them a fiery copper.

Such a strong color. Kind of like her personality. His heart jumped. He wished he had strength like that. What was it like, to not hide? To say what he felt freely, without worrying what others thought?

He saw Nicky say something to one of the older ladies outside—was that Mabel? Looked like it. Acting like a local, practically.

Pretty soon she'd be buying a summer cottage here; a good chunk of the village was seasonal residents. Thank goodness none of the houses were for sale in the central core here. But the suburbs were another story.

He frowned. He didn't know Nicky well enough to make assumptions. He didn't know her at all. He winced. Strong personalities meant drama. And drama meant unnecessary attention called to himself. He needed to stay away from all of that.

"Hi Quinten," Nicky said as she walked up the steps of the porch.

"Thanks for coming."

"Thanks for finally deciding to help me." Nicky laughed and put a hand on her hip.

He shifted his weight.

"So." She met Quinten's gaze.

He could see the hints of green in her hazel eyes. He cleared his throat.

"Like I already said," she continued as she came closer to the screen door that divided them, "this is her diary. You want to know what's inside?" He saw a gleam of daring? challenge? in her gaze and couldn't help the half-smile that flitted across his lips. He kind of liked the fact that she took charge. That she knew what she wanted.

He opened the door.

She stepped inside.

The lace curtains across the street twitched.

Nicky now stood only a few feet away from him and for a second, they simply looked at each other.

Her hair was slightly windblown, and the turquoise blouse she wore looked vintage. It made her skin look—no. That was a detail he was going to pretend he hadn't noticed.

He swallowed and took a step back.

"The zipper's stuck. The lock doesn't have a key." Nicky bit her lip. "And I'm sorry to say I couldn't bring my tool box with me. Do you happen to have a pair of small pliers?"

"Uh..." Quinten blinked. "I think so. If you—" No. He didn't want to make her uncomfortable by asking her to come to the back room. He cleared his throat. "I have some in the workshop. Let me just check."

He exhaled softly as he walked into the back room. Breathe. Just breathe. She was just another person. She was just needing his help. He was just being a good neighbor.

But curiosity and heat nudged at him despite himself. She looked *really* good in that blouse.

He rummaged around in a drawer on his workbench.

Here was a pair. He picked them up and headed back out to the store front.

"Found them," he said unnecessarily.

Her eyes lit up. "Great." She handed him the diary. "Here, maybe if you hold it, I can get a good angle."

"Okay. Uh, sure." He took the small book from her and studied its cover. Would there be anything in here that would clarify things? Or mention a will?

Why hadn't Grandma Viv ever wanted to talk about her life before she'd come to the island? Had she really been...hiding something? He felt a small stab of hurt in his heart.

"Hmm, I think it'd be better if you flipped it over," Nicky said as she reached for the book. She stood so close to him that he could see a small freckle on her collarbone. He moved his gaze to the diary instead.

She gripped the pliers in one hand and held onto the book with the other. Their fingers were nearly touching. He noticed the ring on the forefinger of her left hand.

He cocked his head. Another vintage piece. She appreciated things with history, he noted with approval.

That ring, though...it looked somewhat familiar. And in a flash, he remembered. That old black and white photograph of Vivian that she'd shown him when she was in the nursing home.

He caught his breath. She had been wearing that ring when the picture had been taken.

But how...?

He put the speculating out of his mind as he tightened his grip on the book and watched Nicky grasp the zipper pull with the pliers.

Gently, she tugged on the zipper. At first, nothing happened. But then, slowly, slowly, the zipper began to move.

He held his breath as the zipper inched its way down the long side of the book and then across the bottom.

"We did it!" Nicky grinned at him.

"Looks like it." He found himself grinning back. She didn't give up, did she? He could appreciate having someone like that to work with.

"Well," Nicky leaned in and he could feel her breath on his skin as she said, "we have to find out what's inside, don't we?"

"CAN I JUST..." Nicky indicated the diary with her free hand and Quinten startled. "Uh, sure."

He released the small book and Nicky opened it as far as it would go.

"But the lock's still there. See? It went underneath the flap that keeps the diary closed, and then the clasp locks over on top of that," Nicky said.

"Hmm." Quinten studied the small lock. "Well, I have a bunch of keys somewhere in a mayonnaise jar. Be back in a second."

He turned and headed up a stairway that Nicky hadn't noticed before, tucked as it was in a nook near the cash register.

Nicky heard floorboards creak overhead. A minute or so later, he came back down the stairs, mayonnaise jar with the label ripped off, in hand.

He placed the jar full of keys of all sizes on the counter where the cash register sat. Nicky saw a package of yellow jelly beans beside it. "Do you sell those too?"

"That's a good idea I hadn't thought of." He chuckled. "No. I actually bought those for my cousin's little girl. Her mom's birthday's next week and I wanted to give Rosie something to make sure she didn't feel left out."

Nicky's heart fluttered. That was sweet of him. "I've been a fan of jelly beans since my very first Easter."

"Me too. The chocolate shop here has a great selection. I've always bought mine there."

"I'll have to keep that in mind." She turned her attention back to the keys. "Let's see. Might be easier if we dumped it out."

Quinten glanced at her as a small smile formed on his

lips. "I was just going to say that. Great minds think alike."

Nicky couldn't help but respond with a smile of her own at his compliment.

She picked up the jar and upended it. Long, thin, ornate skeleton keys were jumbled together with newer flat brass hotel room keys that looked like they'd been forgotten in purses and pockets. Some even had fobs imprinted with motel logos and room numbers.

"Quite the collection you have here," Nicky murmured.

"Grandma Viv was a bit of a pack rat," Quinten admitted. He began to sort them out by size. "Makes sense to look for the tiniest keys possible..." He trailed off as he concentrated on the jumbled pile.

Nicky came to stand beside him to help sort. "They all look pretty much bigger than what we need."

"Mmm." Quinten deftly kept sorting. "Sometimes you just have to be..."

He rummaged around between a pile of bolts that had somehow gotten mixed in, and a set of what looked like five or six motel room keys on a fob.

"...persistent." He grinned as he held up the tiniest key Nicky had ever seen.

The happy look on his face probably echoed her own, Nicky realized. Excitement filled her. It was fun to try and figure this out together. "Let's give it a try."

Nicky put the book on the counter and Quinten fit the key into the lock. But it was too small.

"Damn," Quinten muttered.

"Like you said, we just have to be persistent." Nicky scanned the pile of keys again. She reached out and picked up another small key. But that one didn't fit either.

For the next thirty minutes, they went through almost every key that could possibly work. Except none of them did.

Nicky shoved her hands into her pockets in frustration. "Now what?"

"Well," Quinten said, "we could just cut through the leather."

Nicky's eyes widened.

"Or not," Quinten hastily added. "That would sort of wreck the historical aspect of the book."

Hmmm. She appreciated his perceptiveness.

"Well," Nicky said in a joking tone as she pulled her hands out of her pockets and came up holding her keyring. "We could always try these." She laughed as she jangled them.

Quinten chuckled. "As long as we're trying far-fetched ideas, I might as well get out my own keys, too." They went through all of his keys, and most of hers.

"No luck." Nicky smoothed her bangs. "Not that I seriously expected anything to happen."

"What about that tiny little one on your keyring?"

"This one?" She shrugged. "Okay." She plucked up the tiny key and fit it into the lock.

Quinten leaned closer to watch. Nicky could feel the warmth of his nearness that carried a hint of his lemony cologne.

There was a snick as the key fit and a click as it turned.

Nicky gasped.

Quinten whistled. "There's no way—where did you *get* that key?"

"Inside a hidden inner pocket of a vintage jacket I bought on P.E.I. last summer. I just thought the key was cute, so I put it on my keyring as a knickknack."

"Oh?" Quinten raised his eyebrows.

"But now that I think about it, it makes total sense that this little key would fit Viv's diary."

"Why?"

"Because the jacket must've been Viv's, so..." Nicky said, almost to herself.

"The key obviously was too," Quinten said.

"She must've forgotten about it in the jacket pocket. Or purposely hid it there, since the pocket was concealed?" Nicky tapped a fingernail against her chin.

"Either way," Quinten said, "it worked to open the diary."

"Mmm. Come to think of it, that letter was in there too."

"Letter?"

"Written to your grandmother during the war."

Quinten glanced at her, a guarded look on his face as he said, "Was it signed with just the initial 'A'?"

"Yes. But how did you know that?" Nicky said.

"I saw a letter written to her too," Quinten said.

Nicky grinned. "We'll have to compare notes on the letters at some point." She turned her attention back to the diary. "But maybe for now we should see what's inside here?"

"Sure."

Nicky kept her eyes on the diary but couldn't ignore the slight buzz in the pit of her stomach from the brush of Quinten's breath against her cheek.

She gently opened the front cover and saw the faded words.

For Vivian

Love, Mother

Christmas, '38

Quinten traced a finger along the name and then flicked his eyes to hers. He moistened a fingertip and turned the page over in one fluid motion.

June 3, 1939

The heat has settled over London something fierce. Today was my first day in my new position at the Office. I suppose it won't hurt to say that I'm thrilled.

But more than thrilled, it's the feeling that we are achieving some purpose here. Me and the other girls. Though the room I'm in with them gets quite hot even with the fans blowing. And all the papers have to be weighed down or they would blow around and that would be a sorry muddle!

My skills are actually put to good use – maybe more so than they would've ever been had I taken a high school math position back in New York as Mother wanted – and hoped – I would. But war has a funny way of changing things, doesn't it?

So the fight must go on. We must win. And I intend to do my part, whatever the cost.

Quinten met Nicky's gaze and he wondered if her heart was racing too. He noticed her pulse beat at the base of her throat.

He forced his mind back to the journal. This proved that his grandmother had been involved in the war effort in England. Somehow.

"It's your grandmother," she said softly and handed the book to him.

Something about the look of compassion? empathy? in her eyes made him say, "You know, I never felt like I knew who she really was, exactly." He hesitated, then glanced her way and added, "She always seemed to have this part of her that somehow...eluded me."

"That must have been hard."

He felt a nudge to keep going, to say something more, to respond to her openness. But he couldn't. She'd judge him, tell him he was wrong to show emotion, to feel what he felt. Just like his father had judged him.

So he only nodded and thumbed the edges of the pages. Bits of ink showed themselves to him and he felt his pulse quicken. Wait a minute. Quinten drew in a sharp breath.

Nicky glanced at him.

There might be more about Grandma Viv in that letter Nicky had. She'd said they could compare notes on the letters, anyway. Hmmm. What if they went through all of his grandmother's things more thoroughly? Together? Maybe in there somewhere would be some sort of documentation that would help Nicky? And some papers his grandmother had written, indicating a successor?

It was worth a try.

"I'm sorry to stop here but I have to open up my shop in not too long. Tour buses coming in. I do have a day off tomorrow. Pretty much all my grandmother's stuff is packed away, but it might have more answers that would help us both. So why don't we meet at the chocolate shop in the morning, get some good coffee and then dive in to all those boxes together?"

YESTERDAY NICKY HAD left the diary with Quinten at his music shop. He said he'd be more comfortable with it there.

And she couldn't argue with that.

Nor could she argue with herself when she indulged in a memory of how his breath had brushed her cheek; the look of his solid chest as he'd stood so close; or the thrill up her spine when they'd unlocked the diary together and he'd met her gaze.

But more than that, she'd appreciated his persistence in their key hunt. Reminded her of herself when she chased down a piece of research. She also liked his perceptiveness... She toyed with a strand of hair. They'd worked well together yesterday.

She needed to concentrate. She'd gotten about fifteen hundred words down of a first draft. She checked her watch. Already Saturday. And nearly 9:00 a.m. She was making pretty good time.

Once she got to read through all the entries in the diary, she'd have a much better picture of Vivian.

After reading that first entry, it felt as if Vivian was talking right to her. In a way she was, Nicky mused.

And that was the type of story the magazine's readers loved. One that showed humanity, vulnerability... and, well, history. The *Historical Woman* believed that history was no different than the present, that people were people no matter the era.

And that was exactly what Vivian's diary would prove.

Nicky made a few last-minute notes to herself on the steno pad by her computer before she shut the lid.

She glanced out the window. Buttery yellow sunlight

streamed through the gauzy white curtains; and the crystal clear blue sky seemed brighter than she'd ever seen it.

She changed out of her pajamas and pulled on a pale pink cashmere sweater.

She paired it with a pair of dark wash denim jeans—her favorite—that had a rip at the knee and were so soft and worn in that they felt nearly as good as cashmere.

Her phone bleeped and she glanced at the notifications. A text from her landlord. She bit her lip and opened it.

Nicky, don't forget the rent money by the 19th. That's in ten days.

She fought down a flutter of panic. She'd get the money. *Ivory* magazine had to come through. She chewed on a hangnail for a second. She'd tried again to get ahold of them but they *still* hadn't responded. They hadn't replied to that post she'd left on their social media platform, either...

She picked up her hairbrush and pushed down the nudge of worry. She couldn't do anything more about it, she told herself, as she ran the brush through her hair and fluffed her bangs.

What good would worrying do? Nothing. It would only make her nervous. She slicked on some lip balm and grabbed her purse with her notepad, keys, and her Nikon, then headed out the door and up the street to Island Chocolates.

QUINTEN WALKED UP the steps of Island Chocolates. Not too busy yet this morning. He opened the door.

The staff was working on a big batch of chocolates. He could see Gemma's brother Derek busily filling molds through the workroom window.

But Quinten wasn't the only one inside.

"...on my tab. Two espressos for now, please," Nicky said to Gemma.

"Quinten's usual, eh?" Gemma said with a grin.

He saw Nicky head to his favorite table by the window.

"Thanks. I could've bought them." He winced. That sounded far more accusatory than he'd meant. He followed her to the table.

Nicky shrugged. "I wanted to. Besides, I have to butter you up somehow as a thanks for helping me." She sat down. "And between you and me, I could use a cup of strong coffee at this point. I've been up for awhile. Got a start on a draft, anyway."

"Oh, good," Quinten said.

"You two want any cream?" Gemma came over with a small tray that had a tiny jug of cream and two spoons on it.

Both Quinten and Nicky nodded.

On impulse, Quinten found himself saying, "Gemma, can you bring us some chocolate waffles, please?"

"Two orders then?" She looked from Quinten to Nicky and back again.

"Yes, please," Quinten said.

"They're delicious," Gemma told Nicky as she put the tiny cream jug down on the table.

"Great," Nicky said. "I love breakfast. And I haven't had any this morning."

Gemma left them to their coffee and Quinten cleared his throat.

"So." He shifted slightly in his chair.

Nicky picked up her demitasse cup and wrapped her fingers around its steaming contents. The ring on her finger caught the light.

"That's a really intricate pattern of vines and leaves. It's pretty," he found himself saying.

"My ring? Thanks." A look of pleased surprise flicked across Nicky's face. "I love vintage jewelry."

"Where did you get it?"

Nicky glanced down at it and then extended her hand, fingers spread wide. "At a flea market in Nobo a couple summers ago. My friend, and former boss, Maggie—oh, hey, you might know her? She's from P.E.I. Kilhoughery's her last name."

"Mmm. Don't think I do."

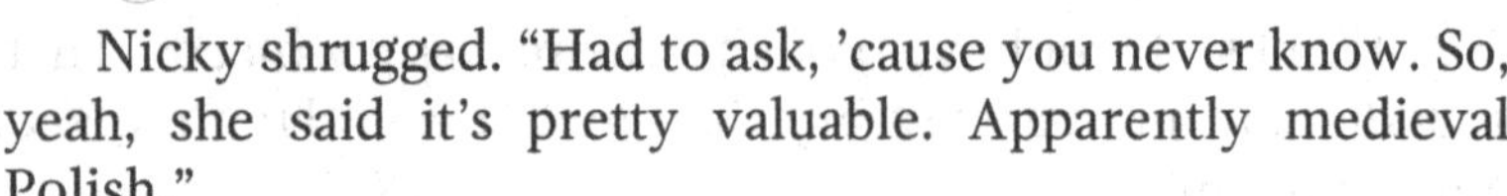

Nicky shrugged. "Had to ask, 'cause you never know. So, yeah, she said it's pretty valuable. Apparently medieval Polish."

Quinten's brows shot up.

Nicky slipped off the ring and held it out to him.

He took it, the metal still warm from her skin. "Someone knew what they were doing when they made it, that's for sure," he commented.

"I know, right? That's what I love about vintage jewelry."

Quinten leaned toward her. "That's the thing with historical pieces. The craftsmanship's always excellent." He studied the ring. "That's partly why I got into the piano tuning business, actually. Because I love history. Being able to preserve that sense of heritage and pass it down to future generations. It's important."

"Right. To keep that connection to the past so that we know where we've come from."

"Exactly." He raised his eyes from the ring to her face. "It's more than that, too. It's being able to share it. Share the stories embedded in the wood, in the strings, in the whole piece..." He tensed and busied himself stirring his coffee. Had he said too much? Exposed too much of himself?

He risked a glance at Nicky and saw a flare of excitement in her eyes as she said, "That's how I feel when I'm writing my articles. Sharing stories, the truth, with the world."

Quinten's shoulders relaxed as a few moments passed in silence. Maybe he was safe to open up a bit?

He cleared his throat. "There's a photo my grandmother showed me when she was in the nursing home. She's wearing this exact ring. Or, if not this exact one, then one that looks identical to it."

"Wow."

"I'd never seen her wear it but the photo looked as if it was taken in the 1940s. And on the back of the picture, all it said was 'Last day at the Office.'"

Nicky's brows furrowed.

But before she could comment, the waffles arrived.

"Yum. These look delicious," Nicky said.

"Told ya." Gemma grinned. "Need anything else?"

Quinten shook his head. Nicky did too.

"Enjoy, guys."

Quinten spread honey butter over the waffles. Fresh whipped cream and a handful of island blueberries were scattered across the waffles. Rich, creamy, warm Nutella had been drizzled over the entire concoction.

Nicky took a bite. Then four more. "These are amazing," she said around a mouthful. "Especially the honey butter. I could eat all of this in one bite, practically."

He took a sip of coffee but his gaze lingered on her lips as she wiped off a trace of honey butter. He preferred to savor things...

He forced his eyes away, lest she catch him looking. "Eating them for the first time's almost as good as eating them every Sunday for brunch like I do. I always eat them by myself. But it's more fun to enjoy them with someone." He tensed as soon as the words left his mouth. What was he doing? Why had he just confessed that to her? But the admission had felt good.

To distract himself, he took another forkful of his waffle and the rich chocolate taste lingered on his tongue. But that didn't help.

"So what do you think it means, us having the same ring?" Nicky's words cut into his thoughts. She had finished her whole waffle and studied him over the rim of her coffee cup.

He tried to look busy as he finished the first half of his waffle. "What do I—oh, about the ring? I'm not sure. You know, I'd call it coincidence, but I don't believe in that sort of thing."

A speculative gleam came into Nicky's eyes. "Well, with what you said about the writing on the back of her photo, I'm thinking 'the Office' meant the Special Operations Executive headquarters at 64 Baker Street in London where she worked with a group of other cipher girls."

"Really?"

"Yep." Nicky grinned as she leaned forward and rested her forearms on the table. "The SOE actually recruited quite a few civilians for the codes department, which is something I hadn't realized until I looked at Viv's file."

"Mmm-hmm." Quinten rubbed a hand across his jaw to hide a smile. Her enthusiasm was cute. She loved history, didn't she?

"There's even a photo attached to her SOE file. But it's only a headshot, so I can't see if she's wearing any jewelry."

Quinten put down his fork. "But if she was wearing that ring in that other photo, maybe she got it from somewhere in London?"

"Or from someone in London?" Nicky grinned at him.

"True."

Nicky took a sip of coffee. "Then somewhere along the line she decided to get rid of the ring? Or maybe she had to sell it because she needed the money? Times were tough back then—the Depression was before the war. Or maybe she lost it somehow and it made its way to that flea market?"

Quinten picked up his coffee and said quietly, "She did, at one point, mail all her valuable jewelry to the Salvation Army." His fingers tightened on the cup's handle. "But like I said before, I..."

"It's okay." She hesitated a second, but then touched his hand.

He sucked in a soft breath as her fingers made contact with his skin. He opened his mouth, then closed it. What was he saying? He couldn't remember.

He met her gaze.

Her expression was one of empathy mixed with sadness. His heart softened and his throat tightened. Had she lost someone close to her, too? He swallowed. What would happen if he opened up more to her?

No. He couldn't risk that. He had to focus. With an effort, he managed, "Thank you."

"You're welcome."

He drained the last bit of his coffee and stood up. "Ready to go?"

He picked up both of their plates and carried them to the register, which was right by the doorway to the kitchen.

"Thanks, Quinten," Gemma called from around the corner of the door.

He pulled out his wallet. She waved a hand and then stuck her head around the doorframe. "No need to pay for the waffles. Already on your friend's tab."

A surge of pleased surprise coursed through Quinten.

Gemma added in a conspiratorial tone, "She told me to add on whatever else you might order before you came in."

He darted a glance at Nicky, who stood near the front door and examined what looked like a small piece of paper she'd pulled from her purse.

He grinned. "Oh, uh... Right." He put away his wallet.

"Have a good day, Quinten," Gemma said with a note of laughter in her voice.

"You too," he replied. He noticed that Nicky looked conflicted about something. But she put the scrap of paper back into her purse as he headed over to her.

"Shall we?"

Nicky, her expression now resolute, picked up her camera. "Let's."

THE STAIRS CREAKED as Nicky followed Quinten up the narrow steps. "I still have the ladder up here because I was going through Christmas decorations for the recycling. Which is due to be picked up tomorrow." Quinten glanced over his shoulder at her. He looked slightly sheepish and the tips of his ears turned red. "And now I'm rambling."

She couldn't help but notice he wore exactly the same expression as his photo on the stairwell beside her. What was he there in the picture? Twelve? Eleven? Something like that. Nicky hid a smile. His embarrassment was kind of cute. Some things don't change. "Hey, no worries. I do that a lot myself sometimes." They reached the landing and Quinten set up the ladder. That cobalt blue shirt was such a great color for him.

What was she thinking? She had a story to write. Information to gather. That's all she was doing here.

She wasn't going to evaluate the merits of the way he filled out his button down. Even if it was very nicely, she admitted to herself, with another sidelong look. Or the way he seemed to appreciate her view on history. Something Ben hadn't appreciated in her at all.

A blush crept over her cheeks as he glanced at her. That cobalt color really brought out his eyes. "I'll just remove the trapdoor hatch here."

Nicky couldn't help but admire the play of his back muscles as he put action to words. He turned and offered her a hand up the ladder.

That was considerate of him. She took his hand and tried not to think about the implications. Was he interested in her? No. He just wanted to make sure she didn't fall and break a limb, that was all.

As she maneuvered through the opening, he said, "Watch yourself. It's a bit tricky to navigate if you're not used to stepping over roof rafters."

"Thanks." She paused. "It'd be great if we could find something, wouldn't it?"

"Mmmm." Quinten raised and lowered his wide shoulders as he joined her.

Nicky felt a stab of annoyance. Was he always this noncommittal? But the man had to have emotions way down deep somewhere...didn't he?

She forced herself to focus on the task at hand. "So all these boxes were hers?"

"Most of them, yeah. I haven't gone through ninety-nine percent of them."

Nicky felt her stomach flutter. "So we have a lot of digging to do."

Quinten glanced at her. "We need to proceed with caution. Like I said, she didn't exactly talk about anything about her time during the war. She made a reference one time to almost having met Churchill. When I pressed her about it, she acted like she hadn't heard me. So I let it go." He paused. "Of course, that only made me more intrigued."

He picked up a box marked *Viv's Things*.

Nicky came to join him.

Quinten looked inside. "Not a whole lot in here. Just a bunch of photographs—you know, I think the one I mentioned should be here—and a few letters she wrote to her mother back in the States."

"Can I take a look?"

Quinten handed them to her.

Nicky leafed through them. "Just daily chatter."

Quinten poked around more in the box. "That's about it for this one...some gloves, stockings, and a hat or two."

Nicky put the letters back. "Can I look at the photos? I'm going to need some for my article and since she isn't here anymore, I can't take her picture. So if we could run the article with some of these, that'd be great."

"Sure." Quinten took out the photos and handed them to Nicky.

They were mostly candid shots, out of focus with parts of people instead of whole bodies. "She wasn't much of a photographer, was she?" Nicky mused.

Quinten shook his head. "She loved math. Puzzles. Crosswords. That sort of thing. She could do square roots and long division in her head. She had pretty much a photographic memory. I was always asking her how she did it and she would just shrug and say it came naturally. She went to school to be a math teacher but ended up with the music store business instead. That was something else she loved—music. Almost as much as math. But," he continued, "there's actually a lot of math in music if you think about it."

"Yep, that's true." Nicky jotted a few things down on a tiny notepad she'd pulled from her back pocket. She thumbed through the rest of the photos. "Here it is. You're right." She pulled out her Nikon and snapped some shots of the photo from close up and farther away. That way she wouldn't have to scan the image into the computer but they could still run it.

She held the photo closer. "That ring does look identical." She studied the ring on her own finger. "Huh."

She threw a sidelong glance at Quinten. "Did Hitler's gold and diamonds really end up on P.E.I.?"

"I can see Mabel's been talking to you. She's utterly convinced." He tugged at his earlobe. "That's what the rumors say."

"So you don't believe it."

"You sound disappointed."

"Just want to cover all the angles for my story."

Quinten crossed his arms. "That stuff about Hitler's treasure buried here is just an island legend. Being a journalist, you should know the difference between fact and fiction."

Now Nicky crossed her arms. "But what if it's true?"

"And what if it isn't?"

"What if I have proof?" Nicky countered.

Quinten raised a brow.

Nicky held up a small silver coin. It glinted in the light.

Quinten's eyes widened. "That's a *Nazi* coin."

Chapter Five

QUINTEN LEANED FORWARD to examine the coin and Nicky caught the slight citrusy scent of his cologne. Something in the way he studied the coin, how he seemed to take in every detail like he wanted to really understand it, made longing swoop through Nicky. What would happen if she let him know her, understand her, like that? No. She was only here for the story.

A strand of his blond hair fell across his forehead as he looked down at the coin now resting on her palm.

As he reached out and picked up the coin with his thumb and forefinger, his fingertips brushed Nicky's palm. She couldn't ignore the fact that she liked the sensation.

"Where did you get this?"

"Mabel had it. She told me I could—"

"—use it to convince me to go treasure hunting with you?"

"Something like that," Nicky smiled.

Quinten laughed and murmured, "She's always been a matchmaker. Half the island, I think, has benefitted from her convictions about true love."

Nicky shifted her weight and tucked a strand of hair behind her ear as she avoided Quinten's eyes. Mabel's matchmaking skills wouldn't be put to use here, that was sure. He was too stoic—which made him too much like Ben—for her liking. Wasn't he?

"So?" she said.

Quinten blinked.

"Hitler's gold," Nicky supplied.

"There's nothing to that. Even with this Nazi coin."

Quinten handed it back. "It could've come from anywhere. There was a German POW camp up in New Brunswick, after all."

"But there were supposed to be U-boats in the waters around P.E.I." Nicky put her hands on her hips. "That's what the online database of archived Charlottetown newspaper articles told me."

"You've been doing your research, I see." Quinten gave her a sidelong glance.

"I *am* a journalist." Nicky tapped her finger on the notepad.

Quinten sighed. "You're not going to let this go, are you?"

Nicky's eyes gleamed. "Not if I can help it. It's the perfect add-on to the article about your grandmother."

"Why? She had nothing to do with Hitler's gold."

"I have a hunch there might be a connection. A good journalist examines all possible related angles. Besides, Mabel didn't say your grandmother was in love with a Nazi for nothing."

"So she told you that, did she?" Quinten's shoulders stiffened. "It's entirely untrue. The whole thing."

Nicky made an expansive gesture. "You don't know that for sure."

"Neither do you."

Nicky pursed her lips. "You just don't want to believe the evidence that's staring you in the face."

Quinten crossed his arms. "It's circumstantial."

Nicky lifted her chin. "There's only one way to find out for sure."

"What are you saying?"

"I'm saying we find the treasure."

Quinten laughed. "There's nothing to find."

"And you're not taking me seriously."

Quinten held up his hands. "It's not you I'm worried about. It's Mabel. It's this whole village. There's a propensity to believe what you hear, around here."

Nicky raised a brow. "So?"

"So," Quinten repeated, "there's nothing to it. There's no gold, there are no diamonds, and it certainly had nothing to do with my grandmother."

"BUT—" NICKY STARTED to say, but the sound of a chime from downstairs interrupted her.

Quinten glanced at his watch and swore. "That'll be the first busload of tourists. I need to go tend the shop."

Nicky tucked her notepad into her purse and hiked her camera bag over her shoulder. "Right. Of course."

They headed down to the kitchen on the first floor of the house.

"Here," Quinten said. He handed her the cream-colored book. "I thought we'd have time to go through this after we finished in the attic. But since we didn't get a chance to, why don't you take a look at it? If you find anything, let me know."

Nicky took the small book. "You're sure you want to let this out of your sight?"

Quinten studied her for a second. "I'm willing to take a chance."

She blushed under his gaze. "Thank you. For the journal, for letting me take the pictures, and for your time."

"You're welcome. That's what I do around here—help people out."

She crossed into the showroom, Quinten behind her. "Once I finish a draft, I'll have a few more questions for you."

"Sure." Quinten held the screen door open for Nicky. As she left, the tourists came inside.

NICKY PICKED UP her laptop from her room. She headed across the back lawn of the Orient Hotel, careful to avoid the croquet wickets, and then down Nelson Street.

She could type up her notes on the boardwalk. There was a nice bench in the sun that she'd spotted yesterday. From what she recalled in one of the Victoria-by-the-Sea pamphlets, it was near the customs house.

She sank onto that bench a few minutes later and looked around. To her right, she noticed the customs house, its bright red siding faded and its windows boarded up. Wouldn't it be nice if someone restored it?

Her thoughts turned to Quinten. Her shoulders drooped a little as the sun warmed her. She'd hoped he would've at least considered the possibility of the treasure...

But it didn't really matter what he thought, now did it? This was her article. But it was his grandmother.

She chewed on a hangnail.

But what she'd told him back in the attic was right. This would provide a great twist to the story. Give it real depth if she delved into the supposed Nazi treasure aspect.

What if they found out the truth about all of it? Didn't Quinten deserve to know if his grandmother had been mixed up in it? Vivian deserved to have the truth known about her. And wasn't it up to Nicky to put that all out there for the world to decide?

Nicky watched the seagulls call and dive over the water. Yes, she realized, it was. And that was exactly what she was going to do.

She picked up the journal.

The second entry was dated two years after the first.

February 2, 1942

It's been so busy at the Office – it's hard to believe I've been here nearly two years now. Time has a strange way of contracting yet feeling unbearably long as well... But I know we are making a difference – I know we are.

Every little piece counts. Everyone here has a specific task, and I know mine. And though sometimes it feels like the war will never end, I need to have faith that it will – that we will come out victorious.

Because the alternative is not an option. And though the girls sometimes disagree about where to aim the fans – oh, how it gets hot in those vast rooms with so much paper and so many hushed conversations as we work to make heads and tails of everything – the overall sense amongst all of us is kinship. Women working toward a common goal, a common good – valued for our minds and our skills; at last.

Though some say it won't last – this newfound freedom we have gained – I prefer to think that perhaps, just perhaps, we could influence our daughters and our granddaughters – to usher in a bold new era.

But I go on too much now!

Nicky turned the page.

March 29, 1943

I have to share my news, if only with myself. I have been meeting him for nearly a year now. It feels treasonous to say so, but it's true.

I am in love with him. And he, with me.

And even though we were specifically told not to acquaint ourselves with those whose work we are entrusted with, it is what has happened.

I did not intend for it to happen. It simply did. I can close my eyes and picture him, standing there, in the hours before he left. In his moss-green jacket, the collar turned up against the London rain, his brown eyes full of warmth. Trust. Hope.

Hmmm. Vivian worked in the codes department, which handled agents' traffic. So it stood to reason that whoever this was couldn't be a Nazi. Why, then, had Mabel said Vivian had been in love with a Nazi?

Nicky rubbed her temples. She could wonder about that later. Right now, her primary focus needed to be getting clear on the truth about Vivian, not sidetracked by who she was in love with—as tantalizing as that was to speculate about. She read the rest of the entry.

I take some comfort in the fact that the politics within the Office here are such... that certain things have the outward appearance of rule-following when, indeed, they are not so. Things are done behind closed doors. People turn a blind eye; say one thing and do another. Such it is in a time of war. I blush at the recollection of what I myself saw one particu-

lar midnight!

Nicky looked at the next page. But the entry wasn't in English. She squinted at it. In fact, it wasn't any language she recognized...

She turned the little book this way and that. No. It wasn't in a language at all. It was some sort of cipher or code. She'd have to tell Quinten about this. Maybe he'd have an idea as to what it was. He had good suggestions. She liked that he seemed to be reliable like that.

Well, she'd start with these first two entries, anyway...

Several hours later, Nicky stretched and looked up. She rubbed the back of her neck. It had gotten a bit chilly out and the wind had picked up.

But she'd gotten a completed rough first draft. She grinned. Very rough. Lots of holes she'd have to go back and fill in with relevant quotes and more in-depth research.

At least now she had the shape of the story. Something she could look at, work with, mold until it was exactly right. Until it conveyed exactly what it needed to say. Until all the voices were heard.

Speaking of...

She uploaded and saved the photos she'd taken of Vivian's picture onto her laptop. She studied them a minute. No distortion or discoloration. They'd work just fine.

Job done, she got up and tucked the laptop under her arm. Her heart lifted as she watched the fishing boats bob in their moorings at the wharf. It was so charming here.

She glanced around. A line of tourists and locals snaked out the door of the Lobster Barn Pub & Eatery. Must be near dinnertime. She'd heard their lobster rolls were excellent. Her stomach rumbled as she headed over.

Nicky passed a tiny wharfinger's hut as she crossed the first few hundred feet of pavement toward the pub. She walked over yellow letters that read Fishers' Parking Only as she passed stone crab traps piled up along the edge of the wharf.

She reached the end of the line at the pub. Its shingle

siding was a naturally weathered gray. But the bright turquoise trim set off the building's best features.

The chatter of tourists drifted to her along with the scent of fried clams and French fries.

Her mouth watered as the line inched forward. Nicky finally made it inside and told the girl at the bar she wanted a table for one.

"Usually it's a three-week waiting period for dinnertime in our busy season. But October's a good time to be here. A bit quieter. So more seating options."

She led Nicky to a table by the window that overlooked the water and a bluff that had a smattering of houses. The server noticed Nicky's glance.

"You can see Crescent Beach and our new subdivision from here."

"Nice." Nicky took the seat facing the window. "Think I'll enjoy the view."

The chatter of other diners and the clink of silverware washed over Nicky. The long, wooden table beside her held a group of laughing, loudly chatting people. She recognized a few by sight and waved. They waved back.

She turned back to her table and twisted the amber ring around her finger. Why had Vivian been wearing it? How had she gotten it? Maggie had said it was from medieval times... Nicky pulled up the search engine on her phone and typed in *medieval Polish amber rings*.

She scrolled through the results. Hmmm. Amber price and value information. How to assess vintage jewelry. Three ways to clean amber jewelry. Oh. *That* could be useful. She bookmarked the page and continued to scroll. Amber jewelry and souvenirs from Krakow, Poland.

Hmm. Nothing was really—

Wait. Her fingers hovered over a link that read Polish Art Center: The History of Amber Jewelry.

She tapped the link and scanned the headline. A history of the use of amber in jewelry in Poland. She skimmed the article and her eyes caught on the final subhead.

The Stolen Riches of Princess Magdalena Jola Piast

It's been compared to the theft and disappearance of the Amber Room during the Second World War. But few have heard the story of Princess Magdalena Jola Piast's stolen riches.

In 1241, Princess Magdalena Jola Piast of Poland married Philippe Capet, a cousin of Louis IX of France. Her wedding dowry—diamonds, a beautiful jewelled mirror, and several pieces of amber jewelry, including a large, rare, green amber ring with matching earbobs, as well as an untold amount of gold—was commissioned and sent along with her to France.

Nicky leaned forward in her chair and kept reading.

Amid the back and forth of European royal intermarriages over the next several centuries, the dowry came back into Poland. It ended up with the prominent Gobell family, direct descendants of the princess's line.

Because the pieces originated in the Middle Ages, some started to believe a legend that said the jewelled mirror held the power to reveal the secrets of lasting love.

But after the fall of Poland in 1939 to Germany, the entire dowry went missing.

Some speculate it ended up as a private collection in North America after being smuggled onto a U-boat during the height of the war.

Other scholars believe the dowry was used as a bargaining chip by Hitler's personal secretary, Martin Bormann, to raise funds to support Hitler's secret plan to create a Fourth Reich.

Still others think the dowry remains in Germany,

since its last known location was the Reichsbank in Berlin, Germany in 1943.

Whatever the case, the fact remains that the dowry, and all its valuable cultural and historical significance, has been lost.

Much like the Amber Room, after the war, the dowry simply vanished. No mention of it, nor its location, has ever been discovered.

Nicky scrolled a bit further down and saw a painting of a beautiful, black-haired woman wearing a gorgeous, burgundy silk gown.

The caption read *Princess Magdalena Jola Piast.*

Nicky noticed the small jewel-encrusted silver mirror the woman held in one hand. That same hand also sported a large green amber ring set in a sterling silver band with a pattern of vines and leaves.

Nicky's heart pounded. She glanced down at the stone set into the ring on her own finger. Her eyes widened. Every detail was exactly the same.

Nicky's lobster roll sat forgotten on her plate as her mind whirled.

She had to tell Quinten. He had to believe her now. But was her hunch right? Did Vivian *really* have something to do with all of this? Or had she simply seen the ring, thought it pretty, and bought it unawares?

Either way, Nicky was going to find out.

QUINTEN MADE ONE final adjustment and examined the piano. Pretty much it for this one.

He smiled in satisfaction but then his lips tightened as he fought a sinking feeling. He wasn't going to jump to negative assumptions.

The will had to be somewhere. Or at least, some sort of

documentation. They just hadn't gone through all the things in the attic yet. Monday was a few days away yet. There were still more papers to look through...

The tourists milled around the small space. Quinten dusted some shelves behind the counter and rearranged a stack of sheet music.

With so few customers last month, he'd had lots of time to fine tune all the instruments in the shop. So if anyone bought them, they'd be in perfect playing order.

But for some reason, this month was quite profitable. Which was good. Because from his most recent conversation with his accountant, it looked like he'd need a fair amount to get the business back into the black—

"Excuse me? How much?" A man in a Panama hat pointed to a hand-carved miniature piano. Quinten checked the price and told the man.

"I'll take twenty. You have?"

"Sure. Let me get the rest of them from the back."

When he came back with the lot, the man pulled out his wallet. "You ship?"

"Yes." Quinten rang up the sale. This would certainly help things along, added to the increase in sales margins he'd seen over the last couple weeks.

A few more tourists bought some sheet music and then the cluster of people dispersed.

As Quinten started to close up the shop and quiet settled over the space, his mind wandered.

What was Elliot up to? Would he actually buy this place out from under him? He couldn't let that happen.

Quinten started to count the till.

There was always another option, another way. He drummed his fingers on the counter as he finished the till count.

Wait a second. He'd helped Mrs. MacPhail's husband Al upload that video for his crowdfunding campaign to rebuild his vintage Harley. Could Quinten do something like that for this business?

His heart beat a little faster as he turned to his computer. It was worth a shot. He'd set up his own page right now. He could make it something about Victoria heritage. Make people aware they could help save a historic, family-owned business from going bankrupt.

The squeak of the screen door's hinges made Quinten look up from his computer. His heart jumped when Nicky rushed in with windblown hair and a gleam in her eyes.

Quinten straightened the hem of his shirt and brushed a hand over his hair. "What is it?"

She waved her phone in his face. "This thing goes even further than I imagined."

"Oh?" He came around the counter and took the phone she handed him. After he scanned the article, he glanced over at Nicky. For a moment, he said nothing. "How do you even know this is true?"

"How do you know it's not?" she countered, as she took a step closer to him. "It's the official website of the Polish Art Center."

He reread the article. "That ring certainly seems like it could have something to do with all of this."

Nicky nudged him. "Just seems like? You're not entirely convinced, are you?"

Quinten couldn't help but chuckle. "You got me there."

"Well." Nicky began to tick points off on her fingers. "First, we have the fact that my ring was Viv's ring."

"Mmm."

"Which, thanks to this portrait, we now know was originally Princess Magdalena's ring."

"Uh-huh."

"And then," Nicky said, "the ring went missing during the Second World War."

"So you think," Quinten said, as he raised his brows, "that because my grandmother had this ring originally owned by this princess, that means Hitler's treasure, which is rumored to contain this princess's dowry, is hidden somewhere on P.E.I.?"

"Exactly. Have you heard anything about this jewelled mirror?" Nicky's brows furrowed.

"The only thing I'd ever heard was about Hitler's gold and diamonds. As for my grandmother being involved in all of it, well..."

Nicky made an expansive gesture. "That's why it's time to go on a treasure hunt."

"WHOA, WHOA. TREASURE hunt? I admit, the evidence is compelling. But it's probably just circumstantial."

Nicky rolled her eyes. "That's why we need to prove it. Follow the facts and hunt down the truth. Think of it as a quest for truth, instead of a treasure hunt, if that makes you happier."

Quinten tugged at his earlobe. "Mmmm. That *is* a point." His heart jumped. What would happen if he spent more time with her on this?

He saw Nicky glance down at the article on her phone again, then pull up the photo of his grandmother and study it.

Vivian looked happy. Excited, even. What had she been up to? 'Last day at the Office.' Maybe she was deciphering messages. But maybe...

"She *must've* known something about the treasure." Nicky breathed.

Quinten's heart pounded. "What makes you so sure?"

"Well, I was going to show you at the chocolate shop earlier but thought you might change your mind about helping me, so..." Nicky said.

"What is it?"

"If you don't believe that legend about gold and diamonds, you're going to—" She interrupted herself and started to rummage through her purse. Her reddish-blonde hair fell in a smooth curtain that hid her face as she looked down. Ironic, really. Because she didn't hide at all. She wasn't afraid of her vulnerabilities. He respected that.

He thought back to her expression of enjoyment as she took her first bite of waffle. And the excitement on her face just now.

Every emotion was so clearly telegraphed. That took a certain kind of courage. Quinten rocked back on his heels. He had to admit he admired that simple, yet powerful ability in her.

He shoved his hands into his pockets. She had the kind of courage he wished he could express. Would he ever be able to?

He noticed the small frown between her eyebrows as she rooted around in her purse.

Could there actually be something to that legend? He hadn't heard too much about it growing up, really. Just that Mabel was sort of the village eccentric and was liable to say anything just for the stir it caused.

But then his mind flitted back to that old article he'd found about the U-boats. That was certainly fact. As was that crumbling letter to Viv...

He rubbed his jaw.

"Here it is," Nicky said. She held up a tiny scrap of paper. "I didn't really know what to make of it. But then that was before."

She pointed to a tiny black circle.

"That looks like a period at the end of a sentence."

"That's what they want you to think." A glint came into her eyes. "But it's called a microdot. They used them during the Second World War to pass information. Confidential information."

"You mean secret messages?"

"You said it, not me." She picked up her notepad and flicked through it. "Let's see. What did I... Here." She pointed to the page where she'd copied the lines. "I found these phrases on this microdot."

Quinten leaned forward and read Nicky's handwriting.

The secretary marches
To a tune unplayed
But the pianist's journey
Mirrors a plan well-laid.

He shook his head. "I still don't understand."

"The microdot was on the scrap of paper. That scrap of paper was concealed in this ring." Nicky held up her right hand. Then she tapped the photograph. "And this ring? Your grandmother had it."

"Oh," Quinten said. He raked a hand through his hair. "*Oh...*"

Some sort of trick? But Grandma Viv hadn't been a trickster. She'd always been a practical, plain-speaking, if somewhat romantic at times, person who believed in facts and figures, not rhymes and secrets.

But this...he darted a glance at the microdot again...was possible? His grandmother did love puzzles.

He shook his head and crossed his arms. That was a completely fanciful notion. Or was it?

"I mean," Nicky said, "you're right. It could just be circumstantial. It could even be that someone entirely different put that there and it had nothing to do with Vivian at all."

"That's exactly what I was going to say."

"I know. That's why I said it," Nicky replied.

Quinten rubbed the back of his neck. But if this riddle was valid, and if there was some sort of connection to his grandmother, well, that meant he had to do something about it.

It would be like helping Grandma Viv. And maybe, just maybe, it would help him put to rest the regrets about her that haunted him.

He uncrossed his arms. "It sounds like some sort of rhyme or riddle or—"

"—code?" Nicky said.

NICKY SAW A flash of excitement in Quinten's blue-gray eyes as he studied the lines.

"Did you know that a coded message," Nicky said, "is what people usually mean when they say an enciphered message? But they're actually two very different things."

"Really?" He looked up, a gleam of interest in his eyes.

"Yep. A coded message means that there's significance in the words themselves—one word actually means something else. Like they did with the BBC broadcasts during the war. The SOE agents would tune in to the BBC's service station and listen for pre-arranged phrases from the broadcasters. Those would confirm arms, supplies drops—"

Nicky suddenly forgot the rest of her sentence. Her pulse fluttered as Quinten studied her, a look of admiration plain on his face as he said, "You know a lot about this stuff."

"Thank you." A swell of warmth filled her. "I'm doing a lot of reading. I love research. It really brings people from history to life. Especially if I find something like your grandmother's journal. That's what makes this whole thing so exciting to me."

He was a good listener. Didn't interrupt to interject his own viewpoint. Didn't try to get her to hurry up so he could go back to his sports show or science magazine. "I also believe in being informed," she said.

"Knowledge is power, and all that," Quinten murmured.

All Nicky could do was nod as her breath hitched. He could see more of her than she'd ever shown anyone before, couldn't he? It was like he wanted to know who she really was. Her heart hammered.

There was a beat of silence as they simply looked at each other. Heat rose to Nicky's cheeks. "But I'm getting side-tracked here. We're supposed to be solving this riddle."

Quinten cleared his throat as he turned his eyes back to the piece of paper. "We're pretty sure this is a code then?"

"Which probably has to do with the treasure? I think we can safely assume that, yep. Your grandmother's job description was deciphering messages. So her writing a coded message isn't that much of a stretch. And, like I said earlier, the ring was in her possession. Not only that, the dowry had disappeared. And German U-boats had been spotted around the island here, which is also where the treasure was supposed to be lost. Plus, in that love letter to Viv that I have, whoever A is makes reference to shared secrets, and something about having been trained to withstand the enemy."

"Right," Quinten said. "So do you think A was a Nazi?"

"Mabel seems to think so." Nicky paused. "But in your grandmother's diary, it implies she was in love with someone she worked with. And in that letter I have, it seems he got captured. So I think A is an SOE agent, not a Nazi."

"Mmmm."

"My theory at the moment is that maybe he was an agent using a code name for the letters. After all, your grandmother was assigned to several agents. One of them had the code name Ash."

"Oh."

"But to make it even more confusing, each agent was assigned not only a code name for their time in the field, but also one for reference when their traffic was being handled."

"Yeah, I can see how that'd be confusing." He rubbed his chin. "But I like your theory."

"Thanks." She blushed. She couldn't help but remember the look of admiration he'd given her a minute ago. No.

Everything was going better than planned. She couldn't afford to get distracted by Quinten. No matter how much she appreciated his listening skills. She'd be gone in a couple of days.

Nicky pushed those thoughts aside and turned her attention back to the riddle. She tapped a finger against her chin. "Let's see. It might be a good way to approach it if we work backwards line by line."

For several minutes they studied the lines in silence.

"*Mirrors a plan well-laid*," Quinten murmured. "I think we know what plan."

"Yep, seems pretty clear," Nicky agreed, "thanks to that Polish Art Center article."

"The plan to use Hitler's gold and diamonds to fund the Fourth Reich," Quinten said.

"Exactly."

"What about this?" Quinten tapped a finger on the word to underscore his point. "*Mirrors*. It's being used as a verb in this sentence, but what if it is really a noun?"

"A reference to the jewelled mirror."

"Right," Quinten said.

Nicky's pulse fluttered. She liked this. Playing detective with him. Working together to put the pieces into place. "The mirror was part of the dowry, after all," she added.

"Mmm-hmm." Quinten grinned.

"We work pretty well together." Nicky grinned back. His eyes were almost the color of a stormy day at sea, weren't they? Yet on him, there was a softness about the shade that—Focus.

She needed to focus on the work. On the words. She took a breath. "So the line above: *the pianist's journey*... Well, the slang term for a W/T operator was a pianist," Nicky said.

"W/T operator?"

"That's a radio operator. W/T stands for wireless telegraphy."

"Hmm." Quinten rubbed his jaw. "That could fit but I—Oh."

"What is it?" Nicky touched his arm.

"Hang on just a sec." He pulled out his phone and started to scroll through his photos as he murmured, "No, no...Okay. This one." He showed a picture to Nicky. "You know how I said I had a letter from A to Viv?"

"Yeah."

"I found it in an old suitcase up in the attic in pretty bad shape. It basically fell apart after I read it. I did manage to snap a photo, though. Look at this line." He zoomed in on the bit of text and showed her.

Nicky leaned toward him. A thrill went up her spine at his nearness. "From what I can make out there, it seems like he's saying he was an actual pianist."

"Which means the pianist reference is probably talking about A," Quinten said.

"And so if the pianist went on a journey...this A was going somewhere," Nicky said.

"P.E.I."

"Bingo," Nicky said.

"Also, Viv would've known he was a concert pianist. And if we're assuming Viv wrote the riddle, which makes sense since it was secreted in her ring, then this line *has* to be referring to A."

"You know, music keeps getting mentioned all through this riddle. That must be significant."

"Viv loved music. That's why she and my grandfather started the piano tuning business." Quinten rubbed his jaw. "She was always playing music. I have reams and reams of sheet music that I've actually just put in the recycling because there's so much..."

"Really?"

"Yeah." He pointed to an upright in the corner. "Every day she'd sit at that piano."

She turned to the window and caught her breath. "That's some piano." Light gleamed off its polished wood surface.

"It's a Princess Royal. Supposedly modeled after one in Buckingham Palace. From what I've heard, they made the original for the princesses, Elizabeth and Margaret."

"Really? Wow. So do you think any of these musical references have something to do with that piano?" Nicky blurted out.

"Maybe," Quinten said. "But I've been over pretty much every inch of it... Found a crumpled scrap of paper with a few letters scribbled across it, but that wasn't anything musically related that I could tell." He shrugged.

"Hmm. Okay. Well, let's look at the first two lines."

"*The secretary marches/to a tune unplayed.*" Quinten mused.

"An unplayed tune..." Nicky said. "Since we figured out that the pianist is this A, then could an unplayed tune mean some sort of plan of his that went wrong?"

"Or maybe it's some sort of signal that means...something?" Quinten spread his hands, fingers wide.

Nicky cocked her head. "Maybe that part'll make more sense if we figure out the first line: *A secretary marches.*"

"If we're talking World War II, there were lots of secretaries doing lots of things."

"But not probably marching to a tune unplayed." Nicky made a wry face.

"No," Quinten agreed. "Probably not."

"But..." Nicky said. She picked up her phone again and opened the web browser. "Wait a minute. In the Polish Art Center article—didn't it say something about a secretary?"

As she scanned the piece, her eyes widened. She glanced at Quinten and then read aloud: "...*Some scholars believe it was used as a bargaining chip by Hitler's personal secretary, Martin Bormann, near the end of the war.*"

"So the secretary in the first line must mean Martin Bormann," Quinten said.

"It must. Now if I do a quick search for Martin Bormann..." She started to type, turned her phone horizontally, then back vertically. "Maybe that'll pull something up."

"Here." Quinten strode over to the door, flipped the open sign to closed, then walked over to the doorway to the workroom.

Nicky watched him disappear into the back. He reappeared a moment later with a silver MacBook Pro laptop in hand. "This is better than that tiny phone screen. Plus it'll be easier for both of us to see at the same time."

"Good idea. Thank you."

Her heart swooped at the warm way he said, "Happy to help." He opened the computer and made a few keystrokes before he hit the enter key.

Nicky was too busy watching the smooth play of muscles in his forearms to pay full attention to what he was saying.

"—we get."

"Huh?"

"I said, let's see what we get."

"Right. Sorry." She blushed. "There's a bunch of hits here." She leaned in to read over his shoulder. "Let's go with the top result." It read, *Nazi Loot for a Song?*

Quinten clicked on it and skimmed a finger down the screen. "*The Nazis started to get nervous and decided they needed to put aside funds—gold and diamonds.*"

"*In case the Third Reich fell—*" Nicky murmured, as she resisted an urge to put her hand on his wide, strong shoulder, "*—the Nazis could reorganize in secret and come back to power by creating a Fourth Reich. They stashed the gold and diamonds in a location that was known only to Bormann.*"

Quinten read the next paragraph. "*The only clues to the Nazi loot were on a piece of sheet music Bormann had. After Hitler committed suicide in the Fuhrerbunker, Bormann fled the bunker and tried to get out of Berlin.*"

"But," Nicky finished the passage, "*he died before he could escape. The sheet music was lost but it supposedly points to the location of the gold, a collection of Hitler's personal diamonds, and the dowry of Princess Magdalena Jola Piast.*"

Quinten ruffled his hair.

Nicky sat back.

There was a beat of silence.

After a second, she spoke again. "You know what this means, don't you?"

"What's that?"

"It means this is more evidence the treasure exists. That it includes the dowry, which Viv had a piece of. And," Nicky lifted her chin, "that she and this A were involved in it somehow."

"I can't argue with that. So, "*The secretary marches/to a tune unplayed* has to be referring to that piece of sheet music Bormann owned."

"Exactly." Nicky caught her breath. "So this means—"

"—we need to find the sheet music," Quinten finished.

Chapter Six

SHE AND QUINTEN spent the rest of the evening making speculations. Then she returned to the hotel.

A glow filled her. Quinten was good at figuring things out. He might not be overly talkative but he'd asked thoughtful questions. He'd taken the time to ask her what she'd thought, too. She appreciated that. His attention to detail. His attention to her opinions, her ideas.

But they'd been so busy doing research about Nazi loot that they'd gotten carried away and totally missed the obvious primary source. Viv's diary.

Nicky picked it up and sat cross-legged on her bed in the Orient. She'd changed into a pair of ultra-soft yellow cotton pajamas.

She traced a finger along the cover before she opened the diary again.

She flipped past the unusual encrypted entry and read the next one, pencilled in neat, tidy handwriting.

May 31, 1943

My heart is breaking. But I must hold my head up and be strong. It does no good to wring my hands when I came to England to roll up my sleeves, against Mother's advice.

It's her homeland, after all. And I love it nearly as much as a native Englishwoman. Because of Papa, though, I am forever American. Thank goodness for the other girls at the Office.

I am grateful for my duties, for the distraction the numbers and letters bring.

Oh, it's so easy, though, to dwell on the love that we shared, and mourn what now shall never be. I am glad mathematics cannot break a girl's heart. I pray we not find ourselves in too deep over here. I must not think on it overmuch.

I am not sure I will find myself writing on these pages again. Too many memories.

Nicky turned the page.

Oct 7, 1945

The war has finally ended and I cannot help but feel a strange burst of sadness as to what my future holds.

I believe I will get a high school math teaching position after all, as we women are expected to resume our "regular lives." As if anyone could do that now, after all we have experienced. We have been sworn to secrecy so only I will remember what I have been involved in...

I have also decided I shall marry Wallace. He is a good man. A Canadian. From Prince Edward Island.

We met at the train station just after victory had been declared. Somehow our suitcases had gotten mixed up. He had mine and I had his. The way his blue-gray eyes sparkled with amusement when he'd realized what had happened made me think, wish, hope...

He proposed not long after.

I know I can make a good life for myself on the island. I do love him, and I believe I shall love it there. He has described the tiny village of Victoria to me and I am looking forward to seeing it ever so much.

Nicky turned the page but there was nothing there. At some point, it seemed, the glue had given way and the remaining pages had fallen out when someone had opened it.

Nicky turned to the very back of the diary.

A piece of lined spiral notebook paper, folded in thirds and then folded in half again, was wedged between the last page of the little book and its back cover.

It looked much newer than the journal. She saw, as she reached for it, that it was written in blue ballpoint pen.

She plucked it up with a pounding heart.

May 29, 2000

It must be something about this time of year that brings him to mind. The scent of the spring rains on the wind. Or the sound of early morning birdsong...

Whatever it is, always, this time of year, I remember.

I remember the night he told me. He'd just come back and then he'd had to leave again. We'd shared a Coca-Cola and a cigarette. I'd tried not to look at the gold signet ring on the pinky finger of his left hand. He only wore it when he was getting ready to leave. Because it contained his L-tablet.

I'd forced myself to smile when he'd turned to me with those brown eyes of his and took my hand. "Sweetheart," he'd said, "I don't want you to worry. That's why we need to arrange something between us because I'm taking a little trip."

"Oh?" I'd said, lifted an eyebrow: a fragile effort to make light of what surely was a dark situation.

He'd nodded. "Thirteen letters. That's what it'll be." He'd touched the gold signet ring and swallowed. Then he'd gently touched my face. "If I, well, am somehow...delayed. You get my meaning?"

"Yes," I'd whispered. He would use a key word of thirteen letters in length if he was taken by the Nazis, to signal to me that his cover had been blown and he was taken prisoner.

I'd understood his meaning perfectly that night.

And today, well, I can finally say it.

Nicky glanced at the date of the entry, 2000. By then, the official oath of secrecy had been lifted, so being able to tell about what she'd gone through must be what Viv was referring to in the last line of this entry.

She reread it.

L-tablet. That was shorthand for cyanide capsule. So this entry proved beyond any doubt that the man was an agent for the SOE.

In fact...this person had to be the A of the letter. Nicky put the diary in her lap, picked up her purse, and pulled out the letter. Yet if the A in the letter was also the agent whose code name was Ash, then why did Mabel talk about Vivian being in love with a Nazi? Perhaps she'd just made up the whole Nazi lover thing.

Nicky skimmed the entry's lines again. They must have run into each other when he'd been at SOE headquarters at some point.

Though according to her research, it was against the rules for girls in the codes department to know the real identity or any other information about the agents whose traffic they deciphered...

Obviously, someone had been ignoring the rules. When it came to love, you couldn't really confine it with rules. In fact, that was when it most easily died.

Nicky frowned. At least in her own experience. She sighed and put the page back where she'd found it.

What was she going to do now that the rest of the diary pages were missing?

Her brows furrowed. Maybe Quinten had some idea. She could show him the encrypted entry, too. But that would have to wait until tomorrow.

She put the diary on the nightstand beside her phone, which she'd just plugged in to charge.

She picked up and reread the letter to Viv. Finally, she put it down, leaned over to the nightstand and clicked off the lamp. Nicky closed her eyes and tried to calm her mind, but lines from the letter kept repeating in her head.

...the summer wind in our hair and shared secrets in our eyes...they cannot know what is in my heart...they cannot destroy my soul, though undoubtedly, they shall try...I have a cause to fight for...

Nicky's eyes flew open. Why hadn't she seen that connection before? Viv hadn't just been in love with this agent—she'd handled a lot—probably *all*—of his traffic, too. Whoever he was.

In Viv's file, it listed the code names of agents whose traffic she'd deciphered. Oak. Ash. Maple.

She was pretty sure A stood for Ash. But... Nicky sat up. Her heart pounded. If she cross-referenced all three of those code names with more SOE agent files...she might be able to find out A's real identity.

Not only that, if Nicky could find his enciphered messages sent to Baker Street HQ, she'd know exactly what Viv and this agent knew.

Did the National Archives in England have copies of the SOE agents' traffic? She'd have to find out. Maybe that would explain what was really going on.

SUNDAY MORNING, NICKY took a sip of the thick rich hot chocolate she'd ordered.

She adjusted her seat at Island Chocolates so that she had a better view of the street and the leaves that had begun to fall in the light breeze that smelled of sea air and limitless potential.

She inhaled a big breath. She could get used to a place like this. Okay, who was she kidding? She could get used to *this*.

She loved it here. She loved the fact that everyone was so friendly. That when you walked down the street, people said hello to you—she was tired of the anonymity of New York City.

And more than that, she wanted to be seen, to be acknowledged, to be noticed for who and what she was. For what she offered others. And people really seemed to appreciate that here.

Especially with all the local shops and artisans and just the overall *feeling* of the place. People actually seemed to care here in Victoria.

She took another deep breath and looked around.

Sure, people here had their problems—just like people everywhere—but here, at least your neighbor would probably help you out with it rather than climbing over you to get to the next rung on the career ladder.

She winced. Okay, that was pretty cynical but—she shrugged a shoulder—that was how she felt right now.

She took another sip of hot chocolate as she riffled through her notes. From what she'd been compiling and gathering, and from her first draft, well, things were really shaping up into a second draft. Excitement zipped through her.

She'd threaded in what she'd discovered from the journal, as well as the love letter. Perhaps she could even feature as a secondary side bar a bit about the history of the SOE and the role that women played in the organization. Just some facts and figures to give the story some more depth and dimension.

She had enough research information here to write a book, practically. Her lips lifted. That was the mark of a good journalist. Gathering as much research and as many primary sources as possible so as to write the best article possible.

She pulled up the National Archives website and typed her message into their contact form.

Hello,

My name is Nicky Stendahl. I'm a journalist in the U.S. with the Historical Woman magazine. I'm looking for information regarding the messages that Vivian Robinson deciphered during her time with the SOE from 1940 until 1945. Specifically, I'd like to review the traffic related to the three agents she'd been assigned: Oak, Ash and Maple. I don't know their true names or any other information about them. Thank you!

Regards, Nicky

Looked like the response time was usually four business days. Well, with the time difference, it was practically Monday over in England now anyway.

She tapped her fingers on the tabletop. Hopefully, they'd get back to her within that timeframe because she only had about a week left 'til the deadline.

How should she work in the treasure angle? That wasn't the original gist of the story, exactly.

She would run it by her editor, but it would no doubt be fine. After all, the woman had said to get as much in-depth information as possible.

If she incorporated the parts about the treasure into the article about Viv, that actually made the story more important from a cultural and historical standpoint. Especially if Viv and this A were trying to recover it.

She pulled up her email and sent her editor an update.

A BLAST OF cool, fall air stirred Nicky's hair and she looked up. Quinten had walked in to the chocolate shop.

Her heart jumped as he saw her and nodded his acknowledgment. No. She couldn't get carried away. Being single was just fine.

He ordered something from the front and then approached her table.

"Is this chair taken?" There was a twinkle in his eye as he said it.

"Yep. By you."

He sat. "How's it going then?" He indicated the stacks of books and piles of papers that covered nearly the whole tiny table's surface.

"Really well. I've done a second draft of the article."

"That's great. So you're making progress then."

"Yep." Her heart warmed at his acknowledgment of her efforts. "I thought I'd look up this A that Viv had received that letter from."

"And?" Quinten leaned forward in his chair. A strand of hair fell across his forehead and she resisted the urge to reach across and brush it out of his eyes.

"Still waiting to hear back from the National Archives in England," she said instead. "Could take awhile."

"Well, while you're waiting...do you want to go to Charlottetown with me?"

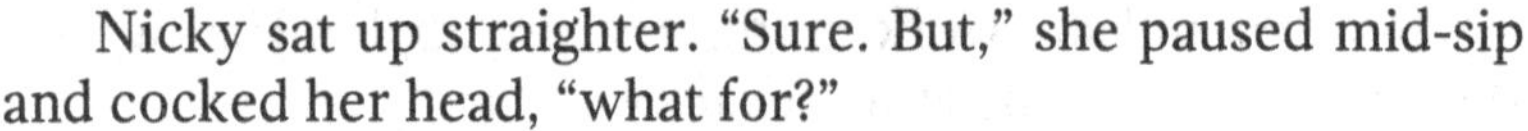

Nicky sat up straighter. "Sure. But," she paused mid-sip and cocked her head, "what for?"

"Are you always this suspicious?"

She laughed. "Just being a journalist."

"The U-boats." Quinten glanced around and lowered his voice. "I was thinking about it in the context of Mabel's story. That the Nazis were here on P.E.I. Well, if we want to find some sort of solid lead on that, and how it might connect to the sheet music and Viv, the library might be a place to start."

"Okay," Nicky said, and drained her mug. "Let's go."

Nearly an hour later, Quinten pulled into a parking spot along Queen Street in the downtown heart of Charlottetown.

Nicky got out and followed Quinten up to the library.

Bright yellows and oranges of marigolds swayed in the light breeze. The sun warmed Nicky's face and the chatter of outdoor diners drifted to her from nearby Victoria Row. And suddenly, she wanted to take Quinten's hand, wanted to hold onto this moment, this feeling, forever.

Quinten must have felt her looking at him because when he glanced over, she saw warmth in his eyes.

"Thank you," she said suddenly. "I appreciate your help."

"My pleasure."

He held the door open for her as they headed inside the library and up to the reference desk. An older man with wire-rimmed glasses and a slim build looked up from his computer.

"How can I help you?" His staff badge read 'Jerry.'

"Well," Nicky said, "I'm looking for some information about P.E.I. during World War II."

"Great! I'm a bit of a World War II buff, so you've come to the right person."

"Did you ever hear of Nazis on the island?" Nicky asked.

"Or anything about a piece of sheet music in relation to that?" Quinten added.

"Nothing about sheet music." Jerry paused for a second

and his eyes narrowed. "As for Nazis on the island, you have to untangle the facts from the fiction with that tale."

Nicky and Quinten took seats on the chairs in front of his desk.

"The story about Hitler's gold and diamonds hidden somewhere on P.E.I. fits in with the local Nazi lore. The facts, though, go something like this:

"One specific German submarine, U-262, was on a mission to rescue German naval officer POWs from a prisoner of war camp in New Brunswick, near Fredericton, called Camp 70. Apparently, the sub planned to rendezvous with them in North Cape."

He glanced at Nicky. "That's at the northern tip of P.E.I. Up west, as they say around here. I imagine the sub didn't meet the POWs in New Brunswick because the Germans didn't want to go any farther into enemy territory than they had to. Anyway, U-262 was actually the *second* sub they'd sent on this secret assignment. The first one, U-376, was reportedly sunk off the Bay of Biscay in France earlier in '43. April, I think it was."

"Okay," Nicky said.

Jerry continued. "So the second sub was tasked with the mission called Operation Elster. Means magpie in English."

He paused and took a breath. "Odd thing was, even though the second sub made the rendezvous point, the POWs didn't. A persistent piece of island folklore even says U-262 got caught in a pretty heated naval battle near the northwest tip of P.E.I. before it headed back to Germany. But *that's* the sub rumored to have been carrying Hitler's gold and diamonds."

Nicky's eyes widened.

"Now, whether that's actually true?" Jerry chuckled. "Well, that's part of the allure of the story." A gleam came into the librarian's eyes. "Personally, I like to believe that it's possible. Makes life interesting. What actually happened, though, no one knows for sure because no conclusive evidence has ever been found. Have you tried searching on the internet for that sort of thing?"

Nicky shifted in her seat. "No. I did see some archived articles but never came across anything like that specifically."

Quinten spoke up. "I found an original article about U-boats on P.E.I. from what I'm guessing is the early forties." He paused. "But it didn't mention anything about these two."

"An original, wow," Jerry said as he reached for a Post-It and a pen. "Here are the web addresses of a couple of online archives: the Robertson Library at UPEI and Charlottetown's paper—*The Guardian*." He handed the sticky note to Nicky, who tucked it into her purse.

"We also have a file down in the basement about the POW rescue attempt. I can go grab it for you." He straightened in his chair.

"Sure," Nicky said.

"That'd be great," Quinten echoed.

About ten minutes later, Jerry returned with a slim manila file in hand. "This is all that we have on record here. It goes into a bit more detail on what I just told you. Some newspaper articles in there, too. You know what? I almost forgot. There's also a P.E.I. heritage database called Island Voices that has a lot of World War II stuff that's searchable." He jotted that web address down on another Post-It and gave it to Nicky. "So. If you check out all those digitized archives, you should at least have a good starting point. You can photocopy whatever you like out of there." He gestured to the manila file folder. "Just be sure to bring it back."

"Here," Quinten said, "I can go run a copy."

Nicky's heart melted a little. Mabel was right—he was a good guy. "That'd be great. Thank you, Quinten."

A few minutes later, Quinten returned. He handed the file back. "Thanks so much, Jerry."

"Yes. Really appreciate your help," Nicky added.

"You two come back any time if you have more questions. Or want to solve any more mysteries," Jerry said.

Nicky followed Quinten as they stepped out into the warm sunshine on Queen Street. "That Jerry guy really knows his stuff."

"Yeah, he's been the head reference librarian there for a long time." Quinten stuffed his hands into his pockets. His habit of doing that was kind of cute, Nicky mused, as they headed over to his car.

She felt a thrill as she gazed at the red-brick buildings from the 1800s, the iron lamp posts, and smelled the scent of sea air. This island just kept getting better and better.

Especially in October.

Bright yellow oak, rich red maple, and russet-brown horse chestnut leaves scattered on the breeze and swirled around the car as they got in.

Quinten turned the key in the ignition and then turned his attention toward Nicky. "Listen, it's just about lunchtime." He adjusted the cuffs on his maroon button down. "Do you want to get a bite to eat somewhere and talk about what we've found so far?"

Nicky couldn't help the look of surprise that flitted across her face. "Umm," she said, "I mean, yes, that'd be great." A surge of excitement ran through her. "Where do you want to go?"

"Wherever you'd like to go is fine with me. I'm not picky," Quinten said.

"Well," Nicky laughed, "I have no idea what's good in this town, so it makes sense for you to choose."

"I hate making decisions, so I find it's easier if I let the other person decide." Quinten looked a little shocked at the words that had just come out of his mouth. "Did I just say that out loud? I didn't mean to do that but I. . . Okay, now I'm digging myself into a hole. I'm going to stop talking."

THEY GOT OUT of Quinten's car and headed down the sidewalk.

Quinten saw Nicky look around with interest and couldn't resist playing tour guide. "You know, downtown here didn't always look like this."

"Really? When I came up here for Maggie's wedding last summer, I just assumed it'd been this way forever. Charming, quaint and trendy."

"Nope. Twenty, twenty-five years ago, Charlottetown's core here was pretty run down. The city's done a great job, though, in changing all that and bringing in tourists every summer and fall. That's one of the things I really love about this city, about this island. Islanders don't give up. We just look for ways to revitalize." He paused and murmured, almost to himself, "Which is what I need to do in my own life. I'd always thought I'd get a chance to do a bit of traveling, have some adventures in my twenties..." He darted a glance at Nicky. Best not to share too much. Right? "...but with all my schooling and then running the shop, I never did." He shoved his hands in his pockets.

"I know what you mean," Nicky said, as she fiddled with a strand of her hair.

Quinten couldn't help but smile at that rather endearing trait.

"I couldn't wait to get out of the tiny Michigan town I grew up in. But living in New York isn't really doing anything for me anymore."

"No? I've always wanted to visit New York," he said. "There are a couple musicals I'd love to see live on Broadway."

"Certainly a great theatre scene there. Guess the grass is always greener, and all that."

"Guess so."

They walked farther down the street. The scent of fallen leaves mingled with the salt air and the chatter of passersby.

"This time of year with the leaves changing, people come from all over," he said. "Sometimes people show up in September thinking the leaves have already changed. But that actually doesn't happen until October. September is basically a bonus summer month, since June's usually pretty cool."

They passed red-brick façades with hand-lettered signs

declaring clothing boutiques and a jewelry store.

"Autumn's my favorite time of year," Nicky said.

"Mine too."

"I love how the sky looks bluer, the air smells like fallen leaves, and the coffee shops have pumpkin pie lattes." She laughed and looked so happy that a sudden swell of longing to connect with her surged through him.

"When I was growing up, Grandma Viv, Grandpa Wallace, and I would always go apple picking this time of year. I loved it. Used to race back to the house and make caramel apples with the fresh ones we'd just picked. Something about the combination of salty and sweet..."

"P.E.I. seems like such a great place to grow up. That sounds like a great childhood memory."

"I was pretty lucky to have them for grandparents."

"I've actually never gone apple picking."

"No? There are some great orchards around here. You should go."

With me, Quinten almost blurted out.

But before he could, Nicky said, "The restaurant's nearby?"

"It's just around the corner here on Sydney Street."

They crossed to the other side of Sydney Street and passed Sim's Steakhouse on the corner. The building's third floor contained his attorney's office.

His shoulders tensed as he recalled Thursday's meeting and Elliot's words. Quinten shook his head. Elliot wasn't going to get the business. Not if he had anything to do with it. His crowdfunding page had even gotten a few hits. No donations. But still, hits were a start.

They continued a little farther before they came to a three-story red brick house with a sign on its lawn that read The Gahan House.

"They also brew their own craft beer down in the basement," Quinten said. "I'm not a beer drinker, but it's kind of neat to see the machinery."

Nicky grinned. "Don't worry, I'm not a beer drinker either."

"No? I wasn't sure what to make of you."

"Most guys don't."

He headed up the short flight of steps to the house, Nicky behind him.

"Two for lunch?" the maître d' asked.

Quinten nodded.

"Follow me." She led them past the wood-paneled bar with its flat-screen TVs and over to a round table with brown velvet wingback chairs nestled up against a bay window that overlooked the street.

Quinten pulled out the chair for Nicky.

She glanced at him and Quinten couldn't help but notice the way her lips formed a perfect O of surprise.

He simply smiled at her.

He sat down in the seat next to her and picked up his menu. The server came and took their drink orders.

Quinten always got the same thing every time he ate here. The blueberry mixed greens salad and the chicken and chorizo penne.

Nicky ordered the maple balsamic salmon.

She took a sip of her raspberry iced tea and Quinten couldn't help but notice the way her bottom lip pressed against the curve of the glass's rim.

His eyes lingered on her mouth and he tried to think of something else. Anything else. But he couldn't. How long had it been since he'd kissed anyone? She'd taste like raspberries...

He cleared his throat. Forced his mind back to reality. "So how's the story going?"

Nicky's eyes sparkled. Quinten felt a glow of satisfaction. He'd asked her the right question. A swell of courage filled him.

She leaned forward. He caught a hint of her vanilla perfume as he leaned forward too.

"Really well," she said. "I hope my editor likes it. This is one of the first longer pieces I've written and I want to make sure I'm doing it right, you know?"

She cocked her head as she regarded him. She wasn't

afraid to speak her mind—that was one of the things he'd begun to really admire about her.

"I do, yes. Because when a customer asks me to fix a piano that's been in the family for, oh, I don't know, a hundred years, I know that if I mess it up, I'll feel like..." Quinten averted his eyes and traced the pattern of the table's wood grain with a fingertip, "...I've destroyed a part of their heritage, a piece of their own story, in a way." He slowly brought his eyes back up to Nicky's face. Expecting to see a frown, a smirk, some sort of doubt or disagreement on her face.

But warmth and relief filled him when he saw only understanding.

"I know exactly what you mean. Because there's nothing that's more important to me than honoring people's stories, telling their truths, sharing that with the world, and being able to have people know that, see that, acknowledge that. For their own sakes, and for the sakes of the people being written about."

She paused. "I think that your grandmother was an important person. She did a good thing, a strong thing, during the war, and I think that people should—no—deserve to know about it. So that it can perhaps help people now. So that it can inspire people to perhaps draw strength from a time of darkness and know that no matter what, things indeed do get better; that no matter what, there is a light in the darkness. To give them hope. To give them some sort of...comfort. To drive them to do better in their own lives."

Quinten's heart felt full as warmth wound its way through him at her words. He opened his mouth to respond, but suddenly Nicky's phone dinged.

"I GOT AN email from the National Archives," Nicky said.

"Wow. That was fast," Quinten said, before he took a few more bites of his penne.

"I know, right? Guess the time difference doesn't hurt.

Listen to what it says."

Dear Ms. Stendahl,

Thank you for your query. Finding records of agents' traffic is tricky. It will take some time to search and retrieve all pertinent documents. There will also be a fee, but as soon as you have paid that, we can move ahead.

I've looked up the agents whose code names you mentioned. Unfortunately, both Ash's and Maple's files are sealed until next year.

As for Oak, most of his records are sealed for another two years. But part of his file has been officially opened this year. As such, that section is now available and digitized. The link below will direct you to that information.

However, I must warn you that it is incomplete, as at some point, files for X section had partially succumbed to fire.

Regards,
Greg Scott
Research Curator
The National Archives

Nicky scrolled down to the link and opened it. Pieces of type and text were blackened or missing, obscured by the fire damage.

<u>R M   C.R.1.</u>

TE: 7.41   INTERVIEWED BY: C. GU

Surname (in block capitals): *GOBELL*

Christian names: *Andrzej Dawid*

Rank or ti

   orations:

1. <u>ORMER NAMES(I</u>

2. <u>PERMANENT ADDR</u>
      <u>TE</u>

3. <u>IF SERVING</u> (Regiment)

4. <u>DATE & PLACE OF BIRTH</u> *9 November, 1917, Gdansk, Pol*

5.   <u>ATIONALITY</u> At birth *Polish*
       At present *German/Polish*

6. <u>EDUCATION</u>
      (a) Schools atte
      (b) Universities *University of Bonn, Ger*
      Oxford University, England
          rees taken *classical music studies (Bonn)*
      linguists degree (Oxford)

7. <u>MARRIED OR SINGLE</u>? *single*

9. <u>RELIGION</u> *RC*

10. <u>PEACE TIME OCCUPATION</u> *translator, concert pianist*
          <u>ION SINCE 3.9.39</u> *translator*
          <u>NGUAGES</u>
       at languages do you spe
        an w fluently? *German — fluent, Polish — fluent, English —*
      fluent.

1 WHA̲   N̲T̲R̲I̲E̲S̲ H̲A̲V̲E̲ Y̲O̲U̲ V̲I̲S̲I̲T̲E̲D̲? *Austria. Switzerland.*
Czechoslov
   (other than in passage)

15. A̲N̲Y̲ S̲E̲R̲V̲I̲C̲E̲ E̲X̲P̲E̲R̲I̲E̲N̲C̲E̲? *German naval ensign. left for personal*
reasons

16. P̲O̲L̲I̲T̲I̲C̲A̲L̲ V̲I̲E̲W̲S̲

17. H̲A̲V̲E̲ Y̲O̲U̲ M̲A̲D̲E̲ A̲ W̲I̲L̲L̲? *No.*

18.   RSON T̲O̲ B̲E̲ I̲N̲F̲O̲R̲M̲E̲D̲ if you bec   a casualty
         A̲R̲A̲N̲C̲E̲
) height *6'1"*
   (b)   ght *191 lbs*
         hair *brown*
   (d) Colour of eyes *brown*
   (e) Complexion *medium*
   (f) Distinguishing Marks *none*
             former neighbours
          know your whereabouts? *No.*

20. DO YOU:-
   (a) Ride? *yes*
   (b) Sail a boat? *yes*
   (& member of Oxford crew)
   (c) Fly an aeroplane? *No*
   (d) Read & transmit Morse? *yes*
   (e) Drive a car/motor cycle? *car*
   (f) Run? *no*
   (g) Box? *yes*
   (h) Mountaineer? *no*

21. H̲A̲V̲E̲ Y̲O̲U̲ A̲N̲Y̲ E̲X̲P̲E̲R̲I̲E̲N̲C̲E̲ O̲F̲ P̲H̲O̲T̲O̲G̲R̲A̲P̲H̲Y̲ O̲R̲
C̲I̲N̲E̲P̲H̲O̲T̲O̲G̲R̲A̲P̲H̲Y̲? *no*

22. <u>HAVE YOU ANY KNOWLEDGE OF MAP READING, FIELD SKETCHING, ETC?</u> *map reading & field sketching during time in German navy*

<u>OWLEDGE OF WIRELESS?</u> *yes*

<u>WITH WHAT DISTRICTS ARE YOU VERY FAMILIAR?</u>
      at home? *Gdansk*
  (b) Abroad? *London*

25. <u>SPECIAL KNOWLEDGE.</u>
  (a) Propaganda *No*
  (b) Technical *translator abilities*

26. <u>ACCOUNT OF PAST HISTORY</u> *particulars as discussed*

<u>F O R M X/89612</u>

Field name: Matthias Grynberg

Code name: Oak

Cover occupation: Nazi in the German navy;
rank, ensign

Real occupation: agent for X Section, SOE

Dates of employment: January 17, 1941–June 7, 1943

Nicky blinked and looked at Quinten. "I just realized something."

"Oh?"

"A didn't stand for Ash." She raised her eyes to the ceiling and shook her head. "It stood for Andrzej."

"The first name of this agent?"

"Not only that, but June 7, 1943...I think that's the same date that the letter had been written to Viv." She pulled the letter out of her purse. "Yes. Which means that was the date he was captured... So. This must be the right person."

She continued reading.

```
Mission Status: Seven missions compl

 urrent mission: Op    Black Forest

           ee Form 6. b)
```

Nicky frowned. This section had been badly burned. She scrolled farther and noticed that in several places, it looked like names had been cut out of the document.

<u>Notes</u>:

```
   disagreed with principles and ideals set
forth by Fascist regime

        t, an Oxford school friend in London;
was approached for interview by

Accepted into SOE and dispatched back to Germa-
ny as agent.
```

Quinten finished his penne and wiped his mouth with his napkin. "What is it?"

Nicky handed her phone to him. "I hit pay dirt. So. His real name was Andrzej Dawid Gobell. But the SOE's file on him is partially burned. And censored."

A gleam came into Quinten's eyes.

"Better than a spy thriller, isn't it?" she asked.

"Definitely."

A surge of excitement ran through Nicky. She didn't know if it was from the warmth of Quinten's gaze in her direction or from the fact that they were getting closer to real answers about Viv, Andrzej, and this supposed Nazi treasure. Probably both.

Quinten looked thoughtful as he handed her phone back. "It says he was a concert pianist. So this confirms we were right."

Nicky's heart fluttered as Quinten held her gaze. They *would* figure out this historical mystery together. It didn't matter, did it, that he didn't always say everything he felt or thought. He said what he felt he should. That's what counted, wasn't it?

"What if we use his real name to do a check online for anything else about him?"

"Good idea." Nicky reached for her phone. A second later she said, "Here's a Wikipedia entry."

Andrzej Dawid Gobell, born November 9, 1917, was a secret agent during World War II. He worked for Britain's Special Operations Executive, X Section (Germany).

Because of the dangerous nature of the work at the heart of the Nazi regime, the SOE ran very few operations in Germany. Gobell was one of only a handful of SOE operatives in that country. For most of the war, the SOE's X Section worked with the Political Warfare Executive's German sector and concentrated mainly on black propaganda and administrative sabotage.

Gobell used the code name Oak, and the field name Matthias Grynberg, from 1941 until his death at Nazi headquarters in Berlin, Germany, in June of 1943.

Trained as a concert pianist in Germany, he also had a passion for the water, and he served with the German navy before obtaining his degree in linguistics at Oxford University, England.

Little is known about his early years, but he grew up in Gdansk, Poland. (During the war, Gdansk was considered to be in Germany and was called Danzig.) Though he was Polish born, he was both a Polish and a German citizen due to the German-Polish border shift in that region.

But as the Second World War approached, he became disillusioned with Germany's politics and returned to England to work as a translator shortly before the war broke out.

His time in the German navy as well as his dual citizenship served him in good stead, as the SOE recruited him and sent him back to Germany to work undercover as an ensign in the German navy.

In the hope it would defer suspicion, Gobell's cover

professed he was a Nazi supporter. Gobell was quiet and reserved, but when needed, became charming and assertive—the perfect combination for a secret agent during World War II.

Nicky glanced through the Wikipedia entry again. "That's interesting. Andrzej's cover had him pretend to be a Nazi supporter."

"So I bet that's why Mabel said Vivian was in love with a Nazi," Quinten said slowly. "It was part of his cover story." He was silent a moment as he rubbed a hand across his stubble. "Speaking of, I wonder if looking up the U-boat crew manifest would yield any additional information?"

"That's a genius idea." She reached for her purse and pulled out the photocopied article. "Let's see. This lists the name of the U-boat as well as the commanding officer. So if we look that up, we could determine if Andrzej was part of that crew..."

"...and then we could hopefully figure out what he—and Grandma Viv—were up to." Quinten finished.

"Once we find that out, maybe we can find..." she glanced around and lowered her voice "...the sheet music."

"If it's even still around," Quinten amended.

Nicky threw him a look of exasperation.

"Hey," Quinten said as he spread his arms, "I'm just trying to be practical. I'm part Scottish, you know—"

QUINTEN'S PHONE RANG.

He ignored it. Usually people knew not to call him at lunch. It rang again. He glanced at the caller ID. His lawyer. He'd better take the call. "Sorry, I have to get this." He answered his phone, pushed his chair back and headed to the foyer.

"Pardon?" He pressed the phone to his ear over the noise of the other diners. "I can't hear you. I was just in the middle of something and..." He made his way over to a quieter corner.

"Quinten," his lawyer said in a louder voice. "I'm sorry to interrupt your day but I have some more bad news."

Quinten swallowed.

"Elliot's come into the office again."

Quinten nodded. Then remembered his lawyer couldn't see the motion. "Okay," he said slowly.

"He's told me to tell you that he wants to null your agreement from the other day and buy you out now instead. If you give him sole control of the business, he said he'll get you out of bankruptcy." He paused. "Have you found some documentation that proves ownership?"

Quinten's stomach knotted. How had Elliot even found out about the bankruptcy so fast? Then again, why was he wondering? Word traveled fast in a small place. Plus, his crowdfunding page... "I haven't. But I hope I don't need to make a decision right this moment?"

"No. But it needs to be soon. Listen, think about it—but not too long—and let me know."

"Okay." Quinten ended the call. He wasn't going to give in that easily, he knew that much.

He schooled his expression to polite friendliness as he came back to the table. "Sorry about that."

"No problem." She studied him. "Everything okay? I hope it wasn't bad news."

Quinten's shoulders tensed. Had he showed too much of his true feelings on his face just now? "A bit of business is all."

"About your family's shop?"

"Yeah." He caught Nicky's steady gaze. Something about the expression in her eyes made him realize, suddenly, that he wanted to tell her. Connect with her more deeply. Unburden himself. He took a breath and said, "I guess I'm just a bit...afraid that I'll lose it." He rearranged the silverware. "Grandma Viv loved it and put her heart and soul into it. That's the other part of why I started to work at the shop. Because I feel like the shop is somehow...a connection to her." He looked across at her, saw softness and compassion

in her eyes. A warm glow filled him. She understood.

"I felt that way about my aunt when she passed away," she said softly. "She had a beautiful vintage pin she always wore and when I lost it after her funeral, I thought I'd lost her, too." She swallowed and fiddled with her purse straps.

"That's, I, uh, thank you for sharing that," he said softly.

"You're welcome," she whispered.

The server came back to fill their glasses and Quinten's mind drifted back to the conversation with his lawyer.

He had to think of something to say to Elliot. But he had to come up with just the right thing. Time was ticking.

Nothing like putting things off to the last minute. He grimaced. That was a habit he should really get around to breaking.

Maybe tomorrow.

"So." He leaned forward and rested his forearms on the table. "We have something much more historically important on our hands than we ever thought. You think?"

Nicky's lips curved up and she raised her eyebrows at him.

A tingle zipped up Quinten's spine as she leaned forward in her chair too. "What do *you* think?" Her cheeks flushed with excitement and her eyes sparkled.

Quinten felt heat creep up the back of his neck as she held his gaze. "I've already told you what I think." He opened his mouth. Closed it. "Uh, I mean, um..."

Confusion flitted across Nicky's face and she sat back, a small frown between her brows.

Damn it. This was what being direct and speaking the truth did. It made things awkward. It messed up dynamics. It hurt people, strained relationships to the breaking point. Like it had with him and his father.

The silence stretched. He cleared his throat.

He'd put his foot in his mouth again. Why was he always doing that?

He shot a sidelong glance at Nicky, who now looked a little bewildered. Or was it bemused?

Either way, she seemed to accept him. His shoulders

relaxed. Another thing that he appreciated in her—No. This line of thinking wasn't going to get him anywhere. It was unproductive.

She herself had mentioned she was only in Victoria for this story. So what was he doing? Going down this road wouldn't help him stay safely away from her.

Quinten felt a tug of disappointment as he turned his attention to the server who'd returned with the bill. "Here. You've been working hard these past few days. Lunch is on me."

THE SERVER CAME back with Quinten's Visa. That was kind of him to buy her lunch. Nicky's heart fluttered. Another thing she liked about him—his generosity.

The two of them headed out into the street and the bright sunlight once again.

She followed Quinten across the pavement and couldn't help but notice the long lines of his back underneath his neatly tucked in maroon button-down shirt.

That color looked really good on him too. Jewel tones suited him, she decided.

Over these past few days, Quinten had been so helpful. Kind. Working with her on the riddle. Listening to her thoughts, opinions, views. Tracking down research. Holding open doors for her... Maybe, just maybe, she didn't have to hold her heart back, with him?

Gah. She bit her lip. No. She was better off single. His issues, whatever they were, would eventually come up; so would hers. So this spending time with him was just...for the story. She was almost done with it. Well, at least, the original assignment, anyway. Then she'd have to leave. Wouldn't she?

Of course she would.

She just needed to figure out how this whole treasure angle could be worked in without having to write an additional 3,000 words and go way over the length limit.

Maybe it was a follow-up piece she could pitch to Susan? That could work. And now that everything was shaping up so nicely, once it was published, the article could really begin to grow her name and reputation.

Chapter Seven

QUINTEN DROPPED NICKY off at the Orient Hotel and drove back to his own place.

He headed to the back door of his house and over to his workbench. It'd be a good time to tighten the strings on that guitar his friend and neighbor Tate had brought in.

But as he worked, his mind kept returning to Nazi submarines and that crumbling newspaper article he'd found.

If there was any concrete connection between the Nazi treasure, P.E.I., and the U-boats, then that website Jerry the librarian had mentioned would be the place to start. That'd be a big help to Nicky.

He put down the guitar and opened his laptop.

He clicked open his web browser. Now, what was the name—

Oh right. Island Voices. The website popped up and he scrolled through it.

Looked like you could search for whatever piece of island history you wanted. It was divided up by years, dates, and types of people, as well as subject matter.

Mabel's legend was one thing, the silver Nazi coin was another, but these first-person eyewitness accounts to history were something else entirely.

He typed in World War II, Nazis, and U-boats and hit enter. Hmmm. There were lots of P.E.I. regiments' accounts of fighting in the European theater...

He kept skimming.

...Canadian naval officers, shore leave, liberating France...

What was this? He scrolled down to the final hit. Ger-

man submarine on P.E.I. He clicked on the listen icon.

"Well, it was back in the summer, no, the late spring of 1943. I remember it well because the spring lobster season was promising to be a good one. I'd been fishing the waters off the eastern side of North Cape for near-on twenty-five years at that point, ya see.

I'd heard the stories—well, everyone in these parts had—about the U-boats in the waters. Been rumors even of a sighting near Victoria. Can't say as I believed any of it, mind. But well, I had fish to catch and lobster to trap. What else was I to do but take a chance, every day, on my fishing trips? That year turned out to be one of the best lobster seasons I'd ever have.

But where was I? Oh, yah. Was near midnight, I think it was the 3rd or 4th of May.

Terrible rainy. But I figured it'd blow itself out. The RCMP had just the prior week come round and told us to keep a watch out for U-boats. They'd been working with the Coast Guard, ya see? We were told, "If ya see 'em, report 'em straight away."

Sure enough, bad weather did blow over. Moon was just beginning to come out from behind a cloud.

Out on deck I looked northwest and saw something breach. Far, far off in the distance.

At first. I thought it was a whale, so I grabbed my glass.

But then I looked through it. Made the hairs on the back of my neck stand up.

A swastika, plain as plain. I nearly fell overboard, a-tremblin' as I was. Pretty much just me out there in that little fishing boat, ya see.

Near as I could tell, it was headed inland and I caught a few numbers on its side: 262.

I think that the U-boat captain or whoever he was musta cashed in on the thought that no one was around, seein' as how the bit of cloud cover that night'd been thick as gravy.

But that little puff 'o wind did it, 'cause that was when I saw a flash. Out of the corner of my eye.

I turned about real quick. And sure as the nose on my face but that flash was comin' from something on shore.

Musta been north of Seacow Pond, near as I could figure. Way up the beach. Like moonlight hitting metal. Bright metal. If I squinted through my glass, I could see it looked like a couple of men in uniform standin' on the sand. Busy doin' nothin' but standing there. Like they were waiting for orders or the like.

Headed as fast as I could for shore 'n got myself back home. Telephoned up the precinct right quick and told 'em exactly what I'd seen.

They thanked me, I hung up the phone, I had my supper 'n that was that. But then, well, when I heard about the sub's supposed connection to Hitler's gold, well, my convictions grew that there was summat goin' on. I could never be sure, but I always did wonder.

Never got the courage to go dig up the beach or anything to see if I couldn't find something."

The recording ended there and Quinten's heart pounded. More proof.

Maybe the German Navy had declassified military records from the war that he could look up to see the cargo manifest for U-262?

Some World War II military buff had a whole website dedicated to German U-boats in the North Atlantic that he'd linked to the archival records from the German Navy.

After thirty minutes of searching, Quinten found the right manifest. He started to scan it. Crew rations. Extra diesel. Tanks of oil. Gas masks. Shovels. Pick axes. And one crate which had neither a contents description nor dimensions listed.

Hmmm...

What had the sub's orders been?

Looked like the orders had been sealed, so none of the

crew knew what the actual mission was.

He brought up the crew manifest. There was an M. Gryberg listed. Had that actually been Andrzej, aboard to carry out a secret Allied mission? The one that it referenced in his file? Looked like the dates matched.

The jangle of the bell at the door cut through his thoughts and he shut the laptop. Good. More customers. Or Nicky? He hoped it was Nicky.

He stepped into the shop, a grin on his face. But he ran right into Elliot.

Quinten took a step back.

Elliot crossed his arms. "You haven't given me or the lawyer any answer yet."

Quinten averted his eyes, grabbed a soft cloth from under the counter and began to polish an already-shiny oboe.

"Quinten." Elliot's voice held a note of exasperation. "You can't keep procrastinating. You need to give me an answer."

Quinten just kept polishing.

"Your avoidance of the situation isn't going to make it go away," he continued, as if Quinten had acknowledged him.

"And your pushing me into a corner about it isn't going to make me decide any faster," Quinten replied, making every effort to keep his voice calm. "It's only been a few hours since I learned about your offer."

"Look, you know how much this business means to me."

Quinten's head whipped up. His eyes narrowed. "No," he said through clenched teeth, "I don't know that. Because you were never around. You never even once paid attention to Grandma Viv or anything to do with this business," he spread his arms wide, "until now. When it suits you. When it fits in with your agenda and your—"

"Go on, say it. I want to hear it from you." Elliot tapped his foot. "I dare you."

Quinten's mouth snapped shut. He'd already revealed too much of himself, of his real thoughts and feelings. His hands clenched at his sides.

Sometimes he let his stubbornness get in the way of his ability to self-protect. He sighed. "Listen, I—the last thing I want to do is argue with family. We should all just get along."

"Why, when we fight so well?"

A chuckle escaped Quinten and he rubbed a hand across his jaw but kept his gaze averted. "I just need...more time."

"Fine," Elliot said and turned to the door. "You have forty-eight hours. Or else the business is all mine."

NICKY SAT ON the deck of the Landmark Oyster House on Sunday afternoon. She picked up her last oyster and drowned it in sauce before she popped it into her mouth.

She wished Quinten was here right now. He'd probably have some great brainstorming suggestions about that piece of sheet music supposedly owned by Bormann.

Where could they look for it? Hmmm. If Bormann had something to do with it, then perhaps she should do a bit of research on the man. She ordered another iced tea and pulled up her web browser. Time to settle in for some research.

An hour and a half later, after reading through several articles and resources about Bormann, Nicky stretched and yawned. She'd found some good background stuff. Enough for now.

She bookmarked it all and looked up from her phone. Hmmm. Quinten had said Viv had loved music. All kinds.

...Wait a minute. He'd also said Viv had a huge collection of sheet music. Some of which he'd saved.

If they started there, maybe that would spark some sort of inspiration?

She picked up her phone and dialed.

"QUINTEN? SORRY, HOPE I haven't interrupted you in the middle of something important."

"Just about to close up shop for the day. Had a chat with Elliot. He's gone now, though."

"I was thinking about the sheet music, that we could brainstorm some things together." She sounded a bit breathless and excited.

"Oh?" He felt a tingle go up his spine. Would she ever sound like that over...other things...if he suggested them?

He cleared his throat. Forced his mind back to the conversation.

"Yes," Nicky continued. "I was thinking that you said Viv had a pretty big collection of sheet music. What if we meet up in say, twenty minutes, if that works for you, and start going through it?"

"That would work," he replied, as warmth washed through him. She wanted to spend time with him. She wanted his help. She appreciated his actions toward her.

"Great! See you then," Nicky said and hung up.

He whistled a few notes to himself as he put his phone away. He had to take out the recycling. Today was Sunday. He checked his watch—the recycling truck was due in about an hour to come pick it up.

He headed to the foyer, picked up the three clear blue plastic bulging bags of recycling and put them out by the curb.

TWENTY MINUTES LATER, Nicky walked into the shop. As she closed the screen door, the chatter of tourists drifted in behind her.

Quinten was cutting a square of wrapping paper. Must be that gift for his cousin's daughter. He was so thoughtful.

Though she tried to avoid it, her gaze traveled over him as she walked toward him, a grin on her face.

Hmmm. That yellow T-shirt he wore looked really good on him. Something about the pale shade brought out the highlights in his hair. And accented his chest.

He looked up from the bag of jelly beans he'd just finished wrapping, his expression happy. "Hi."

"Hey," she replied. Her heart pounded and she fluffed her bangs. She was leaving Tuesday—the day after tomorrow. She couldn't get carried away.

"The sheet music stockpile is in my living room. Over this way." He led the way to a door that was at the end of a short hallway near the entrance of the house.

The rumble of an occasional passing car sounded in the background.

He opened the door and Nicky felt his hand brush hers accidentally as he held the door open for her. She wished he'd keep his hand there.

Because she wanted to stand in the doorway with him all day. A longing filled her. She didn't want to leave. She wanted to stay. To spend more time with him. To get to know him better. To have him show his true self to her. And to share her true self fully with him.

But she walked through the doorway instead. She'd need to go; it was inevitable. The story was getting closer and closer to being finished, after all.

"WHAT'S WRONG?" QUINTEN touched her shoulder.

"I..." Her eyes widened and for a second, he saw a look of...panic? on her face.

Quinten's heart stuttered as a surge of protectiveness swept through him. He wanted to help her, take care of whatever it was that was bothering her. Fix it for her. Make it better.

Her eyes darted to and then away from his before she spoke. "I really like this place and don't want to leave." She shifted her weight. "And, your noticing my sadness about that, well," she met his gaze, "I really appreciate it." She bit her lip. "Everyone else—and by that. I mean men I've been involved with—wouldn't have wanted to listen to how I felt.

That would've meant they might've had to talk about how *they* felt too. They found it easier to avoid hard conversations and lie about what they thought."

She looked at him for a brief second from under her lashes as pink spread across her cheeks. She put a hand to her mouth.

He squeezed her shoulder. "It's okay," Quinten whispered. "People have said I'm easy to talk to. I think it's because I like to listen. Somehow, it's very easy to just listen. So I do." He ducked his head and chuckled. "Guess it comes naturally. Sort of always has."

What he didn't add was how his listening to others made it easier for him to not have to share his own thoughts and feelings and fears with anyone.

"What about you?" Nicky asked. "How's it going with the business?"

Quinten's eyes darted to and away from her face. He shrugged a shoulder. "A bit stressful."

"That good, huh?" Nicky nudged him. "I think I saw Elliot up the street as I headed over here."

Quinten rubbed the back of his neck. "Probably did."

"Well," Nicky said, "I'm not exactly a student of human nature, but I've lived a bit of life." She paused and studied him. "And I'd say..." She paused again, "maybe you're afraid," her voice softened, "that if you lose this business, you'll lose your grandmother, her memory, and all of the love and legacy that she gave, that she put into this business. But the truth is, Quinten," Nicky put a hand on his arm, "her love for you will still be in your heart, no matter what happens to the business. You're just hurting yourself if you think otherwise." She searched his gaze.

He tensed and felt his defenses slide into place. Why did she act like she wanted him to say something? Far better to keep his mouth shut and not share more details than other people absolutely needed to know.

Because otherwise, it just put you in danger. Of being analyzed. Of being criticized. Of being judged—and thus, declared not good enough.

"I know you can figure it out."

Quinten shifted his weight.

"You'll think of something."

He took a breath. She was trying to help him. Understand him. Be there for him. "Thank you," he managed at last.

He studied the floor. By not saying more than what others needed to know, he could stay safe. He could stay in control. Of how people saw him. Of how he saw himself. Of his vulnerabilities. Because if he didn't show any vulnerabilities to the world, to anyone else, then he wouldn't get hurt.

He looked up again. His heart jumped into his throat at the expression on Nicky's face. She looked so...sweet. With her face turned toward him like that. So willing to share, to be vulnerable.

He swallowed hard. He could *show* her what he felt. His gaze flicked to her mouth. Raspberries. If he leaned forward, he could finally taste her lips and—

"SO WHERE'S THAT piano again?" Nicky backed up a step.

Quinten hadn't actually responded to her last statements, had he?

She tried to ignore the clench of anxiety in her chest. He'd only shrugged and nodded. Hadn't actually told her how he was feeling. She swallowed. Just like Ben.

A flutter of panic filled her as she glanced at Quinten. What was she doing? She couldn't let her guard down; she couldn't get involved.

"Oh, um," Quinten cleared his throat. "Just, uh, to the left, by the window."

She forced aside her tumbled emotions and turned to the window.

"Elliot's bought it and had me do a last tune-up. He's scheduled to have the piano movers come to take it to his place on Monday. It was Grandma Viv's. She always told me it was special."

Nicky's fingertips brushed the glossy wood as it shone in the afternoon sunlight. Would Quinten's skin feel as smooth?

She forced her mind back to reality. "You have a few pieces of sheet music here." She waved a hand at the books of sheet music that lined the music rest.

"Those are all mine. I've picked them over the years. My grandmother's collection is here." He crossed to a small shelf right next to the piano and pulled out a thick stack, blew off the dust and set it atop the piano. "I've done a fair bit of culling. She'd owned things that I already had copies of. I didn't feel the need to keep it all, so I've recycled all the duplicates."

Nicky scanned the titles. "Bach. Handel. Schubert. Looks like she liked her German composers."

"Always did," Quinten said thoughtfully. "Maybe now we know why?"

HE SHOOK HIS head. "But that's kind of terrible, since my grandfather was a wonderful man, and she loved him very much. How could you have room in your heart to love more than one person at a time?"

Nicky rubbed at a nonexistent spot on the flawless surface of the wood and then took a seat at the piano bench. She ran her fingers across the keyboard, careful to avoid his eyes.

He shuffled through the papers and cleared his throat, "I guess we're looking for German composers then?"

"Yep. That makes the most sense, since that article we read earlier didn't mention what the piece of music was called."

"We have to remember, while it said Bormann had the piece of music, he didn't actually compose it."

"Okay," Nicky said.

The beep of a large vehicle backing up pierced the silence. Sounded like the recycling trucks were on his block.

"So what are we looking for?"

"Pretty much anything that looks kind of unusual."

"Wait," Nicky said. "I don't know why I didn't think of this before, but if I look up Bormann and coded sheet music, I bet I could find out what it's called."

"Good point," Quinten said, as Nicky pulled out her phone. "There must be a copy of that sheet music floating around on the internet."

After a minute, she said, "Okay, I think I have something here." She turned the phone toward him. "Looks like, no, Bormann didn't write the music himself. He just marked up a copy of it."

The beep of the recycling truck came closer. Quinten noticed its outline through the kitchen window.

Nicky angled the phone so he could see it better. A whiff of her vanilla perfume floated to him. "You're right. It looks like the composer was named Gottfried Federlein." He paused. "Appears he was a German-American. Interesting."

"And the piece that was used looks like it was the second movement in—"

"Marsch Impromptu," Quinten finished. His eyes widened and he jumped up. "I threw it out."

"What?" Nicky's head shot up.

"I threw it out." Quinten crossed the kitchen at a jog. He saw the recycling truck pulling up to the curb outside his house. "It's gone. Unless we act now."

QUINTEN RACED TO the screen door at the front of the shop, Nicky right behind him.

The recycling truck parked. Its side door was wide open. One of the workers got out.

Quinten shoved through the screen door. "Hey!"

The worker walked toward the bags of recycling.

Quinten pounded down the steps, Nicky close behind. The screen door shut with a bang.

"Wait!" Quinten shouted.

The worker glanced Quinten's way as he leaned down to pick up the first bag of recycling.

Quinten jogged over to the man. "Don't touch that one."

The man stopped and his head jerked up. "What's the matter? Got a load of gold in here you changed your mind about?"

"No, more valuable," Nicky called out as she darted past Quinten and snatched up the first blue bag.

"Okay, okay." The man held up his hands. "Don't get yourselves in a twist."

Nicky's heart pounded as she clutched the bag to her chest and looked over at Quinten. His hair was disheveled and he was slightly out of breath.

So was she. She watched him rake a hand through his hair, which caused his bicep to flex. Her pulse sped up as she watched the motion.

His blue-gray eyes blazed as he slid his gaze to hers. For a second, she couldn't remember to breathe, couldn't remember anything except the way his eyes held hers. A shiver went up her spine.

"Got anything else?"

"What?" Quinten tore his gaze away from Nicky. "Oh." He rubbed the back of his neck. "Uh...no. Just, um, these two bags, thanks."

"Right." The worker shook his head, threw the two bags in the truck, and got back inside. With a lurch, the truck pulled from the curb and lumbered on to the next house.

Quinten closed the space between them with a couple of strides. "That was close," he said. He still sounded a little breathless. "But we did it."

Nicky's pulse jumped and she just nodded, unable to trust herself to say anything. She caught a whiff of the clean laundry scent that clung to his soft cotton T-shirt.

She held out the bag to him.

"No," he said, his voice gentle, "you take it." Something in his stance and the tone of his voice suddenly reminded Nicky of that moment when they'd first met. How he'd radiated that quiet strength. That solidness. Her heart hitched.

"We can sort through it in the house," he continued. "Don't want anything to blow away in this wind."

Nicky nodded again and they headed back inside.

A few minutes later, a rather crumpled piece of sheet music lay between them on the kitchen table.

"Wow," Nicky laughed. "Your grandmother was pretty clever."

"How's that?"

"I just realized. That very first line of the riddle is *The secretary marches*. "Marsch Impromptu." The piece of sheet music is literally a march."

"You're right."

"The more I find out about her, the more I realize just how, well, vivacious she must've been."

Quinten's gaze softened. "She was, that. I remember how she'd insist on swimming at the wharf on the very first day of summer. No matter if the water was freezing."

Nicky grinned. "Wow. That takes guts."

"Good for the soul, she always said, with that little gleam in her eyes."

"I did something like that one time."

"Really?" Quinten leaned forward.

"Yep." Nicky laughed. "I'm from Michigan originally, and I jumped in a lake in December on a dare in high school."

"In high school I was pretty awkward. Never did any dares."

"No? They bring something out in you... At least they did for me."

"Sounds like you two would've gotten along great," Quinten replied, a light in his eyes.

"Thanks. I think maybe we would have..." A warmth curled through Nicky's chest.

"She was always doing things like that. Until she got dementia." His face fell.

"I'm sorry," Nicky said. She placed a hand on his arm.

Quinten looked from her hand on his arm to her face. "Thanks." He paused, then said softly, "It was really hard. I never expected to be in that position this early in my life."

"What do you mean?" Nicky saw a flash of vulnerability in his eyes as he looked at her and then away.

He took a breath. "My mom left when I was a toddler. And my dad died when I was in my mid-twenties. So I spent a lot of time caring for my grandmother by myself." He cleared his throat and glanced at her. "Anyway."

Nicky saw the guardedness come back into his expression. She took her hand from his arm and turned her attention back to the sheet music. "It looks pretty normal to me."

"That's the point," Quinten said. "To someone with no musical training, it would look normal."

Nicky's eyes widened. "So the idea is..."

"That this piece of sheet music is hiding something."

"The question is, what?" Nicky tapped a finger against her chin and studied the page. "Well, where should we look first?"

Quinten studied the piece of sheet music.

She couldn't help but notice the way that the sun caught the streaks of gold in his sandy hair. It looked soft. Touchable. What would it feel like to run her fingers through it and—

"Maybe the best place to start is here. Look at this." Quinten pointed to words on the page.

"What is it? Those are just the lyrics to the song."

"No," Quinten said. "Look again."

```
Edelweiss grows at the Black Forest
Where Matthias plays the chords
Northwest of the crown.
```

"It's another code," Nicky murmured.

"Exactly." A gleam came into Quinten's eyes and Nicky's pulse jumped in her throat.

"Just like the microdot riddle," she whispered.

"It must be."

"So who's the writer?" Nicky asked.

"Well, Bormann. Question is, how do we figure out what it really means?"

"Let's work backwards," Nicky suggested. "The last line, *northwest of the crown*. Northwest is a direction."

"Well," Quinten mused. "That fisherman did say U-262 was headed northwest."

"Fisherman?"

"I found a sound byte on the Island Voices database," Quinten said. "He recounted a story about seeing that U-boat in the waters near North Cape and some Germans on the beach there in May of '43."

"Okay. As for crown," Nicky said, "could that mean royalty?"

"I think you're right. In fact, princes wear crowns."

"And this is Prince Edward Island, after all." Nicky grinned.

"That fits perfectly."

"Plus," Nicky said, "if Andrzej was on U-262, which we know from the crew manifest you told me you found, then it's more than likely the treasure was on that sub."

"Right," Quinten said.

"So then the second line, what do you think about that?"

"Not sure."

"Matthias..." Nicky murmured. "Why does that name seem kind of familiar?"

Quinten's brow furrowed and for a second neither of them said anything. "Oh!" He looked at her. "Remember?"

"What?"

"His file. Andrzej's. Can you pull it up?"

Nicky did.

Quinten pointed to the lines. "See? Alias: Matthias Grynberg."

Nicky gasped. "And Matthias is the name used in the second line here, so that fits. But what does it mean, when it says *plays the chords*?"

Quinten shook his head. "No idea."

Just then, Nicky's phone beeped. She glanced at the notification. "Another email from the National Archives."

"Open it," Quinten said. "It might help us out here."

Nicky tapped the screen.

Dear Ms. Stendahl,

Thank you for your further inquiry into the traffic from Agent Andrzej Gobell. The fee has been received. The pertaining document has been obtained. The bulk of Gobell's traffic that Vivian Robinson deciphered was in 1943. The first part has been digitized.

However, we are still working to scan and upload the second and third parts for that timeframe.

As the volume is quite substantial, this may take some time. You will be notified when the second and third parts are completed. But I do hope that this first portion meets your needs.

Regards,
Greg Scott
Research Curator
National Archives

Nicky opened the attachment, turned the phone to Quinten, and they read together.

<u>F O R M 6. B)</u>

<u>C.C. AGENT TRAFFIC</u>
<u>AGENT:</u> OAK
<u>COUNTRY SECTION:</u> X
<u>DECIPHERED BY:</u> ROBINSON, V.F. (File #5234)

INITIAL DROP SUCCESSFUL LOCATION AT SAFE HOUSE
ESTABLISHED ASH AND MAPLE HAVE MADE CONTACT
MORE ARMS ARE NEEDED WILL WAIT FOR NEXT MOON
PERIOD TO SEND NEW DROP LOCATION WILL BEGIN
INQUIRY INTO OPERATION ELSTER

OPERATION ELSTER AS COVER FOR OPERATION EDEL-
WEISS CONFIRMED. USE OF STOLEN FUNDS TO CREATE

```
4R CONFIRMED. PLAN FOR TRANSPORT AND DEPOSIT OF
CACHE OF STOLEN GOLD AND DIAMONDS CONFIRMED G &
D USED AS FUNDING FOR CREATION OF FOURTH REICH
CONFIRMED CACHE LOCATION UNCONFIRMED PLAN AND
FUNDING INITIATED BY BORMANN

PREPARING TO ABORT OPERATION EDELWEISS AS OR-
DERED AND RETRIEVE STOLEN FUNDS CACHE BEFORE
TRANSPORT ACROSS NORTH ATLANTIC ACCESS TO U-
BOAT GAINED ASH AND MAPLE TO ACCOMPANY

UNABLE TO RETRIEVE CACHE AND DISMANTLE STOLEN
FUNDING SOURCE ASH AND MAPLE TAKEN WILL FOLLOW
SECOND ATTEMPT AS ORDERED ONBOARD U262 DEPART
FIRST MOON PERIOD IN MAY

AFTER U-BOAT MISSION WILL PROCEED WITH ORDERS
TO SABOTAGE REMAINING ELEMENTS OF FOURTH REICH
CREATION BY BORMANN UPON ARRIVAL BACK IN BERLIN
BORMANN DRAFTED CODED MESSAGE INTO MARSCH IM-
PROMPTU TO SECURE LOCATION OF GOLD AND DIAMONDS
HAVE BEEN PLACED IN CHARGE OF U262 CARGO
```

Nicky looked up from the screen and over at Quinten.

"Wow," Quinten whispered. "I feel like I'm there."

"I have goosebumps," Nicky whispered back.

There was a moment of silence.

"This is how you feel, isn't it, when you're writing." A mixture of awe and seriousness came onto Quinten's face as he looked at her. In that second, Nicky realized, he got it. He understood exactly what she meant. He understood *her*. Emotion swelled in her chest.

"So, what do you think these transmissions mean in relation to the second line of the riddle?" Quinten asked.

Nicky tapped a fingernail against her chin. "Well, we know that Matthias was Andrzej's alias."

"And Bormann was the one who wrote these lines..." Quinten's brow furrowed. "Plays the chords." He looked up suddenly and snapped his fingers. "It's like, pulling strings. I bet it means Andrzej was in charge."

"That makes sense. Bormann must have trusted Andrzej to carry out his orders. And since this is a piece of sheet music, Bormann decided to cloak it in a musical reference."

"Exactly. Because see?" Quinten pointed to the phrase. "Andrzej says here he's been placed in charge of the cargo."

"Which contained the treasure," Nicky said. "So then what about the very first line? *Edelweiss grows at the Black Forest.*" She frowned.

"Black forest seems very specific," Quinten mused. "Do you think that it's supposed to represent an actual place or—"

"A meeting point." Nicky scrambled for her purse.

"What?"

Nicky dug out her phone. "I got curious and did a bit of research on Bormann earlier." She scrolled through her bookmarks. "It's here somewhere..."

Quinten leaned closer and Nicky could smell the citrusy scent of his cologne.

"Here it is." She skimmed it. "See? It says here that he headed some sort of secret Nazi meeting in the Black Forest in early 1943."

He studied the screen. "You're right. And according to these transmissions, Andrzej said Edelweiss is the name of Bormann's operation."

"So this line is Bormann's way of signing his name to this project, and this treasure, too. He's essentially saying that he created Operation Edelweiss at this Black Forest meeting."

"That makes total sense," Quinten said.

Her heart beat a little faster at Quinten's nearness and she couldn't help the heat that crept onto her cheeks. She liked this, she realized.

Being with Quinten, helping him to work out these riddles, it made her feel...alive in a way she'd never experienced before.

But it wouldn't last. It couldn't last. Because she was only here for the story.

With an effort, she turned her attention back to the riddle.

"So," Quinten said, as he got up to pace, "it seems like Andrzej was ordered to stop Edelweiss from going forward."

"And prevent the creation of the Fourth Reich," Nicky said. "Since the sub with the treasure was headed to P.E.I."

"And he went undercover as a crewman on the U-boat to try to prevent the treasure from being moved," Quinten said.

"And Viv knew all about it."

"So why," Quinten rubbed a hand across his chin and Nicky could see the flecks of gold in his stubble, "did she end up with this piece of sheet music that Bormann encoded?"

NICKY'S EYES WIDENED. "Because she was the one reading Andrzej's traffic."

"Andrzej probably knew that. Maybe he gave it to her?"

"And she knew that it was encoded," Nicky said.

"So then she wrote the first riddle," Quinten said.

"Because she knew what was going on and wanted to help," Nicky finished.

Quinten suddenly stopped pacing. "You still have the riddle from the microdot?"

Nicky pulled out the scrap of paper.

He examined it. "So she wrote this." His eyes raced over the lines. "But what if it has multiple meanings?"

Nicky frowned. "What're you saying?"

Quinten shook his head. "Not multiple meanings. I meant... Okay." He slowly exhaled. "Look at the third line: *the pianist's journey*. We know Andrzej was an actual pianist."

"Yep."

"But," Quinten held up a finger, "what if it meant another type of journey, too?"

"To P.E.I.?"

"No."

Nicky gasped. "He was a pianist, so you're saying we should take a musical journey. Play the song."

"Exactly."

"You have plenty of pianos." Nicky got up and headed to the door that led to the showroom. "Let's pick one."

"Well, that Yamaha has a nice tone." Quinten crossed over to it. "I have an antique Steinway in the back I'm refitting." He looked around the showroom. "But Grandma Viv loved to play on her Princess Royal—Oh."

"What?"

"Princess Royal..." Quinten said slowly. "I think maybe there was more than one reason Viv loved that piano."

Nicky raised her eyebrows.

"The dowry was from a Polish princess," Quinten said.

"So you think the name of the piano is significant?"

"It's not a coincidence that the dowry's from royalty—a princess, in fact—and that the name of Viv's piano is Princess Royal."

"So you're saying...?"

"We need to play the song on *her* piano."

"Then let's—"

Just then there was a knock at the door. Quinten glanced at Nicky and made a wry face. "'Scuse me just a sec."

"Sure," Nicky said. She couldn't help admiring his retreating form as he walked toward the door. She caught sight of a gaggle of tourists farther down the street.

Two big burly men stood on the porch. Quinten stepped outside to join them. Snatches of conversation drifted to Nicky.

"...take it Monday."

"A bit of...mixed-up schedule."

"...over this way." Quinten opened the screen door, followed by the two men with *MacBeth Bros. Moving* written across their navy blue polo shirts.

"Hi, how are yah?" one of the men said to Nicky.

"'Lo," the other one said.

"Hi there," she replied but hid a smile at their Maritime accents. She couldn't help but feel a bit of a thrill. This place was so much better than the city.

"So here it is, boys. But can you give us just a second? We were going to play one last song."

"Sorry, Quinten. We'll be loading it right away. On a bit of a tight schedule. You said it goes to Elliot's, yeah?"

Quinten nodded.

Nicky's stomach dipped and she started to open her mouth. Wasn't he going to put up more of a fight? Argue with them that it would only take a second? But she bit the inside of her cheek. It wasn't her place to say anything.

Quinten's gaze slid to hers as the movers started to load up the instrument.

Just then, the gaggle of tourists walked up onto the porch. One of them asked Quinten a question.

There wasn't anything she could do about the movers taking the piano and she didn't want to get in their way.

"Quinten," she said in an undertone as she approached him during a lull in the conversation. "I'm gonna head back to my hotel room to finish up my story."

"Okay." Was that a flicker of disappointment on his face? Or just the light shifting in the shade from the apple tree outside the window?

She clenched her jaw. Of course, she couldn't tell what he was actually feeling. He was too stoic for that. And that was why she had to protect her heart and stay away from him.

Well, she'd just go write up what she'd seen here and add it in to the final draft of her story.

She took a breath. It was better this way. She needed to concentrate, to get away from being distracted by Quinten's presence...

She picked up her purse. "But we can wrap things up here first thing tomorrow?"

"Sure."

EARLY MONDAY MORNING, Nicky hit save for the final time

on her Word document.

Satisfaction curled her lips upward. Done with the story. But a slice of disappointment edged its way into her mind. She'd had to modify it a bit. She'd had to take out the treasure angle, now that they'd hit a dead end.

She sighed. That would've been such a great secondary thread. But maybe she could file that away for a future issue? Maybe even a book? She had enough information about it, that was for sure.

But all in all, she'd done what her editor had asked. She'd completed the story about Viv. Almost a week ahead of deadline. She grinned. She'd send it off here in a second.

Then she'd need to stop by Quinten's to...say goodbye. A knot formed in her stomach.

A beep from her phone interrupted her thoughts. She pulled it out.

Some sort of email from Susan. Probably wanting to know the status of the story.

Well, she'd have good news for her. Though Nicky had sent her an update a couple of days ago. What if the word count had changed?

Or maybe she wanted to run the piece in a different issue?

Nicky opened the message.

From: susanolmsted@historicalwoman.com
To: nicky.stendahl@gmail.com
Sent: Mon Oct 11, 8:12 a.m.

Dear Nicky,

Nicky frowned. Susan never started her emails like this.

I know you're busy with the assignment, so I'm sorry to interrupt you with a message. But unfortunately, as the Historical Woman magazine is owned by Umbrella Group—

That was the same company that owned *Ivory* magazine,

who *still* hadn't paid her. She turned her eyes back toward the email and kept reading.

—you will find attached to this message an official affidavit for a libel suit against you.

Nicky's hand started to tremble.

Your social media post to Ivory Magazine on Thursday, October 7, indicates to our lawyers your unhappiness and dissatisfaction with our payment methods. Furthermore, your implication that said publication, which also takes into account Umbrella Group, does not treat its writers with timely and professional financial dealings, is hereby considered libelous and further action will be taken.

As per the work-for-hire contract you have signed, though you no longer own the rights to your work, you are liable for all attorney fees and potential court costs incurred by said situation.

Additionally, as per your contract, your current story will not be run and you will not be paid.

I await your response.

Susan Olmsted
Editor-in-Chief
The Historical Woman Magazine

Nicky wiped her sweaty palms on her ripped jeans and reread the email. Once. Twice. And a third time, as anxiety and panic clawed up her throat.

THE SCREEN DOOR opened and Quinten grinned. "Nicky. You're right on time. Come on in. I know that the piano's not here now. But we'll think of some way to..."

He saw sadness flicker across her gaze but she gave him a smile anyway. "What's wrong?" Quinten touched her arm

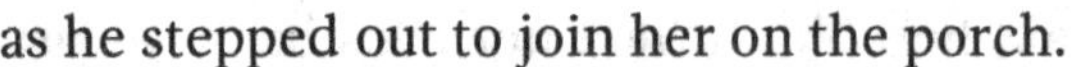

as he stepped out to join her on the porch.

"There isn't really anything else to think of." Nicky rolled a strand of hair between her fingers. "We couldn't play the song. And I have..." she bit her lip, "some bad news."

Chapter Eight

ICKY TOOK A jagged breath. "I'm being sued for libel."

Quinten's brows shot up.

Nicky shoved her hands in her hair. Wasn't he going to say anything to that?

She suppressed a tremble in her tone when she added, "I'm actually pretty freaked out about this whole thing." Relief filled her at being able to share her anxiety. "Has anything this unnerving happened to you?"

"Not exactly, no..." He trailed off and averted his eyes.

Worry nudged at her. Wasn't he going to say more? But she forced down the thought. He probably had his reasons. Right?

"What happened?" he asked.

She rubbed her forehead and said, "I made a mistake on social media. I was doing a bit of, uh, venting. It got out of hand."

"Okay."

"A periodical I wrote for awhile back, *Ivory* magazine, was behind on their payment to me. Beyond the contracted pay period." She began to pace. "So I posted a query, naming that magazine specifically, about how I wondered about my payment being late. They took it, apparently, as libelous. Decided to sue me for it."

"Mmmm," Quinten said.

"The thing is—" Nicky bit a hangnail "—that magazine and the *Historical Woman* are owned by the same parent company. Because of all that, my story on Viv has been axed."

Quinten's jaw tightened, but still he said nothing.

A flutter of panic raced through her. He wasn't responding to her.

"Since I don't have liability insurance," Nicky shifted her weight from one foot to the other, "I have to figure out a way to fork over money for lawyer fees and court costs related to that." She glanced at Quinten and twirled a strand of hair around her finger. "For something I don't even own anymore."

Quinten pressed his lips together and remained quiet.

The gnawing worry mixed with disappointment only grew inside her. Why wasn't he saying anything? "So I'll need to go back to New York and deal with this."

"Right now?" Quinten asked. He shifted his weight. It seemed like he wanted to say something else. And yet...

"I changed my flight to today, yes." Nicky glanced at him. She took a breath around the band of anxiety that had begun to tighten in her chest.

He shoved his hands in his pockets.

"It's just that, well..." Nicky fiddled with a strand of hair again, then tucked it behind her ear. She glanced at him and then glanced away. Cleared her throat. "It seems like I've been disappointed," she whispered, "so many times. After I moved to New York, I was so hopeful. Got that job with Maggie at her jewelry company. But that went up in flames. Then I drifted around pretty aimlessly for awhile. But when I got my journalism certificate, I was so excited. I'd finally found something that I love to do, something that I'm good at. And things were going so well, too. I'd begun to see my writing dreams come to life. But now?" She bit her lip. "I could lose that. All because of some tiny little thing I did that I thought had no importance. I feel like I messed everything up. I feel like if I had only done things a tiny bit differently, then I wouldn't be—"

Nicky's eyelids trembled as she closed her eyes. She took a breath and opened them again. "What I'm trying to say is this story is really special to me. Your grandmother is special to me. She had perseverance, persistence. She wasn't afraid to go out there and do what had to be done at such a dark time; she kept going despite fear, despite disappointment." Nicky took a shaky breath. "No one had any idea when or how the war would end. But to keep going in the face of all that? That takes a kind of strength, a kind of courage, that I'm not sure that I really have. That's why I admire your grandmother, that's why this story is so important to me. That's why I feel so drawn to her. Inspired by her."

Nicky stopped talking and shoved her hands in her pockets. She tucked her chin to her chest and studied the floorboards of the old porch. Paint had peeled off in some places, which exposed the bare, naked wood beneath. The only sound was the tinkle of wind chimes from a house up the street, and the rustle of leaves in the wind.

She'd done it again. She'd just made herself vulnerable, put herself and her emotions on the line...

Quinten swallowed.

...And he still wasn't saying anything in response. He wasn't going to, was he? The band of anxiety squeezed her chest tighter as it mixed with slivers of hurt and disappointment.

Who was she kidding? She'd been stupid to allow herself to start to feel anything for him.

Because if he didn't tell her how he was feeling or what he was thinking now, if they ever got involved, he wouldn't tell her how he felt or what he thought later, with really important situations and decisions that could impact herself and her own life. Just like Ben.

She tried to take a calming breath. Maybe Quinten just wasn't responding to her for his own reasons? Oh no. Full-blown panic hit. No. She *did* know the reasons. Very clearly. He was withholding from her. On purpose. He didn't have the capacity to be vulnerable. When it counted.

When she'd shown so much of her own vulnerabilities to him, the least he could do was reciprocate. Yes. He was purposely withholding what he really felt. What he really thought. Just like Ben had. And withholding was basically a lie of omission.

And then one lie would lead to another and another... Until she wouldn't ever be able to trust Quinten to tell her what was going on inside his head.

Her heart pounded. Because if Quinten had his guard up now, he obviously didn't trust her. And that was no foundation to build anything on.

The silence stretched on.

Nicky's lips quivered despite her best efforts. She tugged on the ends of her hair in frustration. If only he'd say something to her. If only he'd actually voice his opinion.

What would happen if they ever started a relationship? Not that they had. And now they probably never would. The hurt settled deeper. A relationship should be a two-way street—both people had to be willing to share equally.

"Why aren't you *saying* anything?" The question burst from her.

Quinten's head snapped up and his eyes widened.

"Like right now. About your grandmother. About what I just shared."

QUINTEN PRESSED HIS lips together. She wanted an answer. Deserved one. But somehow, watching her be that vulnerable with him just stirred up all his own pain.

He crossed his arms.

He didn't deserve to have the story pulled out of him like this. All the ways he'd thought, wished, hoped that if only he'd taken better care of Grandma Viv then things...would somehow have been different between him and his father.

Because then he wouldn't be afraid to say how he really felt. Wouldn't be afraid to speak his truth. Wouldn't be afraid of being judged or criticized or told he wasn't good enough.

He shouldn't have to tell her that like this. Not when they were basically just friends. She hardly knew anything about him. And whose fault was that? His. He didn't have her courage. He didn't have her strength.

He tightened his jaw. He should be able to tell her when—*if*—they ever became closer. He had hoped they might've... Pain pinched in his chest. But now that she was leaving, that had no chance of happening.

He shouldn't have to tell someone he knew so little about the pain that he guarded so closely in his heart. He hated that. He hated being pried open like a nut or prodded like a turtle who had pulled its head into its shell.

It was none of her damn business. It was none of anyone's business what he'd gone through.

He felt the old pain bubble up into his throat, almost close off his airway, as he tried to speak.

Because that's what love did; it caused pain.

He swallowed hard. So he couldn't let Nicky get to him like this. He couldn't let anyone affect him like this. It was too risky, too dangerous, too vulnerable for people to know his secrets, to know his pain. He had to keep people away. He had to push them out to a safe, comfortable distance. He had to shut them all out.

Because if he let them in, he'd drown. He'd suffocate. He wouldn't be able to function because he wouldn't be able to know what was real, what was true, how to trust or who to trust...

Because his father—he pushed the thought away but still it intruded—hadn't loved him. He'd never said "I love you" to Quinten, so Quinten must not be very lovable. Had never praised him, so he must've never done much right.

His dad took out his own pain, his own hurt, his own suffering about his wife leaving them, on Quinten. He'd been too trapped in his own personal hell, too stuck in his own unhappiness, to show his own son any real affection.

Quinten dragged his thoughts away from that, forced himself to focus on the present. Forced his mouth to move.

"SHE HAD DEMENTIA, all right? She didn't know who anyone

was. Least of all me. I'd come in and she wouldn't recognize me. Wouldn't—" He broke off and blinked rapidly. "It was hard. Really hard."

He crossed his arms over his chest and the flash of hurt in his blue-gray eyes as he turned his head away from her brought to mind a little boy whose parents had gone missing.

She reached out to place a hand on his arm. "I'm sorry. I didn't—"

He flinched away from her. "Never mind," he said far too quickly.

She pulled her hand back as if burned. Her gaze darkened.

He had too many fears and too many demons in his own heart and his own mind for her to waste any more time trying to understand him, trying to reassure him, trying to help him.

He was too damn stoic for that. She held back angry tears. He wouldn't let her in. He wouldn't let her help him. He just had too many walls up to allow her to be close to him. He was too damn afraid to do that. Too much like Ben.

She wasn't going to do this to herself any longer. She was going to free herself from this whole ridiculous, sorry situation.

She was going to leave.

She glanced at him. His face was averted from hers and he was typing something into his phone.

Sparks of indignation lit her blood. He was exactly like Ben. She'd been stupid to think anything else.

She snatched up her purse. Fine, then. She would stay as cool and stoic as he was.

She slung her purse over her shoulder. "Thank you for your help." She forced the words out in a falsely bright tone. "I appreciate your time. And if there's any chance the story will actually be published, I'll do my journalistic best to attribute the letters and such to you and your family."

A shadow crossed Quinten's face but it passed so quickly Nicky knew it must be a trick of the light.

When he met her gaze, his expression was simply polite, his tone neutral. "Thank you."

She turned and walked down the porch steps.

QUINTEN SWORE UNDER his breath and dropped the curtain as he watched Nicky's rental car turn left and head out of the village.

He hadn't said anything. Again. He bit his lip.

And now she'd taken his heart.

He swore once more. This situation was entirely his fault. His fault. He couldn't fix his relationship with his grandmother. He couldn't fix his relationship with his father. And he couldn't fix this.

He'd tried. He'd thought, back in the restaurant, that maybe he did have the courage, the ability, after all. But no. He couldn't express himself. He couldn't explain how he really felt.

It was like there was some sort of vise around his throat, preventing the words, emotions and feelings from coming out.

He'd just let a woman who'd become pretty damn special to him, walk away—well, drive away—from his life. And he'd stood by and done nothing.

He slammed a fist onto the table.

He'd done *nothing*. Just like all those other times before. When he'd listened to his father's criticisms, or stood by his grandmother's bed in the care home, feeling helpless to do or say anything that would make the situation better.

He took a breath. He needed to calm down. He couldn't go back and undo the past. He needed to move forward.

Well, there was one thing that was still in his control, at least. Finding the will. Or sorting through the rest of those things in the attic anyway. He headed upstairs.

As he worked, he tried to fight off his gloomy thoughts, but failed.

He'd lost Nicky. And he was about to lose his business.

He chewed on a hangnail and surveyed the mess.

He'd go through everything else up in the attic here. It was the best distraction he could find that wouldn't remind him of Nicky.

Except everything reminded him of her.

He forced that thought away. There had to be a ray of hope somewhere...

His phone beeped. He glanced at the notifications. There'd been a donation to his crowdfunding page.

See? Things weren't as bad as he'd thought. He checked the app.

Twenty-five dollars. Well, it was better than zero dollars. He shoved his phone in his pocket and set to work.

NICKY BLINKED BACK tears as she walked out of JFK airport early Monday afternoon. The smell of rain on blacktop only made the scent of ocean air seem that much farther away.

She sighed. How had things ended up this way? No. She wasn't going to give in to self-pity.

It wasn't all bad. After all, she could sell the article to some other publication.

The story. That's what she needed to concentrate on now. Not on Quinten.

She forced an image of him out of her mind. He surely wasn't sparing any last thoughts for her, so why should she bother with thinking about him at all?

She clenched her jaw as she headed to the city bus that would take her back to her apartment.

What if it wasn't even hers anymore? She still didn't have the rent money. Her throat constricted. She only had a week left. And now with this lawsuit hanging over her head...

She winced. It wasn't like she could ask her parents for money. They didn't have much.

She hated to bother her friends. And the bank wouldn't give her a loan because she didn't have regular, stable income.

She swore under her breath and rubbed her temples. It didn't do much to ease the headache forming there.

She blinked back tears as she stepped out of the bus and headed up to her apartment.

She sighed in relief as the key turned in the lock.

But as she started to unpack her carry-on, reality settled in. She'd kept her phone off for the return trip but now she powered it back up.

She also turned on her computer. Time to try to do something about this. There must be some lawyer in this town who did pro bono work? A tiny flicker of hope built in her chest. It was worth a shot.

THREE HOURS LATER, Quinten headed downstairs from the attic for a late lunch.

He paused mid-step. Maybe the reason he hadn't raised any money was because no one had known about the fundraiser.

He headed into the kitchen. Some homemade soup would be good. He reached for the tattered and stained cookbook wedged between a diet tome on one side and his grandmother's recipe box on the other.

Yes... Why hadn't he thought of this before? What if he posted it all over his social media accounts? Put up posters around Victoria—Charlottetown, too—as a way to build awareness of the crowdfunding for his "Save-a-Heritage-Business" campaign?

He pulled out the yellow-and-blue recipe book and flipped to the soup section.

That could work. If he told all his friends here in the village—Brian, Anna, Tate, Gemma, Mabel, Derek, Mrs. MacPhail—they'd pass along the word to their extended circle of friends.

That was something Islanders were excellent at— banding together in a time of crisis to help each other out.

And certainly this village knew how to do that.

He now had less than forty-eight hours. He'd better get started on those posters.

He turned his attention back to food. Hmmm. He had chicken broth. He checked the fridge and walked back to the cookbook. So maybe cream of chicken soup...

He looked in the table of contents, then turned to the recipe page.

What on Earth? This looked like the same type of paper from...Grandma Viv's journal? Still held together along their back edge with ancient glue, from the look of it.

He felt a pang. She'd done that, near the beginning. When the dementia had started to close in on her. Car keys in the freezer. Cereal in the linen closet.

He picked up the bunch of blank pages and riffled through them. But they weren't all blank. There was writing here.

January 20, 1947

If I close my eyes, I can still see him in the hours before he left, that final time...

He stood there in the glow of the streetlight: the whoosh of traffic suddenly seemed very far away. His fingers, gentle on my face; his kiss, tender; his smile, sweet. He pulled a box from his pocket and opened it. "This is the last remaining link I have to my family's heritage, to my history." As he slid the ring on my finger, he whispered, "Keep it safe for me, so that when I come back, we can make our own history—together. I love you."

There will always be a place in my heart for Andrzej, one that no other man could ever fill. But he is dead. I still have the amber ring he gave me on that night; oh, it seems so long ago—almost in another lifetime...

But I shall wear it. I do not have to say from where I obtained it, now do I?

Maybe some day I will find out what happened to the treasure. But I know I must put that part of my life aside, as I need to focus on my life here on the island and on my newborn son.

Quinten swallowed a lump in his throat and turned the page.

July 25, 1948

Oh, how my heart pounded as I saw the postmark. Berlin. June 7, 1943. No return address—of course.

I knew at once who it must have been from.

Five years is a long time for a piece of mail to sit. Though I simply cannot fathom how, he must have smuggled the letter out by courier. Had the courier addressed it afterwards?

I can only think that in all the turmoil since the war's end, it must have been misplaced and finally found its way here. After Wallace and I were married, I did leave this as my forwarding address from New York.

It contained only three things, but I know which one is most precious—his final letter to me.

I will put them all aside for safekeeping; though I know in my heart that I cannot pursue this, as my son and my wonderful piano tuning and restoration business now take up my time and my heart. Perhaps one day I will pass the ring and its secrets along...

Quinten looked up from the words. Three things... The first must be, as Viv said, Andrzej's final letter.

But the second? Oh. Andrzej must've enclosed "Marsch Impromptu" with his letter, which was how she'd ended up with the piece of sheet music.

But what was the third thing? He had no idea. For a second, he wished Nicky were here. His gaze flicked to his phone. What would she think of these entries?

What if he called her? Told her about it and—No. That wouldn't do any good.

He sighed and leafed through the rest of the pages. What was this? He pulled out a brittle yellowed sheet folded in quarters. The edges crumbled as he unfolded it to reveal an enciphered message.

NICKY STARED OUT the window at the darkening New York cityscape after she hung up with the lawyer's office Maggie had put her in touch with.

Their pro bono caseload had been a mile long. But they'd told her they'd put her on their waiting list.

At least it was a step in the right direction. Something she could respond to that email with.

She should have felt happier. She sighed.

All she could think about, though, was a particular shade of blue-gray. One that didn't match the gray tones of the busy city...

The gray sidewalks, the black wrought iron on some of the buildings, the rush and flurry of people, so many people. Too many people.

She sighed. New York. She was tired of it. Tired of its hurry. Of its buzz of activity. Tired of its anonymity. Tired of blending in, of not being seen, of just being another face in the crowd.

Her mind drifted back to Island Chocolates. That very first day, when Mrs. MacPhail had said, *"We're not above sharing tables with strangers here. That's how people make new friends."*

The sound of laughter and the crack of mallets hitting croquet balls on the emerald-green back lawn of the Orient Hotel. The way that strangers had treated her like a friend from the very beginning. The taste of salted caramel chocolates on her tongue...

And Quinten.

His eyes warm, his smile soft. How he looked at her as if he truly appreciated her, as if he really wanted to listen to her, to know her and who she was, what she was... That connection that they'd shared.

She clutched her mug tighter to stop her fingers from trembling. What had she done?

Why was it that she didn't miss things 'til they were gone, until they were too far away to ever be retrieved? She pressed her palm against the window as raindrops slid down the pane.

She wiped a few drops from her cheeks. She was being ridicu—

A sob broke through her resolve and before she knew it, tears streamed down her face. How could she just have walked away like that?

How could she have let her own issues, her own fears, build up to a point that *that* was all she'd seen; *that* was all she'd allowed herself to see, when in reality…?

In reality, she didn't know because she wasn't a mind reader.

In reality, she realized, as a hard knot formed in her throat and was difficult to swallow, she'd never asked him.

Her gaze strayed again to the window, to the walkers, to the raindrops, to the seemingly endless sea of black umbrellas.

She wished it was a different sea—the coast of P.E.I.— that she was looking at.

But she couldn't go back there. Not now. Not when she'd screwed everything up between them. She couldn't go back, either, because she'd made it clear she had nothing more to say to him, and he had nothing more to say to her.

And that was that. What else was there, when there was nothing to do but remember all the mistakes, all the missed opportunities, all the pain—

She exhaled sharply. She was giving in to misery. She needed to think about something else.

So she picked up her Nikon and started going through the images. She paused on the black and white photograph of Viv. But she couldn't concentrate. She kept seeing the wharf in Victoria, the way the leaves had rustled on the trees, that particular quality of October light that was golden, that was beautiful, that was, at its heart, the essence of Prince Edward Island.

She put down her camera and picked up Viv's journal. She'd remembered to return Mabel's box. So why hadn't she remembered to give this little book back to Quinten? She sighed. She'd have to mail it back.

She opened the book and paged through it. There was

that enciphered entry.

She traced a finger along the lines. She'd meant to mention the entry to Quinten. Or at least, try to figure it out herself. But with everything else that had ended up going on, it'd gotten a bit lost in the shuffle. But now...?

She looked again at the arrangement of letters on the page. Had Viv used one of the ciphers she had been trained to decipher, to write this? It was possible.

In fact, now that she thought about it, hadn't Leo Marks mentioned in his book that agents used the Playfair cipher sometimes? Yes.

She turned to the Internet for the decryption process and then pulled out a notebook and pen and set to work.

At last, she was able to read the clear text writing.

May 1, 1943

We are not supposed to speak of this but I simply must have someone to tell it to, even if it is only to this page. I have taken great care to encipher these paragraphs and hide this journal.

As I deciphered his incoming message, I felt my heart plunge, because the mirror, the gold, the diamonds, have been taken by the Nazis. Worse, there have been sightings of U-boats along the North Atlantic coast and perhaps he is even on one of them, as he spoke to me about joining the German Navy as part of his cover. (Yet another thing that is 'forbidden.')

The Nazis think they can simply take what they want—ruin lives, ruin whole histories, without the littlest regard for anything beyond their own interests. They have stolen his heritage, his culture, his family legacy. Just because of his lineage. In fact, he is proud of his closest guarded secret. Which he entrusted to me to keep. Which I shall.

That is why I promised him before he left last week—his eighth time— that I would do what was in my power to help him. Even if he does not return.

Nicky looked up from the small book. His closest, most-guarded secret... Not that he was Polish. No.

Viv had meant—Nicky's eyes widened and she picked up her phone and scrolled to that Polish Art Center article she'd bookmarked—he was the descendant of Princess Magdalena Jola Piast.

Yes. The article even said the dowry ended up with the prominent Gobell family, direct descendants of the princess's line. Viv said *his family legacy* in this entry, too, which meant he must have inherited the jewelled mirror and—

The ding of a new email notification popped up on her laptop. Nicky's mouth went dry as she saw who it was from.

From: jwhite@umbrellagroup.com
To: nicky.stendahl@gmail.com
Sent: Mon Oct 11, 8:15 p.m.

We have not heard from you in response to our earlier message.

In the interim, we have spoken with our lawyers.

We have decided we do not wish to tie up company time in legal battles. After consultation with our lawyers, we would like to propose the following:

1) That the lawsuit may be considered withdrawn if:

a) you agree to never again write for Ivory magazine, the Historical Woman, or any of the publications the Umbrella Group produces

b) you agree that your article with the Historical Woman magazine will not run and that you will not receive compensation for any part of it

c) you agree not to run the already-agreed-upon article content with anyone else, as the work-for-hire contract for that material had been signed and agreed upon previously.

Your decision must be made within 48 hours. Otherwise, we will press charges.

Jonah White
Executive Assistant to
George J. Starr, CEO
Umbrella Group

Nicky chewed a cuticle. Of course. She'd forgotten that she'd already signed the contract. She sighed. There went her idea to sell the article elsewhere.

She stared at the screen. But what about all the work she'd put into the story? And all her extra research...

How could she just give up all of that?

Nicky pulled out the delicate air mail envelope and stared at Andrzej's final letter to Viv. She traced the neat handwriting with a fingertip.

She couldn't just give up on Viv's story, give up on Viv's life. It was important. Something that had to be said—and shared.

But in exchange for not having to go to court? She swallowed hard. That would be a lifesaver.

She hit reply.

Quinten stepped away from the telephone pole and grinned as he surveyed his work.

The last poster was up. He'd plastered them everywhere between here and Charlottetown, it seemed like. Told all his friends. Posted like crazy on social media.

Now he'd just have to wait.

He shoved the sleeves of his teal blue shirt farther up his forearms.

He wished Nicky could be here to see the progress he'd made on this. She'd appreciate his work. She'd probably even post something about it on her own social media platform that she loved so much.

A sad smile flitted across his face as he remembered the way her eyes had sparkled as she'd sat across from him at Gahan House. The protectiveness he'd felt as she'd stood so close there in the doorway. The way she'd put her hand on her hip, so sure of herself and what she wanted, when she'd come into his shop with the diary.

She wasn't afraid to speak her mind. That was one of the things he admired most about her.

Quinten rubbed a hand across his stubble as he walked back to the music shop and went in the back door.

That was the trouble. His own fears and insecurities had such an iron grip on him. That was part of why he couldn't say what he truly longed to say to Nicky. Truly yearned to say to her.

Damn it. She didn't realize just how powerful of a connection he felt to her.

Somehow, his lips were sealed, his throat wouldn't work. It went beyond an unwillingness to say anything. It was a visceral, almost primal need to *not* say how he felt. Not to risk being seen and thus, be rejected.

He shook his head. Probably related to his father and all those years Quinten felt that he wasn't important. All those years that his father had criticized him. Told him that he wasn't good enough. Told him that he'd never measure up.

His fists tightened at his sides.

That was ridiculous. But that was how it was.

He blinked rapidly. Nicky had been willing to be there for him. Willing to see him. But now she'd gone, he could never tell her.

He *wanted* Nicky to see him, wanted her to know him for who he truly was. He'd been wrong, back on the porch, when he'd been so sure they were just friends; when he'd been so sure he wouldn't—couldn't—open up to her.

He brushed the back of his hand across his face. He wanted...to let Nicky in.

But he didn't know how.

Chapter Nine

ATE MONDAY NIGHT, as Nicky lay awake in bed, she tried to ignore the nagging feeling in the pit of her stomach. No lawsuit. But at what cost?

She rolled onto her side and shoved the pillow over her head. But it didn't drown out the vibrating buzz that erupted on her nightstand.

She grabbed her phone, half-hoping it was Quinten.

It wasn't.

Dear Ms. Stendahl,

I have some unfortunate news. The files request you have made regarding Agent Andrzej Gobell's traffic has run into some difficulties.

The second and third portions, when they were re-trieved from deep storage, have succumbed to mildew and water damage.

We have done our best and were able to digitize one piece of traffic. His final transmission. It is enclosed. Thank you, and best of luck with your research.

Regards,
Greg Scott
Research Curator
The National Archives

Nicky jumped out of bed and went over to her desk. She'd be able to see it better on her laptop. Besides, her phone battery was almost dead. Again. She really needed to replace it.

She pulled up the file.

```
SUSPECT COVER COMPROMISED COULDNT ALERT OSS TO
CACHE LOCATION HAVE TAKEN PRECAUTIONS WITH
CACHE REMEMBER AMBER IMPRISONED ON CROSSING
BACK HAVE ESCAPED IN BERLIN SAFE HOUSE BEING
WATCHED HAVE SENT SHEET MUSI
```

The message ended mid-sentence. Nicky's chest tightened.

If Andrzej had suspected his cover had been blown and the safe house was watched, then...the moment the message was being sent was the very same moment they'd been discovered.

The W/T operator must have been shot partway through the transmission. And Andrzej? Captured and tortured and then killed by the Nazis.

She stared at the last four letters. Goosebumps broke out on her arms. She rubbed them. Someone had died. More than one person, actually.

She couldn't just sit here and not do this whole saga justice. The public had to know. She needed to keep looking for the treasure. Because it had to be returned.

What about Quinten? Oh God.

She pressed her fingers against her lips and refused to let the tears fall. Quinten wasn't going to see her cry. Not even in her own mind.

She clenched her hands so tightly that the knuckles turned white. Damn him and damn her issues. She'd completely screwed it all up with him because of her stupidity and her fear.

She'd been too busy worrying about how he never seemed to open up to her to realize she'd been dangerously close to falling in love with him, anyway.

And now? It was too late. Too late to turn back. Too late to start again.

She couldn't go, she couldn't...

Go?

She narrowed her eyes. That's exactly what she *had* to do. Go back to P.E.I.

She lifted her chin and suddenly she could very clearly see everything about the island, everything about Quinten, and everything about herself that she hadn't seen before.

She'd let her perceptions overrule the truth. She hadn't let him show his true self to her when he'd been trying to, she realized now with a little gasp.

She'd been too busy labeling him, judging him, thinking she was so sure about him when all it would've taken was a little compassion, a little empathy, and—her heart skipped a beat—a little *love* in order to see him for who he truly was.

Yes.

She squared her shoulders. She had to talk to Quinten. And she had to follow through on the story. It didn't matter if no one published the article. What mattered was doing the right thing.

Who knew? Maybe she could rewrite it and put it up on a blog of her own? Maybe she could use all the extra research to write her own book about all of it?

Because she had to do this. For herself. For Quinten and his heritage. And for Viv and Andrzej.

TUESDAY MORNING, QUINTEN picked up his phone. His forty-eight hours were almost up. All that work. The crowdfunding. The social media posts. It had helped. Unfortunately, not enough.

He'd have to call his lawyer.

He didn't want to sell to Elliot. But it looked like he didn't have any other choice.

Quinten's grip tightened on the phone as he dialed his lawyer.

"Is there anything you can do? I mean, I know I'm grasping at straws here but I have to ask."

The other man sighed. "There's nothing I can do. Legally, Elliot can buy out your half, seeing as how you haven't yet found any solid inheritance documentation."

"What about this bankruptcy solution Elliot's imposed?"

"I'll have to do some checking; and I'll get back to you by the end of the day today. Technically, your forty-eight hours don't end until midnight tonight. Remember that."

"Okay, I'll wait to hear from you." Quinten put down the phone and took a deep, yet shaky, breath. There was hope after all.

He rubbed a hand across his face. At least there was some hope. For his business anyway. But what about his love life?

"Nicky," he whispered to the empty room. "I'm sorry."

He had thought that by holding back, by not telling her what he now knew she most wanted to hear, that he was helping her, helping himself.

Doing them both a favor by taking out the messy emotions and the drama and protecting himself.

He sighed. Protecting himself. That's exactly what he had been doing by playing the tortoise and pulling his head inside his shell.

But that wasn't going to get him what he really wanted, now, was it?

He shook his head.

It was only going to get him more of the same. More pain. More silence. More lonely nights and long days filled with work but not much else. There was an emptiness in his heart that longed to be filled.

And the only person who could fill it was himself. There was no one else who got that job. He shouldn't—couldn't—ask that of anyone else.

He had to do that for himself. He had to create his own happiness. Nicky wasn't going to give that to him, nor was anyone else.

He picked up his phone again.

He had to tell her that. Somehow. He had to make himself do it. He'd been wrong. He'd put her through too much pain to hope that she'd forgive him, but at least he had to try.

He dialed.

NICKY PICKED UP her to-go hot chocolate off the counter at Island Chocolates late Tuesday morning and turned toward the door.

She pulled out her phone to check her messages but then realized the battery was dead. Again. This was the third time in a day. She'd have to buy a new battery for it—

"Nicky!"

"Mrs. MacPhail." She tossed her dead phone back in her purse.

"Sorry to startle you, dear." She patted Nicky's shoulder. "But I'm so glad I ran into you. You know, I haven't seen you around lately."

"I, uh," she cleared her throat, "was away for a bit." She took a sip of coffee. "But now I'm back." She glanced at the door.

"I've been trying to find Quinten today but you'll do just as well. I'm sure you'll see him so if you could give him this..." She started to dig around in her purse as she kept talking. "It's just that, you know, Quinten's crowdfunding campaign got me to reminiscing. His grandma and I used to write letters to each other, back when I was overseas teaching in Ethiopia."

"Uh-huh."

Mrs. MacPhail continued, "Well, I threw most of them out. Al didn't like all that junk, as he called it, just sitting around." She flapped a hand. "So what did I do but listen to him? Anyways, that was awhile ago." She paused. "But then just yesterday, I was cleaning out my kitchen. You know how you always have a drawer that sticks? Well, that one's in my kitchen. It was driving Al batty—frankly, me, too—so I decided to fix it."

Nicky hid her smile around another sip of coffee.

"Ah-ha. Here it is." Mrs. MacPhail pulled something out of her purse and held it up. "I found it stuck in a drawer. The darn thing wouldn't shut and when I pulled out this crumpled piece of paper, that's what it turned out to be. So here you go, dear." She passed the mangled page to Nicky and straightened up.

"Thanks, Mrs. MacPhail." Nicky tucked the paper into her own purse. "Nice to chat and, uh, hope to see you around later."

"I won't keep you now. But I just wanted to say that everyone in the village here, well, we're so happy that you decided to write about Viv. You know, if you're ever looking for something else to write, my mother was in the Women's Royal Canadian Naval Services during the war. Went over to New Brunswick, near Moncton, to a place called Coverdale. All very top secret, of course, at the time. But it was actually an outstation for Bletchley Park back in England. The women who worked there, including Mom, intercepted and transcribed German messages from the U-boats running around the North Atlantic, then sent 'em over to Bletchley to break."

"Wow," Nicky said. "I'll keep it in mind. I really should run now..."

"Alrighty. One other thing, dear. We're preparing for the annual Victoria Village Christmas Stroll. Happens near the end of this month." She patted Nicky's shoulder. "Maybe you'll be around for it?"

"I hope so," Nicky called over her shoulder as she hurried out of the chocolate shop.

QUINTEN CHECKED HIS crowdfunding app. His eyebrows shot up. People had actually donated more? He gave a shaky laugh. Things were looking up.

He would need to organize the prizes and get that together, but it should be easy enough to do. Maybe he didn't have to wait to hear back from his lawyer after all?

He glanced at his phone and tried to ignore the fact that Nicky had not replied to any of his texts. Or the call he'd made.

He had to harden his heart, snuff out that hope. At least

things with his business were looking up—he should just focus on that and—

He jerked his head up as the floorboards creaked.

NICKY STOOD ON the porch of Quinten's music shop. She put her trembling hands in the pockets of her denim capris and shook back her hair in an effort to feel nonchalant.

It didn't work.

She took a breath, pushed open the screen door and stepped inside. Quinten met her gaze from across the counter.

Sunlight shone through the window and highlighted the gold in his hair. She wanted to reach out, touch it, smooth it under her fingertips and then lean forward and kiss him; tell him how she felt; tell him her deeper feelings and deepest desires.

She shook her head. Bit her lip. Those gestures wouldn't be enough. She had to show him.

So that he would truly know and understand, so that the embers in his heart would catch fire again and they could both be bathed in the warm glow.

She let out a shaky breath and twisted a strand of hair around her fingers. She began to speak very quickly. Maybe if she talked fast enough, he wouldn't kick her out before she'd said what she had to say.

"Listen, while I was back in the city, I had a lot of time to think. In between worrying about paying my debts." She gave a quick laugh. "I started to wonder why the song would have to be played on that specific piano. And since we're thinking it did have to be played on that specific instrument, well, that could mean there's something more to the song than notes. What if there was some sort of connection between the melody you were going to play and something unusual about the piano itself?"

Quinten opened his mouth to say something but Nicky hurried on.

"Because you'd said yourself that your grandmother loved puzzles, so maybe she engineered something about the piano to hide a clue? Or maybe she just used what was already there and connected the melody somehow with—"

"Whoa, whoa." Quinten crossed the room in a few strides and put his hands on Nicky's shoulders. "Slow down. We'll figure this out together."

Nicky blinked. "You're not...mad at me?"

"You sound disappointed."

Nicky made a strangled noise.

"Did you not get my text messages or my voicemail?"

"My phone died and it doesn't hold a charge and I didn't have time to replace the battery or anything so I've just been using my laptop to check emails and such."

"Well, that explains that."

"Listen, I'm sorry, Quinten. I...I acted like an idiot and I need to fix this." She looked at him with a hitch in her chest.

His face was unreadable. For a moment Nicky felt the old anger, the old fear, return.

He blinked rapidly, averted his gaze, and shoved his hands in his pockets.

But then she realized, there in that second, that she'd read him all wrong. The lack of expression on his face, the stoicism, wasn't that he didn't care...

It was that he was working twice as hard to hide the fact that he *did* care.

"Oh..." she whispered.

QUINTEN JERKED HIS head back in her direction. Saw the look in her eyes.

She'd come back because she actually might care about him? Care about him so much that she'd been willing to be vulnerable with him, set aside her own fears, her own hang-ups, for the sake of reaching out to him.

That was real love. That was true love, he thought, as a bitter taste filled his mouth.

And he'd gone and stomped all over her sweet, good, kind intention, back when he hadn't opened up, been vulnerable, or reached out there on the porch. He'd shattered her heart, and his own in the process.

But he couldn't just apologize to her for that. No apology was going to change that, was it? Words weren't enough; action, hopefully, would fix things. Right? There was only one way to find out.

QUINTEN SQUARED HIS shoulders and cleared his throat. "You're right. There's something about that piano. We'll need to go see it at Elliot's."

"Um." Nicky shifted her weight. "We'll have to figure out how to...arrange...that." She tucked a strand of hair behind her ear.

"Looks like we're going to have to do a little—"

"—breaking and entering?" Nicky's pulse raced. She'd never done anything illegal before and it seemed a bit extreme.

He chuckled as he picked up a wrapped package Nicky recognized as the yellow jelly beans. "I was going to say pay a house call to drop this off." He hefted the package. "And check the piano now that it's been moved. Because, you know," he paused and lifted his eyebrows, "it could be out of tune."

Quinten grabbed his car keys out of the basket by the back door and "Marsch Impromptu" off the counter. "Let's go play a song, shall we?"

FIVE MINUTES LATER they came to a stop in front of a large old Victorian two-story house with a box-bay window and a wraparound porch.

Quinten got out of the car. "They moved this house to Dunrovin Estates here from my other grandparents' farm,"

Quinten said to Nicky.

"Wow. So picturesque." The yellow house stood on the edge of a small bluff that overlooked the Northumberland Strait.

Nicky followed Quinten as he walked up to the front door and knocked.

Elliot opened the door. "Did you come by to say you've decided sell to me?"

Quinten swallowed and took a breath. "Um, no." He glanced at his watch. "Technically, I still have until midnight tonight."

Elliot crossed his arms.

Quinten forced himself to sound casual. "I, uh, wanted to check that the piano made it through the move okay."

Elliot didn't say anything.

Quinten added, "I won't charge you."

A silent few seconds passed. Elliot tilted his chin in Nicky's direction. "Who's your girlfriend?"

Heat crept up the back of Quinten's neck. He thrust the wrapped package at Elliot. "I, um, also brought these for today. They're for Rose."

Elliot took the package and said a terse, "Thanks."

"Honey, who's at the door?"

Elliot turned at the sound of his wife's voice from the back of the house. "It's Quinten," he called back.

"Good, he can tune the piano for my birthday party. Come help me move the table before the guests start arriving, please."

"Sure, sweetie!" Elliot yelled in reply. To Quinten, he said, "Fine. Come in then. I'll just be in the kitchen. Piano's in the living room." He opened the door wider to let them in. "You have ten minutes," he added in an undertone before he left.

QUINTEN PICKED UP the rather brittle and somewhat crumpled sheet of music and placed it on the piano's music holder.

Nicky couldn't help but admire his long, strong fingers.

He bowed his head a moment before he placed his fingers on the ivories. He glanced at her for a second and Nicky caught a wistful expression that lingered even as he turned his attention back to the piece of music.

He began to play.

Nicky watched as his eyes closed and he lost himself in the piece. Her throat tightened as she saw his concentration deepen, his focus narrow, his body sway ever so slightly in time with the melody. Her heart squeezed as she was again reminded of one of the trees along the street here. Solid, strong. Deep-rooted.

She closed her eyes too and listened as if the music notes themselves would tell her something, would reveal some hidden, deeper meaning...

But all she heard was beautiful music. What was Viv trying to say? What was Andrzej trying to convey?

The pianist's journey, she mused, *mirrors a plan well-laid...* What if there was no plan at all?

Was there even a treasure? Or was this some sort of elaborate diversion designed to distract the Allies from whatever the Germans were planning in relation to D-Day?

Nicky's stomach dipped.

Quinten played the final notes. They echoed in Nicky's heart as they faded into silence—

Her eyes snapped open. What was that? She held her breath. Had that noise been from the clock on the mantel? Or the piano? She listened again.

Now nothing. Just the chirp of birds and the rustle of the leaves on the maple tree outside the window.

She met Quinten's gaze. "You play very well."

"Thank you."

For a moment, neither of them spoke as the silence filled in the words between them.

Her heart pounded. Was he thinking the same thing she was?

As he looked at her, a softness filled his expression and she swallowed. Was she thinking the same thing he was?

But he was the first to avert his gaze.

"DID YOU HEAR that?" Nicky whispered and glanced toward the kitchen. The sound of Rose's laughter, the clink of dishes, and the murmur of Elliot and his wife's conversation drifted into the room.

"Hear what?" Quinten said in a low voice.

Nicky sat down beside him on the piano bench, so close her hair brushed his upper arm. "A noise at the very end of the song. Like, a click?"

She turned her head toward him. Quinten's heart jumped into his throat at the excited expression on Nicky's face.

He swallowed hard. She was so close. His gaze flicked to her lips. But so far away...

His mouth went dry and he swallowed. If he leaned forward an inch—

"I bet it's some sort of secret compartment your grandma rigged up," she whispered, her lips close to his ear. "And the compartment was somehow triggered when the last few notes were played." Her eyes lit up.

He shifted on the bench. It creaked under him as Nicky jumped up then crouched down to examine the piano legs. "I'm trying to remember exactly where I heard it." She frowned. "I think it was somewhere around here."

Quinten joined her. "Let's look for anything that's sticking out or seems oddly fitted," he murmured under his breath.

Nicky ran her hands over the glossy surface. "I don't see anything yet..."

A few seconds ticked by in silence.

"The piano's fairly free of ornamentation. There isn't much of a place to hide anything," Quinten whispered.

Nicky tapped the legs of the piano but shook her head. "Doesn't sound like they're hollow."

Quinten continued with his inspection of the piano. "I've tuned this piano so many times. I can't believe there's something that I've missed."

"Wait a minute," Nicky said, her voice tense and low. "Look at this."

She pointed to the front right piano leg's scalloped edge. "That wasn't facing in that direction before." She touched it, then motioned to Quinten. "I think..." He came nearer. "Playing those notes somehow made the leg rotate a few degrees. What do you think?"

Quinten ran his fingers along the piano's leg to the place that she'd indicated. Smooth. Satiny. Like her own legs...

No. He couldn't think about that now. He forced his mind back to the piano. "You're right. This leg's turned counter-clockwise ever so slightly. I think we need to move it just a bit more... There's some sort of—" Gently and carefully, he swivelled the wooden piece just a hair. "—secret compartment."

Quinten met Nicky's gaze as he slipped his fingers into the darkness. Her eyes widened and he heard the catch in her breath.

Floorboards creaked and they both froze as footsteps sounded in the hallway.

Quinten plucked up what felt like two small scraps of paper from the cavity with his first two fingers.

He did a sweep around the remainder of the small space. No, nothing else.

There was a quiet snick as he rotated the piano leg back into place. Quinten gave a quick nod to Nicky and they both stood up. He tucked the papers into his pocket, then glanced over his shoulder.

Elliot's wife leaned around the doorframe. "How's it sound to you?"

"Great." Quinten dusted off his hands. "You're all set." He walked to the door, Nicky behind him.

"Wonderful," she said. "Thanks so much."

"You're welcome. And happy birthday." Quinten waved as the door banged shut behind him and Nicky.

NICKY SANK ONTO one of the oak captain's chairs at Quinten's kitchen table.

"So. What did we find?" Her voice came out a whisper but her heart raced.

She held her breath as Quinten sat down beside her and pulled something out of his pocket. "It's two pieces of paper."

The scent of his cologne drifted to her as the breeze from an open window brushed her cheek.

"Oh." Nicky struggled to keep the disappointment out of her voice.

"You were hoping for some gold coins?" Quinten's eyes sparkled.

"Never hurts to hope." She wound a strand of hair around her finger and avoided his gaze. "So." She cleared her throat. "What's on it?"

He unfolded the first brittle, yellowed paper.

Nicky peered over his shoulder and frowned. "What on Earth...?"

"It looks like some sort of diagram." Quinten squinted as he turned the paper this way and that. "I think it's from some sort of machine?"

"Two concentric circles. Maybe we can logic it out," Nicky said. "We know it's probably vintage World War II, whatever it is."

"And it's round."

"So it could be from a gun barrel?"

"These look like dimensions." Quinten tapped the page. "See the numbers?"

"I do. It almost looks like crosshairs or something..."

"Mmm." He studied the page. "I think it's bigger than a handgun."

"A tank?" Nicky guessed.

"I don't think..." Quinten picked up his phone and began typing. After a second, he showed the phone to her. "See? Looks like it's from a submarine."

Nicky sucked in a breath. "A German U-boat."

Quinten put his phone back in his pocket. "I think this is

a diagram for the forward and aft torpedo tubes."

"But why stick it in there with..."

Quinten carefully opened the second piece of paper. "A piece of poetry? That's a very good question."

```
The moonlight shone
Down on your face
My heart leapt up
To take its place.

Watch, my love,
For my return.
Though tears fill your eyes,
Though your heart shall yearn.
```

Quinten frowned. "Why go to all that trouble for a poem?"

"Unless," Nicky grinned, "it's not a poem."

Quinten raised a brow.

"Well, it *is*. But it's more than that. Of course." She smacked her forehead. "Why didn't I think of that right away? Andrzej was an agent. He worked for the SOE. The SOE used poem codes to pass messages from enemy territory back to London. It was a system that unfortunately wasn't very secure even though it used double-transposition and key words..." She bit her bottom lip.

"Key words?"

"Five words, chosen at random from the poem, that the agent would use to carry the message. They'd put those five words through a double-transposition system. They'd number each letter of each of the five words and then transpose the resulting numbers into a grid... The SOE asked the agents to memorize their poems. They thought that would make the poems secure."

"But it didn't?"

"No. Leo Marks, head of SOE's codes division, eventually devised a more secure system agents carried with them on silk handkerchiefs that they would then cut away and burn. But they also continued to use poem codes as well."

"Mmm. That makes sense. Old habits die hard, and all that."

"Yep. And there was a lot of internal politics involved, too, apparently."

"But why weren't the poem codes secure?"

"Because the Germans tended to figure out the key words. Either through torture of a captured agent or through a lot of searching through books by trial and error on the part of the German cryptographers. And once they figured that out, well, they could figure out the resulting indicator groups and transposition keys and crack the messages."

"Okay."

"Plus," Nicky continued, "a lot of times the agents were given common poems, for ease of memorization, that everyone, including the Germans, already knew."

"Really?"

"Like Poe or Shakespeare. Once Marks joined the team, though, he got SOE agents to start making up their own ditties, as he called them. He wrote a lot of them himself, actually. Which made it slightly more secure."

"How do you *know* all this?" Quinten watched her.

Nicky felt warmth surge through her at the admiration in his tone. She fiddled with a strand of hair. "Research. And, I read a book called *Between Silk and Cyanide*. It's Leo Marks's memoir."

"So you think someone at the SOE wrote this?"

"It's possible Viv wrote it. Or Andrzej. Or neither of them... But whoever received it would've had, or known, the indicator group. That would've told them what the five key words were that were then used to transpose the message." Nicky glanced at the poem.

"Hmm." Quinten rubbed his jaw and Nicky watched the motion. A blush swept her cheeks. No. There wasn't time for thinking about that now. "Any guesses on what the five words could be?"

"Unfortunately, no." She tapped her fingers on the table.

"Crap!"

"What?"

"This isn't going to do us any good even if we *did* have an indicator group. Because we need to have the enciphered message. Otherwise...there's nothing to decipher. We can't just make the message of out thin air."

"Damn. That's right." Quinten frowned. "Because the poem is what would give us the way to crack the enciphered message... But without the enciphered message, there isn't anything to solve."

"Exactly." Nicky sighed and put her chin in her hands. "We need to have the secret message." She bit a hangnail. "*And* the indicator group."

Chapter Ten

QUINTEN LOOKED AT the poem. "You said an indicator group..." He trailed off. "What does that look like?"

"Well," Nicky said, "the thing is, no one really knows exactly what type of indicator groups the SOE used. The best guesstimation is that they must have labeled the five key words using either letters or numbers. So the short answer is, it has to have either five letters or five numbers."

Quinten frowned and stared at the poem. "Five letters or numbers." Then his eyes widened. "Wait a minute. When I was tuning the piano before I gave it to Elliot, I found the oddest thing under the lid." He jumped up from the table. "It didn't make any sense to me, but I thought I'd try to figure it out later so I put it over here."

He strode over to the door where a low marble-topped cabinet sat. He rummaged around in a shallow wicker basket filled with house keys, sticks of gum and loose change. "Okay, here we go." He plucked out a small square of old yellowed paper and came back over to Nicky.

She extended her hand and couldn't suppress a shiver as his fingertips brushed her palm. She unfolded the paper.

BIOPW

"Huh." A slow grin spread across her face. "Exactly what we need." She met Quinten's gaze.

"It's my grandmother's handwriting," he said.

"Wow." Nicky traced a finger over the letters. "So Viv must've known what indicator group Andrzej would've used."

"You know, I bet there's an app for this," Quinten mused. He pulled out his phone.

"Even if there is, I want to do it the old-fashioned way."

Quinten put away his phone. "Okay."

"It's how they would've done it," she said softly. "I mean, can you imagine all that the agents and the wireless operators went through to get the messages back to London?"

Quinten traced a finger along the faded letters as Nicky continued to talk.

"You had to somehow get your message to the wireless transmitter operator. When the Germans stopped people on the street for random searches..."

"Uh-huh."

"...and if you had anything on you that was suspicious, even just one tiny thing out of place, you were questioned."

"Whew."

"And then the W/T operators...doing the enciphering with just a stub of pencil...maybe in near-darkness in some cramped, airless space...heart racing, one ear listening for the Gestapo pounding down the door?"

Quinten shook his head.

"All the while trying to transpose the letters into numbers correctly when you hadn't slept in three days but you knew you had to concentrate, had to get that critical arms drop location back to London? But one tiny mistake could mess up the whole message."

"It wasn't easy for the W/T operators to transmit the enciphered messages by Morse, either," Nicky said, as she picked up the yellowed scrap of paper. "They had the most dangerous job. The units were usually big and heavy. The only way they could typically hide them were in suitcases. Pretty conspicuous. But they had to send the messages. They had to communicate with the free world."

"Yes."

"The agents and W/T operators didn't let anything stop them—the fear of discovery, the sleepless nights, the constant threat of imprisonment or worse. It's like, when I do this by hand, somehow, I'm part of history, I'm helping history..." Nicky touched a fingertip to the yellowed bit of paper. A few flakes crumbled away from the edge.

"History," Quinten echoed. "You know what...I think I just might have the enciphered message."

"What do you mean?"

He went and grabbed his grandmother's cookbook off the shelf. "Here."

Nicky's eyes welled.

Quinten gently put a hand on her arm. "So now what?" he asked.

Nicky gave a shaky laugh. "This means Andrzej must've sent Viv the secret message along with the final letter he wrote to her."

"Must have," Quinten agreed.

"But she didn't decipher it?"

"Mmm." Quinten shook his head. "I don't think she did. Because in a diary entry of hers that I found in this old cookbook, she says something about not knowing what happened to the treasure."

"That makes sense." Nicky took a breath. "Okay. So in order to figure out the secret message..." She bit her bottom lip but couldn't suppress the happy thrill that ran through her, "...we need three things." She ticked them off on her fingers. "One: the poem."

"Check," Quinten said.

"Two: the indicator group."

"Check."

"Three: the enciphered message."

"And check." Quinten held it up. "So how do we solve it?"

"Well, that's why the indicator group is so important. We use that to figure out the five key words that the message is enciphered with." She took out a pencil and her small notepad from her purse. "So, first thing, you have to label the poem." She picked up her pencil. "You assign a letter to each of the words in the poem, starting with A. So the first word in the poem is 'the.' You write the letter 'a'

above that."

"So we'd label the next word, which is 'moonlight' with the letter 'b' because it's the second letter." Nicky continued, "Then we do that for the whole alphabet." Nicky put words to action until the whole poem was labeled.

Quinten glanced from her notepad to the poem and back again.

B = moonlight

I = heart

O = place

P = watch

W = tears

Quinten rubbed his jaw. "Okay, so that tells us the five key words. I also noticed something... Each of the 'words' in the enciphered message is five letters long. Is that random or is there a reason?"

Nicky grinned. "It's to help out the W/T operator."

Quinten cocked his head.

"The enciphered messages were transmitted by Morse code. To make it easier for the wireless operator to send the coded messages back to London, the enciphered message was sent in 'words' that were five letters long."

"Ah," Quinten said. "Now what?"

Nicky tapped her pencil on the page in her notebook. "Now we write these five words out all strung together. Like this."

M	O	O	N	L	I	G	H	T	H	E	A	R	T	P	L	A	C	E	W	A	T	C	H	T	E	A	R	S

"Then we label each of the letters with a number. We label each letter that's shown, in chronological order. So the first A—it's there in the word heart—we label that with the number 1. The second A, in the word place, would be number 2. There aren't any words with B, so we move on to C until we go through the entire phrase. That creates the transposition key." She started to write. After a few minutes she put down her pencil.

M	O	O	N	L	I	G	H	T	H	E	A	R	T	P	L	A	C	E	W	A	T	C	H	T	E	A	R	S
17	19	20	18	15	14	10	11	25	12	7	1	22	26	21	16	2	5	8	29	3	27	6	13	28	9	4	23	24

"So these numbers we've just generated underneath the letters," she tapped the eraser end of the pencil on the notebook page, "are what we're going to use to decipher the message. This is exactly what your grandmother would've done."

"Wow. I never knew." Quinten shook his head and cleared his throat. "You said it's double transposition. Which would mean we need to use this numbered grid twice?"

"Right," Nicky said. "Which also means we need some squared paper." She ripped out a clean lined page from her notebook and used a spare pencil she'd grabbed from her purse to draw vertical lines down the page so that the page was filled now with small squares. "To keep everything lined up," she explained.

"Okay."

"Now that we have our chart, we look back at the enciphered message. See the first five letters?"

Quinten looked at the page. "I T E I A."

"Right. We take each five-letter group in the enciphered message and put it in the chart. We write it vertically under the corresponding number's column."

"Okay."

"So, since the first five letters in the enciphered message are I T E I A, we put I T E I A under the column with number 1. That corresponds to the A in the word 'heart.' Like this."

M	O	O	N	L	I	G	H	T	H	E	A	R	T	P	L	A	C	E	W	A	T	C	H	T	E	A	R	S
17	19	20	18	15	14	10	11	25	12	7	1	22	26	21	16	2	5	8	29	3	27	6	13	28	9	4	23	24
											I																	
											T																	
											E																	
											I																	
											A																	

"Then you just repeat that process, putting each five-letter group from the secret message vertically under the correct numbered column, until the whole enciphered message is placed beneath the transposition key?" Quinten asked.

"Exactly." Nicky set to work. It wasn't too long before her pencil stopped moving. "So now we have the whole chart filled in. But that's just the first part of it."

"Right. Because you said it uses double transposition."

"Yep. In order to figure out the clear text message, we need to decipher the second part of it. The message, in essence, was scrambled twice. We've gotten the first unscramble. Now we need to do the second unscramble. Which, by the way, is actually the reverse of what the agent did to encode it. So, if I don't make any mistakes, this will give us the actual plaintext message."

She picked up her pencil again. "We take what we've gotten from the first transposition, and read those letters horizontally left to right, starting at the top left. See?"

M	O	O	N	L	I	G	H	
17	19	20	18	15	14	10	11	
D	N	U	H	D	G	H		

Quinten nodded.

"We put those letters, which now appear horizontally in the first table, into the second blank table vertically in order to spell out the actual clear text message." She started to fill in the blank squares.

M	O	O	N	L	I	G	H	T
17	19	20	18	15	14	10	11	25
D	A	R	L	I	N	G		
N	I	A	M	G	O	N		
U	A	N	D	T	H	A		
H	E	M	I	R	R	O		
D	I	A	M	O	N	D		
G	U	A	R	D	T	H		
H	E	R	I	N				

Nicky's pencil stopped moving a little while later.

"So now," Quinten said, "it looks like we have to read the resulting letters here horizontally left to right...?"

"Right," Nicky laughed. "Right."

```
DARLING IF YOU ARE READING THIS THEN I AM GONE
PLEASE KNOW THAT I LOVE YOU AND THAT I HAVE
TRIED TO RETRIEVE THE MIRROR THE DOWRY AND THE
GOLD AND DIAMONDS I HAVE TAKEN STEPS TO SAFE-
GUARD THE HIDING SPOT DONT FORGET THE RING
```

Nicky exhaled a shaky breath and turned to Quinten. "This confirms what we've been theorizing all along."

"You're right." Quinten looked thoughtful for a moment. His eyes widened and he sat up straighter. "So *that's* the third thing that Viv got..."

"Third thing?"

"In that diary entry I found in the cookbook, she said Andrzej gave her three things." Quinten tugged his earlobe. "Andrzej sent her that final letter, which she mentioned in the entry. He also gave her the sheet music. He must've also given her—"

"The poem code and the schematic," Nicky exclaimed.

"Right. So this means the treasure is definitely real." Quinten grinned.

"Question is," Nicky said, as she tucked a strand of hair behind her ears, "is it still there?"

"I know how we can find out." Quinten dangled the car keys from thumb and forefinger.

Nicky jumped up. "Let's go."

Quinten stood too. "Where?"

"That's easy." Nicky laughed.

"North Cape." Quinten chuckled to himself. "Because that's where everyone's been saying it's been for the last seventy-five years."

"And because that's the POW rendezvous spot referred to in that *Guardian* article," Nicky added.

Quinten grinned. "Looks like we're headed up west."

"I'll drive," she said.

"DO YOU KNOW where you're going?" A note of amusement crept into Quinten's voice as he glanced at Nicky in his driver's seat while he tossed a couple of shovels in the trunk.

She shot him a look with brows raised as he got into the passenger seat and stowed a pair of flashlights in the back seat. "I figure with your fancy Apple watch, you can navigate."

"True," he said. "But I'll probably use my phone. It has a bigger screen."

"Speaking of phones, can I charge mine up?"

"Here, I can do it for you." He took her phone and plugged it into the car charger.

"Thanks." She threw a grin at Quinten, put the car into reverse, and backed out of his driveway.

"Let's swing by my friend Tate's place. He has a metal detector he's let me borrow a couple of times. Might need one now."

After they picked up the device, they turned back onto the TransCanada before they changed to Highway 12 West.

"I haven't been up west in awhile," Quinten said, as the rolling hills covered in pine trees flashed by the passenger window in the early evening light.

"No?" Nicky said. "Looks like it's a pretty beautiful part of the island."

"It is. During the war, there was a station up in Tignish. You know, there was some wartime song... Let's see, how did it go?"

He hummed a few bars.

A companionable silence descended between them. He could get used to this, he realized with a jolt. Her. Him. The road stretching out in front of them. Savoring the journey together. He glanced at Nicky.

But did she want that too? His gut tightened.

"We still headed in the right direction?" Nicky asked after a while.

He certainly hoped so. In more ways than one. "Almost there, actually. Just pull into the parking lot here. This is where the lighthouse, restaurant and gift shop are. Closed for the day now, though."

Nicky got out and stretched. "Pretty long drive."

"Yeah. About an hour and a half from Victoria." Quinten rolled his shoulders.

"So what's next?"

"Now?" Quinten pulled out a shovel from the trunk. "We see what we can find."

"But," Nicky said as she turned on the metal detector, "we have no idea where to look. The message just indicated North Cape, which is a pretty big search radius, from what I can tell." She glanced around. "And we're starting to lose daylight."

"No worries. That's what these are for." Quinten handed her a flashlight and pocketed the other. He put one of the shovels over his shoulder and headed toward the beach, Nicky beside him.

"From what that fisherman said on Island Voices, we know that the U-boat didn't come ashore. But part of the crew got the crate to shore somehow and..."

"Buried it. That's what Andrzej said, after all, in the message we deciphered."

"Only question is, where?"

"Right." Nicky came to stand beside him on the wide expanse of beach. Her vanilla perfume filled his senses. "I mean, it seems pretty random as to why a torpedo schematic would be included with the poem code. Unless it has something to do with it?"

Quinten pulled out the yellowed page. "But what?"

NICKY STUDIED THE schematic of the torpedo tubes but found herself distracted by Quinten's nearness.

If she shifted even a millimeter, she'd be pressed up against his solid chest, could wind her arms around his

neck—

"Well," Quinten said, "does anything look different or unusual on this page?"

Nicky forced her attention back to the paper. "Not really."

"Hmm." Quinten studied the drawing again. "What do those numbers mean?"

"Those are just the dimensions of the fore and aft torpedo tubes. It's not—"

She looked up. Their gazes locked.

"I don't think those are dimensions," he whispered. "See? Along here?"

He pointed to the vertical and horizontal lines along the edge of each circle.

"I bet that's latitude and longitude." Nicky pulled out her phone and started tapping. "Yes." She pointed at the screen. "See? When I enter those numbers, it comes up with..."

"Nothing," Quinten finished, as he peered at her phone over her shoulder.

"That's weird." Nicky frowned. "Maybe I entered it wrong?" She tried again. "Still nothing."

"Here, let me try." But Quinten came up with the same result. He rubbed a hand across his jaw.

"But these have to be latitude and longitude." Nicky bit her lip.

"Unless they aren't."

Nicky made a wry face as she gently folded the yellowed sheet back in quarters, as it had been originally. "It's a wonder the paper hasn't completely disintegrated."

But Quinten didn't reply. He was staring at the page in her hands. "Hold it up again," he said, his voice tense.

Nicky cocked her head but did as he asked.

"Whoa."

"What?"

"It makes a compass."

Nicky blinked.

"See?" Quinten pointed at the middle of the drawing.

"When it's folded up like that the lines intersect. That would create a heading..."

"You're right," Nicky breathed.

Quinten pulled up the compass app on his watch. "Let me just confirm it." He glanced up at the horizon. "Yes." He looked back down at his watch. "Right...over..." He consulted the antique paper and then his compass app again. "...there." He pointed to a piece of beach with a pile of red sandstone rocks that jutted out into the surf. "Come on."

Nicky followed Quinten as her heart pounded in her chest. This was really happening?

The scent of the salt air and the whoosh of the surf told her it certainly was real. Her heart skipped a beat as she glanced at Quinten and then back out at the horizon. The full moon had begun to rise.

A swell of happiness filled her and she realized, in that moment, that she belonged here. On this island. With this man. Her heart filled with happiness and joy as she looked over at Quinten. She bit her lip. But did he feel the same way?

"It's over here." Quinten pointed to a spot in the sand, glanced at his Apple watch and compared it to the paper one last time.

"Okay," Nicky said. She swept the metal detector over the area. It began to beep.

They started to dig.

The only sound was the whisper of the breeze, the call of the gulls, and the sound of the shovel turning over sand. And more sand.

"There's nothing but sand here," Nicky said, as she fought to keep the disappointment out of her voice. "I think we've dug down about three feet. We need to—"

His shovel hit something wooden.

"—dig this up," Quinten finished as he grinned at Nicky and knelt in the sand.

She sank to her knees beside him. They began to carefully push away the sand.

The exposed wood was rotten in places. Nicky switched

on her flashlight and frowned. "It almost looks like a case."

"For?"

"I have no idea. Let's open it and see."

Together they pried the partially rotted lid open on its rusted hinges.

"A typewriter?" Quinten said and sat back on his heels, his flashlight in hand.

Nicky dusted off her hands. "Wow. Has glass keys and everything."

"What are these things for?" Quinten pointed to multiple thin black wires that were attached to the front.

"I'm not so sure it *is* a typewriter."

Quinten frowned. "But what else could it be?"

Nicky shook her head.

"And what about this? Above the keyboard? Looks like rotors or something," Quinten mused.

Nicky gasped. "It's an Enigma machine." She glanced at Quinten's raised brows. "I've watched a lot of World War II movies and TV shows," she murmured with a guilty shrug.

"Come on," Quinten said, "let's move it and see whatever, if anything, is underneath it."

"I don't think this is going to be light," Nicky said with a laugh.

Together, they cleared the sand away from all four sides of the wooden box that housed the Enigma machine and reached under it. Slowly, it began to shift as they lifted upward.

"Oof," Nicky muttered. "My grip is—"

"Oops, careful there," Quinten said, as the machine tilted sideways. He gritted his teeth to keep hold of his side. The motion jostled the wires.

"Sorry, I just—there, I think I've got it now—"

"Let's just—be careful and—ooh—this is hard to—"

But Nicky's fingers slipped again, which caused one of the wires to jerk loose. "I think I have the wrong angle now—just don't—"

Quinten swore under his breath.

"What?" Nicky's cheeks flushed.

"Look down there."

"Oh God. Where?" Nicky's eyes darted around.

Through clenched teeth, Quinten jerked his chin at the hole.

Underneath the Enigma machine was a stack of TNT on top of a wooden crate. Wires attached the TNT to the Enigma machine.

Nicky's face drained of color and she almost dropped her end of the machine.

"I've read somewhere that the stuff gets more volatile the older it is." Quinten's jaw set as he grappled for a firmer grip on the heavy device. "And after seventy-plus years, I'm sure it's none too stable—"

Another wire popped loose.

A loud ticking noise started.

"What is that?" Nicky's eyes widened and her muscles strained as she held the machine.

Quinten swore again. "With those two wires that just came loose, I think we've just—"

"—triggered a bomb." Nicky swallowed.

NICKY WILLED THE pounding of her heart to slow but it didn't work. "What are we supposed to do now? I don't think I can hold onto this much longer. My arms are getting really tired."

"Mine too," Quinten said. "We need to put it down as gently as possible. Don't want to risk jostling anything else loose."

Nicky nodded.

"On the count of three," Quinten said. "One, two..."

"—three," they said in unison.

They put the still-ticking Enigma machine back down.

"W-what are we going to do?" Nicky tried to force her voice to stay level but it wavered anyway. She jumped up.

"Don't panic." Quinten jammed a hand in his hair. "That's the first rule of survival. Don't panic." He swallowed.

"I don't suppose you know any bomb squad people?" Nicky said with a shaky laugh.

Quinten shook his head.

"Well," Nicky smoothed a shaky hand over her hair, "neither do I."

He swallowed again and looked down at the rotors. "We don't have much time, either. Hear how fast the ticking is?"

"That's not exactly helping my train of thought, you know."

"Sorry," Quinten said. He jumped up too and pulled out his phone. "We need to call someone—911. The police. An—"

"We need to solve it," Nicky said.

"Huh?"

"The Enigma machine encoded words five letters long using these rotors and pins. We need the right five-letter word that would break the code. We do that, the bomb doesn't explode, we don't die, and we can see whatever's in the crate underneath it."

Quinten rubbed a hand across his face. "Got any favorite colors that are five letters?"

"Not helping." Nicky bit a hangnail.

"Sorry. Just trying to lighten the tension." Quinten tugged his earlobe. "The right five letter word... Well, maybe it has something to do with Andrzej or Viv?"

"There are fifteen billion-billion possible combinations. But we only have one try."

"Don't remind me," Quinten said, as his eyes fixed on the rotors.

"WE NEED TO think." Nicky pulled at the ends of her hair in frustration.

Quinten began to pace on the sandy shoreline. "Andrzej and Viv. What did they have in common?"

"They both knew the treasure was here."

"Andrzej must have rigged this up. In that last transmission, he said he'd 'taken precautions.' This must have been what he meant. To prevent it from falling into the wrong hands...which doesn't really help us now. What else?"

"They loved each other?" Nicky said.

"Love is only a four-letter word."

"Damn it," Nicky said. "What about a name?" She looked up at Quinten.

Quinten kept pacing. "Some sort of name that they both would've known... Andrzej thought that Viv would come find the treasure because after he got caught by the Nazis, he knew that he wasn't going to make it."

"But what name?"

Quinten frowned and stared down at the ground. "Well, Andrzej is seven letters, Viv is three and—Oh!"

"What is it?"

Quinten's gaze locked on Nicky. "The secret message we deciphered said, 'Don't forget the ring.' At first, I thought it was something just sentimental, but I think the ring must have something to do with all this."

"Okay," Nicky said slowly.

Quinten gasped. "The last time I saw my grandmother alive, she looked into my eyes and said with the strongest conviction, 'Remember amber.' I just dismissed it at that point because I thought she was talking about a person. But," he shook his head "she wasn't."

Nicky's eyes widened and her voice lowered to a whisper. "The ring...is *made* of amber."

Quinten sank to his knees in the sand. "And amber? Well, it has five letters."

"I really hope you're right," Nicky said. With shaking hands, she keyed in the five letters.

As she hit the last key, she held her breath.

Quinten tensed.

The ticking stopped.

Nicky closed her eyes and let out a slow breath.

For a second, they both sat there in silence, the moonlight shining down, the only sound the rush of the surf.

Quinten met her gaze and opened his mouth but then

closed it. He cleared his throat and said, "Should we find out what's underneath?"

Nicky nodded.

They carefully cleared the sand off of the small wooden crate. A swastika was stamped on the lid.

"It's nailed shut," Quinten said. "But I have a car kit that might have something in it. Be right back."

He returned a minute later with a hammer and put it under the lip of the crate's lid. Pieces of rotten wood flaked away. The rusty nails squealed in protest but finally came loose.

Together, Quinten and Nicky lifted the lid and peered inside.

Several piles of cotton bags leaned against one side, stamped with the symbol of the Third Reich. The bags were streaked with dirt and grime and smelled of seawater and stale dust.

Nicky reached down and pulled one out. She started to untie it but the rotten cloth fell away in her hands.

The shine of gold winked in the light from the rising moon. "Coins." She examined one. "Definitely Hitler's gold. The swastika is unmistakable."

"He must have melted down the Polish princess's gold and re-minted it. Looks like some of the other bags have silver coins. And these," Quinten lifted out a smaller silk pouch in the opposite corner, "must be the diamonds." He undid the drawstring. "Yep." He tilted it so Nicky could see inside.

"Look. There's something else," she murmured. A small wooden box, with intricate marquetry work on the lid and sides, and small, delicate gold-ball feet, was in the center of the small crate.

Quinten reached a hand out to help her carefully open the lid.

Nestled inside on a bed of plush deep blue velvet were a hand mirror, a pair of amber ear bobs set in silver with tiny diamonds, an amber necklace encrusted with diamonds, and an empty sterling silver ring box.

"The rest of the princess's dowry. We found it," Quinten murmured.

"And the jewelled mirror," Nicky whispered as she picked it up. Its silvery back, carved with a delicate pattern of flowers and leaves, inset with sapphires and pink diamonds, winked in the pale moonlight.

Quinten peered over her shoulder as Nicky turned it over. She could see both their reflections in the antique surface.

She met his gaze in the mirror. And in that second, she knew the secret of lasting love in her heart that she'd been withholding from herself.

Internal confidence, not external confirmation. She could be confident to let love in again, could allow herself to be known fully. She didn't need to have someone tell her everything on their mind; she could simply have confidence within herself that they cared. Quinten had inadvertently given her that gift, in all of this. She felt a glow, a stirring in her heart.

AS QUINTEN LOOKED into Nicky's eyes in the mirror while the moonlight bathed their shared reflection, he felt a deep knowingness rise up within him.

He didn't need to believe his fears anymore. That was just the fear trying to control what he did and didn't do, what he did and didn't say. Which just crowded out his own happiness.

He was done with all this hiding. He was ready to step out into the light of his true feelings, his heart's voice, his own pure, real emotions...

He could be vulnerable. He could speak his truth. That was the secret of lasting love. His fingers curled and uncurled. He swallowed.

He should've known—should've acted on that long ago, with Nicky, when it wasn't too late. But maybe it wasn't?

The soft whoosh of waves and the whisper of the breeze

were the only other sounds besides their breathing.

Suddenly, Quinten's phone blared. He startled and fumbled with it as he pulled it out.

His lawyer? He took a breath, cleared his throat, and answered the call.

"So Quinten," his lawyer said, "you filed the initial bankruptcy motion with me."

"...Yes."

"Now, I've been familiarizing myself with what Elliot's demanding. And I've done some checking. It looks as if there might be a way to rectify things...if you act fast."

Quinten's heartbeat sped up.

"Now, since your grandmother's health was in decline and that had negatively impacted the business, along with the bookkeeping associated with the business, which was also affected by her poor health, there may be an opportunity to look at filing the necessary paperwork with the courts for something called a hardship discharge."

"Okay," Quinten said. "What does that mean?"

"Basically, if granted by the court, it can allow you to have the bankruptcy terms reduced or relieved entirely."

"Wow, that's great. What do I have to do?"

"Well, that's the more complicated part. It would help if you had found the will."

Quinten winced. His lawyer went on.

"Since Elliot's offering to take over the business, thus showing your debtors that they would get their debts repaid, it might be a bit more challenging. But, you still have a chance. You need to show the court official working on your case that you can't pay the debts. But it needs to be due to something outside your control, like job loss. In your case specifically, that situation would be the ongoing medical bills from your grandmother's illness and her time in the specialized care home that provincial health didn't cover."

Quinten exhaled a shaky breath.

"I hope you've kept good documentation about that," his lawyer added. "Because you'll need the medical bills and profit and loss statements to support this filing.”

“I’ve kept everything.”

“Good. I’ll be in touch with Elliot and then go ahead and start on the paperwork. You’ll need to come down to the office to meet with me.”

“Okay. Thank you so much.”

“You’re welcome.”

Quinten ended the call and Nicky threw him a sidelong glance. “Good news?”

He exhaled. “My lawyer’s figuring out how I might not have to sell to Elliot. And how I might not have to file for bankruptcy.”

“That’s great.” Nicky put a hand on his arm. His heart flipped.

“What about your situation with the article?” Quinten asked.

“Well,” Nicky said, “I can’t publish it anywhere. But that’s actually a good thing because I really want to tell your grandmother’s story in depth. And to do that, I realized, it needs to be longer than just some article—”

Her phone buzzed. She jumped. The notification said she’d gotten a message from Shutterstock. She pulled up the message and as she read it, she laughed. “Wow.”

“What is it?”

“I uploaded some photos last Tuesday onto Shutterstock. They’ve gotten enough combined royalties now to cover this month’s rent.”

“What a relief, eh?” Quinten said.

“Definitely.” She fiddled with a strand of her hair and met Quinten’s gaze. “I’ve gotten so much good background information while I’ve been here on the island...” She paused, “...that I’ve decided to stay here for awhile and write a book about Viv and her life and Andrzej and the treasure.” She grinned at Quinten.

“That’s great.” Quinten’s heart jumped. She was staying. He put his hand over hers and squeezed. “I’m sure your book will be filled with some amazing history.”

“Thanks!” Nicky laughed and Quinten’s heart leapt again

at the sound. He leaned closer to her. "Nicky, I—"

"Speaking of history...I almost forgot." She pulled a mangled piece of paper out of her purse. "I meant to give you this earlier but in all the excitement I, uh, forgot about it."

"What's this?" He looked her with raised brows.

She pointed to the page.

Quinten unfolded it.

Most of the writing had faded away, and the ink had blurred. But the last few paragraphs of the letter were still legible.

I know you're not supposed to have favorites. But Quinten is my favorite grandson. I'm so proud of him. And so proud of having a hand in raising Quinten to be the fine young man he's become. That's why I know that when I pass on, there's no one else but Quinten who I want the business to go to.

Love,

Viv

Quinten wiped at the corner of his eyes with his thumb. "Thank you, Nicky."

Nicky placed a hand on his arm. "You're welcome. Mrs. MacPhail cornered me in the chocolate shop and wanted me to give it to you because she couldn't find you."

Quinten chuckled and shook his head. "Oh, P.E.I."

But his expression turned serious as he looked at the treasure. "We'll have to contact the appropriate organizations so we can make sure the dowry, the gold, and the diamonds are given back to the correct people in retribution for the war crimes of Hitler and the Nazi regime."

"It wasn't Hitler's gold or diamonds in the first place," Nicky murmured. "That was all part of the dowry, originally. And the ring. It's time for it to be returned to Poland. Viv and Andrzej went through so much."

"They knew it was worth it, though. They had to. Why else would he take on such a dangerous task unless he had a personal reason?"

"You're right." Nicky caught her breath. "Viv even said

in one of the entries, *I will do what is in my power to help him.* After Andrzej died, Viv must have decided to write that riddle with the hope that someday, somehow, the treasure had the chance of being found and returned to its rightful owners."

"And now it will be." Quinten said softly. "She must've decided not to look for it herself, because in that diary entry I found in the cookbook, she said she had chosen to put that part of her life aside to raise her son."

Nicky slid the ring off her finger and placed it in the sterling silver ring box. "I think that's everything in here, then," she said, as she looked again at the crate.

"Nope, nothing else—wait. What's this?" Quinten leaned forward to examine the spot where the bags had sat for three-quarters of a century.

He pulled out a brittle, yellowed piece of tissue-thin airmail paper that had been wedged between two slats and carefully opened it.

August 29, 1942

Dearest Viv,

You know Fritz? Remember, you said, when I told you that story about him and the champagne cask, that his sense of humor was 'wild!' if I quote you correctly.

He had joined the Nazi Party early and attended their rallies often. He was an old friend of the family, so he knew about the mirror. But I'm afraid it's gone missing.

Our house had been broken into at the beginning of all of this—apparently Fritz let slip about my Polish ancestry, so the higher-ups in the Nazi Party thought it best to liberate objects d'art and make several, shall we say, inquires. Starting with my family home.

I tried to get back there—I'm fearful for my family—what their fate may be, as well as that of the mirror. I have not heard from anyone in months and we're forbidden from trying to contact them.

Once I find out what has happened, I will get it back. They think they would get away with it. They will not. They cannot.

All my love,

—A

"They haven't gotten away with it," Nicky said quietly.

"No, they haven't," Quinten agreed.

"So how does a letter about the missing mirror end up in a crate that contains the missing mirror?" Nicky asked.

"Good question. We might never know," Quinten replied. "Maybe he wrote it and intended to mail it but didn't get the chance, and figured that if Viv found the treasure, she'd also find the letter."

"I think that's as good as an explanation as we're going to get."

As she put down the letter and looked up at Quinten, he caught his breath. Her eyes shone in the moonlight as she gazed at him.

For a long moment, neither of them spoke.

"I feel the same way," Quinten finally whispered in response to the look in her eyes. He reached up and stroked a hand down her cheek. He felt his heart beat in his chest when he placed his hand on top of hers and closed his eyes, savoring the sensation.

He opened his eyes, leaned forward, and tucked a strand of hair behind her ear. "I've been suppressing my feelings for you, Nicky," he whispered. "I'm sorry it took me this long to realize that. To voice them aloud."

She swallowed back tears. "And I was so afraid...I didn't have the internal confidence...which made me hold back with you. I didn't want to fully let you in because I thought you were just like my ex. I didn't feel secure in his love for me, so I never let him in all the way. He was never clear. He never came out and told me what he thought and felt about me, about us. And so I thought I had to protect myself from you, too."

"I'm sorry if that's what you thought." He brushed away her tears with his thumb. "I'd been running away. Putting myself in the way of developing a relationship with you because I was afraid I'd be rejected. Afraid to be seen, afraid to feel and act on the truth in my heart."

"You put yourself through that?" Nicky's breath hitched.

"It's okay," he whispered, "it's okay." He slid his arms around her waist. "How's this for being clear? I'm falling in love with you."

"I'm falling in love with you, too," she whispered, as she slid her arms around his neck.

His heart swooped and he knew, in that moment, that truly, this was real love.

"At last," she whispered, echoing his thoughts as his lips brushed hers, "it's true love."

Thanks for reading!

If you loved the historical eras in this trilogy, then you don't want to miss two great sweet historical romance series by Jessica Eissfeldt—*Sweethearts & Jazz Nights* and *Love By Moonlight*. Turn to the back to find out more!

Author's Note

I've always loved the movie *National Treasure* and the 1940s. So when I found out about U-boats off the shores of Prince Edward Island during the Second World War, I knew I had the perfect piece of history to write the third and final book in the Prince Edward Island Love Letters & Legends trilogy.

When I wrote this novel, I wanted to be as accurate as possible. However, there were some instances where, because of the real historical events' timelines, that wasn't possible.

So I took artistic license to modify some dates, time-lines, historical events and such to fit into this plot.

According to Leo Marks' book *Between Silk and Cyanide*, quite a lot of the SOE's codes department records and files were either destroyed after the war or were non-existent in the first place.

As such, it was a bit tricky to track down information about the codes department as so much of the material written about the SOE focuses on the agents in the field.

But with some dogged persistence, I chased down leads. Thanks to the amazing kindness and help of those who I've mentioned on the acknowledgments page, I located several files for a few women who worked in the codes department of the SOE.

I used some of the documentation in those real-life files as a loose guideline for the forms within Vivian's and Andrzej's SOE files that appear in this novel, as I modified some things and omitted others. Also, no Form C.R.2., Form X or Form 6 b) exist—those are all purely a productive of my imagination.

For the sake of the plot, I have given Andrzej dual citizenship—both German and Polish—though I do not know if that was actually possible during World War II.

According to Steven Kippax, the cipher girls were assigned country sections, not specific agents. But, for the sake of this novel's plot, I gave Vivian specific agents who she worked with.

As for the codes themselves, well, I'm no math whiz. But in order to have Nicky and Quinten decipher Andrzej's secret message, I actually had to reverse engineer the process.

I enciphered it, then worked backwards to figure out how the cipher girls would've deciphered it. I've done everything by hand, as Nicky did in the novel, and, indeed, as the women at SOE would've done, too. So if there are any transposition errors or calculation mistakes, they are entirely my own! (I used the internet liberally to piece together an estimation of how it would've been done, as to my knowledge, Leo Marks in his memoir does not explain the entire process step by step.)

Also in my research, I was not able to discern how the indicator groups for decryption of the agents' messages were, well, indicated, to the person deciphering the message. So I have made my best guesstimation as to how it might have been done.

For the facts I've chosen to use in this novel about the minutiae of the SOE sending and receiving wireless messages to London, I discovered slight differences in my research. In those instances of slight variation, I have chosen the version of details that work best with the plot of this novel.

In addition, the vast majority of the SOE files at the National Archives have not, as of this printing, been digitized. However, for the sake of a streamlined plot, I've made them digital. I've also made some modifications to the National Archives' fee structure for document requests, for the sake of this novel's plot.

The SOE did not begin operations out of the Baker Street location until later in 1940, but in order to fit into this novel's plot timeline of the U-boats around PEI, that date needed to be adjusted.

The legalities described in this novel, while within the (loose) realm of plausibility, aren't considered to be probable. I took liberties with legal realities in order to suit the plot.

In that vein, a hardship discharge for bankruptcy is U.S. law and actually not available as an option for bankruptcy in Canada. However, given Quinten's circumstances, I felt that this U.S.-based solution fit best with that part of the plot. So I have chosen to take artistic license, and give Quinten this option to solve his financial issues by utilizing the hardship discharge.

The U-262's POW rescue attempt is fact. (Of course, Hitler's gold and diamonds aboard that submarine are purely the products of my imagination.)

The Charlottetown's *Guardian* newspaper article I used for research and reference does not specify exactly where in the North Cape area the German U-boat was, so in this novel, the location that the sailor recounts is purely a product of my imagination.

During World War II, German U-boats were spotted in multiple locations around P.E.I. But for the sake of this story, I made the same sub appear on both the north and south sides of the island. That probably wouldn't have been the case in real life, as I imagine the Germans wouldn't have wanted to venture any farther into enemy territory than they had to.

All the shops and restaurants mentioned in this book are real—aside from Leard's Piano Tuning & Restoration. While the house that I've borrowed for Quinten's shop location is real, it is no longer occupied. Island Chocolates is a real chocolate factory and shop in Victoria, P.E.I. (And the chocolate waffles there are definitely delicious! If you ever have a chance, try them.) However, they are only available on Sundays. But, again for the sake of the plot, I've made them available other days.

And yes, the piece of sheet music, "Marsch Impromptu" really does exist. The encoded "lyrics" that Nicky and Quinten solve on that music score are inspired by the fact that real phrases do appear on that piece of sheet music. There are even some people who say the piece does contain clues to the location of a secret cache of Hitler's gold and diamonds.

I first learned about the supposed treasure from the TV show *Expedition Unknown* in an episode called *Deciphering the Last Nazi Code*. My imagination took off after I saw that episode, as I knew that was exactly the treasure hunt angle I could draw inspiration from. I already knew that U-boats had visited the shores of P.E.I. during WWII, so a secret stash of HItler's gold and diamonds somewhere on the island seemed a perfect fit!

And if you happen to find yourself on some sandy stretch of beach on Prince Edward Island, keep your eyes open—who knows what treasures may be beneath your feet...

Acknowledgments

The Special Operations Executive—to all the men and women of the SOE who served their country, and the free world, in so many capacities. Thank you.

The residents of Victoria—everyone's kindness and caring meant a lot, so thank you. I hope that this book, in some small way, honors that.

Dr. Steven Kippax—SOE Society, who very kindly answered my questions and provided me with files of the SOE's "cipher girls," as he called them.

Dr David Abrutat—GCHQ Departmental Historian, who helped point me in the right direction for answers to my historical questions.

Lester Cowden IV—who very kindly took time out of his busy schedule to read through and provide feedback on the legal scenes in the book.

Sabrina Volman—awesome beta reader, who read the story in manuscript form and provided excellent observations that only made this book better.

Shannon Page—line editor, who did a great job with copy editing this book.

Arnetta Jackson—proofreader, whose excellent attention to detail gave this book a final polish.

Jane Dixon Smith—cover designer, who designed the lovely cover on this book.

All the other people, including Lynn Hodgson, who helped me along the way with my research and questions about cipher girls and World War II history. Thank you so much.

Bibliography

Binney, Marcus, *The Women Who Lived For Danger: the agents of the Special Operations Executive* (New York, William Morrow, 2002)

MacKay, Mary. "A Tale of Two Submarines." *The Guardian*, May 5, 2001.

Marks, Leo. *Between Silk and Cyanide: A Codemaker's War 1941-1945* (New York, The Free Press, 1998)

Mundy, Liza. *Code Girls: The Untold Story of the American Women Codebreakers of World War II* (New York, Hachette Books, 2018)

Riols, Noreen. *The Secret Ministry of Ag. & Fish: My Life in Churchill's School for Spies* (London, MacMillian, 2013)

Read on for an excerpt from the first sweet historical romance book in Jessica Eissfeldt's Sweethearts & Jazz Nights series, set in 1940s San Francisco.

Dialing Dreams

Chapter One

ELINDA THOMPSON COULDN'T stand one more moment of this. What was she doing here anyway, sitting at a switchboard at midnight, humming jazz melodies to herself? Melodies that she'd practiced through all four years of high school vocal classes. And then sang for hours more in the kitchen at home, with her heart full of hope and dreams. So shouldn't she be enchanting audiences and singing songs, not answering calls and connecting wires?

But the sound of her father's hoarse cough echoed through her mind and tugged at her conscience. She would not abandon him. She straightened up. She was all he had. She might not want to work as a telephone operator at the Hotel Whitcomb but she could still choose how she acted about it. She would do it—for him. Taking comfort in that, she began the jazz tune again. But it faded from her lips when a call came in.

"Operator. How may I transfer your call?" She cringed as a male voice slurred a greeting.

"No...no tra-transfer. Please, can we just...talk?"

Not only drunk, he's desperate, she thought. Yet his velvety baritone intrigued Belinda in spite of herself. "I'm sorry, sir. You have to tell me who you want to connect to."

"Room five oh...five. Yeah, that's it."

Belinda studied the tips of her polished nails. "One moment, please, while I—"

"No, no, no. No. No...need. I don't...*actually* want to talk to her."

"Sir, who *do* you want to be connected to?"

"There isn't a number. I want...to talk to someone like you."

"I need to connect you. Or I really can't continue this conversation."

"Operator, you sound like a nice girl, and I...need to talk to a nice girl. Claire wasn't—"

A little unnerved, she spoke over him. "That's not my job."

"All right. All right. I...won't bother...you."

The line went dead.

Belinda frowned then shrugged. She glanced at the clock. Time to go. She collected her purse and slid on her trench coat before cinching its belt. She pinned her hat in place and pulled on her gloves before locking up the tiny switchboard office on the hotel's main floor. With a sigh of relief, she walked through the marble-floored lobby, waved a goodbye to the doorman and headed up Market Street, her seven-cent fare in hand. The cable car's rumble and screech told her she'd arrived just in time to jump onto the Powell-Hyde line and head for home.

A LIGHT DRIZZLE spattered the phone booth the following Friday night as Nick Hart ducked into it on impulse. Couldn't sleep anyway. And a walk usually cleared his head. He stared out into the darkness enshrouding the Bay Area as the lights of San Francisco winked back at him, as they did every evening across from his place on the waterfront.

Not so long ago, things were going great. His third record was selling well, and he'd gotten his polished shoes onto the crooner stage at last. But this whole thing with Claire had begun to fall apart. He frowned and shook off the raindrops that clung to his fedora, placed it back on his head, and tugged the brim lower.

Eying the sleek black handset, he ran a finger along it as he pondered last week's drunken call to the Hotel Whitcomb. Was he that desperate that he'd actually tried to get sympathy from the operator? Even though she'd been annoyed with him—he hadn't been too drunk to remember that—he couldn't quite forget her satiny voice.

Read on for an excerpt from the first sweet historical
romance book in Jessica Eissfeldt's Love By Moonlight
series.

Beneath A Venetian Moon

Chapter One

THE MOONLIGHT SLIPPED through the partially open window as Alessandra Velocchi smoothed her amethyst gown. If only her own escape could be so easy. But the binding ties of duty wound around her more tightly than the velvet-trimmed silver mask she wore as she stepped out of her chamber, down the stairs, and out into the waiting gondola.

She gasped as the chill waters of the Venetian canal splashed at her hem like greedy fingers trying to reclaim their prize. She shuddered, putting the childhood near-drowning experience from her mind, focusing firmly on the festivities ahead at the Doge's birthday celebration.

"Does the Contessa have an escort?" The doorman addressed Alessandra at the palace entrance.

Lifting her chin, she shook her head. "Tonight, I am a free woman." She felt her heart swell with gladness. No father to watch her, no boring escort to hinder her. Pure, clear freedom. Just the way she liked it.

Candlelight sparkled off cut crystal chandeliers as she took a goblet of wine from a side table. Winding her way amongst mingling revelers, she spotted familiar faces all around. Laughter and accented voices drifted past her as the pull of duty pushed her to the front of the ballroom where the Doge stood.

As she approached, the Doge's ministers bowed, acknowledging her as the daughter of Venice's most powerful palace advisor.

"Before the Doge begins his own speech," stated one of the officials, "he expects to hear the address your father entrusted you with." He nodded toward Alessandra. "You have prepared?"

"Of course." As she brought her goblet to her lips to calm her nerves, a sudden shadow flickered in her peripheral vision. She glanced sideways. Now nothing. Closing her eyes for a brief second to gather her thoughts, she savored the drink's heady sweetness.

Alessandra took another sip of wine, fiddling with the stem of the goblet, watching the carved facets glimmer in the light. And again, the shadow flickered in her vision, this time closer.

She frowned. Looked around. Returned her attention to the Doge, waiting for him to give her the nod. But just then, the shadow appeared again – this time taking on a form – that of a man. With a black silk mask tied around his glossy dark hair and a velvet doublet trimmed in the same midnight shade.

This time, she openly stared at him. Watched while his furtive glances around the room displayed fear. Watched while his fluid movements wound him between guests. Watched while his steps led him closer and closer to her.

She forgot all about her staid speech as she searched the planes of his face. He was not part of the court. Or the Doge's administration. Or even a member of the Venetian aristocratic circles she'd known all her life. Though he certainly was attractive. And certainly not a boring escort. Her lips curved into a smile.

She continued to admire him, noticing that by now he stood only a few paces from her. But protocol and privilege forced her to turn away, forced her to acknowledge the Doge, who now beckoned to her.

She raised her chin and straightened her spine, pivoting to face the assemblage. As the guests' final murmurs died away, she inhaled, about to speak.

But in that brief hesitation, the masked man leapt toward her. As she startled, stepping back, her name tumbled from his lips. "Contessa Velocchi."

His eyes held hers even as he collapsed at her feet, gasping, his hand pressed to his side. And that's when she saw it. Blood. Seeping crimson onto the polished parquet floor.

She knelt, one look into that sea-green gaze telling her she had nothing to fear. Her heart filled with concern at his wound and she pulled out a handkerchief, leaning forward.

His breath warm in her ear, he whispered low, frantic. "Please...I beg of you...help me. They...want me dead."